Penguin Books

The Destinies of Darcy Dancer, Gentleman

J. P. Donleavy was born in New York City in 1926 and educated there and at Trinity College, Dublin. His works include the novels, *The Ginger Man*, *A Singular Man*, *The Beastly Beatitudes of Baltha-zar B*, *The Onion Eaters*, and *A Fairy Tale of New York*; a book of short pieces, *Meet My Maker the Mad Molecule*; a novella, *The Saddest Summer of Samuel S*; four plays, *The Ginger Man*, *Fairy Tales of New York*, *A Singular Man* and *The Saddest Summer of Samuel S* (published in Penguins under the title *The Plays of J. P. Donleavy*); and *The Unexpurgated Code: A Complete Manual of Survival and Manners*, with drawings by the author. All these are published in Penguins.

The Destinies
of
Darcy Dancer,
Gentleman

J. P. Donleavy

Penguin Books

Penguin Books Ltd, Harmondsworth,
Middlesex, England
Penguin Books, 625 Madison Avenue,
New York, New York 10022, U.S.A.
Penguin Books Australia Ltd, Ringwood,
Victoria, Australia
Penguin Books Canada Ltd, 2801 John Street,
Markham, Ontario, Canada L3R 1B4
Penguin Books (N.Z.) Ltd, 182–190 Wairau Road,
Auckland 10, New Zealand

First published in the U.S.A. 1977
First published in Great Britain by Allen Lane 1978
Published in Penguin Books 1978
Reprinted 1979

Made and printed in Great Britain by
Cox & Wyman Ltd, London, Reading and Fakenham
Set in Monotype Ehrhardt

I

Blue strips of sky between bleak clouds this chill day before Christmas as winter entrenched across the remote midlands of Ireland. With darkness descending at tea time in the north east bedroom of a grey cut stone manor, an ample horsey woman who had the day before been riding to the hounds, groaned giving birth. The news was whispered from servant to servant down through the house and more loudly into the kitchens and louder still out across the lantern lit stable yards.

The husband of this woman, a man as well known for his gambling as he was for his generosity among cronies, had married for money and was, as he was mostly, away in England for the racing. And upon that birth day he had waged one hundred pounds on a rank outsider at one hundred to one, which had come waltzing in by eight lengths, a winner. And upon hearing the news of a boy sent a cable

NAME HIM DANCER

And with this among other names a child was christened in the small chapel at the top of the stairs. Reginald Darcy Thormond Dancer Kildare.

Reached by a mile long winding drive through vast entanglements of ancient rhododendrons, Andromeda Park stood a weather worn cold edifice three storeys tall over a basement on a hill surveying lonely standing oak, beech and chestnut trees in a forty Irish acre field inclining down to a small river. Here three children, two sisters and their baby brother played along the grassy banks of these trout waters and ran as cowboys and Indians up into the higher hills of forest hiding other distant fields and meadows. And when recaptured for meals by nurses and nannies, were led, sometimes by the ears, up wide granite steps through an oak bulletproof door fitted with a small iron barred grill out which the cross eyed butler Crooks asked visitors their business so it could be discerned as to whether they were friend or foe. The latter always being those with a bill who wanted to be paid.

His nurse called this alabaster skinned, blue eyed and black haired boy Darcy Dancer and swaddled, dressed, fed and minded him in his nursery till he was six years old when a groom taught him to ride. And sometimes at the open stained glass chapel casement, with his older sisters each holding a hand, he watched the cattle stampeding as the hunt assembled on their front lawn. Later as darkness fell he saw them through a blue tinted pane of a north east parlour window come straggling back, scarlet coats, black coats and breeches, mud spattered, horses steaming, a few lamed some maimed and all, as Uncle Willie said, relieved to be alive. He counted from the shortest winter's day right into early spring the lengthening minutes of light. Till on midsummer nights a cold glow lurked in the northern sky way past bedtime when in the illumined sunset darkness he listened to the donkeys braying. To be always finally lulled to sleep by the chiming bells of the clock tower from which his mother's father had removed the hands when too many of the locals trespassed to a neighbouring hill to be told the time of day by a man who owned a spy glass. And just beyond this hill he often dreamt there were green and white bearded little fairies with angels' wings who lived and played joyously there in the lonely grassy beyonds and would one day come and bring him into their hidden warm wonderful kingdom where nice little boys could sit with them mending shoes.

His games were to ride the hay top of ricks as they were drawn to the barns at harvest time. And his chores were picking summer berries for winter jam in the hedgerows. He grew taller amid the smells of drying saddles and the whinny of horses and the pounding of their hooves in springtimes out across the surrounding pastures. All moments of this tiny world golden within petals of a buttercup. Till one early morning dawn, falling out of bed, breaking a collarbone and rolling in agony where a rocking chair rocked, I was carried sobbing and trembling in my nannie's arms to her bedroom further down the hall to mend and convalesce. And learn to know that just as poison lurked in the beauteous soft tissue of yellow meadow flowers, so too did pain and sorrow lie before all one's footsteps.

> And only
> Some knowing
> Loving hand
> Could
> Guide you
> By

2

His sisters gone away to school in Dublin, Darcy Dancer was taught reading writing and arithmetic by Mr Arland, a tall, thin, grey suited gentleman who often said between his deep sniffs of snuff, that that was what he was, a gentleman. Who although disowned by his aristocratic father as a child borne by a serving girl, was educated at proper schools in England and later at Trinity College Dublin where he was a sizar and scholar. And often on his lips were his favourite words he used to a disputatious Darcy Dancer.

'Please do not Kildare, be miserably negatory.'

Mr Arland came fetched each day and they sat at ten o'clock for three hours in the tiny schoolroom tucked in under the servants' staircase. And always Mr Arland as he took his cane from the front hall and shoved it up under his arm also took his last pinch of snuff which he sucked from the tip of the back of his hand up each nostril as he stood on the front steps waiting to be ferried by pony and trap back to the village where he stayed in a grim damp room over the pub.

Following lessons, and free to run, explore and hide, Darcy Dancer often climbed up upon the massive bough of a tree where he lay stretched out holding his head in his fists, elbows on the rough bark listening to the creaking cartwheels and trudging horses heading for the underground tunnel which led from the stable yards behind and under the back of the house and way out to the light of day again in the fields. And his horse trading visiting Uncle Willie when shouting to find him there would always smilingly say.

'Ah child, it will soon be for the likes of yourself that you'll be inside looking out over your madeira upon the vistas that do be displaying from this house, and that the beauty and peace of your daydreaming can not be disturbed by the rough movements and noises of carts and men.'

And it was one year later on the third day of spring in the late sunny afternoon, his mother, carried in strange foot shuffling silence by the linked arms of farm hands, was lifted up the steps and through the front door. Her long dark brown riding habit bloodied and tresses of her hair hanging while she was laid upon the horsehair chaise longue, her one green and one blue eye staring at the ceiling of the north east parlour, dead. The smell of baking scones for tea in the air and on the floor of the whim room next to the chapel I had been playing with my trains, lifting the locomotive with a derrick back on the track. I heard a loud scream and choking sobs and went to the balustrade and saw down into the front hall the men standing hunched and silent, caps in their hands, the mud broken away in lumps from their boots and scattered on the black and white tiles. They held me away till I ran in between and around them into the room. And when I looked and looked at her. Her slender ankles and white satins closed by a gold pin around her throat. The blue veins at her temples and the way she always swept through the house, casting friendly orders to the adoring servants over her shoulder, her voice so clear so certain and kind, a pleased smile always ready on her lips. And all had said that although before her marriage she was plump and plain, that following the birth of her last child, she became slender rarefied and beautiful.

The coffin made by the village butcher arrived by the farm road and was brought in through the ivy shrouded basement entrance. And a day later his father had come on the train from Dublin where during the yearling sales he'd been staying at his club. A large gloomy establishment through which once after seeing my first rugby match, I was led. Thawing my chill in front of an orange glowing turf fire and watching members like my father, stand at the great polished gleaming drawing room windows safely surveying over cigars and port the flat green velvet playing fields of Trinity College many of them had attended across the street. And I slept there in an attic room hearing the trams screeching and roaring along the road and in the morning could see the moist glossy rhododendrons and evergreen leaves that grew up from the college grounds the other side of the spear topped iron fence. And midday sat in a smoky carriage pulled by a throbbing puffing steam engine which sputtered and wheezed across a Liffey bridge and gathered speed by the blackened slate roof tops and tiny back gardens. Till out between the furze and heather covered bog lands it raced, whistle wailing along by the banks of the Canal to finally, after two hours chug into the little familiar grey and black painted station with its carefully tended always blossoming flower beds.

And all those other days I knew my father was home, when he could be heard shouting for Crooks that his boiled egg was too soft or hard or the fire to be mended and kept blazing or his newspaper found or that he would not speak to some caller who demanded to see him. And once, his monocle flashing at the bottom of the stairs, he said to me as he saw me at one of my daydreaming spots at the great window on the large landing watching out to the grove of beeches where each evening, black hundreds of wing flapping barking rooks gathered.

'There you are, you bastard.'

Now to see on the thin narrow reddened face his lips drawn tightly as he took his long leather motoring coat from his shoulders, nodded at the members of the household who lurked genuflecting and then blessing themselves as their master entered his study. A whole day passed with his door closed on this shuttered panelled room where he sat in front of the fire drinking whiskey and listening to solemn symphonies on the gramophone. Crooks stationing a stable boy inside the door of the salon across the hall to steal forward as the music began to fade and to wind up the gramophone again and again. And the visitors in the faded blue walled parlour looking down and paying their last respects to the alabaster face cushioned by the soft black waves of hair and those vanished strange gems, the gently closed eyes of my mother.

That fifth day of spring like the first day after the end of the world had come. A storm the night before sending slates flying off the roofs and they lay scattered and broken around the house, some stuck like arrows deep in the front lawn where ancient oaks were blown over, their roots sticking up and their boughs breaking the fence. I came awake as the shutters and window frames shook and a giant stone falling from a chimney sent a great bang trembling throughout the house. The pounding gusts of the gale poured billows of turf smoke into rooms and out into the halls where it gathered high up beneath the skylights. And now heavy rain swept in wave after wave out of racing dark clouds from the west. Crooks bracing with his shoulder and needing help to slam closed the front door. The entrance hall covered in puddles from the dripping coats and umbrellas. With mourners standing backsides to the roaring fire with their dark clothing steaming and some of their chilled blue hands holding brimming glasses of brandy.

Outside lost birds knocked backwards in the sky. Floods of water shining silver below in the fresh green field where the banks of the river overflowed. Motor cars had blocked the entrance drive and wheels were churning and skidding deep into the lawn. His mother's coffin taken from the darkly furnished north east front parlour where the smooth gleaming elm box had reposed two days on an oak wake table under the hunting portraits of my mother's pink coated father and black habited mother. And now borne down the front steps by grooms through a way made between the vehicles and placed upon a black velvet covered cart. The voice of the head groom repeating over and over again.

'Gently lads gently.'

All walked and the dark line of people strung out from the apron of stones fronting the house. To follow the horse drawn coffin a short way down the drive and left on to a farm road which entered the park and wound under a giant oak and down a steep hill to the dell surrounded by a grove of walnut trees. In the small walled cemetery where were buried her mother and father and two of her brothers, the musty mausoleum held coffins of Darcys and Thormonds back through generations and my sister Sybilla. The men had dug my mother's grave by the ruins of the ancient chapel whose thousand year old arched entrance and stone foundations still stood heaped up and roofed over by ivy vines. A place where I had so many times come in summers to sit cooled and shaded by the great yew tree to watch the wasps go and come from their hole in the ground.

Shielding the pages of their bibles from the rain, a priest and a parson in attendance. The first a strange friend of my mother's, whose elegant clerical garments were tailored in Paris, and the latter an even stranger friend, an amateur astronomer and botanist who spoke with the high pitched voice of a woman and who with his long blond curling hair was rumoured to be living in his parsonage with a man. Both usually called for tea and always brought presents, mother of pearl shells, copper boxes, and sometimes statuettes of Wedgwood and Meissen. All placed on tables and admired as the butters melted between the halved scones, and voices ranged upon vases, paintings and opera. My mother as she held the silver pot to pour, reeling off dates manners schools and motifs. And hear the refrain from her gently chewing ecclesiastic friends.

'Yes yes superb I do most certainly agree exactly.'

Standing around the mound of mud and sods were the Master of Foxhounds, twenty three members of the hunt and four neighbouring farmers and their wives. The gombeen man of the village, whose bald black browed wife wore a blonde wig, was sheepishly rubbing his hands. And from the town, six Irish miles away, came six of the biggest shop-keepers. One nearby Earl and two Barons stood under their black umbrellas with their black bowler hats in hand. A Marquis, a widowed Countess, one well known bookie and further, their backs against the cemetery wall, nine members of the household, my two red eyed sisters and twenty working men with their big fingers grasping their caps, as all these heads dripped with rain.

And my blue eyed Uncle Willie, his broad shoulders folded forward, standing next to me behind my father, was sobbing like a child. His big hand reaching up again and again to brush at the tears and rain rolling down his cheeks. And I could hear him say. As the same words were choking up against my silent lips.

I love you
Nettie
I loved you

3

Two days following the funeral Darcy Dancer's father sold ten big bullocks at the street market in the village and without an ounce of petrol for the motor cars he left again by horse and trap clip clopping three miles on the hilly winding road to the station. His two big thick heavy leather cases waiting that morning in the hall and I traced my fingers on the tooled large black initials of R.C.S.K. While Ruby my nurse, who had moved in semi retirement to the top floor, was packed and weeping clutching me, was gone with my sisters minutes later.

The next day a cable came from Dublin. The pale green envelope emblazoned with a black harp. Crooks solemnly brought it on a tray. Standing above me in the whim room intoning.

EN ROUTE VIA LIVERPOOL STOP
IN EMERGENCY ONLY CONTACT RITZ
LONDON

And Crooks retreating with his crossed eyes and now just one of his front upper teeth left to hardly brighten his rare smiles. As he daily, along with six other pairs of hands, continued to run the slowly collapsing household.

And still with each week day at his appointed hour Mr Arland stepped from the trap, lifted his chin and always turned to look down the sloping parkland to the river and then reach into his pocket, take out his big gold watch and regard the time. The stitching threads hanging loose from his little battered briefcase across the top of which he held his cane. His nervous sometimes twisting mouth which always seemed to draw a deep breath before he climbed the steps. Just as I would then speed from the whim room and along the stone paved corridor and down the servants' staircase at the end. To await Mr Arland's arrival as I sat steeped in laborious study. When came his tapping of the blackboard pointer and I would then sit book open over the grim wastelands of Latin as his kindly reasonable voice spoke from his thin white face.

'Kildare, you are being automatically stupid.'

And then as we embarked upon English grammar and punctuation, Mr Arland kept by his left hand a volume of poetry into which he would refer his eyes, patiently waiting for me not to be automatically stupid.

'Kildare, when do we use a period.'

'When a comma is not required.'

'I shall repeat. For the umpteenth time. For the benefit of your inattentive ears. When a sentence is complete and independent and not connected in construction with the following sentence, it is marked with a period. As, fear God, period. Honour the King, period. Have charity towards all men, period.'

'But I do not honour the King.'

'Kildare you're being tiresome, you know. Do you have charity towards all men, period.'

'No, period.'

'Well that is a pity, period.'

'No one has charity towards me, period.'

'Ah you are getting the point, period.'

On wild rainy days he came hunched and huddled up under a naval great coat from which his head emerged to wipe his nose gently against his sleeve. And if the day continued dark and cook brought us up bowls of hot vegetable soup, he would tell his little stories, looking down now and again at his bitten fingernails, his thumb rubbing along his spoon and then pulling his soiled shirt cuffs back under his frayed jacket sleeves.

'Yes my absent minded tutor. He was always nervously rushing hither and thither never fully realizing where he was. Until one day, stepping off a ladder backwards from a book shelf high in the college reading room he was killed. For the

15

world of scholarship it was most sad. He broke his brains. They hopelessly tried to revive the poor man on the reading room steps. But he was as absolutely dead as an old bone.'

And those afternoons following lessons, Darcy Dancer would wander to the stables. To see the big hunting mares bred by his mother in off the grass in their loose boxes chewing hay and waiting to foal. Foxy Slattery the head groom's son, milked the cows and fed the chickens and would be lurking there silently behind the bales of straw glancing up sideways as he made a sucking sound with his lips secretly pulling smoke out of a cigarette. His one or both eyes blackened and his face bruised if not by the kick of a cow then by his father's fist the previous night.

'What is wrong with your face.'

'Ah I have a knock on it now and again.'

And as the herd came mooing in from the fields, udders swollen and led by three goats, Foxy ran back and forth behind them waving his hat, shaking his fist, kicking with his boot and throwing sticks, stones or anything at wayward beasts. When a chicken was to meet its doom he would charge after it, his two hands outstretched, his mouth spitting vile oaths and curses as he galloped crashing and banging through barns and sheds tripping over rakes and ploughs, lashing out with swipes of his sharpened axe at the fleeing hen. And once when he fell full length immersed into the water trough, he surfaced, swinging his axe and roared out two words I had not heard before.

'Fucking cunt.'

Crooks on one of his frequent insomniac tours of the sleeping house, shuffling in an old pair of my father's slippers embroidered in gold with a stag's head, caught Foxy stealing whiskey from the wine cellar. In the struggle, as the bottle broke on the red tile corridor, Foxy kicked Crooks in the shins and shouted that Crooks himself had been stealing the wine and whiskey for years. Next day Foxy's head all wrapped in white bandage and his both eyes closed to two blue little slits. Catherine the cook said his father had socked him like a football all over the Slattery cottage. And when Foxy's bandages were finally gone he celebrated on a bottle of poteen, picking the lock of the cabinet in the tack room where it was specially kept to cure beasts of blackleg. Then half delirious atop an unlit bicycle heading down the drive on his way through the black night to the village pub, he sailed on the first turning straight into a tree. Crooks hearing the news of cracked ribs, fractured skull with various contusions and abrasions as well as a broken arm, announced solemnly to every member of the household.

'That should keep that regrettable rapscallion quiet for a while.'

But before these bandages were off, Foxy, his arm still in a plaster cast, was trying to ride an evil minded stallion which had already attacked and nearly killed two grooms. And every able footed inhabitant of Andromeda Park ran for their lives when Foxy mounted bareback came charging out of the stable lashing the wicked brute on its quarters. Suitably named Thunder and Lightning, the beast bucked, its hooves flashing sparks across the yard with Foxy hanging on like a leech two handed to its mane. Till with an almighty undulation of its equine spine, Thunder and Lightning threw Foxy eleven feet high over the wall into the orchard. Where Sexton, a six foot four inch tall man who wore a black patch over his blind eye, was pruning trees. And who in his great shambling way, produced Foxy back out again crumpled unconscious in a wheelbarrow with a daisy chain wreathed around his skull.

'Here's the hero served up with laurels. Now tell me what will I do with this stupid sack of imbecility. Lateat scintillula forsan. If any of you uninitiated understand me Latin.'

Later when I came into the shed where Foxy, his plaster cast arm brushing away the swinging tail of the cow he milked, had his head again newly wound with gauze.

'What this time is wrong with your head.'

'Ah I have a knock on it now and again.'

With summer, new grasses growing thinly over his mother's grave, where an obelisk, tall as a man, now stood, letters gleaming in gold leaf, chiselled deeply in the grey stone.

In everlasting memory of
Antoinette Delia Darcy Darcy Thormond
beloved wife of
Caesar Reginald Sean Kildare.

When Darcy Dancer went there, he found placed on the granite plinth a fresh bunch of flowers just as were placed freshly round the house on hunting days. When always there was great commotion and feverish activity with the sound of boots down the halls and servants at the windows watching my mother in black and my father in pink be mounted by grooms at the foot of the steps. And Sexton said that her ladyship's favourite mare when it grazed the surrounding field came each morning and afternoon to neigh over the cemetery wall. And I felt a strange loneliness growing. Just as the bright green moss did on the tops of the old deer park walls. And now when some of the stones had fallen and lay there in the growing grass, I'd wonder who would ever come and build them back up again.

For two months now, only the men to talk to in the barns and stables. After Foxy Slattery finally ended up in the hospital. With two broken legs. Got in the course of stealing exotic fruits from a neighbouring Lord's greenhouse one midnight. A crack shot and former colonel of a crack regiment, his Lordship cornered him in the top of a tree in the walled orchard. When Foxy refused to descend, his Lordship blasted him down with the near misses of his shot gun. And now the only excitement stirring was when a foal or calf were born. With men tugging sometimes six or seven of them on a taut rope out a barn door. To all fall thump on their backsides as a calf with one last almighty heave was finally pulled out of a groaning heifer.

'There he is lads a fine big strong bull with not a bother on him.'

It rained till autumn. One unending caravan of clouds after another heading east, carrying mists and vaporous winds across darkened days. When suddenly the sun shone blazing. And Darcy Dancer's father returned for three weeks of harvest. Selling the barley and the wheat as soon as they stood near ready and ripe to be cut and an auction was held for the two hundred cocks of hay. And before he left, ten more big bullocks, fifty sheep and five sows went off to market. And trays of silver egg cutters my mother had collected over the years along with selected pieces of Wedgwood and Meissen were packed by Crooks to accompany my father's luggage.

Two upstairs maids Norah and Sheila and Kitty from the kitchens were given notice. And when Norah and Sheila were miraculously next morning reinstated, Kitty, in tears and howling out the act of contrition, was nearly dragged all the way to the front gate. And times she had minded me, her blue eyes wide like footballs and her red kinky hair electrified around her head, as she said God would get even and had cast a curse on the house because my father a Catholic was raising me as a pagan Protestant. But wherever she was, she would, she promised, pray for the redemption of my immortal soul.

Sexton, in his Sunday best, his black bicycle cleaned and shined to go off to mass, went gently pumping his pedals with his long legs. And shouting as he rode by the front of the house and down the drive.

'Incorrigible, incorrigible cur, that's all he is or will ever be and you couldn't whisper pax vobiscum within a mile of him without being branded a liar for life.'

Foxy had following the mending of his broken legs used one of his crutches to break his father's arm, who, he claimed next morning, punched his mother all night over the house. Catherine the cook said what better hand to administer justice than a husband's and it was about time someone had caught the wench who'd go behind a cock of hay with any stable lad, she with her skirts up and they with their trousers down. With Crooks mumbling as he gloomed through the pantry, nervously scratching at the tiny spots of dried soup and gravy that dotted his livery.

'No good will ever come out of that bunch.'

Mr Arland on recent instructions from my father now came only Monday, Wednesday and Fridays, assigning me work to do alone on Tuesdays and Thursdays when he went instead to the great castle where the heaviest nobleman in the world lived and which could be seen on clear days from the high land of spy glass hill, its turrets and towers nestled distantly between the forested downs. Sexton exaggeratedly said it was where he worked for slave wages till my mother visiting remarked on his most splendid roses and chrysanthemums. And he wasted no time before he got himself fired by levelling a few sophisticated insults to the foreman which had to be made less and less so until that thick headed eegit understood. And soon after he was with cap in hand taking favoured instructions from the lady of Andromeda Park.

'Ah young master Darcy there was no more beautiful woman than your mother. She was a saint, god rest her, a beauty. God speed her soul to heaven. She was a madonna. By god she was a madonna. With the purity of the blessed virgin, sine dubio and the kindest of the master creator's creations, sine ira et studio, as surely as you follow my Latin.'

Days when Mr Arland was absent I found much pleasure climbing in the lofts and searching the attics. And on fine days, followed by my mother's wolfhounds Kern and Olav, I would ride my white pony as far as I could get the stubborn animal to go across the fields. Trying once to make my way fording the streams and around the lakes to the great castle, but with its tower out of sight I would lose my direction and get lost. Returning muddy and scratched and leading my tired sweating pony into his box and fetching oats. I'd wait till Foxy would come in with the cows for their evening milking. Watching him reach in under their bags to hammer out jets of milk with his jerking fists, his woollen hat pulled down over the scars on his brow.

'And where has master Darcy been today.'

'I tried to find the way to the castle.'

'Ah you'd have to know the way around the woods and lakes for that. Sure I'm taking that old Thunder and Lightning for a gallop again and I'll show you the way.'

'Don't you think it's time you stopped getting knocks on your head and your legs broken.'

'Ah don't worry I'll be giving out the knocks soon enough.

And the ones I've been getting will be like taps of a feather compared to the ones I'll be handing out.'

'Sexton says you're a cur not fit to have conversation with the likes of me.'

'That dirty filthy one eyed liar. What's he doing but riding his cycle around pulling his prick into every hedge because not a woman in the countryside would let him near her.'

'What do you mean by that.'

'Now don't go around asking them questions and saying the answers that they came from me.'

'But I do not know what you mean.'

'Sure you're old enough don't you pull yours.'

'I do not know what you are saying.'

'The thing between your legs you piss out of. Haven't you seen the bulls at the cows and the stallions at the mares.'

'I am always shooed away.'

'Well I'll show you sometime, some night when the time's ripe. It's like so, the milk I'm squirting out the teat I've got in me hand. You can come with me over beyond where there's the woman.'

'What woman.'

'The wife of the one eyed one armed man. She'd soon teach you.'

'I'm not allowed out at night.'

'I'll get you out.'

'Crooks locks the doors.'

'Never mind that stupid eegit Crooks. I'll have you out and not a soul will know. And here for a start I'll show you mine. It's only a middling size now but in two seconds it'll be as long as an axe handle and spitting in a minute like a squirt of milk out of that cow.'

'Nurse Ruby said that's wrong till you're old enough and married.'

'Never mind that cross eyed hunchback who'd never find a husband in donkey's years.'

'Don't say such a thing about my nurse.'

'What harm, she's gone now and you're old enough. Sure what would that old crone know. Who'd put a hand to her when there was the likes of Norah and Sheila with nobs on them that would open a treasure chest.'

'You shouldn't speak of our servants in that manner if what you are saying is not nice.'

'Sure nice or not there are goings on in the big house I could tell you plenty about. Four of the girls this last year are gone from there now with their bellies bulging to the nuns in Dublin.'

'And what do you mean by that.'

'That they'll be having their bastard babies before long.'

Darcy Dancer went crossing the cobbled stable yard that night. Pony's bridle draped over an arm. The word bastard blazing on the mind. A distant whistle of the train and a beast groaning out somewhere on the evening pastures. To know now for certain that men did something to ladies. And that Nurse Ruby went red in the face as I sat on a chair by the copper bath. She slapped my thigh when she looked down and saw what Foxy was showing me, sticking straight up at her from my lap. And to know now that a cross eyed hunched back was ugly to the rest of the world.

> And a
> Beauty
> Only
> To me

4

As the autumn days shortened, cobwebs were getting thicker and darker on the ceilings of the house. The crack where the bees made honey in the wall of my mother's bedroom grew wider. And each time I came there to see where she lived and touch the things she owned I found a turf fire glowing in the grate. With Crooks still entering her door with trays and once passing in the hall I heard his voice which suddenly made me stop and shiver.

'Madam I do believe there is a little sun this morning, shall I part the drapes further for you. And I do hope Catherine is making the coffee more to madam's preference, ah allow me, madam to freshen your water decanter. I understand madam it's twenty eight instead of thirty to dinner. The smoked salmon will be at the station at three. Certainly madam, the Sèvres. And the blue candles, of course.'

I tiptoed to the next door down the hall to enter my mother's ablution room to listen. And could see through the half open door Crooks reflected in the dressing table mirror as he stood at the foot of my mother's lace canopied bed. His right hand clasping his left, his chin held high and his head inclined to the side. He stepped forward touching the counterpane, his voice still full of urgent ministration, and a fear crept up my spine. That all in this house had died. And dwelled in an eternal world like heaven or hell.

At nights it took Darcy Dancer hours to sleep. Feet chilled under the damp blankets. Alone, with his sisters and nurse gone away. And now every day to go down the hall and with no one near, to go into my mother's room. See myself in the painting picnicking under our greatest oak tree, my sisters and I seated around our mother. The colours matching the fresh flowers put each day on her writing desk and the tables by her bedside. And in the ablution room her toothbrushes laid out on the pink marble wash stand. The glass shelves of her soaps and bath salts waiting ready for her hand. Her scent bottles wiped and polished gleaming and once even her tub filled with hot steaming water. When I heard Crooks's voice again.

'Norah how many times must I tell you to air madam's towels.'

Pastures growing soft again with rain and grazing cattle shortening the grass, leaving only the clumps of stiff stemmed sharp ended rushes. To walk early mornings wandering with Olav and Kern by foxes' coverts and watch the big dogs bark and dig furiously only to suddenly whirl and chase a zig zagging bounding hare, the great hounds stretching across the turf pounding furiously in pursuit. And wandering back up the hill towards the house I'd detour down into the servants' entrance. To find Sexton cutting stems and filling vases in the basement flower room.

'Why does Crooks draw my mother's bath.'

'Ah Crooks doesn't know he's half gone daft. The man's sine dubio as mad as a hatter. But your mother, Master Darcy is with us nevertheless, living and breathing like life and any man who doubts that will have to reckon with a fist in the gob from me.'

A lead drain around the domed skylight of the front hall began to leak and in the worst rain storms would make floods on the black and white tiles. Until basins and finally buckets were all over the floor. And with water seeping in, mushrooms were flowering up from skirting boards and carpets in the cloakroom. Where when Mr Arland was hanging his coat I asked him what he meant by his Latin remark about Sexton, insanus omnis furere credit ceteros.

'Kildare does it not ever dawn on your lazy head to refer yourself to your dictionary if, as is clearly the case, you cannot translate even the most simple of phrases.'

'My mind goes blank at the thought of Latin.'

'Pity.'

And Mr Arland smiled as I presented my sheet of paper.

EVERY MADMAN THINKS EVERYONE ELSE MAD

'Good for you Kildare.'

I found Sexton in the kitchen gardens coming out of his potting shed where inside the Latin names of flowers were pinned up on sheets of paper. And inscriptions were written under a little altar on which stood a statue of a blue robed woman. Holding it up to his tall face, I showed him the Latin. He peered at it. And I said now you know what it means.

'Ah now I'm not going to bother meself about translating another man's Latin.'

'I translated it. And do you want to hear what it says.'

'Sure if you've nothing better to do, I'm not against encouraging scholarship. Life is short art is long, and the beauty of the sirrepedium lasts forever, if you understand me.'

'It means every madman thinks everyone else mad.'

'Is that fact.'

'Yes and it's what Mr Arland says about you.'

'He what. The insolence of him. Shoot me down would he. Make a mockery of a poor old horticulturist, would he. Madman is it. And he is the sane one is he. I'll soon teach that cheeky pup to address his intellectual betters with more respect.'

'I thought you might have something in Latin to say back to him.'

'In Latin is it. It'll be in English delivered on the end of an Irish boot that that sasanach bastard will hear from me.'

'But you said Crooks was as mad as a hatter.'

'And so he is, completely demented.'

'And now you are angry that someone has said something about you.'

'I am by God I am.'

And then as I stood there, Sexton's one eye grew moist and brimming and suddenly, from under his eye patch, tears streaming down his face. As the giant man bent and broke into convulsive sobs.

'O God almighty I'm not mad, don't say that, never say I'm mad. I'm not that. I only love the flowers and nature and the beauties of the world with my whole heart, my whole soul. And I conscientiously do my religious duty. And any man who would say I was mad has no charity. O God and his only begotten son, save me.'

Darcy Dancer reached forward to touch Sexton's arm to comfort him and he drew away. His hands pushing up over his face and his whole body racked with more sobs as his shoulder leaned in against the wooden panels of the shed wall knocking a stack of clay flowerpots from the shelf which broke hitting the ground. His voice came muffled out between his moans.

'Leave me be. Leave me be.'

Day after day Catherine the cook scraped together chicken scraps and boiling turnips and dished out cauldrons of potatoes covered in slabs of melted butter for the men to eat who had too far to travel back to their cottages for lunch. And Darcy Dancer still sniffed the smell of freshly baked bread coming up the stairwells. But slowly the bacon sides and hams hanging and curing from the basement ceilings vanished. Sexton now left the apples, pears, damsons and plums falling from the orchard trees for the birds to peck till they were rotting brown on the ground. The clock chimes stopped sounding in the stable tower. And the one bell outside the kitchen that all watched and listened for. Hoping to hear it ring, jangling back and forth on its curled spring. Its brass turning green. And its unused wire through the house, grown stiff with rust. Where it went turning corners on little wheels under floorboards and joists to the pearl inlaid ebony knob in my mother's silent room.

Crooks who read his bible aloud each evening in his quarters, shuttered the ballroom and closed up half the top floor, locking off chambers where he said the chill would snuff out a candle. He would sit, on the cold evenings, thick woollen dressing gown pulled over his livery and a heavy pair of white boot stockings pulled up over his trouser cuffs. And once when I came to his room to ask him for the hot bottle that was usually there warming my bed, there was a strong smell of whiskey and I pointed to a door bolted with a large padlock which he said was the hanging room and haunted by a previous butler who had hung himself from the ceiling.

'It is cursed, and should never be entered. Furthermore Master Reginald, it is not done for you to come to my chambers, it is proper you should summon me to yours.'

'I rang the kitchens. And no one came.'

'Still, it's not done. And stay away from Foxy, he sets a bad example with every broken bone in his body.'

The electric light which always faithfully glowed pale yellow in the filaments of the light bulbs was wavering weaker and weaker each evening, and now went out. The generator set on the hillside in the woods received visit after visit from the amateur engineers among the men and was given kicks, nods, pats and clanks and spins and turns but stayed still. And a man from Dublin would not come till all of Andromeda Park's unpaid bills were paid.

Candles now gave their flickering glow as the winds groaned along the stone paved corridors. And the shadows moved and loomed and maids, those with locks and those with keys to their doors, tried to make them work. With Crooks still at large midnights or dawns trying all the doors. And when my mother's father's portrait crashed down on the main staircase, Crooks stood there with a lantern and said the ghosts who have risen this night from the grave are guilty of this. And one more maid frightened into her senses was gone fleeing the next day.

The walnut grand piano began to warp and rust. The huge gilt mirror on the chimneypiece of the back drawing room fell forward where it lay crashed, broken and untouched on the floor. While slowly his mother's fortune and estate declined with the further sale by his father of their shrinking lands. From six thousand acres down to three. And now several more and larger and nearer fields were auctioned. Neighbours' boundaries coming closer and closer and arguments over trespassing sheep and cattle more and more frequent. With Crooks announcing himself at the schoolroom door as Mr Arland and I would look up from our books.

'Mr Arland please forgive my interruption. Master Reginald, while his father is away, should have announced to him callers whom I am sure you do not wish to entertain the thought of seeing, but we must at least pay them the courtesy of inquiring that this is in fact the case.'

'Thank you Crooks, I don't wish to see them.'

'Very good Master Reginald.'

Autumns, winters and a distant war, and his father's absentee and indifferent farming spread weeds and left dead sheep and unmended fences and pot holed roads. With irate farmers now threatening violence and bloodshed on the front steps. And upon his infrequent brief returns, he would immediately following lunch, reconnoitre the remaining crops or livestock. To be heard cursing as he did when the men let the hay ricks collapse or a thoroughbred horse get loose which a buyer was coming to see. And it had to be chased as it ran wild for miles. And always following three days of these continued catastrophes he would be gone again, not to be heard of for weeks and weeks. As more wagon loads of hay, sheep and bullocks disappeared, lost or stolen. But just as the grumbles would deepen, a money order would arrive for the agent, a swarthy beetle browed gentleman, to pay the back wages of the servants and men who lined up outside the old rent room.

And the evening following one such departure, and the recent hiring of a new lady housekeeper, I lay awake thinking that meaner men than my gambling father were getting closer and closer. Shouting out and shaking their fists at Crooks. And to feel I wanted to run. Gallop up over the hills. Take my pony and my mother's dogs and find a round tower made of big stones where I could climb up into and be safe. From this new woman who went poking around the house snapping orders and commands at the servants and throwing Crooks into frequent door slamming rages. And a creak of boards made me listen and then I heard a little knock and a voice.

'Are you there.'

And I thought some thoughtful ghost had come who heard me thinking. And the black knob with the golden circles, turning. A wind rushing up against the window and rattling the casement. And I sat frightened in my bed as the door slowly pushed open with a shadowy head under a cap peeking round it.

'It's me Foxy, are you awake.'

'What are you doing here.'

'Sure didn't I tell you I'd come and get you. Keep your voice down and I have it all fixed.'

'Go away.'

'What way is that to talk when I near kilt meself getting in to get you out.'

'I don't want to go.'

'Suit yourself but there'll never be another time. As ripe as right now I'm telling you. I'm going meself whether you come or not. With whiskey and all. And don't breathe a word of that. It's me own whiskey and not out of the house. Are you coming.'

The wind high and a full bright moon above the grey speeding shadows of clouds. Foxy looking back over his shoulder. For any signs of the now two major domos of the household. With Miss von B's room at the upper end of the corridor. Who had that day in her flowered silk dress and white cloth gloves sent Foxy to the town to get men to come and mend the leaks in the roof. With Foxy standing in the front hall, his cap in hand and pulling his forelock as he said yes ma'am, that's right ma'am. And then she called for Crooks to have the crashed mirror on the back drawing room floor cleared away. And her voice was heard raised and shouting.

'I am in command of zis household and you should do what I say.'

And the mirror remained. With the seven years bad luck Crooks said anyone would get cleaning it up and he put his nose in the air and walked out. And as I came down the main stairs with Crooks slamming another door somewhere down the end of the hall, I could hear Miss von B still in the salon as she called it.

'Swine. Dirty filthy swine. You are all swine in this house.'

I stood in some alarm and disbelief on the stair. Miss von B came out in the hall and saw me there. Composing herself, she stretched her neck, looking over both her shoulders from which she brushed imaginary debris. Then putting her white gloved hands to her throat she stood staring at me across the black and white tiles. I thought it appropriate one should adapt Mr Arland's cool measured words and deliver them accordingly.

'Ah Miss B.'

'It is von B thank you.'

'Ah, Miss von B. Do I perceive that you are aggrieved. Is there something I can do.'

'What can you do with swine. It is squalid. These people are nuts. They are completely nuts.'

'Nuts.'

'Yah, nuts.'

'I'm sorry but I do not know what you mean.'

'Cuckoo. Batty. Loony bin. Fruity cake crazy. I am speaking perfect English. Do you understand.'

'Yes.'

'Vell den. I am thinking I am in a madhouse. It is falling down. The dirt. It is pushed under the rugs. The greasy fingers. They go so on the doors, on the lamp shades, on the objets d'art. The mud. It come off the boots. It go all over the floors. The hair off the dogs. The rain through the ceiling. Your father, he wants spick and span. It will be smudge and stain he will get.'

'I am sorry. But we in Ireland do not think it unfit for there to be some dust and cobweb about.'

'Dust and cobweb. Ha ha. That is a good one. You are dirty people.'

'How dare you.'

'Dare. Of course. Look at my gloves. They should stay white when I touch so, and look. My finger, it is dirt. A chicken it run back and forth downstairs, in the corridor. It come in the broken window. Then there is one dead in there behind the curtain. With the feathers all over the floor.'

'Why don't you go if you are unhappy.'

'Go. I have just come. Sixty miles. I tell your father how I am treated too.'

Miss von B passed by me up the stairs. I thought perhaps

on her way to her room to pack. But later she was in the blue walled north east parlour taking afternoon tea and perusing the colour plates of my mother's large vellum bound volumes on pottery and china. Her only ally being Sexton who daily brought her a bouquet of flowers and said, by god she's a woman of culture come in her innocence to this temple of defective intellects. And von B appreciating this attendance upon her, stood patiently but dumbfounded at Sexton's stream of Greek and Latin. And one wonders now. If she lay asleep up the hall contemplating how to escape back to civilization again. Or if she sits up trembling at the creaks Foxy and I make, shoes in our hands, and stealing past her door. To proceed down by the west stair landing. The shadows of the grove of big beech trees out there. Through which we can run. To haunt the countryside this night.

'Follow me now, and never breathe a word of where I'm taking you.'

'Where are you taking me.'

'Out by the tunnel.'

'How can you get to the tunnel.'

'Ah now haven't I tolt you I'd get you out. It is how the priests got in and out of the house long ago. Quiet now, that ould eegit Crooks will be coming drunk out of his bedroom and falling on his head. Now watch where you're going over these bottles I put here on the stairs.'

'You could hurt someone.'

'It's only to know if Crooks was following me. He'd only get a little tumble and knock on the skull. Sure there are carpets over the timber. And wood never did any harm cracking your head. It's stone and cement you might feel if you wasn't used to it.'

Touching the wall, following the way behind Foxy. His stale smell of dogs and stables. Go tiptoeing down past the great window, the moon silver against the leaves and bark of the birch trees. The unhappy moan of a cow out somewhere missing its calf. Through the swing door from the main hall where the grandfather clock chimes half past the hour and down the stair to the basement. At the corridor's far end the night's white white light through the arched panes of the transom. And only feet away the bedroom door of Catherine the cook. Whose gnarled hands still toiled over her cauldrons from dawn till all the household were asleep. And she lies loudly snoring.

'Listen to the noise of that ould bitch. In here behind me now. Don't make a sound.'

The cold clammy air of the pig curing room with its shelves and slabs of slate. The heavy clank of a stone as Foxy digging in with all his fingers, prised it up from the floor. Climbing down into the darkness. The earthy damp musty chill air. And Foxy crouched grunting as he pulled on a ring to drag the stone slab thumping closed over their heads.

'No one can hear us now. And never breathe a word. This goes out now to the big tunnel back of the house. And not another soul knows.'

'The smell is not nice.'

'It takes some pipes. And they do be leaking betimes.'

'And you must stop making your unpleasant comments on members of the household.'

'What harm is that to pass a few ould remarks when I'm taking you out to the best lesson you'll get in your life. Sure and that old Catherine owns a forty acre farm and has it stocked with sheep and pigs and is stacking up pound notes in the bank. And how do you know she's not stealing.'

'Our cook is honest.'

'It's none of me business but let me tell you they're robbing the place blind.'

'Do you steal.'

'Ah only ould bits and pieces now and again. But I'm honest in general. I only lie not to get a beating. But when I'm telling the truth they think I'm lying because I'm such a liar. So it's all the same. They love giving a beating. But I don't feel a thing.'

Through the blackness, crouched hobbling forth, and hands touching in the cold mud along the dank low corridor. Water drips on the back of the neck from the roof of the tunnel. A scurrying and scrabbling.

'What's that Foxy.'

'Ah them's only a few ould rats.'

'I don't like rats.'

'Sure they'll do you no harm if you give them a swipe of your hand in the gob. It's only the very big ones that can kill cats, that'll jump for your throat and chew open your vein and take the blood out of you.'

'I want to go back.'

'Ah sure there's only a dozen or so of them in the tunnel. Sure they've only managed twice to take a bite out of me and each time I gave them a wallop with me boot that made manure of their guts. It's not more than a few yards now and we'll be in the tunnel to the stable yard. Mind these slippery steps.'

The great shadowy arch of the farm tunnel as Foxy pulls Darcy Dancer out behind him. And pushes back the stone and lifts another stone. Turf mould spread over the cobbles. The air sweet smelling with hay where clumps of it had fallen from the carts hauling it in from the fields. Down more stone steps and now along another underground passage wide enough for two men to walk abreast and tall enough that you had to reach to touch the vaulted ceiling.

'Mind now the big rats be worst here, kick out if you feel something putting teeth into you.'

'I don't like this.'

'It's not far now.'

In a black mustiness they emerged. Foxy lighting a match. A strange fear. In the chill stillness of death. A room of cob-webbed coffins stacked on stone shelves. Their rusted handles and copper nails stained green. On the oak and elm, brass plates engraved with names. Of Darcys and Thormonds. Bertha, Elizabeth, Esekiel and his own name, Reginald. On the top corbels were smaller coffins near the big ones. And the tiniest one of all. To whom death came at ten months of age. With the same christian name as his eldest sister. Beatrice Blossom Thormond.

'All your mother's lot back till Kingdom come. They'll put you in here too when your time comes.'

'They will not.'

'Ah they will. There be jewels on them in the coffins. That's why they are put here secret the way they are behind them big bars and locked with the size of them locks.'

'How do you know there are jewels.'

'I've heard tell.'

'Did you try to look.'

'I'm not going to go touching in them skulls and bones. But there are others I hear talk of who'd like to get in here.'

'Who are they.'

'Ah I'm not saying now. But they be grave robbers from beyond the other side of the lakes.'

The headstones of the cemetery looming. A breeze rustling the ivy leaves. They stepped out under the massive tangle of vines roofing over the ruins of the ancient chapel. Foxy's breathing heavy as he tugged lifted and nudged with knees and shoulder the heavy grey slab back into place. And reaching under a moss covered rock, he pulled forth a bottle of whiskey. Squatting, he planted his elbows across his thighs and tipped the pale spirit up to his lips.

'Only you're too young I'd give you some whiskey. Now like I said never tell anyone this secret way. Nobody else knows it but meself, the Gaffer and maybe that fool Crooks. I have a good mind sometimes to scare the wits out of that big old eegit Sexton when he comes here simpering to the grave-yard and I jump out at him like the holy ghost and send him blessing himself for miles running across the countryside.'

'You must not do that to poor Sexton. He is not well in his mind.'

'Sure haven't I just said he's an eegit. Bursting into the new housekeeper five times a day with a bunch of flowers. Don't I know he's not well in his mind. Isn't he there up on the altar every Sunday with his grey hair slapped back wavy on his skull and it looking black as coal.'

'And why shouldn't Sexton's hair be black.'

'Because it's as grey as your pony is white. Doesn't he go to the ould can of motor oil in the stable and take a drop. And then brush down a bit of the soot from the stove that keeps

the mares warm when they're foaling. He mixes ι
ould soot with the dirty ould motor oil till he gets
paste. Then he rubs it well in into his skull and plasι
hair back with the iron comb they do be using in the staοιε on
the horses.'

'If he wants his hair black surely that's alright.'

'It isn't the colour that anyone minds. Sure once didn't the
priest wonder on the altar if he was in a place to get petrol
with the smell of him. And then didn't a gob of that muck get
on the bottom of Father Flaherty's gold chalice and make
marks all over the altar cloth. But it was nothing mind like
when he put perfume in it and sold the stuff in jam jars down
the village to Kelly the chemist for a cure to the grey hair.
Sexton's Genuine Compound, the eegit called it. With him
printing out labels for it and all. They nearly kilt Kelly. There
were women screaming at him over the husbands' greasy
black hands they got laying holt of their heads. And the great
mess it made of the pillows. But never mind that now. See the
wood beyond. That's where we're headed.'

Foxy at a trot across the velvety soft meadows. Holding his
arms up against briars and backing his way as he climbed
through the thorn hedges. Jumping streams and ditches. And
down a heathery hillside and around the stony shores of a lake.
Up a steep bracken covered hill and on top Foxy pointed out
across the bleak moonlit flatness.

' 'Tis out there just a little walk. But mind now it's the
worst of our travels. Many coming this way to the woman
have been swallowed up in the bog. Once you slip in there
you're done for. Never to be heard tell of again. But if they
find you even after a hundred years you look like you only
died yesterday.'

'I want to go home.'

'After we come all this way. I am going to sow me oats.
Sure if you keep right behind me you'll get across safe. But
some of the holes go down ten men deep.'

The sound of pigs honking and snuggling about in their
pen. The back of a long thatched cottage standing desolate in
its muddy farmyard. One door and three small windows.

A wisp of sweet scented turf smoke descending from the chimney. Foxy putting his cupped hands to his mouth and hooting like an owl. A candle flickering past a window. One's feet wet and chill. Falling twice up to my knees in the oozing bog. Back of hands torn by briars. And finger bones stung by thorns. Across all this flat haunted land. Like we'd reached another world somewhere the other side of the earth. Huddling near the warmth of a steaming manure pile.

'I'm cold Foxy.'

'Keep in close to the heat of the dung. Won't be a minute now.'

'We've been here ages.'

'Ah sometimes it takes a little part of the night waiting.'

'Why.'

'She might have to give the ould fellow the slip.'

'Maybe he's heard your noises.'

'Ah he's nearly deaf. And the one eye he's left with is nearly blind. But we have to get a spell away over the bogs where we're safe with the woman.'

'If he's blind and deaf how could he find us.'

'Ah he's used to the place, he'd know every stump, ditch and hedge hereabouts.'

'Could he not be lost and sink in the bog.'

'Ah he'd be too wise for that. He'd know by his own steps where he'd be safe. And he could chase you up beyond with a hook and just by the heat of you he'd know where to swipe to lop off your ears. He nearly had me once only I'm too fast. And I had a raw potato I was chewing that I let him have it in the gob. It shut up his shouts with the spud locked in his mouth he was trying to dig it back out with his big ould fingers. I nearly couldn't run with laughing.'

Foxy hooting again. A wind rising. The moon passing behind thickening clouds. A donkey brays and a rooster crows.

'It could be getting morning Foxy.'

'It's not morning at all. Sure the smoke is still coming out of the chimney from the evening fire. And them ould cocks don't know when they're crowing. And if it was morning, that mean rooster in there would be out charging pecking and clawing at us.'

'I want to go home to bed now.'

'I'm telling you wait. Or you'll never clap eyes on your first cunt. And then we'll go back by way of the big castle. There be shenanigans to be had there as well.'

'I'm sleepy and cold.'

'Go then. And be sure to watch where you're stepping across the bog. And it's worse for you falling in the lake. Pike in there ferocious, bigger and longer than you are. Rip you asunder. Sure they snap duck and fox down like flies and a few big rats they gollop is only to make them hungrier.'

'I will stay.'

'And it will be the better for you.'

In the shadowy greys of dawn great wings of a bird flapping slowly across the brown bog lands. And curlews whistling as their flight dipped right and then left under the haunted sky. A snort of a horse. And the wind creaking the rusted corrugated iron roofed stables. As Foxy suddenly turns his head to look behind. And the murmur of holy shit slips from his lips. A face with a black patch over one eye looming over the wall followed quickly by shoulders coming in a giant heaving mass just behind it.

'Ah you pair of dirty little blackguards I've caught you now and you won't hoot again I'm telling you.'

'Run.'

'Run is it.'

Foxy like a streak was up and over the heap of manure. Leaping down the other side and his feet pounding and splashing through the deep mud across the farmyard. A great hand descended clutching Darcy Dancer by the back of the neck. Lifting him up in the air his feet dangling. Then dropping to the ground with lights exploding and comets zooming with sparkling tails as a blow landed on the side of his face.

A voice speaking. The smell of turf smoke and a flickering light. To stare up at a stained panelled ceiling. A hook holding a black kettle hanging over the orange glowing embers of a fire. High on a wall a red flame beneath a picture of a bearded long haired man, upon his chest his heart, out of which grew a cross. Like a statue Catherine the cook had in her damp basement room. And from a bucket of cold water on a chair, a white cold cloth came wiping blood from my brow.

'Ah the poor darling. His eyes is opening now. You nearly kilt him.'

'I did. And I would. And I will. If I ever catch him or that other one Slattery from beyond there in Thormondstown. They'll be in the bog saving the cost of their funerals. They'll be taught coming around here. And if this one needs another lesson I'll give it to him right here and now.'

'Stay away now from the child. Or I'll fix you with a bat in the kisser with this handle.'

> God love
> The poor little
> Defenceless
> Creature

5

In the late dying afternoon, a bird happily chirping just out the window of this dark strange room. One heard hoofs clip clopping far off on the surface of the hard road. Coming slowly nearer and nearer. The squeal and clang of a gate and wheels grinding over the pebbles to halt outside. Then a loud rapping on the cottage door. My head still swirling as I lifted up on my arms. And voices raised outside.

'He fell I'm telling you.'

'Be gob never mind there are pieces of you missing, if you've touched a hair of that lad's head I'll do you here and now. Till you're nothing more than rudis indigestaque moles.'

'Gospel now, the lad took a tumble.'

'Gospel is it. I'll give you gospel and it won't be from St Luke or the Corinthians. Nor will it do your inferiority complex a bit of good.'

A smile of greeting on Sexton's face. His hair gleaming black and wavy. A rug over his arm. As he steps across the earthen floor. And this large bosomy red headed lady wiping her hands in her apron.

'Ah it was only a little blood spilled out of his ear and a cut there he got on the head.'

'That bully of a husband of yours out there. Sure the lad is still in short trousers. And be gob you're priviledged to be having gentry under the roof of this hovel. How are you Master Reginald.'

'I'm groggy a bit. But I'm alright.'

'Didn't I warn you. Tell you. Keep away from the filthy likes of that Slattery leading you in your pure innocence astray. The dirty filthy pup. We had four of us to beat the truth out of him. Come now and we'll get you back to the sylvan setting and dignities of Andromeda Park and far away from the dreadful bogs out here.'

'I knew he was gentry. I knew it.'

'Madam you should be overflowing with gratitude that a Darcy Darcy Thormond related by the best of bloods back to the last kings of Ulster, has crossed the threshold of your humble abode.'

'O I am. I knew by them good boots he's wearing, sopping muddy wet as they were.'

'Come Master Reginald. I'll give you a hand now. Forsooth we are to forthwith about to depart. Without being so much as offered a cup of tea. And I leave whores and sinners to suffer what hell the hereafter has in store for them.'

'Who are you calling a whore.'

'Now woman who said anyone was a whore.'

'You did. You smarmy boot licker to the pagan gentry. Don't you call me a whore.'

'O lord what fools these mortals be.'

'Well this mortal will rattle an iron pot off your head. Get out of here now.'

'I will be gob. Sine mora. Get out and glad. And take this innocent boy away from the lickerishness concupiscence salacity and harlotry.'

'That's all you're good for is them big words. You dirty Casanova.'

Sexton turning back from the half door. A chicken scurrying out and two more shooting in. Followed by a marauding rooster. The rug tightened around Darcy Dancer's shoulders. The gleaming white plates and cups and saucers on the dresser. Steam curling up from the kettle's spout on the hearth. The woman her arms hanging out from her sides. Her bosoms set like two great prows of battleships cutting through waves seen in the war pictures of the illustrated magazine.

'What was that you said.'

'I said and you heard me, you dirty Casanova.'

'Casanova is it.'

'Cycling up to the young girls at every crossroad all over

the countryside. To get them take a ride with you across your dirty filthy handle bars.'

'No bog harlot will call me that. Not while my adoration is daily offered to the blessed virgin who stands righteous above me in her beautiful purity, you won't, be gob make that slander of me I'm telling you.'

'I will. And tell you to fuck off out of here as well. Casanova.'

'Be gob woman Lord have mercy on the souls of your livestock if that's the kind of lingo they hear. But I've said to you now. Don't repeat that aspersion. Call me a homo, a paederast, a sodomite but be gob don't use the word Casanova to me again.'

'Casanova.'

The tears flooding into Sexton's eye. His fist raised shaking as he steps across the floor. A dog barking and a long groan of a beast out in the farmyard. The woman raising her own fist and with the other reaching for a pot on the mahogany sideboard behind her. Sexton grabbing for her upraised arm.

'Get off me you. You big hulking dirty Casanova.'

Two fisted the woman sinking her clutching fingers into Sexton's hair. The writhing figures crashing backwards into the wall. Turning, twisting, pulling and tearing. Looming about in the shadows panting and grunting. Gasps from Sexton as his eye patch comes off.

'O merciful lord almighty god.'

A bell like clink and clang as a flying elbow pokes a metal tureen to the ground. And the chickens run scurrying out of the way back and forth, jumping to the sills of the windows to flap there against the panes.

'Get your hands off me tits you viper.'

'Bear false witness against me will you, you swamp trollop.'

'Get your disgusting interfering claws off me personals.'

'I'm merely clutching at the rubbery fat of you, madam.'

The back of Sexton's coat rent down its seam. His shoulders covered in whitewash from the walls. The woman's hands losing their grip as Sexton, arms free, let loose long looping swings at the red haired head huddling to fend off the blows.

'Mick, Mick the holy greasy terror is having me kilt. Come Mick.'

Sexton momentarily ceasing his blows, pressing both hands down on the back of the woman, and turning his face away upwards towards the heavenly deity.

'Dear lord my god and saviour give me strength as well as your forgiveness to chastise this female savage.'

Out of the grey afternoon, sudden sunlight flashing in the tiny window. As more came flooding in the door behind a roaring Mick with a shovel. His one hand gripped holding it out with the long handled end stuck under his one good arm-pit, as the other empty sleeve of his coat flapped up and down.

'Where are yez Agnes, where are yez.'

The two warring figures hair engripped, waltzing across the room. Mick blindly swiping with the shovel. Missing the antagonists and carving a wide wood naked furrow down the polished length of the sideboard. Splintering a butter churn and smashing divers potteries to smithereens.

'Ah jesus. I missed. Holt him still Agnes till I get a smell of his location.'

Sexton, eyes closed and dentures stuck half out of his mouth. Hanging on to the woman as they tripped over a fallen chair and fell backwards. Crashing into the dresser. A hook catching in the torn tatters of clothing and the falling contorted bodies pulling the dresser plunging forward with cups, saucers, plates and platters crashing on the floor. Now turned white with spilt milk and the feathers of a chicken nailed flapping and cackling beneath the shattered shelves. While its winged comrade flutters down from the window sill to peck morsels from a loaf of bread.

'Me dowry, me dowry. It's ruined. Mick over here. Quick get a smell of him. I've a good holt. Dig him one with the shovel in the guts.'

Darcy Dancer clutching himself in the blanket. Trembling with cold. Squeezing backwards into the corner behind the door. To pray to someone. That Sexton stays alive to take me home.

'Now Mick now.'

'I'll get him Agnes.'

Mick putting his nose forward sniffing. As his next step comes down squarely on a chicken. And he jumps back. With a swing of his body bringing the shovel whistling in a great arc. To slam in mid flight the squawking rooster across the room with glass shattering concussion into a photograph picture of a man in white raiment holding a hand up in blessing.

'You eegit Mick you've smashed in the holy pontiff himself.'

'Ah god I can't see a thing at all without me eyes.'

'Aren't we in front of yez. Haven't I a holt of him. His dentures has his mouth jammed. Now's the time.'

'In this heat of the house I can't get me direction. Agnes let loose of the fucker and duck out of the way and I'll cream him. Say where you are.'

'I'm here, here. With the grease of his hair on me hands I can't keep a holt of him.'

'Ah god with the noise I don't know where you are.'

'I'm here you eegit. With him getting loose.'

'I'm coming now. Say where you are.'

'Here you eegit. Can't you hear the landing of the punches on me all over.'

'I'll put paid to him. Say where you are.'

'Haven't I said I'm here. Stop the talk for mercy's sake. Clout him one with the shovel.'

Agnes doubled over, arms crossed on her head. Sexton with the knuckles of one hand trying to reverse his dentures sticking backwards out of his mouth. Hammering his other fist downward on the crouched back of the woman. Mick holding the handle end of the shovel under his chin and the handle length over his arm as he feels ahead with his hand advancing towards the sound of the struggle.

'Is it him I'm feeling Agnes.'

'You daft thing, wouldn't you know by now the feel of your own wife. It's him just to the left of you there now. The left, the left. Don't you know the left. I've got holt of his arm and another on his belt. Carve his fucking head off.'

The rooster lying feebly flapping its wings as it slowly turns on its back in a circle, feet sticking in the air pointing up at the smashed picture of the man in white raiment. A sheep dog rushing to bark in the door and cowering away again. And Sexton pulling out his dentures.

'Ah god so you bog trotters use language will you and gang up on me like Judases betraying Jesus at the last supper.'

Mick, the horizontal stump of his arm trembling in its sleeve, lifting the shovel up over Sexton's head. Darcy Dancer rushing forward from his corner. Crushing pebbles of sugar underfoot. Two pigs honking and snorting in the door, pink ears flapping over their eyes and biting and squealing at each other as they suck up the milk from the floor. Darcy Dancer pushing with two hands against Mick's rear end. As the blind man's rusty spear shaped shovel descends on the red haired woman's back with a lung thudding thwack.

'I'm kilt.'

'O tempora o mores, no sweeter sound is there than the thump of justice.'

'It's the young one Agnes gave me a shove.'

'What's wrong with ya, ya blind fool. Smash the holy father the pope and now murther your wife.'

The figures crumpled upon one another in a mass of entwining limbs. Gasps of air sucked in and breath heaving out of chests. A shadow at the door.

'Vas is diss. Achtung. Stop. Stop. At once immediately. I call the police stop.'

Miss von B, riding whip in her hand. Smacking it into her glove. The end of the long thong falling over the tip of her black boot. As she stood legs astride in derby hat, white breeches and brown hunting coat. The antagonists slowly standing. Grabbing back pieces of their clothing still clutched in other hands. The pigs rooting and snorting for tid bits in under and around the upturned furniture.

'What ist diss fight. You should be ashamed. Grown people. Do you not know any better.'

Miss von B's blonde hair coiffeured in a net under her hat. Spurs on her boots. A gold pin stuck sparkling with a large diamond in the white scarf at her throat. Upon which she places her hand as the avian livestock flap in her direction to escape. And the woman of the big bosoms points her finger.

'Isn't she the fine one now coming in here. Giving orders. With the heathenish gang of you from over there in Thormondstown raping me.'

'Achtung. Shut up you woman. What do you know about rape. I know about rape. Come. We go.'

Sexton bowing. The pink darkness of his toothless smile. Long scratches dripping blood down his concave cheeks.

'Excuse me Countess for my temporarily suspended phonetics. Occasioned by the recent dislodgement of my false choppers both uppers and lowers.'

Sexton brushing his dentures off on his sleeve. Placing them back in his mouth and taking them out again.

'Ah god haven't they been maltreated out of shape by you savages. Let's out of here now, Master Reginald and leave the habitués of these waterlogged banshee riddled bogs to stew in their ignorance. And madam, my esteemed Countess, a lady of your high standing and dignified status should not have to witness the unpleasant consequences of a common brawl.'

The red haired woman, holding her torn flowered garment together across her chest. Following Sexton out the cottage door, her neck craned forward spitting words between Sexton's shoulder blades as he guided Darcy Dancer with a hand behind the dark haired head.

'I'll be suing you, you cycling romeo, for damages. And the sacrilege of smashing in the face of the pontiff.'

Miss von B shaking the rein of her horse as it pulls its head away to grab more grass. Her backside two gleaming mounds of white under her kid skin breeches as she pulls herself up over her saddle and shifts a thigh over the mare's quarters to seat herself. Sexton helping Darcy Dancer up into the trap, wiping a place dry and placing him snug on the leather cushion and wrapping him tight in a blanket. The woman clutching the leg of a chair in her hand, holding it up shaking at Sexton who wags his finger down at the red fuming face.

'Sue madam, sue if you like. Continue to conduct your hate

and strife. Sure it will be good to hear evidence given concerning this occasion with all the attendant reasons, wherefors and whatfors. And as the searchlights of publicity is placed upon you in the dock and your faulty slanderous testimony is recorded in the books for all time, just remember that there is he, the eternal omnipotence above you, who shall be the final judge. And in the exercise of his great level headedness he will sure as hell put the flames scorching you in your rigor mortis.'

'Don't be talking as if yez are the only saint on earth. I'll get the lawyers to you bunch for the damages. Trespassing, breaking and entering. Rape. Assaulting a blind disabled and altered cripple. I'll have the writs out after you.'

Sexton face up to the skies. His palm raised to the fine falling mist. A sudden beaming ray of sun casting a shimmering blaze of purple green and orange in a rainbow out over the brown bog lands.

'Dear god, to whom these days can we say, dearly beloved. Sure the Prince of Peace himself would break a leg running to escape from the likes of the pair of you. But look at the irony of that now. Beauty in the heavens. Over a miserable bit of landscape the likes of this.'

'Well there'll be bloodshed on earth, yet. Wait and see. I'll get you.'

'And if you do madam you'll only be bringing grief to the pistils petals and stamens grown by a poor humble common gardener. Ah and who knows it may do your lunatic self esteem a world of good. But beware you don't get a fatal fist in the gob first.'

The red haired woman throwing the chair leg whistling past Sexton's ducking head as he slaps down the reins and the barrel shaped Petunia takes off galloping after Miss von B's horse cantering ahead up the pot holed drive.

'Go on you dirty romeo, go home and put more of your black filthy grease on your hair.'

Two small scraggly ash trees on either side of the gate out to the tar black shiny road. Which stretched straight out into the white mists descending from hills ahead. The emptiness in all directions. As we rolled over the steamy smell of Miss von B's horse's dung freshly plopped. And another rainbow now high above the first, spanning all the countryside from one end of the world to the other.

'Ah Master Reginald, you've learned your first lesson in life. Unless you were better off where you've been, you're always better off where you are. But no matter where you've been or where you are you'll never know if you'll be better off where you're going. Are you right, now.'

'Yes.'

'Thanks be to the sacred heart of Jesus your beautiful gentle mother wasn't alive to witness any of that back there. But the real sad horror of it all. Is your blind man. He isn't only missing an arm and like meself, an eye. But didn't a mare he was after beating with a club throw him from her back on to the ground and then come with her teeth, and with one swift awful mouthful like the handiest surgeon who'd ever wielded a scalpel, bite completely off all the things most men are born with between their legs.'

> And you'd
> Not think
> The pair of them
> Back there
> Would need this soon
> Another sample of justice
> Following that

6

His foot treading on one of Foxy's bottles, Crooks in the dawn of the day of the bog fight, sailed on his backside and tumbled on his head down the stairs and broke his left arm and right collarbone. Miss von B heading out for her early morning canter found him groaning at the bottom of the landing that overlooked the grove of beeches.

For many days Crooks looked very poorly indeed perambulating about the house. His face pallid, his arm in a black sling and with one of my father's old purple velvet smoking jackets thrown over his shoulders. He sat many hours at the side of the kitchen range sipping Catherine's cabbage soup and referring the reputedly medicinal contents of a pewter flask frequently to his lips. While Miss von B held sway in the reception rooms above as she stood with her whip over Norah and Sheila on their knees scrubbing their way across the tiles of the front hall. And Crooks, shooing at the cat when it sharpened its claws on the leg of the kitchen table, would announce.

'Of course, when I am back on my feet there will be changes in this house and soon.'

Out in the barn, Foxy was another mass of welts, bumps and bruises, seated on his milking stool slapping away the kicks of the cow.

'I'll get them. All four of them cunts. One at a bloody time.'

Foxy groomed my pony, blacked its hoofs and plaited its mane and turned me out in some splendour each hunting day and I'd find him evenings before by lantern light in the tack room rubbing my boots and leathers.

'But Foxy it will be the worse for you if you try to get revenge.'

'Ah it'll be one full moon and before it's half up in the sky, I'll be gone out of here and be far away. All I'm getting in this place is pennies for wages anyway. Join the circus or something like that. It'll be here now soon at the village. Have you been pulling your prick like I told you.'

'Yes.'

'Did the juice come out.'

'No.'

'You want to keep pulling. Just a few little tugs is not enough.'

The bog fight still the talk of the countryside all these months later. With the maids still snickering behind their hands. And Crooks thinking I had with Foxy put the bottles on the stairs. Now each full moon, with the moist slates on the barn roofs shining silver, I watch out the window across to where I can just see through a valley made by the tree tops. And beyond, the distant darknesses of the rest of the world. Leaving me standing here as the gales come roaring out of the west and bang doors somewhere through the night, making my life all fearful and lonely. And that I, like Foxy should go out and away from Andromeda Park forever.

Appearing white faced and chilled but far more dapper than usual with a reddish moustache sprouting on his upper lip, Mr Arland patted me reassuringly on the back. Repairing as we did now to the salon, daily aired and recently spick and span with its furnishings dusted and the warped cover of the grand piano gleamingly polished. At the big map table in front of a roaring log fire we sat and on the large globe of the world traced the ancient excursions of St Brendan.

'Ah yes Kildare, to be sure, St Brendan discovered the new world long before Columbus did. Quite extraordinary how scholars jump to their sometimes premature conclusions. Even the Vikings were on those nether shores five hundred years before that chap the Spaniard. Although dear me, does it really matter when one considers America's total and abysmal lack of culture.'

And Sexton, prior to rushing as he did all over the house with his vases in the wake of Miss von B was one morning in the flower room cutting and pruning his stems. And arranging his winter greeneries, holly, wild berries and bog grasses, when he held up a catkin.

'Now this unisexual inflorescence would do that intellectual humbug Arland a world of good presenting it to his inamorata he's paying court to away over there on the outskirts of town.'

'What do you mean by that Sexton.'

'I mean the young blue eyed lady with the long golden hair who rides to the hounds like a little queen. Sure she's a distant relation of the Thormonds if not the Darcys. And Baptista Consuelo are her christian names. Now wasn't that fool Arland refused as he asked for her hand in marriage. And he hardly knows the girl.'

'Mr Arland is not a humbug nor a fool.'

'Ah little you know. He was a fool a fool, sine dubio, a fool. Refused he was as he knelt, knelt would you believe it, on the very steps of her house with his nosegay. Sure the decent people inside didn't know what to do answering the door to that besotted suitor. He was lucky it was pouring rain which kept the crowd to a minimum who were spying on the ridiculous spectacle from behind every curtain and abutment.'

'Mr Arland never did that.'

'He did. He did. He did, I'm telling you. Sure he's a perfect stranger to the girl and what would she want with the likes of him when she could have the biggest earl, cattle dealer or duke she fancies in the district. Sure it's divitiae virum faciunt everywhere these days.'

Before Christmas as the wet early afternoon days grew dark, Mr Arland escorted me in the governess's cart drawn by Petunia to the great castle for dancing class. And the first of twelve to be held following lunch on Monday Wednesday and Thursday of each week. Bundled up in rugs and hatted with sou'westers, we fast trotted the five miles by the winding road, the breeze blowing at us warmed by the steamy fat quarters of Petunia. Passing as we did around that half of the village green where I saw the large stone house behind its tall clipped hedge and iron fence. A gravel walk between neat square lawns up to the granite steps. And when Mr Arland turned to look back staring at the grey building, his eyes moist with wind and mist, there came no reprimand as I asked.

'Mr Arland what is the literal of divitiae virum faciunt.'

'Riches make the man.'

Not till we finally came in under the arch of the gate lodge of the great castle, clip clopping over the pebbled drive under vaulted silver branches of the beech trees, would Mr Arland arouse from his silence. And as the road dipped downwards he said, let's have a run. And snapping the whip we'd go hair flying over the remaining winding road through the park land. To rein to a stop on the gravel in front of the entrance door. And there before us with its great towers and turrets rising in grey stone splendour stood the castle I had so often seen in the distance across the countryside.

Mr Arland lifting and thumping the knocker, an iron fist on an iron arm. Letting it fall pounding on the thick slabs of oaken wood. And we waited and waited till he pulled on a gleaming brass knob set in the wall.

'I prefer not to have to use this bell as it rouses too many of the servants who shortly will be at many windows nosey to see, who it is who is calling upon the high the good and the mighty.'

Inside, the sound of heavy beams, chains and shackles being loosed. Scrapes and bumps as the massive portal opens. And we entered this fortified vestibule to go up steps and through another pair of oaken doors and out into a huge hall, its vaulted ceiling high as clouds, its walls hung with flags, weapons of war, portraits and emblems, and the whole chamber as big nearly as all the rooms of Andromeda Park put together. A tall bent grave faced butler called Simpers received us and took our coats. It was said he always examined the cut and fabric of each garment, and would, with apparel offending his sensibilities, hang them in a place which he thought suitable to their inferiority. And I saw him hesitate with Mr Arland's naval great coat before deciding that it deserved to be hung well. And before Simpers returned, Mr Arland gave me a little bow and smile.

'Kildare, don't sneeze, don't fall, don't trip and don't associate with those who do. But waltz well. Ta ta.'

Mr Arland brushing down his waistcoat and lapels, disappeared through a door to another room off the hall where he was lecturing several collected ladies on the architecture of the Byzantine. And I was left standing there in the monstrous semi darkness as Simpers with his permanent stoop shuffled out of the shadows and led me away from these towering walls hung with their vast tapestries, ancient killing implements and where beneath these trophies and in the glow of a log fire I felt awfully sad about Mr Arland and his love spurned by the blue eyed girl with the golden hair who lived in the town in the grey stone house overlooking the village green.

Behind Simpers I went by a door up a candlelit stair hung with portraits to a landing. Then by another door up another staircase to a dark long hall and by pink carpet past endless bedroom doors and intersecting corridors. And yet by another door and up more stairs of more portraits to finally emerge in a large attic hall half way down which was a large room with a skylight and the windows barred. Here, with music crackling out of a great horn of a gramophone, a blond curly haired gentleman stood attired in light blue tights with three prominent little bumps bulging between the fork of his legs where no horse yet had bitten away what men usually had there. And flexing the muscles of his thighs he lisped in his high pitched voice.

'Ah my last little victim has arrived. And who may I ask are you.'

'I am Reginald Darcy Thormond Dancer Kildare.'

'Ah you are already a dancer. Good. O.K. Pay attention. I am the Count Brutus Blandus MacBuzeranti O'Biottus and although I am named after the Greek comic poet I shall stand for no nonsense or comedy. And you will obey me. You will not speak. You will stand like so poised. And you will be fearful of your very life. Understand.'

'Yes.'

'Yes, sir, you say.'

'Yes sir.'

The seven of us, four girls and three boys swirled around on the dusty floor. The Count pounding the worn broken keys of an upright piano. His metronome ticking and his shrill cries. With four white candles flickering in the breeze of his gesticulating arms.

'Dance you silly little children, dance with the élan of the gazelle before I must tear my hair out in agony.'

Tea brought at four. Two great silver trays of scones steamy hot under linen napkins. Golden yellow beaming balls of butter. Honey, damson and gooseberry jams. Soda bread, ham, chicken and egg sandwiches. Silver pitchers of cream. The Count holding the back of his hand stiffly out under his chin to catch drips from his cup. And he stood to bow to our host's mother who called.

'How Blandus are they getting on.'

'Ah the little darlings they are so wonderful. Simply wonderful. Look at them there, won't you, so serenely sitting. But dance, never, they are too much like cattle, the ankles far too thick, my dear lady. Since I am a genius, it is such a waste of my most precious time. Better to teach them to plough and milk the cows. Ah but I am descended from fighters, and I will not my dear dear lady give the poor darlings up as a lost cause. Until of course I am exasperated beyond the redemption.'

A brougham came to call and drawn by two prancing greys, I was fetched back with three other little dancers two girls and a boy who regarded me with the deepest suspicion and I asked to be dropped at the front gates of Andromeda Park from where I could run free and wild by a short cut through the woods scaring up pheasants lurking in the dark passages under the rhododendrons.

And Miss von B upon my closing the front door came strolling out of the blue parlour, her high heels clicking on the tiles and her silk stockinged legs with long sinewy muscles splayed as she stopped and took her ivory cigarette holder from her mouth and blew a puff of smoke upwards into the chill of the entrance hall.

'Ah what use is to clean. You have just come in like to a

barn and make more muddy mess. While I am hoping perhaps to progress in ziss house while that Crook is hors de combat. But when everything spick and span it is quick again dirt and smear.'

'It is my mother's house and I shall do as I please.'

'Ah, of course. Once upon a time. It was your mother's perhaps. But now your father's maybe.'

'It is not. It is mine. Anyway he never comes here.'

'Ah it is no business of mine but perhaps to avoid, how do you say, the misunderstanding, we should change the subject. You have learned by now, have you not, the waltz.'

'I have not.'

'What, you have not. But how come.'

'I do not prefer dancing.'

'O but you will never meet a nice girl.'

'I don't want to meet a nice girl.'

'Ah but that is a pity. Because of course, you must sometime find a wife.'

'I am never going to get married.'

'Ah what a shame. Someday you would live with your wife here in this house.'

'I am not going to ever live in this house.'

'Ah but then what are you going to do.'

'I am going to be a bishop.'

'Ah a bishop. So. But before you become a bishop what will you do.'

'I will be the Master of Foxhounds.'

'Ah. Ah.'

'Or maybe a jockey.'

'Perhaps it is that Foxy who has taught you to be so marvellous a rider. He says he has the horse for me.'

'I should not if I were you go on that horse.'

'Ah he would run away.'

'Yes and he would kill you.'

'Ah tut tut, he perhaps would not kill me. But it is so friendly for Foxy to recommend a horse who would try.'

'Foxy is not particularly keen on members of the household as a matter of fact.'

'I should remind you I am not a member of the household I am a private person here who is in charge. As a guest you might say.'

'You are not a guest.'

'Ah perhaps not exactly. But your father would prefer it so.'

'Why did you come here.'

'That is perhaps not your business.'

'Why did my father hire you.'

'Ah again perhaps it is not your business.'

'Why do you always carry your whip and make Norah and Sheila work so hard.'

'They are lazy. But why I carry my whip. That also is not your business.'

'Should you persist in being what I regard as uncommonly rude to me I shall turn every member of this household against you and drive you out.'

'What is that you say.'

'You have heard what I have said.'

'That is outrage. Outrage. You. Who are you, Bonaparte already.'

'I am a most cunning fellow. But because I am so young and have not come of age I have not got the power to dismiss you. Therefore I must use other means at my disposal.'

'I would slap your little face. How dare you.'

'I am a daring chap as a matter of fact.'

'Ziss. Ziss madhouse.'

'If you stay here, you too shall become mad.'

'Your father is my employer. Until he tells me so to go I shall stay. You of course who have grown a few inches too fast perhaps. Your head it gets too much full of your importance.'

'You watch out, you.'

'Ah you set a trap. Like for Crooks.'

'Good day to you.'

'Good day to you too Master Reginald Bonaparte.'

At night before sleep, as Foxy recommended, I pulled and pulled my penis. With the sheets stiffened in the morning with white stains. Awaking with visions of that other night and day of the red haired woman out across the bogs. And returning home shivering rescued by Sexton, clip clopping up under the mists into the hills again. Past a little group of tinkers at their meal around a fire, like the multi coloured petals of a flower. They watched as we went by from under their tousled heads of hair. Their days spent beneath rainy skies on the chill wet grass. Clustering close to a kettle brewing over burning sticks and ashes. To all go lie asleep huddled tight in under their tiny canvas covering. While their ponies hobbled grazing along the road.

Miss von B made a sudden stir out hunting. Changing from her own usual regalia. To riding side saddle wearing my mother's habit and on my mother's mare. Crooks the following day retrieved the outfit to hide it, shouting loudly, up and down the kitchen hall.

'The sheer brazen cheek of that woman to dare to sully my ladyship's robes.'

And an evening following hunting and her long hot bath, Miss von B was down in the kitchen hall pinning notices on a board under the servants' bells. With dire warnings should her breakfast be late brought to her bedroom. Crooks now limping and quaking in anger again. Buttons missing from his stained livery and with his leg recently sprained in another fall. And following his long silences as he served me as I sat solitary in the dining room, he would always bark out after I'd finished my pudding.

'Kummel Master Reginald.'

'No thank you Crooks.'

'Cigar Master Reginald.'

'No thank you Crooks.'

And then in his specially deep voice, reserved for these occasions, he would lean in close to my ear.

'Well that awful woman thinks that she should now dine with you and she has posted a notice to that effect. Which I, knowing of your preferences, Master Reginald, took the liberty of tearing up.'

And now whenever Crooks and von B confronted there

would be conducted loud shouting matches. The two of them raising and waving their arms. With Sheila running for her life and Norah raising her eyebrows high over her bright green eyes, mumbling, it's a loony bin, it's a loony bin. And I would always speed to the locality to take up my listening post. For as Foxy now said life in Andromeda Park was quickly becoming every man for himself. And the more recent news one had of the goings on, the better.

'You have no right madam, while my back is turned to enter the wine cellar and remove bottles without my leave.'

'And why not.'

'Because not only are you assuming prerogatives beyond your station madam but I must make a note of all bottles in the cellar book.'

'Ha ha, the cellar book. I laugh. It is so much, how do you say fraud, ziss cellar book.'

'Fraud. Before I consult my solicitor, let me tell you a thing or two madam. I won't be spoken to in that or a similar manner under the roof of this house where I have served faithfully my dear mistress, the Antoinette Delia Darcy Darcy Thormond.'

'Your mistress Madam Kildare you mean.'

'I mean my mistress loved by all, the most wonderful charming beautiful lady that ever strode or rode across this county.'

'Of course it is sad but she is dead.'

'She is not dead. As sure as the god above, she lives and breathes in this house. She walks these halls at night. She dances in the ballroom. And she is appalled. Absolutely appalled by you, madam.'

'O god what nuts. Already I know you are all mad.'

And as I sat one evening in the dining room with the winds howling and shutters rattling and Miss von B taking her meals alone served by Norah in the small morning room just across and down the hall, I dropped a potato on the polished table. And as I reached to wipe away the steamy stain it made, Crooks gave a great sigh of his whiskey perfumed breath.

'Ah Master Reginald now, no need for you to bother doing

that. A wipe from me in a thrice will take care of it. It's that woman of course with her rules has us all extremely upset. She will soon be cleaning and polishing the pebbles on the drive. And I do think and fear that I will, should she continue to stay, give in my notice.'

'Crooks please, you must not entertain such a thought.'

'I shall. Believe me I shall. She is quite making my life miserable. I have run this household all these years, O but I simply can't repeat what I have already said so often.'

'Crooks you know I had nothing to do with putting bottles for you to slip on, on the stairs.'

'I heard it told from Foxy's father's lips that indeed you were innocent of that blackguard's attempt at murder. But that interfering woman and I cannot stay in the same house.'

Foxy came riding on the hunt. And where we met at the pub on the four roads, he won bets drinking pints of porter while standing on his head. With folk later screaming at him as he barged by on the untameable Thunder and Lightning, smashing through hedge and fence, scattering sheep and cattle and sending protesting farmers running for their lives.

I rode along with Miss von B and others of the nervous contingent who took up the near rear of the field, next to the terrified contingent who lagged building back walls and closing gates. I saw Baptista Consuelo. On a silver grey mare. A light tinge of red on her cheeks. A bowler set on her golden hair, her smile radiant and blue eyes sparkling in the fresh blowing breeze. And poor Mr Arland with the locals came cycling the roads after us. Dismounting in his naval great coat to approach while we waited for the hounds to raise a fox. As again and again they failed to keep a scent. Mr Arland looked many times in his little queen's direction and once, as he approached, she with a kick of her spurs cantered away. And I wondered if beauty did make a woman very mean.

Sunshine broke out over the fields. Suddenly the hue and cry went up as the hounds found a fox. And the horses and their thundering made the whole earth shake. Foxy in front of the master flailing the quarters of Thunder and Lightning. The brave contingent in hot pursuit. Down across a pasture towards a high bank and ditch. And suddenly one saw a horse and rider somersaulting through the air and both thudding to the ground. And as I got closer I could see it was Foxy, still tightly gripped to his rein, Thunder kicking and lashing hoofs in all directions and one knocking Foxy flat. I approached thinking he was done for. But again he was up and mounted and hammering away with his crop.

'Come on get going you four legged cunt.'

Back in the stables that evening, Foxy said Thunder's kick was only a feather tap on the belly and with the briar scratches on his face caked over with dried blood, he finished rubbing down the legs of my pony with his clumps of straw. Beckoning me as I stood taking my saddle and reins to the tack room.

'Come here till I tell you now while the time's ripe. Let me back in the house behind you. Sure I could be carrying up an extra basket of turf for your fire and none would be the wiser. And maybe I'll show you something you won't forget.'

Foxy following me lugging a basket of turf. Catherine giving him a dirty look out the door as we passed the kitchen. And an even dirtier look and a distinct growl from Crooks on the landing next to the schoolroom. And up the servants' staircase we went and down the hall to my ablution room.

'Take off your boots now and come this way.'

In stockinged feet following Foxy up two more flights and tiptoe along the cul de sac hall with all its closed up servants' rooms. Foxy carrying a chair to a small window aperture shaped in a fleur de lis high on the wall. A faint light glowing beyond inside. The sound of a splash and water. Foxy standing on the upholstered chair his finger over his lips for me to climb up behind him to look.

Darcy Dancer holding on to Foxy Slattery's hard muscled shoulder. As they peered in through the glass and through an open closet door. And diagonally across and under a bed tapestry and downwards, there was Miss von B lying stretched with her face and bosoms floating in the steaming bath water.

'Got to wait till she gets out before we can catch a good

sight of her. Anytime about evening that I could get into the house I've had my eye full of plenty from here I'm telling you.'

Miss von B pulling herself up by her hands on the edge of the tub. Her bosoms expanding forward.

'Ah now look at that. Didn't I tell you. O what I wouldn't give to get a handful of one of them.'

Miss von B climbing out of the copper bath.

'O Jesus O Jesus now will you look at that.'

The gleaming whiteness standing drying in the candlelight. Seeming so much bigger and more of her than when she wore clothes. The white curving contours shining wet and dabbed and rubbed pink and bright. The chair wobbling with the shifting weight of an excited Foxy.

'Ah Jesus it would put sight in a blind eye. Will you get that now. Will you look at them fine bags on her.'

Miss von B her foot up against the edge of the copper tub, breasts shaking gently as she spread cream up along her thighs, knees and elbows. And pushes her feet in red slippers to move out of sight. Foxy groaning as he stretches craning to look. The fabric of the chair creaking and the cracking sound of wood. With a loud collapsing crash. A whisper coming from Foxy out of the blackness.

'Fucking cunt.'

And from the other side of the partition, a voice sounding nervous in the stillness.

'Who's dat.'

As I fell backwards. Landing on the fundament. My legs suddenly without feeling. With more challenging shouts from within the bedroom. And just as I was sensing in the dark with my hands to see if the bottom part of me was still there, my legs began to feel again. With pounding sounded coming up the servants' staircase. Foxy already taking his leave on all fours. With only one way to go or be trapped back down the cul de sac hall. Or turn left along the corridor now echoing the steps of an approaching von B or else a recent new ghost wearing slippers.

Darcy Dancer pressing back into a bedroom doorway. Foxy

crouching next to a large glass fronted cabinet. Stored with stacks of dishes of patterns and styles disused over the years. Crooks arriving at the top of the stairs dimly silhouetted by the moonlit landing window below. Until the light of a candle held high in the hand of von B wrapped in a towel throws more shadows down the hall. And illumines to Crooks the sight of Foxy pressed up to the side of the dresser.

'I've got you, you brazen hooligan.'

'Like hell you have you ould crippled cunt.'

Foxy springing up and out with a growl. Colliding with Crooks's and the two of them in a whirl engripped, falling backwards against the dish cabinet. Crooks hanging on for dear life. Foxy dragging him back and forth on the clamouring floorboards as Crooks loses and regains his hold and in one grand embracement locking his arms around Foxy as the two fall with a massive thump against the cabinet which smashes against the handrail of the banister and breaks it from its anchorage in the wall.

'You ould stupid eegit let loose or I'll fucking well brain you.'

'I've got you now.'

Crooks's strange shrieking grunts with his arms grabbed around Foxy as the pair of them again and again crash into the cabinet. Von B raising her candle higher over a nicely rounded pair of shoulders. The tall dark shadow of the piece of furniture and its entire breakable contents slowly moves, creaking, breaking and with a splintering of wood pitches through the balustrade. A female screech as the cabinet plummets. A moment's silence before it crashes. And a thunder as dishes, bowls, sauce boats and egg cups shatter in pieces everywhere down the flight of stairs below. With Crooks still bellowing and holding on.

'You'll not get away from me this time you blackguard.'

From my redoubt I had a rear view of the silhouetted bifurcation of Miss von B's legs. Wondering when she was going to shout stop. As she did the day out on the bogs. While Foxy tore at Crooks's grip and dragged him thumping down the stairs to the landing. Where with one massive wrench Foxy broke free. Sending Crooks flying and momentarily stunned against the clanking rusting metal of a suit of armour from which as a tiny boy I always thought I saw eyes peering out. As Foxy stood with all his escape routes blocked. The cabinet wedged between wall and banister. Von B above and sounds of more feet coming up the servants' stairs.

'You'll none of you get me you bunch of cunts.'

Foxy turning and facing the casement window, took two steps backwards and with his arms and elbows held up in front of his face, leaped crashing through. To descend three storeys down into the darkness. With the sound of breaking branches followed by a thud and thump. With Miss von B suddenly apoplexed bare arsed without her towel. And Crooks surfacing from his dazed condition on the floor.

'That should be final good riddance to that blackguard. Bury him we will. And be delivered forever of his infernal nuisance.'

Crooks getting to his feet. Turning to pick up and hang back the metal codpiece knocked off the suit of armour. And carefully stepping over the pieces of glass from the smashed casement as he wrings his hands in the fresh breeze blowing in this recently widely opened window. And slowly raising his head to look up. To see the apparition standing in its candle light at the top of the stairs.

'Jesus Mary and Joseph. As if death out the window isn't enough. Haven't we got up there the kraut herself in the buff.'

Naked
As the day
The
Almighty
Made her

7

Foxy following his jump from the window had a broken finger. And his jacket hung caught between the branches of a yew and ash tree high above the deep impression he left of his feet arse and hands in the soil of a flower bed where he landed. Miss von B had shrieked and grabbed up her towel, rushing away back down the hall. Leaving Crooks, lame as he was, dancing over the broken glass in circles of joy. Till he fell groaning with a twisted ankle. To be escorted under the armpits by Norah and Sheila back to his chambers.

And I had made my way along past the bedroom door where von B had taken her bath. Foxy said it was the room where the hottest water came up from the kitchen range. And where, after a day's hunting my father used to come to bathe in the medicinally beneficial big copper tub.

For some time after her impromptu nudity Miss von B was bundled in shapeless sweaters and often took till noontime to appear at all. And when she did I found my trousers poking out nearly popping my fly buttons. While I disported myself with an academic air carrying about my person books Mr Arland recommended I read from the library. And he gave me promiscuous exercises in Syntactical Parsing.

'Kildare, take this down. To live long, ought not to be our favourite wish, so much as to live well. By continuing too long on earth, we might only live to witness a greater number of melancholy scenes, and to expose ourselves to a wider compass of human woe. Got it.'

'Yes sir.'

'Good. Resolve syntactically into its elements, analyse and describe.'

Mr Arland's quoted exercise seemed to me to make much

sense, especially since the next night after the débâcle, Foxy's father chased him all around their cottage pounding him with his fists. Until Foxy grabbed a hammer and clouted his dada senseless. To then run back across the fields to the farmyard and go up to the tiny bedroom loft over the stables, from where watch was kept on foaling mares. And there he jumped upon Luke the sleeping groom, who had been one of the four upon whom he had sworn vengeance. Punching his face black and blue and tearing one of his ears half off.

Next morning Foxy was gone. The rumour was he'd run away to join the circus. And then one late afternoon a week later I was out galloping my pony up over and down the other side of spy glass hill. When I heard this shout. Coming from behind an entanglement of gorse and brambles. And as I reined round there was Foxy cold and shivering, a big old macintosh over his shoulders.

'Ah is there no sign yet of his funeral.'

'No, he woke up this afternoon.'

'Ah I'm glad to hear that. I was sure he was murdered with the guards out after me. But I didn't want to do me poor old father any permanent harm, just to keep him quiet a bit so's the whorer wouldn't always be after landing punches on me.'

By darkness accompanied by Kern and Olav, I brought Foxy butter bread cheese and turnip slices. And watched him over a fire, burn the feathers off a chicken he caught the night before roosting in the barn.

'The doctor said you put dents in your father's head. And he still doesn't know where he is. He may be invalided to bed.'

'Ah sure after a while they will clear up and he'll feel the better for it. I've had them dents all over me skull and it only would make you that bit giddy now and again. Sure half the time I don't know where I am meself.'

In mild moist westerly breezes the white snowdrops were poking up in the long sheltery grass under the chestnut trees. Foxy was again back milking and making himself as his father said, useless around the farmyard. And just before Christmas my father sent a wire that he was detained in Dublin. My two sisters now taken from school and sent to live with an elderly maiden aunt in Devon. From them came a stamped and addressed photograph. Where they stood wearing wide straw hats by a beehive in a winterish landscape in an orchard, holding between them a comb of honey. On the back of the picture a message scrawled.

WE MISS OUR SMALLEST DEAREST
BROTHER

Early on Christmas eve, Uncle Willie came. In a black glistening gilt trimmed brougham drawn by two splendid black mares. The top hatted coachman's face reddened by the wind and Uncle Willie's by the indoor consumption of malt. And I saw him from the whim room walking back across the front lawn where I knew he'd been visiting my mother's grave. Foxy told me he'd handed out half crowns round the household and gave him a pound. And that it was grand that there was such a decent skin as my uncle and didn't his race horses deserve winning races everywhere across the countryside so that his pockets were stuffed with stacks of them big hundred pound notes that farmers peeled off at the markets.

Uncle Willie sat with me in the recently dusted library, where the spines of the old bound volumes had been wiped and polished by Miss von B. His blue sad eyes under bushy black brows looked round the shelves and his big hands took a glass of whiskey brought by Crooks.

'Ah in spite of the depredations the old place is holding together. It would still take a lot to tumble all this in a heap.'

'Crooks is threatening to give his notice if Miss von B the housekeeper stays.'

'Ah don't mind Crooks. He'll go to his grave here. And you wouldn't be doing too badly either if you went to yours beyond as well.'

'I don't want to stay here to die.'

'Sure this is yours. To keep you living. Every last pillar and post and beyond there for well over a thousand good fattening Irish acres or more.'

'Do I own these books too.'

65

'Ah your mother's father was a great one for the books. He got them I'm told from all over. Sure them's yours. Along with every blade of grass every stone and brick and beast breathing out there on the land. In trust as you might say. Ah in spite of all the housekeepers it misses the hand of your mother. It needs a mistress like that marvellous woman. But now you're growing into a young man. I hear tell you've been raising some hell out there in the bogs. Ah don't mind that a bit. Sow your wild oats. Sure your father's still sowing his.'

And as Uncle Willie slammed the carriage door closed and put down his window to say it's been grand grand grand, he kissed me on the brow as another carriage came up the drive. My mother's two strange clerical friends. To call. And I sent a reluctant Crooks quickly for Miss von B to assist receive them. And ordered tea in the blue parlour. Where the four of us sat. With Miss von B in a pink flowered dress talking excitedly of opera. And the two clerics frowning their eyebrows as their eyes, between mention of Verdi and Wagner, swept the empty spaces and table tops that had once held the objets d'art they so often had declared they adored. And when I said that my father had stolen these things from the house. And I would demand their return. There was much awkward silence and reference to their large gold waistcoat watches. Till they politely bowing and stuffing hankies back up their sleeves, took their leave.

'That was not proper for you to say, that your father steal from this house.'

'He's a dirty thief.'

'Grosser Gott, shame on you.'

On the suddenly grey cold misty Christmas morning all the household and estate workers assembled in the front hall. Kern and Olav getting many pats on the head and wagging their big grey tails. Mr Arland came by his bicycle early to stay to Christmas dinner. He stood nearby sniffing from his knuckle his little speckle of snuff and overseeing as I shook the hands and gave each an envelope out of the black strongbox brought from the town bank the day before. First in line was

66

Foxy's father now able to limp about. With two red healing imprints of a hammer's head on his brow. Followed by Luke the groom who wore a bandage over where his ear had been sewn back on. And last came the ancient white haired washer woman Edna Annie with her gnarled face and hands, who never left her two steamy laundry rooms where she ate and slept. Now made her little bow and gave her toothless smile.

'Ah may the god almighty save and love you you're the spitting image of the mother.'

Shortly after Crooks rang the dinner gong Miss von B appeared from around the grand staircase just as Mr Arland and I, proceeding to the dining room, came along the hall. We stood aside for her. She wore a flannel skirt, string of pearls and a flimsy blue blouse through which one could see the white shapes of her undergarments and there was a heavy perfume in her wake. She awaited my seating and as I gently tucked in her chair she gave me her first smile ever. I nodded but couldn't smile back. But found myself stealing glances at her sitting there to my right, her hair brushed back straight from her forehead, and a gold bauble hanging from the lobe of each ear. As I felt a thumping in my beating heart, she was suddenly and strangely looking pretty. With Mr Arland on my left glumly looking sad.

In the course of my carving I sent a goose leg skidding into Miss von B's lap. She tweezed it up with her napkin covered fingers and without a murmur placed it on her plate. And finally in my embarrassed anguish, I dismembered the bird, chopping off the remaining limbs piece by piece. Crooks clearing his throat in a pained manner and pretending to look out the shuttered window as the grease and gravy slopped all over. Till he finally retreated to serve the wine. The bottle wrapped in white linen and each drip carefully blotted from the pouring. And then his chin loftily raised surveying matters before ushering Sheila and Norah to serve the sprouts. Seemingly the nude sight of Miss von B did something for his morale and he mostly now passed her silently by. While Mr Arland asked in his best quizzical manner.

'I understand Miss von B that you rather had a difficult time escaping from Warsaw.'

'What do you mean, I have not escaped from anywhere.'

'O I am sorry, someone had told me you had.'

'Do not believe all you hear Mr Arland. There is much rumour and story I am sure.'

Darkness fallen and the tallow candles, made by Catherine, lit and smoking in the hall. Coffee and brandy served by Crooks in the salon. The polite conversation continuing as I drank my lemon barley water and the fire blazed. Miss von B seated on the sofa. Her long angular fingers brushing a speck from the recently laundered flowered cover. And smoothing her skirt down, her legs stretched crossed, with two tiny mends now on her silk stockings, from which I caught Mr Arland withdrawing his eyes as he stood sipping his brandy at the corner of the mantelpiece. We spoke of horses and hunting and Mr Arland referred once more to the prewar beauty of Warsaw and Miss von B said somewhat testily that she came from the Salzkammergut and was born in the small town of Durnstein on the Danube. And was not and had never been from Poland. And later that evening we played each other in chess, Mr Arland finally winning against a battling Miss von B and I thought, as I enjoyed the evening's society that perhaps this would be the only family I might ever know.

Mr Arland said he had to be up early in the morning. If he were to be ready in time to come and see us all off to the meet. He rose and bowed at the salon door to Miss von B who inclined her head gently in his direction. He thanked me in the front hall as I helped him on with his naval great coat.

'You know you are, Kildare coming along quite nicely. Your chess game is lively. And despite a little slip here and there with the goose and a few other small lapses regarding your French irregular verbs, you promise to be a most worthwhile member of society. Indeed to use your sobriquet, one might say, the destinies of Darcy Dancer, gentleman, are foretold. And I must thank you again, and for the marvellous cravat. I shall wear it often.'

The sound of rain on the skylight. Faint embers of the hall

fire. Mr Arland keeps so secret all his woes. To return back to his lonely room. Into which he would never invite me. And once I saw his cracked ceiling as he kept me waiting in the governess's cart outside when we were on our way to the big castle and he had detoured to collect prints to show the ladies he lectured. And he told me. When I was stammering over some words. That he had stammered. So much so that he could not speak. And remained mostly silent during all his school years. Until upon entering University, he had changed his rural Irish accent to an English one. And never stammered again.

'Kildare, I wonder might I trouble you with the request of a favour. I fear of a rather personal nature.'

'Most certainly Mr Arland.'

'It is somewhat of an imposition but would it be asking too much. I should like for tomorrow's hunt to borrow kit, should there be any spare lurking in the household.'

'Ah Mr Arland shall you come out with us tomorrow. After the fox.'

'Yes Kildare, after the fox.'

'That would be so splendid. You'll be my guest and most welcome. We have drawers and closets full of breeches, jackets. I'm sure we'll fit you out. Crooks will see to everything. I didn't know you hunted.'

'Well Kildare, I don't actually. To tell the honest awful truth. At most I've been on a horse. And when given a little luck, have stayed thereon. And I might just manage I think not to give too much offence if I turned up.'

'The scent should be good tomorrow. O that's exciting. You're coming out. That really is.'

'I'm not quite so sure about that, Kildare. As I think I am very likely to break my neck.'

'Foxy will have a very safe mount for you. We'll saddle up Petunia.'

'Thank you Kildare.'

Watching from the open door Mr Arland affixing his candle lantern to the front of his handle bars and disappear down the little hill beyond the rhododendrons. The world so dark wild

69

and windy out there that you could not think that it would ever blossom so green again under grey skies at morning.

And Mr Arland now, who would come, perhaps even hard riding by day on the chase and hard drinking by night. And who had brought me once to have my hair cut. To the fox hunting barber he said was the most erudite in the county and with whom he often discoursed in the pub. And Mr Arland asking him why he hadn't seen him having a pint for some time. And the barber stopped cutting my hair and looked up at the ceiling.

'Now I'll tell you Mr Arland, I had to give up the hunting and abandon the drink for a bit, as I drank so much the scissors of a morning was jumping like a live fish out of me hand.'

And as I sat there I felt the nip of the leaping shears taking bites out of my scalp. With Mr Arland grinning behind his sleeve.

And tonight to walk back over these worn, chipped and cracked black and white tiles. Push ajar this heavy mahogany door into the salon. Its warmth of fire and light. Miss von B, a tome open across her lap, turning the pages.

'Miss von B may I offer you further refreshment in the way of another liqueur.'

'O I couldn't. It is my third brandy.'

'It will as a matter of fact be your fourth. But of course I'm not counting.'

'Ha ha.'

Darcy Dancer taking the stopper from the decanter. Crossing the creaking boards under the carpet to pour the pale brown liquid with its sweet aroma into the balloon shaped glass.

'Miss von B I don't believe I have had the pleasure of hearing you laugh before.'

'The occasions are perhaps rare, I admit. Nothing has been very funny for some while. Today it has been very nice. And you, you can be a perfect little gentleman when you choose.'

'I hope you have not been too unhappy here.'

'Ah but anywhere you can be unhappy.'

'Have you been very unhappy somewhere.'

'I have seen much and been through much. So much awful things. Here at least there is a little peace.'

'And madness.'

'Ha yes. But it is mostly foolish madness. It is not evil madness. Maybe there is evil madness but I do not see it yet. You turn the water tap it say cold and out come hot. It is dirty and the people are stupid but what matter. Maybe it is better that way.'

'Mr Arland is not stupid. Nor is Sexton.'

'Mr Arland no he is not. He is very clever. He speaks such perfect German, such perfect French. But Sexton O tempora O mores, he says. With this black mess on his hair. It come off all over the cabinets in the flower room and everywhere it gets on the vases. He is charming. But quite insane.'

'He would not appreciate it to hear you say that Miss von B.'

'No Sexton, poor man he would not. He is so easily upset. Ah but it is beautiful, the hills, the fields so green. And when sometimes you want it to be, life can be so slow. That you do not do today what you won't do tomorrow.'

'That is because cattle never stop eating and the grass never stops growing.'

'Yes perhaps that is why.'

'And we have rainbows.'

'Yes you have. And it was nice that you call me when the priest and parson come. You and I, I think we could be friends. Perhaps. But you should not call your father a thief.'

'That's what he is. If he is stealing what is mine. And all this belongs to me.'

'Ah you are a funny little one.'

'I'm not so little. And I don't think I am so funny.'

'Ah but you are. Come. Sit by me here on the sofa. I will not bite you.'

Two candles guttering out on the mantel. And the glow of the fire waving on the moss green brocaded cloth of the walls. The wind still blowing hard beyond the panes and shutters. Darcy Dancer placing a log on the fire and pushing the big embers together. Letting the tongs lean against the cold marble chimneypiece. To go sit on the sofa. My jacket tight, my sleeves short and trousers hiked up round my ankles. And Miss von B pats a seat beside her.

'Ah but you can sit closer than that. Come. Here. Beside me.'

'I don't mean to be unfriendly Miss von B but I do think I am close enough. I have an aversion to being too close to people.'

'Ah what is that word aversion. I do not think I know it.'

'It means repugnance. I have a slight repugnance to other people.'

'Ah repugnance, now my English is not that specialized. This repugnance, what is that.'

'I suppose incompatibility. Not getting on with others.'

'Ah but you get on. Perhaps it has not been too good between us. But it has been better like now and today.'

'Why does Mr Arland think you come from Poland.'

'As a matter of fact, as you say, that is a long story. I shall tell you sometime. But now you tell me something.'

'What.'

'About that day in the bogs. You don't want to tell.'

'No.'

'I understand you were over there to learn something about life.'

'Who told you that.'

'Ah I have perhaps ways of learning these things. You have such big innocent eyes. With the beard coming on your face. Your voice it is getting deeper. And you do not know about women.'

'I know about women.'

'Ha ha, you know nothing.'

'I do.'

'I could teach you about women. As Mr Arland, he teach you Latin. But you might make it difficult.'

'What would you teach me.'

'You are so young. And there is so much to learn. Perhaps it would be better for a start, that I ask you what you would like to know.'

'Are women cruel.'

Miss von B taking her long ivory cigarette holder which stuck out from her gold mesh opera bag. Delicately pushing a cigarette in its end. As she raises it held between the very tips of her fingers. She stands up to step to the chimneypiece. Putting down her glass and leaning to light the cigarette in the flame of a candle held in the blue pink and gold candelabrum just as the clock tinkled the time. And she regarded the tiny watch on her wrist.

'Ah that clock is only two hours wrong.'

Picking up her glass again and turning, as she used to do in the front hall, and lifting her chin to blow out a puff of smoke. She crosses to the decanter.

'May I, Master Reginald.'

'O yes of course.'

Her eyelids flutter as she removes the stopper. Closes her fingers around the neck. Lifts and pours out the liquid into her glass. Squinting as smoke from her cigarette curls back in her eye. Squaring her shoulders back. Her chest rising and her bosoms stretching out white under the light blue gauzy fabric of her blouse. And she downs nearly all the brandy in one gulp. As something gets awfully stiff and pointing distinctly upwards in my trousers.

'Yes perhaps they are. Women are cruel. They are much crueller than men.'

'Are you cruel.'

'Yes at times I am cruel. But if I am not cruel. Cruel people they are cruel to me.'

'How old are you.'

'Ah you ask the personal questions. How old do you think.'

'You are thirty.'

'Ha I am not going to tell you how old. How old is Mr Arland.'

'He is quite old too.'

Miss von B's eyes seem blue. When always they were colours I could not remember before. She smiles around her lips. And one brow rises. She stares down at me. Like a matador must do at a bullfight. Only I have never seen one. But Miss von B appears to be crossing the arena with her gently shifting hips. And she goes. With her long legs. So slowly. Back to her seat. With her brazen bosoms. To turn. Blazing them at my eyes. And then so carefully. To sit. And raise one thigh and knee over another.

'Old. My dear boy. What do you mean. I am not old.'

'Mr Arland is twenty six.'

'That is young, my little fellow. Surely he is older than that.'

'Mr Arland is a little balding on the front of his head and that makes him look older than he really is.'

'He takes this what do you call it.'

'Snuff.'

'Ah, der Schnupftabak. His Taschentuch, it is brown from wiping his nose. Sexton says he is in love. With the little beauty on the hunt with the golden hair. That he follows on his bicycle when she is on her horse. And he goes with the banjo to play outside her bedroom window in the rain at night. Sexton says it make the cats and dogs of the village howl while he sings.'

'Sexton is a shocking liar, sometimes. I don't really think it is anyone's business what Mr Arland does.'

'Ah, you are loyal.'

'Yes.'

'And you are so young.'

'Please stop saying I am young.'

'But so you are.'

'You are really trying to say that I do not have knowledge of the world.'

'Yes perhaps.'

'I have more sense and intelligence than people twice or three times my age.'

'Yet you do not know about women.'

The candles flickering low. Miss von B raising her glass to

me. Signalling for another brandy. I watched her return the chess pieces to the game box, one by one placing each in its proper place, and with her fingers gently on the veneer, close the leaves and snap the top shut. She rises tireless to adjust a drape or straighten a picture on the wall. And now I smell her faint perfume as I lean towards her to pour. And she asks raising her smiling face up to mine why I didn't have one as well. And I spilt a little of the spirit in a glass and twirled it round as my father did. During other wintery evenings as he sat alone in the library in front of the fire, long sticks of incense burning on the chimneypiece, a cigar in one outstretched hand, a glass of brandy cupped in the other. As he lay back his head on the chair pillow, his eyes closed, listening to choirs and mournful singing chants on the gramophone. And once with his brandy bottle empty he sent me for another and I woke him as I clonked it on the table marble. His one eye opening and his monocle slipped to rest on his chin. And without moving lips or a muscle, he bid me pour him a dram. I took a considerable time to engineer the contents of the bottle into the glass, and he turned to see me sniffing my nose in the strange aromatics. And then told me to get another glass and pour myself a drink and bid me take a cigar from the humidor and light it up. I stood there sucking in the horrid smoke and feeling the liquid sting my mouth and burn my throat. Holding the distasteful things away. And he said be a man about it, take a good long puff and a good deep drink. I exploded coughing in smoke and spluttered out brandy across the room. My father put his monocle back in his eye and informed me.

'Well you little bastard, you're not much good at smoking and drinking either.'

Next morning I came back down again to the library before the shutters had been opened or servants attended the room. And as I made my way across to a window to let in some light I felt brittle broken matters underfoot on the carpet. And saw bottles and glasses smashed in bits. Chips knocked out of the marble where they had hit the chimneypiece. A side table with its ormolu embellishments blasted as Sexton would say to hell. The pages of books ripped out, strewn and torn all over the floor. And taste this brandy now as I had planned to do again that morning till a strange fear made me leave that musty book lined chamber.

'I have not had the occasion to know about women.'

'Ah they are funny ones.'

'Are you funny Miss von B.'

'Ha who is to know or who is to care out here in all the rain. But please. Can we not now no longer say Miss von B. Is it not time now that we drop such formality.'

'If you wish.'

'I think it would be more camaraderie, for you to call me by my christian name. Yes.'

'That might set a bad example. Crooks may come along and call you by your christian name.'

'Ha Crooks. The crook.'

'He is no such thing.'

'Ah his room, in there he has a locked door. Behind the locked door is kept the whiskey. His breath all the time it smell of whiskey.'

'That is the room where our butlers commit suicide and it is always kept locked. But your breath too I have noticed on many an occasion smells of drink.'

'Ah but of course. I admit I have the little bit of sherry perhaps or I would commit suicide. Or would you want me to freeze to death. Tonight I am warm perhaps for the first time. But now you must call me Gwendolene. Ah you are a little love dove. So sweet. I want to take you up in my arms and be a mother to you.'

'Don't you dare. Attempt such a thing.'

'Ah I frighten the poor little boy.'

'Madam I do think you are taking liberties with me. Assuming as you do that I am young and innocent and not able to protect myself.'

'Ah but this madam, she knows something.'

'What do you know.'

'Ah that you have spied on me.'

'Who told you that.'

'I have no need to be told. I saw you. You went down the hall after the fight of Crooks and Foxy. What is the matter. Have you not got something to say. Of course I understand. It is entirely natural. That you should climb up on the chair and look through the little window. It is merely playful. But of course it is not what a gentleman would do.'

'I think, if you will excuse me Miss von B, that I shall retire for the evening.'

'Ah what a pity. Why don't you wait a moment and I shall sing for you.'

'There's the meet tomorrow. And I have promised Mr Arland that he would be fitted out.'

'Ah Mr Arland is to hunt. We all shall have, how do you say, a merry spin. But I would like to sing for you. Please. Sit down. And listen. Just a moment.'

Miss von B opened her lips and a low humming voice came out. Growing slowly louder. And turning into German words. As the vein on her throat grew big and blue. And I feel that clearly this is the most terribly embarrassing moment of my entire life. Especially when one is fuzzy in the head and so little schooled in music. And hardly knows what a rondo is. Ich liebe dich. I do believe she is singing. Was seen escaping down the hall. Nothing one does in this house is private. With blame whispered up the stairwells and in every nook and cranny. Eyes always watching. Every footstep heard. The window boarded over that Foxy jumped through. The landing dark now both by night and day. And worse haunted by the staring suit of armour. Her ankles crossed. The black shiny leather of her pointed high heeled shoes. With small silver sparkling buckles. In the shape of a butterfly. One does not know quite where to look during this aria. And I feel that somehow any second now Count MacBuzuranti Blandus O'Biottus will, with pink ribbons flying from his wagging extremities, come dancing and skipping through the salon door entirely otherwise unattired in the altogether. With the three of us dancing a quadrille.

'Ah you like the buckles on my shoes. Did you also like the song.'

'Yes it was quite nice.'

'Come with me have another brandy. It is so marvellous. It is only now my fifth.'

'I think it may be as a matter of fact your seventh.'

'Ah as all the English gentlemen say, that is what they always say. As a matter of fact.'

'I am distinctly not English. And really I should be going Miss von B. I must search out kit for Mr Arland.'

'But one, just one little brandy. It is so nice here. It is the first night that I have found it pleasant. Peace, it is as beautiful as war is horrible. And why did you come to look at me when I bath. Is it because you want to see what a woman looks like.'

'This is a rather mournful line of questioning you are pursuing Miss von B. It really is.'

'What did you see.'

'Nothing. I was merely.'

'Merely, merely what. What merely.'

'Merely. I was merely.'

'Ah merely. Merely what. So you were there. Of course you were there. How dare you. Spy upon me. Disgraceful. And your father should know. But then. Ah then. I am not what you call the tattle tale. But it is what is wrong with this place. So much taboo. Like a woman's body. Maybe it is because it is so wet and cold.'

'I am rather now proceeding to bed Miss von B.'

'O well who cares. Goodnight. Bye bye. Sweet dreams. Toodle ooo. So long sonny boy. Baby.'

'I do think you are being rather vulgar.'

'Ha. Vulgar. I am being nuts. That's what I am being. And are you still to be a bishop.'

'Goodnight.'

Darcy Dancer bowing. Taking a pewter chamberstick from the chimneypiece to light the way. Turning towards the door. One last look at her slender legs crossed. Her calves come out of bigger stronger thighs. She licks her lips as she speaks. And Foxy brought me all the way over the countryside to nearly get killed in the bogs. To teach me about women. And

my sisters' naked bodies that Nurse Ruby would never let me
see. The sting of her slaps raining down on my legs. Each time
she washed around my prick and it stuck up in her face.
Creaking of floorboards. Open the door now quickly so that I
can catch whoever is crouched there listening. Nothing but
the cold breeze of wind pouring in from the hall. And perhaps
it is rude of me to be so abrupt.

'Miss von B.'

'Yes.'

'O it is nothing.'

'Is there something you wish to say. You must say it.'

'I hope I have not been discourteous.'

'But of course you have been. But then I have been provo-
cative. But why do we not both go together. We go by the
same light and not waste two candles.'

'That is a very good idea.'

'Well then I shall finish my brandy.'

'O do please.'

'And then I shall be promptly right with you.'

'O there's no hurry, none at all.'

'Ah but we must not diddle dawdle though, must we.'

'No perhaps we must not.'

'Then I come.'

'Shall we use my light or yours.'

Miss von B blows out her candle. Crossing from the sofa to
put her cigarette into the fire, her glass on the mantelpiece
and her ivory holder back in her purse. She walks, her hips
swaying, and I think her lips smiling too, right straight at me.
As my hand shakes holding the chamberstick. The chain of
her opera bag over her wrist. Some curls of her hair loose from
the bun at the back of her head. And my candle light throwing shadows across her face. If I stand up on my toes I'll be
taller than she. Only it makes such awful cramps in the backs
of one's legs. I keep swallowing down my throat. She stops.
Takes off her shoes.

'That's better. Isn't this how you and that Foxy go around
the house.'

'You are making fun of me.'

'No. I am being what is known as discreet. We should not make a sound. Take off your shoes. Now we go. Blow out the candle.'

Turning right out the salon. On the cold stone floor. Towards the beech grove stairs. In the chill air of the front hall. Sound of rain up high on the skylight. She takes my hand. Presses her breast up against my arm. Soft and like something you feel when your fingers want to touch. Wind blowing against the landing window. When summer comes the tree tops out there will be full of screeching jackdaws. And I was rather angry for that moment when I saw Mr Arland's eyes viewing Miss von B's lower limbs. They say love hits you a blinding flash between the eyes if you are a gentleman. And between the legs if you are not. Making me at this moment a rather shameless cad. Right here on the landing. Where she's putting her arms around me. A shoe in each hand. Pressing her face on mine. And opening her lips and parting mine. Her tongue pushing long and big and hard into my mouth. Embraced with the housekeeper. Fattened with the butter she eats and the cascades of cream she pours over everything. Her breath breathing against my neck. Her tongue digging in my ear. Just as I drop a shoe. The heel landing ouch right on my toe. And whoops. Now goes the chamberstick bounding back down the stairs.

'Are you alright my little darling.'

'Yes.'

'Quick now my lovely. Come.'

Darcy Dancer's hand held up to Miss von B leading the way. My shoe left behind. Plus a chamberstick over which Crooks is not likely to fall especially with his legs in their invalid condition and the memory of his last bottle skidding keeping him in some seclusion. But his midnight melancholia could sometimes drive him to pouring cold water over his head and crawling on all fours along the midnight halls. And perhaps right past Miss von B's room, into which I follow her. And to where she had moved after much demanding complaint. With its canopied brass bedstead on which my sister Beatrice Blossom had slept. And with whom on the pink silk of the love seat along the wall, I played draughts on summer evenings. Her favourite dolls kept in the heavy iron chest. That Crooks said came from a Spanish ship which sailed in the Armada. Birds and sprays of flowers on the wall paper. Blue and green on white. And I'm so trembling. Just me and my heart. The shadow of von B at the door and hear the click of the key turning in the lock. She must see the shape of me shaking here with my back against the window sill. Breathing in the dark. The movements of her arms. Buttons opening. Stepping out of her skirt. The rustle of her clothes. A white slip like a ghost rising up and coming off over her head. Her hands behind. And her undergarment falls away. Her bosoms out right here in the room. My penis hurting hard in my trousers. Heart now jumping when before it was only thumping. What I saw that night is right up close and warm to me. With the splatter of rain on the window panes. Imprisoned. And really worried out of one's wits.

'Where are you going.'

'Miss von B I must go.'

'Go. Silly child. Why do you go.'

'I must soap my boots.'

'Luke the groom or Foxy will soap your boots.'

'Neither of them do it properly.'

'Are you frightened.'

'No.'

'You are. You must not be. Come. I am going to get in bed before I turn to ice. Ach du grosser Gott, there is no warm bottle. I have got the key. You must stay. I will not let you out.'

'You are imprisoning me. That is quite illegal.'

'Ha ha. I did not make you come here.'

'You did.'

'I did not. And I do frequently lock the door at night. Once the dog come in and push his big cold nose on my face and I jump up to scream.'

'If I come into bed with you, is it not the case that with such intimacy you might then take advantage of me.'

'What. What do you mean.'

'I mean that you might assume you are no longer a servant.'

'How dare you. I am not a servant.'

'But you are the housekeeper.'

'So who are you.'

'I am the gentry.'

'I too dear boy am gentry. I am plenty gentry.'

'You are not.'

'Well get out. If you are gentry and I am housekeeper. Get out.'

'Give me the key.'

'Go find it for yourself.'

'Where is it.'

'I have it right here, under the covers. What do you know about gentry. You are all peasants. With everything falling down around your ears. Who teach you these stupid things to think you are so magnifico.'

'They are not stupid. It is how people like me are brought up to live. I am gentry and you are not.'

'Shut up. Shut up you stupid boy. I am a Schlesgluckwig-sonderstein, a princess before your ancestors could piss properly into the pot. You are nothing but a little peasant pig. Take off your clothes and get into bed. Or else I sock you. You are to be sure, so full of shit.'

> You need
> How do they say
> Das Klistier
> The enema

8

The day dry and fit for fine hunting. Everyone who was anyone among the gentry and peasantry was hacking, walking or staggering to the pub at the crossroads from all over the countryside. With members of the hunt, their mounts plaited beribboned groomed and gleaming.

The early activity at Andromeda Park was feverish. With the clank of spurs and boots down the halls. Shouts around the stable yard for bindings for manes and bandages for tails. Crooks rummaged through my father's wardrobe and fetched out a pair of cavalry twill breeches and polo boots. And a top hatted Mr Arland looked rather smart up on Petunia, overly fat though she was.

Our little contingent left in the blazing blazing blue of mid morning, preceded by Luke and Foxy's father and followed by Miss von B, Mr Arland and lastly my exhausted self and Foxy. The latter up on top of the eighteen hands high Thunder and Lightning whose tail was tied with a great scarlet bow. Warning all to stay well out of kicking distance.

Beneath the bright chirp of birds up in the tall pines, making our way along the drive. To where it turned between the thick rhododendrons. And upon my shouted instructions we went through a gate to short cut across the old deer park field. Hooves pounding on the velvet soft pasture to the entrance gates. Where most of the lodge had recently further collapsed with a tree fallen through the roof and now could hardly be seen under this new mountain of beech branches and ivy.

Heading westwards. By a babbling swift flowing brook. Then along a straight road with its little hills. From the top of each, one could survey miles across meadows, bogs and lakes. The yellow and moss green lichen spotting the grey stone walls which went criss crossing the distant green. Tiny puffs of clouds sailing the horizon. A chill in the slight breeze. And joined now by other members of the hunt heading out their gateways or coming down lanes and connecting roads. The sound of horses' hooves thickening. Past two cows and three grazing goats and the cart of a shawled old lady, a nail stuck in the end of a stick prodding it into the haunches of her donkey. As Miss von B turned back to stare in disapproval. Till finally ahead were the pink walls of the pub on the village crossroads. And the scarlet coated hunt servants armed with their horn handled hunting whips.

Miss von B's face this morning looked pale. Last night when she finally fell asleep she lay snoring. Her head deep sunk backwards and her long flowing hair across the crisp linen pillow. I lay crouched under the mountain of her blankets. A rather unpleasant stale smelling breath coming from her open mouth. Wondering what I had learned about women. And she cried out something like wo sint do, followed by much other German sounding words. Tossing herself up and over again on her side. As I watched the light of dawn breaking on the tinted blue window panes. Her bottom, two big cool mounds pressed against my knees. And now I see her lean forward over the neck of her horse to fix her stirrup. Her blonde hair all neatly gathered in a hair net under her bowler. Her thighs snug in her white leather breeches parted over her saddle. The whole thing strange that was down there between her legs. If every woman had one. Soft and wet inside. Covered by crinkly curly hairs. Where she pushed my hand and brought it back again each time I pulled it away. And she leaned on her elbow watching me in the shadows undress. I said please don't look. While I filled her pot with pee. And as I shivered towards the bed she threw back her head and shook her hair. She climbed all over me, her head crushing down with kisses and German words whispering in my ears out of her lips. Furiously pumping on top of me. Telling me later in my long silence to speak. When I couldn't think of a thing to say. About her brothers and parents killed. And her husband, a blue eyed army lieutenant, crushed under the tracks of a tank. And a second brown eyed husband, a captain disappeared somewhere around Smolensk on the Russian front. Her family's town house flattened by a bomb. And their country Schloss desecrated. Soldiers shooting holes in the eyes of family portraits and trying on their silk underwear and sleeping with their muddy boots on their silk sheets while swilling champagne from the cellars. Rape drunkenness and death. And that she lied to Mr Arland. She had escaped from Poland. With her diamonds up her arse and twat. Through Czechoslovakia. Hiding in Prague deep down in the cellars under the old town square. And in Vienna in another cold basement. To Salzburg. Till she got to Switzerland, to Italy, France and to Spain. And seasick all the way on a ship she finally landed nearly destitute in Dublin. And there, calling herself Miss von B, she established in an attic where she slept, ate and designed and made fashionable ladies' hats. She met my father surrounded by women in a pub they called the gilded cage. After he had a winning day at the races. Stood buying everyone drinks and quaffing black velvet. Said he needed a housekeeper who could saddle and ride a horse. He peeled off her first three months' wages and the next day she bequeathed her hat business to the landlord and stood freezing in the gloomy cold station for twelve hours waiting for the train. And when she saw me first she thought I had such startling and stunning eyes.

Locals leaning against the pub wall and standing in little groups huddled whispering under their dark rain stained and weather beaten trilbys. Their collars upturned in the sunshine and taking long sucks on their cigarettes. Girl pumping a pail full of water at the village pump. Her big pink knickers showing on her fat legs as she bent over. The green telephone kiosk to which a person not afeared of speaking over wires, was dispatched from Andromeda Park, to ring westwards to find out when the train was coming. And when with the birds singing I was climbing out of her bed, Miss von B said don't go, don't leave me. Her soft blonde skin, a mole on her throat growing little blonde hairs. And her eyes in her face looked as if at any moment she might laugh. But down deep in all the specks and flecks of colour they were eyes full of fear. And I slipped from the covers and stood with one foot tripping over the piss pot on the rug. And she said why did you have to do that. And I said shut up.

The masked singers, the wren men, came and went into the pub with their tambourines and spoons. The dogs barking and wailing in the pub yard when they began to play. And the hounds arrived. Noses in a row sticking out the slats of the cart. From down the road with a clatter of cantering hooves, Baptista Consuelo approached. Accompanied by three top hatted pink coated gentlemen. And as her horse went prancing by. It chose to blast out several farts. Right at our Andromeda Park contingent. Bang, boom, bang, boom. Bringing, I thought, some dispirit across Mr Arland's face. Haughtiness upon this champion hunting day was quite prevalent. But I discerned at close range that Baptista had a somewhat stupid looking and quite unnoble little upturned nose. Unlike the firm straight features and nicely curved nostrils of Miss von B. Who was also astonishingly strong and able to hold my arms pinned. As she did while banging down on top of me in some kind of crazed delirium out from under which I tried to get in case she'd suddenly gone nuts like everyone else in the household. But after some prolonged gasps groans and wails she lay quite content for a while before trying it again. And during these between times with my head and ear pressed on the soft soothing flesh of her breast, I felt a lazy cosy comfort as her arm tucked me in.

'Come come, pay up now. I won't have any of this shoddy dodging.'

The hunt secretary collecting people's caps. Making a stack of notes in his hand. I thought he was going about it rather rudely. In the loud offensive way in which he asked for mine and that of my party. There being perhaps some feelings regarding my father not having contributed to the hunt for some time. Nor since my mother's death did we plant coverts or hold a hunt ball. In a manner overly familiar, the Master of Foxhounds on an enormous bay mare came up to greet Miss von B. Along with him trotted the first whip also smiling with a large assembly of teeth which I'm sure were bought off some itinerant dental salesman who was temporarily out of his size. And together with the huntsman and a hunt servant, all made a distinct fuss, mouthing compliments concerning my housekeeper's smart appearance. I found their fawning close proximity rather tiresome. While Miss von B rather revelled in it.

'Ah Princess you are looking so devastatingly radiantly beautiful.'

'But you are just too kind, Master.'

'The stones in the walls, ma'am, you make them smile.'

'Ha you give me how do you say, the blarney.'

Just before moving off a group of riders stopped near by in a field. Some with saddle flasks at their lips. And village boys running with the bottles to refill them at the pub. Till one of them fell clean backwards out of his stirrups off his horse. Landing with the flask still held to his lips where supine he drained it. Upon seeing this, a ruddy faced chap known as the Major although he was never involved in anything the least military, cantered over. Sitting high on his horse accusing the prostrate gent of inebriation. Who now slowly arose from the moist morning grass and staggered a little about the field. The Major shouting.

'Go home sir, you are unfit to hunt.'

'Bugger you.'

'I said go home sir, you are drunk and a danger to the field.'

'Bugger you you stuffed twit.'

'Having long emerged from my school days, I shall not be buggered sir, and direct you to depart without giving more disgrace than you already have. And I say go home. You are too drunk to hunt.'

'You mean I'm too drunk not to hunt. And who the hell are you telling me.'

'I am a member of the hunt committee.'

'Well fuck the committee and bugger you.'

'There are ladies sir, mind your language, there are ladies.'

'There are crumpet and fluff and brazen arses and horny old devils like you sniffing their saddles.'

'I shall teach you a lesson sir.'

The Major raising his whip brought it lashing down knocking your man's bowler off to the ground. Whereupon your squiffy chap on the turf rounded with his own whip to land a swipe across the nose of the Major's mount. The big grey gelding rearing bucking and kicking. Sending the Major skywards and eastwards pitched on his back, boots in the air. The locals deserted the crossroads with this sign of action. And came aswarm over the walls of the field, smiling and giving each other joyous digs in the ribs. As there was nothing to be enjoyed more than seeing the gentry go berserk. In the quickly man made arena the florid faced Major gathered himself from the ground. Tightly stretching his whip between his white gloved hands he circled round the squiffy chap. And the two of these red coated gentlemen started belabouring and slashing each other from toe to ear. As their shouts roared out over the countryside.

'Cunt.'

'Cad.'

'Cunt.'

'Cad.'

It was rare to see such delightful justice being done. For, according to Foxy, both protagonists were eegits of the highest order and the meanest bastards imaginable you could find in the district. Where they'd been for years guilty of giving nothing away free. I manoeuvred my small mare Molly to a nice vantage point, a grassy mound, to witness from. And right next to a highly perfumed Baptista Consuelo. Madly licking her lips at every blow. And as a clean swat of the lash landed across the Major's left cheek she gave a sucking hiss of her lips followed by a satisfied smile. Just as Miss von B came trotting and reining up between us. Turning to me as if the whole thing were my fault.

'Ah grosser Gott such savages.'

Baptista Consuelo looking round to Miss von B and pulling her mount back a pace. She seemed to let the morning air purr down the nostrils of her bumpy little nose as she uttered her vowels in a very superior manner indeed.

'I think it most jolly good that one gentleman chastise another should he need it.'

'And you, you little bitch should get a good hoof up the backside.'

'Why you dirty foreigner, you, speak to me like that.'

'It is of course darling the language which exactly you deserve.'

Baptista Consuelo turning her nose up and backing her chestnut stallion away. Just as the squiffy chap with his horse grazing near, was lashed to the ground. The locals cheering and the gentry handclapping. The Major, florid cheeks puffing, and adjusting his stance for maximum leverage, continuing to flog your man.

'Tally bloody ho, take that you sod. And that.'

'O god, what are you doing to me.'

'I'm thrashing you sir.'

'You cunt.'

'You cad.'

The squiffy chap rolling arms wrapped round his head. The gentry's pukka shout of shame and a chorus of encouragement from the locals as the Major landed a boot thump in the ribs. Your man curling up from the concussion and then lying groaning and still. The crowd fading back. And Mr Arland's voice.

'You sir, are a pathetic bully and coward striking a man who is down.'

'Poppycock sir. He got no more than he richly deserves. And perhaps you too should like a whipping.'

'If I get down sir, from my horse, I assure you that you will never again get up on yours.'

The hair standing up on the back of my head at Mr Arland's quietly delivered words. The Major grunting and turning away. Foxy said the randy Major would jump up on his own grandmother in her coffin and had put every scullery maid in his house up the pole. And he was widely known for his particular skill in administering indoor punishment to servants. When he wasn't otherwise busy himself dressing up as a woman. And was now prancing about the meadow with victorious self importance. Stopping only to pose in the gaze of the mounted ladies. With Baptista looking down admiringly as he slapped the ivory of his whip into his white gloved hand.

'I should venture to suggest that that should teach the sozzled insolent chap some manners. And I apologize to the ladies if this unbecoming fracas gave offence.'

The Master and Huntsman leading the field off down the road and into a boreen. Through rusting iron gates and across two fields. To the first covert which drew nothing save pigeons. Nor the second in a grove by a bog from which snipe flew in their shifting flight. But the third, a wood atop a stone strewn hill roused a fox. Skidaddling goodo pronto. The Huntsman blew his horn. The echoes sounding back from the nearby hills. The chase was on with the usual curses flying amid the whoops and hollers, and the rather more staid remarks of the elder members.

'I say there, I do believe that that ruddy fox is departing.'

'Yoikes, yoikes.'

'After the bloody little bugger.'

Uncle Willie said hounds take their character from their Huntsman and this pack was splendidly disciplined. The sunshine bright up on their backs. Barking and bounding off north west, nose to ground, white tips of sterns bobbing. Foxy on Thunder and Lightning leaping to the forefront of the field between Huntsman and Master. On the heel of these, the brave contingent, already pounding half way down across a great spreading meadow. Hooves slapping the grass. Chunks of dark tan turf flying up behind in the sky.

The first minor casualties were the Slasher sisters. Two raving redheads, who both fell off in a deep flowing brook. Smiling, they remounted, water spilling from their boots and wet hair flying. And lips loosing rather not nice words. They charged up the hill. Fighting Murphy the Farmer was next. His horse going down at the gallop in a rabbit hole. And poor rider, he was flung like an arrow head first into the ground. Where he lay, believed to be soundly dead. Till someone hoping to borrow a nip from his small brandy bottle awakened him. He was soon up and mounted again and minus only his memory which it was agreed he never used anyway. And back at the crossroads this morning one saw various sober persons secreted behind hedges vomiting. And others minus their flasks, taking their courage in great gulps of whiskey in the pub. Some of whom now formed the courageous gang looking for a way through the thick tall tangle of ash briar and blackthorn at the top of the field. Till Foxy crashed a hole in the hedge big enough to bring an army through. And the Mad Vet himself said.

'That pup Slattery would ride an elephant between two atoms stuck together.'

I kept mostly in the middle of the field with my Molly who did not like to get her feet wet or her coat scratched by briars. Being as she was a rather proud and delicate lady. Miss von B I could see ahead at the rear of the brave contingent. The twin acorns of her gleaming arse bobbing over her saddle. And closely behind Baptista. Who kept turning to look back at her most unpleasantly. And I stretched Molly's legs galloping two fields with the nervous contingent before dropping back to lurk a little behind in the forefront of the cowards. To see that Mr Arland came to no early harm. And no one sniggered at him now aboard the barrel shaped Petunia.

'Are you alright Mr Arland.'

'Thank you yes Kildare. I am merely trepidatious.'

'Uncle Willie says always take your first fall as soon as you can to get rid of your fear.'

'Unfortunately Kildare having only one life, I think I may prefer to stay mounted and frightened out of my wits.'

The Major smugly smiling to each side of him at the ladies as he now passed forward through the field, having officiated over the farmer Murphy who since his amnesia was on every side proclaiming he was an African prince with a harem, instead, as someone said, a bog trotter with a paddock of scrawny pigs. And the Major while galloping by circulated the news.

'That silly sod Murphy thinks now he's a rich nigger.'

I sat on a hillock pausing in the sunshine with Molly puffing somewhat out of condition and viewing the Major just as he galloped up and over a high mound near by roaring 'Gung Ho' and then plummeted down the other side. Where his horse most wisely, but extremely abruptly, refused at a very wide deep ditch on the edge of the bog. And the Major, without wings was sent aloft. Landing stretched full face in the oozing deeply brown mud. Accompanied by the echoes of his Gung and Ho. And as he half raised himself up from the clinging muck the humorously inclined Mad Vet cantering past, suggested loudly.

'Sir it appears that it is you who is now the nigger.'

I twice caught sight of the poor fox. Making his skulking way along the edge of a wood. Jumping a little to left and right. His red and brown coat so plain against the green. The sight of which would instantly alert these blood thirsty pursuers howling and shouting in the wake of his scent. With the pack of paws and hoofed avalanche of horses pounding upon his canine heels. To be in a breath atomized by flashing fangs. Sad fellow.

With most of the brave field gone ahead, the Major, his mouth spitting mud, was dragged by the boot heels back up to dry green land. He stood up, his hands pressed at the kidneys. And then with a long groan, keeled over backwards into the bog again. Baptista holding his horse and still levelling her best dirty looks in Miss von B's direction and that of any member of the Andromeda Park contingent. The Major now mostly surrounded by the elder ladies making their inane remarks. And very much distracting the Major's attention from his task of sloughing off his person the bigger chunks of clay. As in her haughty supercilious manner Baptista looking down at the Major keeps loudly uttering.

'O I say what foul awfully bad luck.'

And the Major mumbling as he dug further copious muck from ear hole and nostril.

'Yes quite.'

The baying of the hounds now seemed to have changed

direction. And Baptista, right as we were enjoying the splendid view of the stricken and ooze encrusted Major, barged straight into Miss von B. Who spun round and gave the quarters of Consuelo's horse such a slap of her whip that I thought I saw smoke rise where it burned into the hair and I would have sworn that Baptista this time farted in fear as her horse bolted, for she gave, as Uncle Willie called it, a backside bark and left behind a fume something entirely unhorsey. And as the sweeter air from green things swept it away, one was rather aware that it could be a fracas between females soon. This day already being most full of the unexpected. Just as last night had amply been full of most useful discovery.

I tried my best to warn everyone out of the way as Baptista came galloping back, her steed blasting out steamy puffs from its nostrils and her riding crop raised to strike Miss von B. And as the horse's hooves began thrashing round his prostrate figure a loud scream came up from the mud and the Major. As Baptista Consuelo's swipe missed. The ducking von B, in the same instant caught the young golden blonde beauty with the most marvellously disguised back hander which landed a stunning swat across Baptista's backside just as that part gleamed exposed from under her jacket flap. The splash of mud from the flying horses totally obliterating the Major. Whose protesting voice now seemed to come out of nowhere.

'Stop it. I'm secretary of the hunt. Stop it.'

The fox had doubled back. And must have crossed over this bit of bog. For the scent mad hounds were sailing at us. And even trying to sniff under the mud bathing Major. Now came thundering the whole field, the brave contingent foremost. The nervous contingent following not far behind. Even caught up were a few of the cowards, all pounding straight towards this newest mêlée. Foxy still in front of the Master who was shouting most angrily and now obscenely shrieking for him to stay back out of the way.

'Get behind me you brazen cunt.'

Fighting Murphy the Farmer said if his senses still served

him there was no doubt that a devilishly clever fox had put the hunt to rout. And reined up together on a knoll over the débâcle were the parson and priest friends of my mother who were both clearly disturbed by the curses flying and the imminent maim about to be wrought. The parson tendered a glinting silver cup of refreshment to the priest as these two clerics made ready to help each other administer the last rites of their respective churches to those recently quickly becoming in need of same. Two bogged down riders were already making unbrave noises as they sank atop their struggling horses. While Luke and Foxy's father were either side of the rather eccentric Lord otherwise known as the Mental Marquis in a yellow hunting cap who carried American six shooters hidden under his coat and always volunteered his vocation as being that of a debauchee. Following him close was the mad veterinary surgeon carrying a vastly long amputation knife in a sheath stuck down his boot, so, as he said, to give quick treatment to any hunt member who had hopelessly mangled a limb in the field. Being that it always made the injured chap lighter carrying him to the hospital. And when the begrimed Major saw this bloodthirsty gentleman closing down upon him he was vociferous.

'For god's sake don't let that tree surgeon at me. I'm merely temporarily incapacitated and I don't want to be permanently disembowelled.'

'Tally ho.'

Someone said it was the first sensible utterance heard in a long while. And it was out of the Master's lips who was pointing with his whip. At the ruddy fox. Who, would you believe it. Was now suddenly in the midst of us. And wouldn't he know it was the safest place. Running in a circle from the converging hounds through horses' legs and even some human. Of those recently dismounted to assist the Major. And Baptista now striking out with her fist at von B. Who was a consummate expert with her crop. Swatting Consuelo again and again. And even thwacking one back handed across Baptista's face where a red welt blossomed smarting across her cheeks and nose.

'O my god you've struck me. Someone please, kill her the filthy bitch. She's not fit to be out with civilized people.'

'You, you little bitch, are the bitch.'

'I'll show you yet who's the bitch.'

Baptista raising her own whip. Slamming her heels deep into the sweat stained flanks of her chestnut stallion. This sixteen hand monster charging forward straight at Miss von B who raised her own whip and spun my father's once polo schooled horse round. Both whips landing. Foam flying from the equine mouths as they churned in a circle digging deep gouges in the turf. The mud bespattered Major, hands waving as he stood.

'I say ladies, ladies. What is the difficulty here.'

The Major attempting to rapid step out of where he stood between. Turning round and round to avoid the orbits of the flying hooves. Arms raised to ward off the stray blows landing from the lashing leathers. Which the Major quickly decided was the least of it as these quadruped wild tramplings and stampeding could be curtains not only for him but for everybody.

'I say, quicko, let's have orderliness.'

'Ah jasus in a second you won't have your quicko testicles.'

'Who said that. Out with it. Who said that.'

A dowager lady riding side saddle, a winter hot house rose in her lapel, her black skirt spreading midships on her horse and the shadow of her veil across her face, let out a holler as her mare bolted and ran away with her. And two more horses bucked and threw their riders. Just as Miss von B, her vast diamond sparkling from its setting in the gold pin stuck through the folds of white satin at her throat, took a grab of Baptista's lapels, and both ladies' bowlers bounced off. Poor Mr Arland, his hands over his face. Von B pulling Baptista forward. Makes one remember the strong tapering muscles in her arms bigger than mine. And all the polishing and dusting and holding open of large books she does.

'Let go of me you filthy foreigner.'

'You common commoner, I shall teach you a lesson. You will not again try to ride me down.'

'Let go.'

'Ladies, this is most ungracious, can we not determine what is the difficulty here.'

A dismounted local squire rumoured to be erudite, stepping innocently forward to mediate and as Baptista's mount reared with a massive erection he wisely jumped instantly backwards. With the great chestnut stallion taking bites out of the air. Von B backing away her mount and again catching Baptista by the collar, dragging the fist flailing girl backwards from her horse. The long blonde tresses, stuck with large tortoiseshell combs now hanging loose around her head as she fell. Landing smack on her bottom, hands and legs asprawl on the squelching boggy ground. And her mount galloping off rigid pricked, blasting farts, its hind hooves kicking in the sky.

All but Foxy and the Mental Marquis of the brave contingent took off after Charlie the Fox. And both the nervous and coward contingent contentedly remained behind to watch the fight. All nicely arranged in the sunshine in a safe semi circle. Foxy sitting there among the gentry, a great grin on his face. And I believe I heard him shout at the height of the mêlée.

'Up the Republic.'

And just as the huntsman's horn away in a copse beyond the bog sounded the quick pulsating notes of a tremolo to signal that the hounds had killed the fox, Baptista was feeling around her on the grass for a stone. Gathering up instead a fistful of grass to throw at von B.

'You horrid horrid person you.'

'You brat you are spoiled.'

'You are a whorish servant.'

'Ha ha, you make me weep.'

'You disgusting foreigner.'

'Now you make me laugh.'

'My Lord Marquis just don't sit there, shoot her, you've got guns.'

'My dear Baptista, I also retain the very vaguest of morals. One mustn't fire upon unready ladies.'

'She's no lady. She's a tramp.'

Baptista knelt on the moist turf her knees staining brown.

Mr Arland dismounted, was crossing to where she'd lost her bowler and picking this up and brushing it clean with his sleeve he approached, bowing gently forward, his own top hat with suitable respect sweeping from his head, and leaning down to the rising Baptista he proferred his assisting hand.

'Please may I at least as a possible peacemaker return your hat and help you to your feet.'

'As for you, leave my hat alone and get your hands away from me you wretched damn tutor to those land stealing Kildares.'

On the edge of this barren bog. And on the inclining side of this rushy meadow, some yellow little gorse blossoms opened by the sun. The sweet of their coconut scent lost on this crisp air. Through which this girl's two eyes were blazing hatred. Making me feel as if great welts were blotching all over my skin. And Mr Arland, poor Mr Arland, my noble kind tutor, who froze in his tracks. And stood there dumbly. And then slowly took back his outstretched hand and put back his opera hat on his head. And as someone had now led back and held Baptista's recaptured horse and she unravelled a stirrup, I could in the clear winter light see the sparkle of moisture in Mr Arland's eyes. And his voice was something I heard in me saying.

> O god
> I'm hurt

9

The weather stayed cold crisp and sunny an entire fortnight. With mornings of frost whitened meadows. I was getting used now to being squire of Andromeda Park. And that my father would not suddenly enter the door and thereupon I would have to hurriedly stand. With Crooks indisposed with severe gout, I enjoyed to walk the corridors listening to the sound of my heels striking the floors. Sheila or Norah stopping momentarily in their work to address me with the time of day. My only childish action was whenever I heard the haunting squeal of swan wings. I'd rush to the window to watch these great white birds cruise across the sky, all their strength and power whistling just above the trees of the front lawn. And the sight filled me with loneliness and a feeling I would like to be gone somewhere far away.

And then on a grey rainy cold morning, the mailman came urgently on his bicycle with a special letter. My father from whom no one had heard except that when after more cattle and fields were sold, money orders arrived to pay the servants and men, was now writing to tell Mr Arland that I must attend a young gentlemen's school close to Dublin, and that his services upon my gaining entry would no longer be required. Although I was furious and Mr Arland was extremely sad at the news, he counselled me that I should go. And when he complained he could not sleep these recent nights over the pub, I invited him to take a room at Andromeda Park.

Three weeks later we departed just before lunch, bundled up and wrapped in scarves. Miss von B as she stood tweedily attired in the hall making sure again and again that I had all my necessities and that I was smart looking, held her fists clenched at her sides and her lips drawn tight as if she were about to cry. Outside on the steps Sexton presented himself to say goodbye, giving us four winter stored apples he had brightly polished. I could sniff the usual smell of soot and motor oil on his hair and I perceived moisture in his eye as he touched his patch and seemed overly hearty expressing his words.

'Up there in the roaring metropolis you'll soon be getting Latin aplenty Master Darcy sine dubio. And Mr Arland, what harm was there in our little differences. God bless the both of you now and safe journey.'

Our bags followed on a float driven by Luke and Foxy's father. And Mr Arland in his naval great coat sitting high in the governess's cart was chewing the last of the apples as we arrived at the faded grey station. Standing lonely and bereft as it did down at the end of the tree lined drive, its apron of gravel surrounded with its neatly tilled flower beds. Its large clock suspended over the platform was said to have the most accurate time in the county. That is if anyone had the correct time to compare it to.

Although we'd learned earlier by the crossroads telephone that the train for certain had left the previous town, we waited two hours. And every time Mr Arland opened his coat and pushed into his waistcoat pocket for the silver box to take a liberal pinch of snuff, he would also take from his baggy grey suit, his big gold watch to regard the hour. And with his battered briefcase resting against his ankle, he would peer up at the station timepiece.

'Good lord that damn clock is losing a minute every ten minutes and it was made in Leicester.'

And when finally we first heard and then saw the puffing engine rounding the bend between the hills, there was a great self important flurry from the platform porter. And the Station Master with his whistle and green flag kept shouting.

'All aboard now, don't keep the train waiting.'

The man sitting on a box of pigeons stood up and spat into the stones between the tracks. Another sitting on a crated squealing pig, dragged it along the platform. Then a gentleman lugging a suitcase perforated with holes and full of squawking chickens said to these other two owners that their livestock could just as soon be dead cooked and eaten after themselves were already killed with the waiting, and then he pointed towards the locomotive and then announced.

'Sure that yoke would be flying if it only had a bit of coal.'

There were faces I recognized from the town. The bald headed and dour demeanoured owner of the drapery shop who was rumoured to be buying some of our land. And others whom I saw look at me and then lean over and make whispers in each other's ears. Quite disrespectful and most uncomfortable making. Especially with some of the monstrous bills we owed. But one elderly gentleman, who said he served my grandfather for forty years in the stables of Andromeda Park, had the courtesy to salute us and hold open the train door as we boarded. And with turf being flung into the boilers we made eastwards at a steady pace along the banks of the canal and between the stretching dark bog lands, stopping at the little stations to collect the patiently waiting passengers some of whose faces were blue with cold.

With my sleeve I wiped clear the steam of my breath collecting on the window. Out in the gathering darkness all one could see were shadows and sometimes a lonely light. My feet growing cold, I daydreamed of von B. Mostly of her body. And just as we finished eating our buttery ham thick sandwiches a priest came in to our compartment and regarded me out of the corner of his eye. In some strange way I seemed to irritate him. Perhaps upsetting him with my lascivious thoughts. He would squiggle up his nose and frown and make nasty faces. And especially so when I took out and wrote in my recently begun blue leather diary. I had found it in back of one of the cupboards of medical instruments with its pages empty and under another diary my mother's father had kept and in which I found great interest to read. I carried both and mine was locked with a silver tiny clip. And because this could easily be broken open I thought it would be prudent on the frontis page to write.

Herein lies the truth of The Daring Dancer's activities and a curse shall be on him and his heirs who shall open without my warrant and peruse these pages.

The click clack of the train slowing as we made another stop. Then the mournful whistle wailing as we approached road crossings. A gentleman entered in a stiff wing collar, and sat with the priest across from us. His red glowing face lit by the ceiling light. And perhaps many whiskeys. By the cut of his jib not to mention cutaway coat, striped trousers and black gartered socks, he appeared to be of the legal profession. And from time to time he regards Mr Arland who only lifts his head up from his book to try to read the name as we pull into yet another tiny station.

The legal gentleman seemed to entirely approve of me and once smiled as I wrote in my diary. Which really alarmed me to blushing because I was writing that last night I had four emissions with H.R.H. which initials I used to refer to Miss von B. We stopped at sidings along the great bog to load turf into the tender from the great stacks by the track. And I detected a certain smugness in the legal gentleman who cleared his throat as the conductor who was coming by the carriages asking for the lend of a hand, but who when looking into our window, instead saluted from his cap. Then the legal gent spoke for the first and last time, giving us a flash of his best French.

'Premier class passengers are not asked to help unless they volunteer.'

We heard concerned voices shifting boxes. And back along the train there was the roaring moaning of cattle as they were beaten up into a livestock car. Then the train slowly chugging underway again and I thought back to that fox hunting day of von B beating Baptista. And making, with those splendid lashes landing on the latter, the occupants of Andromeda Park, persona non grata. And we chose to miss a meeting or two of the hunt. Who had four more fixtures during the splendid weather. Which produced grumblings around the stables at the lack of action. All except for Foxy, who said as he cantered Thunder and Lightning around the farm buildings.

'You can the rest of you do what yez like but I'm going to hump after that fucking fox.'

And off he would gallop. And from Foxy came the information that it was rumoured that Baptista's solicitors in the town were intending to call half the hunt as witnesses when they went to trial to ask for damages for assault. Although no writ had yet arrived upon the heels of their threatening letters to Miss von B, more of these unpleasant communications continued to come. Over which Mr Arland and I would pore in the schoolroom between bouts of geography and my recent course on American history.

Dear Madam,

Our client is not satisfied to grant further unappreciated courtesy to await further your obtaining legal representation, the time for which is now long past due, and we call upon you to remit the damages required and give the written apology demanded, or we shall, per our client's instructions, institute proceedings without further notice.

Yours faithfully,
Fibbs, Kelly, Orgle and Fluthered

I could not help but feel as Mr Arland toyed with and touched these distressing letters that he made seem that they were in some remote way secret coded friendly messages to him from Baptista Consuelo. I kept imagining that he might pick one up and kiss her solicitors' signature which I had seen times before provocatively suggesting legal redress against my father for selling some outlying land which some small farmer, claiming squatters' rights, had decided to quietly fence off for himself. But as we all sat over Catherine's piping hot buttery scones and damson jam served by a limping Crooks for tea he dutifully upon lengthy consultations with Miss von B composed replies. And in his high mock pompous voice, putting the final sheet in front of me. Saying.

'I think that out of some authorities who write on such

matters, we may have produced here a thorn or two for them Kildare.'

> Dear Sirs,
>   I write in response to your latest letter and on behalf of Her Royal Highness, The Princess Schlesgluckwigboomsonderstein, that she is, due to a recent indisposition, unable to make the trip to Dublin to instruct her legal advisers not only in answer to your client's claims but also in the matter of the malicious slanders uttered in the disparagement of Her Royal Highness in her present vocation and further reckless imputations of unchastity published in the hunting field by your client with the words hereinafter following. To wit: 'You are a whorish servant.'
>   And additionally:
> 'She's no lady, she's a tramp.'
>
>   Yours faithfully,
>   Mister Arland
>   (Tutor in residence to Master Reginald Darcy Thormond Dancer Kildare.)

Touching this cold clammy train window. The thick leather strap which holds it closed scratched and worn. And now miles back there those evenings after dinner, when it wasn't quite jolly for us three to be in cahoots constructing these letters, it was for me altogether quite mournful. As I took the imputation of Her Royal Highness's unchastity much to heart. Especially as I did now, more than occasionally, sneakily detour to sleep in her bed. But with Mr Arland making one of his funny faces and placing his head on one side to say.

'Ah I think that that nice flourish, imputation of unchastity, may, when the enormity of its ramifications penetrate their thick country skulls, put those rural legal chaps to rout.'

One would at these words be amused and the flush of embarrassment I was sure was on my face would fade. While at the mention of Baptista, Kelly, Fibbs, Fluthered or Orgle, Miss von B merely sniffed down her nose and gave a high pitched false laugh. And with Crooks finally hors de combat with two gouty feet, she was these days a power of activity and made what she said was a pre spring clean. The great big ring of clanging jangling keys on her forearm, pulling open the long closed cupboards in the walls of the ballroom and putting her hands on her hips as she surveyed the shelves full of ancient medical instruments. Her eyes growing wide as she said in her excitement Vas is diss, when her German accent became quite pronounced. And I replied with some relish.

'Ah Princess Gluckswittlebocksonderboomstein, dem ist der blood letting blades, dat snap out to cut zee two rows of incisions to let zee patient's or victim's, however you prefer, to let zair blood flow mit some profusion.'

She would when I used that accent try to clobber me behind the ear. The strength of her was quite amazing. And once I saw stars followed I was pleased to feel, by her kisses bringing me back to life. And then I would with forceps and other evil looking contraptions, try to apply and attempt to operate with them on the more intimate parts of Miss von B's body and she, quite unreasonably scared I thought, would shriek and run, bosoms bouncing, as I chased her all about the ballroom, making my most horrid faces and looming in my most contorted and frightening manner. Till caught she would say, as I flung her down on a dusty window seat with our feet entwining in the great heavy drapes and my hand searching to tug down her undergarments.

'Not here, not here, you little fool.'

Now with every click clack of this cold train I get further away from von B. Who wanted to tie me up and whip me. And when I let her once and it hurt, I asked her was she not disgusted with her behaviour. And especially of indoctrinating one so young as myself. She said that all the better bred older ladies of the deeper continent kept young boys to whip and make love to them. In Vienna it was quite the custom. And she asked would I ever wed. I said no and certainly I would not contemplate such a thing as marriage to an older lady. Not if they did that kind of thing. But with all my responsibilities these days I thought that a wife, one of the quality of Miss von B, would be quite suitable. And save me paying wages. She is so good at cleaning and keeping everything in its place. She sews, mends and crochets. And even knows considerable about cooking except that Catherine hates the sight of her in the kitchen. She is an accomplished horse woman, and jolly good at diagnosing their troubles. Pity she is quite unknowledgeable when it comes to cattle. Had to tell her the difference between a Friesian and Hereford. Of course I could teach her these agricultural things. Just as she has taught me how to make love to ladies. Touch them where they like it most. With these my fingers, which wipe the window and I watch out into the passing black night. And look at my fingernails she manicured. On my third trip to Dublin. Way back there now in the countryside, Andromeda Park sitting lonely on its hill. Strange, how when you leave a whole world behind, you worry that who will see that gates are closed in the far off meadows and mend where the fences are broken. Her Royal Highness will keep the home fires burning. Especially if Crooks will uncomplainingly serve her tea. Although not really himself, he was quite attentive as we dined those evenings. And seemed, always at the end of the day, to be able to manage to arise from bed and bring up from the cellars to table some of our most very best wines, in particular the great booming reds of the Côte de Nuits which he briefly aired and decanted for drinking. But I had noticed recently that not only had he become considerably more cross eyed but that he was particularly monosyllabic with me. Holding awkwardly out from his side his previously broken left arm and answering. Yes master Reginald. No master Reginald. I'll see to it, master Reginald. And one late evening as I was heading to fetch my atlas from the schoolroom to get an impromptu geography lesson from Her Royal Highness nakedly waiting for me upstairs, I stopped to watch the three bats flying in the front hall. When Crooks, stooped forward in his dressing gown and slippers, confronted me in the moonlit darkness. I must admit that there was prevalent a religious mania which seemed to affect to some degree, all the servants, especially those in their less menial and more polite pursuits above stairs. And this I now detected in Crooks as he growled and then with his whiskey smelling breath spouted polysyllabic at me.

'Good lord my God who hath made my legs weak and big toes pained, beseech you deliver us from fornication, and all other deadly sin and from all the deceits of the world, the flesh and the devil.'

'Is that you Crooks.'

'Yes.'

'Are you speaking to me Crooks.'

'I speak to my God first before I shall speak to any earthly master. There's too much and enough going on in this house already. What good would it do to speak to you Master Reginald.'

'Well you are speaking to me.'

'And I regret to see the bad evil influence of that hooligan Foxy coming to flower. And now with that kraut herself disembowelling the very house and sacrilegiously dislodging your great grand uncle's medical instruments from their repository. O there will come the day.'

'What are you trying to say Crooks.'

'I'll say it. And when I have it said and done, the good Lord will then judge. Meanwhile I can only beseech he deliver us from fornication.'

Crooks's slippered footsteps shuffled off down the hall into darkness. And it always rather amazed and alarmed me at how unconcernedly he would, without being summoned, march at any old time through any old room of the house when the fancy took him as it obviously took him now, his voice mumbling as he went.

'O this house, this house. Where I have served so faithfully my dear departed mistress, would that you o great god have the mercy to resurrect her. The all pure and holy Antoinette Delia Darcy Darcy Thormond. God bless you dear. God bless you, you wonderful charming beautiful lady.'

Whenever I looked up in his direction, the priest in our train compartment seemed as if he were about to suddenly speak or more probably shout at me. Clearly to him both Mr Arland and I were agnostics at large or something, or even worse, protestants. Whom Sexton said, were at least well bathed and honest while any good catholic worth his salt didn't go near a bath tub and would treacherously lie sooner than look at you. And Crooks and Sexton were easily the most devout among our male staff, both wearing crucifixes under their tunics which they oftentimes took out and kissed. And I thought any day I'd see the two of them dancing a jig down the hall each with a winter bouquet of Sexton's night scented flowers and screaming hail mary up at heaven. But all that happened back that night confronting Crooks, was that my erection went down and when feeling around in the dark for the atlas I fell over a broom sticking out wedged between a table and the wall in the schoolroom. But it was the first time ever that I heard Crooks pray for my mother's resurrection. It was not however, the first I had heard of him speaking of his miraculous visions. Vouched for on one occasion by Sexton, who only that I knew he was somewhat touched with an equal mania, I might have nearly believed them both. Their urgent hysterics about the apparition told all over the farmyard, that my mother had appeared where the altar used to be in the ancient ruin of the chapel in the cemetery. Or Sexton when he stood in his potting shed imploring with his hands.

'Ah it was a blinding brightness of light and that immaculate lady, sine dubio, the very virgin replica of the Blessed Virgin herself, stood there with her fair hand raised till the explosive vision blinded us. I myself with me only one good eye left threw meself prostrate to the ground. Then when I looked back up, there stood a vase right out of Catherine's kitchen cupboard with the loveliest of deep red roses in it. A miracle.'

And on this bumping ride now. The train to Dublin. Photographs of the great hotels enveloped in smoke over the legal gent's head, as the priest puffs on a cigarette. And all the waste land and barren bogs out there in the darkness. And upon the journey from Andromeda Park to the station we were discussing the niceties of legal jargon when I asked Mr Arland if it were not proper for me to address Miss von B by her title. He frowned slightly as he said.

'Of course in mere courtesy you might. However, although she is, Kildare, according to the *Almanach de Gotha*, high born, I regret to say that, in fact, she is not entitled to be referred to in the style and manner of Her Royal Highness.'

We had on that subject a good jolly laugh when letter composing. For Mr Arland, when we sat alone without Miss von B, further and better revising our letters to those naughty solicitors, would place his pointing finger under the words Her Royal Highness and then double up his hand into a shaking fist. And how in this carriage he slumps a little, there in the corner, his head nodding off to sleep, his book open across his grey knee with the thumb of his pale scholarly hand held between the pages and I could see the nosey priest trying to see its long complicated title.

A Domestic Homoeopathy
Its Legitimate Sphere of Practice
Together with Rules for Diet and Regimen

Mr Arland often read and quoted to me from this volume with such advices as, 'Nightmare often occurs after a hearty supper.' Although he said he should be sorry to no longer be my tutor, I felt he might be glad to be departing. Especially with his advances towards Baptista Consuelo so poorly and unsportingly received. But recently he seemed to have come out of his tendency to long silences. Which I felt had resulted from his deep and spurned love for that little bitch. He had moreover, met me, as nearly every bloody member of the household now had, on one of my rather late evening expeditions to Miss von B. I was about to babble out a whole stream of ridiculous excuses as to why I was to be found tiptoeing in my dressing gown upwards on the beech grove stairs, my noisy slippers tucked under each armpit, when he bowed in the candlelight and instead made his excuse to me.

'Ah Kildare, I am unable to sleep and I am on my way to the library to choose a book. And ah I see you were just like me as a boy. I too often went at night to go catch moths attracted by a light I'd put at an attic window.'

'Ah yes, Mr Arland, yes, precisely what I am doing. As a matter of fact. Catching moths.'

'Of course you'll find moths more plentiful in summer. But have a good catch, Kildare, goodnight.'

Now Mr Arland slumped over in his seat lets out a little snore. Which clearly the priest does not appreciate but at which the legal gent kindly smiles. Just as Mr Arland did that night on the stairs. When I knew that I had blundered by saying anything about catching moths. But I am sure he felt it beneficial for me to have it off with Miss von B even though he could not contribute to the furtherance of that aspect of my education by his tutoring. And noting the fact in my diary, I was astonished as to how well used I was becoming to sleeping with her. We could get nice and jolly warm together. And I liked her stories. About the Barons Princes and Duchesses, and the naughty goings on in the tottering Royal Houses of Europe. And the way she would suddenly in the middle of them jump up and go guzzling and kissing all over me with her mouth. I could nearly think of nothing now but climbing on top of her each night or she upon me as we did occasionally till dawn or our utter fatigue finally intervened. Resulting then in my being unable to stand up during the daytime. Sitting there in the schoolroom or across the table from Mr Arland in the library, with my pained and strained prick pushing my trousers out like a tent. And at lunch when I walked bent over behind Mr Arland to the dining room, he turned to regard me.

'Good grief Kildare, what on earth's the matter, you're bent over like an old man, are you alright.'

'I believe I may just have a small rupture.'

'Good lord, we had better summon the doctor.'

'O no I'll be quite alright, it easily passes off.'

'Rupture Kildare, does not pass off. Indeed you can get a strangulated hernia.'

'O I'm sure it's perhaps not rupture. Colic or something. Quite temporary.'

'Colic, o well, my *Domestic Homoeopathy Manual* has just the jolly job for you. Hot flannels applied on the belly. And you must abstain from green vegetable and other flatulent food.'

Yet, having it off with Miss von B had so much changed one's life. For a start my voice was considerably deeper. And I was able to wear my foreskin back. It was worrying however that nearly nothing else entered one's mind. And there might be something going wrong with my brain. For even as I used to do, watching the rooks, or tramping for a walk up over spy glass hill, everywhere in front of one's eyes was the moaning writhing body of Miss von B. And I must admit that not everything was pleasure. Those first few times I blushed and shivered and trembled and at times was revolted. Indeed a whole fortnight passed before I was able to avoid vomiting usually once before heading up the stairs and again in her room and again when I returned to mine. And dear me, once right on top of her. Later of course, when I returned to the privacy of my own chamber, I did nearly laugh my head off. It was the extraordinary panicky manner in which she tried to get out of the way of that evening's digested dinner. Since I was in her we were rather pinned together, and she would move one way just as I was trying to move the opposite. I had also to get used to one or two regrettable things in the way of her personal smells occasioned when she could not bathe. When, as a result of a two week visit from the plumber who went round scratching his head and twisting and banging the pipes, finally had water flying out of everywhere but where it should. Although she retired behind a screen to put some contraption up her I always found it rather disconcerting especially as she would with equanimity loose farts. However when she did this under the covers she did explain that if such gas should therein remain bottled up there could result one awful battle to finally bust it out. As I got used to her ways I laid a few myself and we would both lie there listening together to see who could make the most interesting bang. She was most remarkably handy with her tongue as well. And would put it around things and in places that most surprised me. And just so that she would not think I was as sordid as she was I thought it appropriate to mildly remonstrate.

'Even though I like you doing that to me isn't it filthy and disgusting.'

'You Irish, your minds are as stupid as your bodies are usually dirty.'

The train now passing by bleak black rooftops and over a trestle bridge in the misty darkness. Lamplights up streets glowing on the shabby red bricked tiny houses. Smoke curling thick from chimneys into the hovering fog. And as the train pulled into the station, the legal gentleman again smiled at me. He also civilly bowed to Mr Arland who bowed back as he was leaving the carriage. The priest however appeared to like one even less now at the end of the journey and took his black case down from the rack with an impatient long sigh.

The great glass roof over us in the terminus. A porter, already shouting his services to the emerging first class passengers, pushed a noisy iron wheeled barrow in front of him and at Mr Arland's direction took our luggage. Turning continually to speak back to us.

'This way now gentlemen if you please.'

And Mr Arland absent mindedly turned right down grey granite steps. To then hear the porter calling after us from the top, to say he had a carriage waiting at the other entrance. Where he hefted our luggage up on the brougham's roof and then made vague mutterings over his tip until Mr Arland gave him an extra shilling.

'Well there you are Kildare, evidence of the greed overcoming modern society.'

The horsecab driver with his big crimson nose sticking out from under his top hat, folding his whip and climbing up on his perch to sit pulling an old piece of burlap across his legs. Giving his thin nag a feeble belt across the quarters, and off we trotted down this incline, the candle fluttering behind the gleaming glass of our sidelights. Turning right, out through great grey gates to suddenly stop. This morning Kern and Olav loped beside us all the way to the lodge and then just sat, their great hulking shaggy shapes, disconsolate as we disappeared down the road. And this city street aswarm with bicycles. Coming by in a great wave as we waited. And here and there were motor cars. The huge garda finally putting up his white gloved hand to halt them all. And we pulled out, passing this policeman nearly as tall as the roof of our horse carriage and as wide as a full grown bull across the shoulders.

'Well Kildare, we made it multa gemens. Five hours nearly, to go sixty miles. Translate please.'

'With many an agony.'

'With many a groan Kildare, with many a groan.'

A sign at the door of a dirty red bricked building said Coroner's Court. And next to it written on closed big dark wooden gates, City Morgue. Newsboys on the street corners shouting out *Herald* and *Mail*. Their tattered jackets too small and their white naked legs and blue white feet on the wet blocks of granite, phlegm streaming from their noses. The evening herd of cold pinched dark coated figures waiting to cross at the pavement's edge, their breath making steam from their mouths. The strange purple of the sky. A ship hooting on the river. Great stack of barrels quayside being loaded by a ship's derrick under lights. And bouncing on the cobbles, clattering huge carts tugged by massive horses. Followed here and there by impatient automobiles. Must be sadness where so many of the lower orders live inside the big broken windows. Behind these mournful unloved walls.

'Kildare cheer up. It will appear much better to you in the morning, I assure you.'

'It looks so appalling. Down those streets.'

'In a moment or two and just over this bridge we shall be in a better part of town. A bath, a little supper in you, will put a completely new complexion on it. Now in that building there, once when the college baths were closed, I cleansed myself as an undergraduate.'

Past pubs, a coal merchant, gentleman's clothiers and a shop selling yeast. And on the right, a massive edifice with porticoes and pillars blackened by age and bleached by rain. Another garda even as big as the previous one, his nose and face red in the cold mist, directing traffic outside the gates of the college. At which Mr Arland seemed longingly to look. Beyond the railings either side of the entrance path, a statue standing up out of lawns flat velvet and green. And we trotted on behind a tram, clanging its bell, roaring and grinding on its track. Indeed one felt without being jubilant, at least a little more hopeful. And now the tram with its two tiers of dim yellow lighted windows, turning as we head straight. The horses' hooves slipping on the wet wooden blocks.

'That Kildare is the Provost's House and here we are now in the lap of elegance. On your left, Mitchell's for yummy creamy cakes and tea. Now Brown Thomas's for the best in silks, cashmeres, lace, linen and I suppose ladies' knicker-bockers. And coming on your right. Bewley's Oriental emporium of coffee, spice buns, butter balls and jersey milk.'

Turning left at the top of the street. The winter shadowy trees of St Stephen's Green. Trotting along, a sweet smell of turf smoke pushing down from the roof top chimney pots on the terraced row of tall Georgian houses. Standing cheek by jowl like the giant faces of people who sit with big empty eyes staring. Pulling up in front of a big red brick building. The doorman opening the horsecab, assisting Mr Arland to alight. Two porters attentively collecting down our luggage. Mr Arland plonking two half crowns into the jarvey's upturned hand. And turning to me as we mounted the step under the hotel's glass awning.

'Well Kildare, whatever amenities this city may possess most are, to use that favoured expression of Sexton's, sine dubio to be found right in here.'

There was welcoming warmth and bustle in the lobby of the hotel and faint smells of ladies' perfume passing. And with some interest I regarded their legs. And with much interest their bottoms, especially those well delineated by snug tailoring. Mr Arland made reservations for dinner, while a boy much smaller than myself, hair slicked back and parted in the middle, carried my bags as the porter led me with his big key into the cage of the lift and up we went three floors. My room long and narrow. Thick crimson carpet on the floor. I could see out my window across the winter trees of the park and all the way to the far outskirts of the city. And beyond the faint outlines of the rising mountains. And there downward just below on the street, those tinker women to whom Mr Arland gave a coin, squatting on the wet pavement with the patched red and blue skin of their legs showing and babies held in their arms. And their toothless mouths begging.

'Give us a couple of coppers mister, will you now, and may no burden after ever be too much for you.'

Darcy Dancer holding aside the curtains from the window. The sky clearer, the clouds moving. Patches of blue purple and pink. Down there, a lake and a summer house. And big dark buildings the other side of the large square of Stephen's Green. Small figures scurrying along the park's black fence. Without friendly company. In this city. Where my father somewhere is. And where behind walls and under roofs, books and records are kept. Juries sit and cases are heard by big important judges. Mr Arland seemed so pleased when we passed his University. There behind its high wall and railings. I hear a seagull cry. This port where ships come up the river. And away in the world across the water there has been all sorts of war. My feet still chilled and hands cold. And as I always wished at the whim room window, like my mother did when February came. That soon it would go.

> And come
> Summer
> With your
> Swallows
> Swimming in
> The air

10

Stylishly wrapping a towel at my throat and after peering to see that no one was about to witness my rather tattered dressing gown, I hurried to bathe in the piping hot waters of a monstrous tub down at the end of the hall. The steamy slightly brown water came blazing out of the taps. Lying back in the liquid comfort, my red knob was soon sticking out of the water like a periscope. If Miss von B were here she would lunge with her mouth upon it and I think I might howl with rapture. As I did anyway when I pulled it. Feeling warm once more.

All spiffy and tingling just that little bit with moral evil, I went down in the iron cage of the lift. Watching the green uniformed attendant with his little lever lowering me from floor to floor. Thinking apropos of nothing at all that Nurse Ruby was forever pulling my sister Beatrice Blossom's pigtails and making her cry. Just as she used to play with my penis and make me laugh. And Miss von B. She wanted to kiss me goodbye as we stood with the breeze blowing in the front hall. I kept leaning back quite naughtily out of her reach. And then, the moment Catherine retreated from delivering our sandwiches and Mr Arland had gone down the steps to mount the cart, she grabbed me. Said I was looking elegant. Her lips soft. Quite substantial tears came into her eyes. I was glad. Clearly it meant I would be missed.

In the lobby, within the space of only a few minutes, I saw three monocles being worn and shudderingly thought each time it was my father. I lurked by one of the pillars and watched into the great high ceilinged lounge. Crowded now with tweedy gentlemen looking like human branches of hawthorn. They sat, walked and loudly talked. The constant refrain, yes yes, quite quite. And when not discoursing on horses, they seemed to be speaking of snipe, fox, grouse, salmon or pheasant. And it appeared that they were, as Mr Arland suggested, hysterically pukka. And had hunting fishing and shooting appointment books instead of souls. And matters of cultural beauty could not possibly cross their outdoor minds. Except if it had wings. And then it would be promptly blasted from the sky.

I followed Mr Arland through a small cosy sitting and writing room of flower covered deep soft sofas. Up stairs to a balcony and out into a hall and down stairs again and into another hall. Through curtained french doors we stepped into a blue large room, white splendid medallions on the walls. The colour seemed that of our faded blue north east parlour when on winter sunny mornings the sun flooded in our tinted window panes. A blonde lady with her undulating curves held voluptuously in a long blatantly orange gown, swept in. Her gently bouncing alabaster bosoms nakedly swelling forth and nearly popping out. Her nose repeatedly sniffing upwards and hooking a little as if she were smelling a fume drifting in over her left shoulder. She joins a red haired moustachioed gentleman at the bar who bows deeply, kissing her hand. A cigarette between her lips wagging up and down. Her voice reverberating.

'Ronald, Ronald. You are so pleasantly flattering with your attentions. Especially when I feel I shall faint with the noise and the people. Buy me a drink quickly.'

'For you madam, only a bottle of the house's best champagne will do.'

'O Ronald darling you are dear dear.'

In here under the soft white marble mantel, a turf fire roared. The cold black bleak city shut out. Hiding all those poor and hungering, all those cold and lonely. And hunched backs carrying their tattered garments. The gentleman called Ronald dressed for dinner. His dark elegance and long ivory cigarette holder. As we sit at our glass topped table in our wicker chairs. In this warmth and safety. One other gentleman in the corner reading a book which, judging by his concentration, must be saucy indeed. The waiter retreating backwards out of our presence. To bring us sherry. Mr Arland with his one usual grey suit, sporting a tie I had not seen before.

'What is that tie, Mr Arland.'

'Trinity College. I wear it while in Dublin, Kildare. In some places it would get you excellent service, in others perhaps, you might get a kick in the pantaloon.'

Following our first sherry and upon completion of half our second, the lady in the fiery gown was tippling back the last drops of her champagne. And then both Mr Arland and I faltered in our conversation. For it appeared that the shapely lady had pulled down that part of her dress which previously covered and now prominently exposed her left breast. Pressing it up with her hand, showing it to Ronald.

'You see Ronald can't you, where that wretched stallion bit me. I can't help that I arouse horses. Look, one two three teeth marks, quite black and blue. Even geldings get into a frenzy when they sniff me.'

Ronald then, quite deliberately slowly I thought, took a pair of spectacles from his inside pocket. Placing them half way down his nose. He leaned deeply over to make a lengthy inspection. All the while making suitable sympathetic noises through a large gap between his protruding front teeth.

'Indeed quite so my dear, you were well and truly bitten. Clearly however, if I may say so, judging by the tooth marks, by a thoroughbred.'

'Yes, a Derby winner, he just missed my nipple.'

'Yes, he did. I rather noticed that.'

Following more of Ronald's scrutiny and a final appreciative pat, the breast was replaced under its coverings. The gentleman in the corner, no longer regarding his book, absolutely gaped with his mouth open wide enough for doves to fly in. And the waiter and bartender brought their eyes back down again from the ceiling. Mr Arland and I departed through the passage crossing the little sitting room once more.

'That lady back there Kildare, acts also upon the Dublin stage. Where her performances are not nearly so good. And that chap Ronald, I'll tell you more about later.'

The dining room waiters in plenty scurried around us. For starters we had saumon fumé. I ordered steak, spinach and chips. And felt quite pleasantly inebriated taking a glassful of the Pommard Mr Arland ordered with his roast beef, as I, even with my rudimentary French, pointed out mistakes in the French menu. Mr Arland saying wistfully.

'They mean well but it would be so much better and accurate if things were said in English.'

'What if they were said in Irish, Mr Arland.'

'The gentry would starve Kildare.'

Great crimson drapes drawn closed across the windows. The faint sweet smells of cooking sprouts, cabbage and other green things. Sauces pouring from the sauce boats. Wines of sacred vintages cradled carefully across the carpets. Altogether the sort of setting of which Crooks would approve. The most distinguished looking of black tail coated waiters, giving their lofty orders down through a chain of command. Till it reached some little boy who had to run and do all the dirty work. And was stationed standing by some empty table adding polishing touches to the silverware and sneaking looks at the nearby guests. Or rushing back and forth following urgent hisses from under waiters to fetch this or that. As still other little boys went pageing by mournfully intoning people's names.

Throughout the meal I still had the uncomfortable feeling that my father was somewhere near. Half expecting him to suddenly turn round and be one of those tweedy thin gentlemen who kept pausing to look at the Fox Hunting fixtures posted on the wall in the hall. Mr Arland eating with gusto. Smiling at me, and shaking his head in agreement as I smiled back and chewed down another chunk I'd sliced off my slab of blood rare steak. Dublin suddenly most agreeable. Mr Arland happily putting his nose over the edge of his Pommard. But I could tell he was still distressed over Baptista Consuelo and he would apropos of nothing at all refer to the subject of fox hunting. Asking me of lady Masters of Foxhounds.

'Sir they do frequently want to have that honour, especially as the one who leads the hunt gets no splatter. And a lady might then appear at the end of a day's hunting just as splendidly fresh and radiant as she was at the beginning.'

I was nearly on the verge of launching into the more scandalous aspects of hunting. Of how ladies with their blood up were constantly attempting to entice even the Master at the end of the day into some seemly copse and there dismounted to have lively congress with him upon the cold wet moss and grass. But I was so distracted with the arrival of my favourite pudding, trifle. And while Mr Arland was having cheese, port and a cigar, I with fork and spoon rapidly shovelled it with accompanying scads of thick cream, most deliciously between my lips. But soon as I was finished, Mr Arland, never one to waste time when he could be imparting knowledge, discoursed upon the Constitution of the United States. When suddenly who should leap up from a distant corner in the room smiling ear to ear. And waving as he came, cross over to our table. Barging quite unceremoniously between the other diners. One of whose elbows was knocked sending a fork into that part of his face where there was no mouth. And leaving I think four little bloody puncture holes. The Count Blandus MacBuzuranti O'Biottus pausing to somewhat hysterically commiserate and apologize. Until he finally reached us flushed and red faced but bubbling with excitement.

'Hello, ah hello. How are my dear friends. How good to see you. And how are you, my former little victim. The very worst you were. Yes, the very worst little pupil that I have ever had the insanity to try to teach. Who now looks so grown up. Have you yet got the élan of the gazelle, my little darling. O I know I push by accident of course that poor man's fork into his head. But his elbow it is too far stuck out. But surely you have come to attend my marvellous party I am giving this evening to celebrate the opening of my new school. But of course my dear friends you are coming.'

Mr Arland and I sat there waiting till the Count was out of breath. Which was clearly not going to be tonight. As he shifted his weight from leg to leg, and continued to be heard by the entire dining room. Many of whom were whispering in somewhat awestruck tones that the Count had received thirty curtain calls when he last danced in Milan. I found the attention paid us quite pleasing. And even Mr Arland, not one to be showy or grand, was sitting just that little bit more upright. The Count's blond handsome looks and white flashing teeth. And I could see at the table from whence he had come that there sat a dark haired woman of austere beauty.

'O but I must go. But come. Of course you shall. And bring all your nice friends with you. And even those who may not be so nice.'

The Count reeled off an address which he said was merely around the corner. And dancingly returning across the dining room he executed an attitude alongée on point followed by a grand jeté. Some of the more cultivated and easily amused diners politely clapped but most ducked. The Count bowing before he sat down at his table across from the dark beauty. Who reached out to pat her hand on his and smilingly formed her lips into a kiss. And they kissed. While we retired to the lounge for coffee. I told Mr Arland how the Count used to scream at us, 'Let us have for god's sake the perpendicularity, the natural elegance the ethereal lightness, the carriage of the body and arms, the motions graceful and easy.' But Mr Arland seemed rather in a dither. And said, completely straying from the point in question, that the Count was not so entitled, and might merely be a papal count but that there was no doubt but he was related to some very splendid people indeed and could, if one stretched the point, be considered ennobled.

'Of course, I can't bring you to a party, Kildare. Not that sort of party.'

'What sort of party.'

'Well I don't really know, but I'm sure it's that sort of party.'

'Sir. O but you can.'

I insisted, when Mr Arland had said that we had already been too extravagant, that he should sample some of the house's best brandy. And I had the waiter go fetch from their cellar such a suitably dusty bottle. Mr Arland said that kind of party could give one a reputation. And people like the

Dublin actress attended them and that Ronald was a chancer and a notorious fortune hunter. And that he'd marry a witch if she had the price of a pint of stout and that he was most suitably nick named Rashers Ronald. And each time I reached to refill Mr Arland's glass he would put his hand forward to the rim. But then he would smile.

'Now now Kildare, you are a devil. I really have had quite enough.'

When I was sure that Mr Arland had indeed had a sufficiency, I had our coats fetched from our rooms and it was not at all difficult to get him out the door. To freshen up a bit with the night air. But I did indeed once or twice quite forcibly push him forward in front of me. Past the still begging tinkers who thrice blessed him. And the more he started to laugh, the more I pushed. Till I was really shoving him, right, as the saying goes, around the corner. But we had to walk yet another street. Which seemed quite pleasantly and thoroughly protestant. With a big grey Masonic lodge. And societies for the protection of Indigent Widows of the Gentry. Then crossing over into another narrow street we came to the door. Open on the latch.

Again I had to push Mr Arland forward. And also upwards as he kept stumbling still highly amused on the narrow stairs. Groping as we were noisily through musty blackness from landing to landing. Till at the very top we could hear voices and singing and light flooding out. We stood in the doorway. And then came the Count's voice over the throng of assembled heads.

'Hello my darlings. Come in come in. Of course you will know no one here. And it does not matter. Nobody I know admits knowing anyone else I know. Shall we just leave it that way and get you drinks.'

Candles burning in this low ceilinged room. Sound of corks popping. A bottle of stout shoved in my hand. Hanging between gilded framed mirrors, four illumined oil portraits of Popes of the Roman Catholic Church. One of St Gregory the Great. His light blue painted eyes staring out over the pillow stacked chaise longue. And there, away in a tapestried corner were the courtesan and her red haired friend Rashers Ronald from the Shelbourne rooms. While another blonde lady was eyeing me. Making me most uncomfortable. And as I eyed her right back, she crossed the room towards me pushing between the tight packed people.

'You're a bit young aren't you, dear boy, to be here amid all these flagrantly perverted people. But I like your eyes. Are you with your parents.'

'I was in fact invited with my tutor.'

'You were what.'

'I suppose as part of my education. There he is, the tall gentleman talking with that lady who's wearing that large blue hat.'

'O you are a rich young man then are you. Having a tutor.'

'I don't think so.'

'O you must be. Although you certainly don't look it. But you sound to the manner born. I am an impoverished artist late of Bloomsbury, Bloomsbury Place, Bloomsbury Square, London as it happens. And I want you to buy my paintings.'

'I should be quite happy to see them but I do not have much money to buy.'

'I think you must be lying or else you're totally bereft of culture.'

'And you madam are lacking in manners.'

Darcy Dancer stepping back a little from this lady whose face juts forward. And turning to apologize as his heels landed on a rather robust young woman's toes. Who shoves him off. Right up against the artist advancing upon him in her green voluminous sweater. A look of some consternation in her eyes. Streaks of grey in her bundled blonde hair. Moist red lips and quite good quality teeth. A pronounced strong nose and flared nostrils and a blue vein throbbing on her temple. And pleasantly sweet smelling breath as it wafts on my face.

'I say who the hell are you. I really want to know. I have a son older than you are and I would not let him attend such a gathering as this. But you do have rather feminine eyes. They attracted my attention the instant you walked into the room. Yes you're quite extraordinary looking. Who are you.'

'I'm from the country.'

'That's quite clear from that coat and suit you're wearing, and your rather overly large ears. Not that I'm that pristine, but your hair is washed I hope. Let me smell. O I say it's quite clean. At least you're not one of those awfully dirty Anglo Irish always doing something greasy with axles or water pumps or if they're not wringing chickens' necks in the drawing room then they're sticking their arms up cows' arses.'

'You are impertinent, madam.'

'Impertinent. Good lord, you've got your damn nerve coming in here among many of my personal friends and telling me, a lady three times your age that I am impertinent. Who the hell are you.'

'And you've already asked me that three times and I have my good reasons for declining to say.'

'Cheeky little chap, aren't you. It's your immaturity of course. But I think I like you. Yes, there's just the merest trace of hair on your upper lip. You shall have whiskers soon, won't you. I am one of those dangerous women they call divorcees. Whose husband was a confirmed pederast. Which put it into my head to corrupt little boys such as you before he did.'

'Why don't you try it.'

'What. What did you say. Try it. Surely you little fellow, you're having me on. I wouldn't dare. Corrupt you.'

'I thought not. You're all talk aren't you. That silly kind of thing ladies like you of the Bohemian set think is the modern fashion.'

'In one second I think I shall slap your little face.'

'And should you madam, I will in turn, slap yours.'

'Just who the hell are you, you brat.'

'My father frequently refers to me as a bastard, but I don't suppose that information will enlighten you much.'

'It enlightens me a great deal. But I think you should be got out of here.'

This lady leaning close to Darcy Dancer's ear, her lips touching to whisper. The softness of her mouth. Makes me rather shiver pleasantly. Just as Thunder and Lightning must do when Foxy on cold winter nights rubbed and squeezed his ears to make him warm and calm.

'Dear boy, there is an unwholesome element. Not to mention the many mediocre minds present. But see those men. They are gunmen. Quite ruthless. Not the sort of type a young man such as you ought to be rubbing elbows with. The Count should be ashamed of himself for inviting you. Come. Come with me immediately.'

'Why should I.'

'Because I shall, dear boy, besides showing you my etchings, make you the most marvellous cocoa you have ever had.'

The lady casting her eyes for Darcy Dancer to follow across the room. Past a hefty bruiser wearing a red carnation in his buttonhole. A gentleman they said was a champion boxer. And a red haired beauty they said was his girlfriend who used shoes to bang his head as he used fists to bang her face. They were called all over Dublin the Bruises United. And to three gentlemen in caps and macintoshes standing about sucking on the ends of cigarettes, looking furtively at the doorway and indeed unpleasantly in my direction. Certainly cocoa as a beverage is not to be dismissed lightly. And always was, after wild blackberry jam that Nannie Nurse Ruby specially made for me, my second favourite food. Coming hot in a jug up from the kitchens snug under a tea cosy on the chill winter nights, when Nannie Ruby told me my bedtime stories of big green dragon monsters and wise old billy goats. There stands Rashers Ronald brushing a speck from his dinner clothes as he loftily intones to a shabby rain coated gent beside him.

'Would you mind awfully getting out of my life, I prefer the company of people creative in the arts rather than criminal in the crafts.'

And now bodies jumping in the centre of this smoky room. The floor as well as the whole building shaking. A roaring shout.

'Give him violence or give him death but don't give the greedy fucker another bottle of stout.'

'You'll give me another bottle of stout by gob or I am going to kick the living bejesus out of you back and forth across the border till not a vestige of that division is left, you cunt, you.'

This wavy haired gentleman in a mustard coloured sweater, his fist gripped tightly round the neck of a Guinness. And mounting and standing on the delicate fabric of a chaise longue.

'Shut up now while I'm talking to you. And let me hereby assert to every bollocks here assembled, my inalienable, indefeasible and sovereign right to drink and fuck myself to death from one end of the national territory to the other so help me satan and to let it be said once and for all across Ireland that never in the history of the nation has so much been drunk by so few or so few fucked by so many. More power to the intelligentsia. Up the Republic.'

A chair suddenly flying from the direction of the three outspoken gentlemen. Goes crashing through the window and falling to the street below. Where, unhappily, as was reported by someone leaning out watching it, it landed on a guest just arriving with a parcel of drink. And knocked to the pavement, bottles smashing, he lay in a large pool of dark foaming beer. A voice calling down.

'Binky darling, o what a nuisance for you, are you hurt.'

And brown foam slipping down the sides of the glasses held in all these hands. Two voices singing. Someone shouting pipe down. And between the weaving heads and parting shoulders I see in a more peaceful corner, an animated Mr Arland talking to none other than the courtesan. He really looks so jolly pleased. Must be telling her my best jokes for normally he is never that hilarious. And the Dublin actress is laughing. Bosoms heaving with her alabaster arms nearly flapping out of her flame radiant dress. Could cross over to say that a kind lady was snatching me from the present mayhem to preserve my virtuousness. But poor Mr Arland, after all his mortifications at the hands of that bitch Baptista, I'm sure does not want to be disturbed. Especially in what might be some new romance in his life. Just as I would not approach when lonely he played our corroding out of tune piano. The compositions of Sergei Vassilievitch Rachmaninoff as Mr

Arland insisted he be called. Nor may he see this lady artist as my saviour and might feel he personally should escort me back to the Shelbourne.

'Come with me. And call me Lois dear boy. You see I told you. About these men. They are quite frightening. But what would you know of an artist's fears or suffering. And the awful sacrifices one makes for one's work. Especially when one is without patrons. My milk bill, gas bill, my rent. Who's going to pay them.'

Darcy Dancer following Lois out to the landing and into a back room. The sound of heavy breathing and rolling and pitching bodies in the darkness. Digging in the heaving shadows, Lois unearthing her coat. Tugging it from beneath a lady and gentleman who were seemingly transported in a groaning moaning paroxysm.

'How dare you do that on my coat you filthy people. Get off. You see don't you, dear boy, the kind of monstrous shamelessness I am rescuing you from.'

Lois pulling me back with her into the hall. I held her leather string pouch and helped hold her heavy garment as she plunged her arms into the sleeves. She stands pinioning the front together with elongated wooden buttons and then pulled a hood up over her head.

'Only good thing my husband left me. He used to wear it on the bridge of his ship. He was a lieutenant commander dear boy. Ah but I've got you now, haven't I.'

A strange dreamy smile coming over her face. She grabbed me by the head and shoved her tongue deep into my ear where it went burrowing around. We nearly fell down the stairs and her saliva left me quite deaf for a moment and I wondered if she could taste my wax. And I look at her legs. Where I had never seen a lady wear trousers before.

'Don't look at me as if you think I'm bizarre dear boy. I just am.'

On the landing below, past another room from which came the smell of incense, she stuck her tongue again deep in my ear. And as we proceeded downwards, she reached upwards backwards to apply a momentary squeeze to my privates. My heart surprised me as it pounded with some excitement descending the last flight and out the door to the street. On the pavement more guests arrived and stood standing over the gent Binky as he sat groggily regaining his senses. With his raincoat open showing him entirely stark naked underneath. And he cried out when spotting my Bohemian artist friend.

'Lois, my dear, where are you going you naughty girl with that frightfully attractive young innocent looking boy.'

'Never you mind Binky, it's a pity you can't keep out of the way of falling chairs.'

'I may be felled my dear but I shall be erected soon.'

Lois hurrying Darcy Dancer past several shops and doorways and a pub with polished brass fittings outside. We turn left and up this shadowy thoroughfare, hardly a soul on the street, save a tiny barefoot boy yelling out to sell his newspapers to a man staggering in front of a furniture shop window, speaking earnestly and gesticulating vehemently to his reflection in the glass.

'O god dear boy, everywhere people are roving insane out of their minds in this city.'

The gesticulating gentleman struck one or two classically proper stage poses and obviously had a sense of theatre. But as I tried to slow down to watch his performance Lois pulls me forward along another alley with a fragrant smell of coffee. And then left again. Street called Chatham Row. Ahead a great grey granite building Lois says is a hospital. How will I ever remember the way to get back to the Shelbourne. A voice from somewhere calling.

'A penny, the oranges.'

As I pause Lois again catching and pulling me by the arm. Moving as quickly around another corner. At an alley entrance she stops. Turning to look back. Her voice coming out of her nose.

'I'm sorry to rush like this but I simply hate being followed as I sometimes am. By these hordes of sexually frustrated people. Such a bore. And that old wicked queen. Serves him right to get banged on the head with a chair. He'd just love to get his hands on you. The Count should be ashamed. Inviting you, and your tutor taking you, a mere totally innocent boy. Thank God I was there. Think what might otherwise have happened. Someone should tell your mother.'

'I do appreciate your rescuing me. Madam.'

'And so you should be. And why do you keep using that madam. You're not a shop assistant are you.'

'No madam.'

'Well then stop it. My name is Lois.'

Up this dark narrow alley. Past tall warehouse doors. A chill wind blowing up behind our backs. The wails and hisses of a screaming cat fight. And bells tolling as I count up to nine, ten, eleven. The only life now through the empty city streets. Illumined by the near lamplight ahead stuck high on a wall, its gas mantel flickering. Lois rummaging in her leather pouch. Taking out a key on a long white string. And pushing it in the lock of this pale green door on which a brass number says four. I waited standing on the wet glistening cobbles till she reached and pulled me rather forcibly in. And a draught of wind suddenly slammed the door thunderously shut. Lois stumbled backwards falling over milk bottles. And landed with a thud on her bottom. I really laughed.

'You think that's funny. I certainly don't appreciate your sense of humour. Here help me up damn you.'

'I apologize madam, I really do, but you did go down as if felled by an axe.'

'I'll fell you with an axe. And stop that damn madam. And get me up. I think I may have crushed a vertebra. Or dislocated my hip. O god, does anyone know, does anyone realize, the trials and tribulations of the sincere and dedicated artist.'

Darcy Dancer in this darkness, lifting Lois upwards under the armpits. Only a few hours in Dublin and I've attended a party and am dragging a lady limply along this hall knocking over more bottles and trying to lower her gently seated on the bottom step of the stairs.

'At least I'm glad to see you are quite strong.'

'Thank you.'

'Well I think I'm alright. It's my diet which has been so poor. So wretched. I'm quite nearly starving sometimes you know. That's why I go to those awful parties. To eat. And one hardly ever can because all they do is drink. Every penny I earn must go towards buying more paint and canvas.'

Lois slowly getting to her feet and holding a banister rail to lead Darcy Dancer feeling his way up the narrow steep staircase. The sound of a box of matches opening. And Lois strikes one once, twice and three times. And finally a flame. To light four candles. A large tall room. A big pot bellied iron stove in the centre. Glassy blackness beyond a great skylight. Paintings stacked everywhere.

'I nearly have a good mind to send you away laughing at me like that. And not to let you see my etchings. But of course I will give you some hot cocoa. Well, don't just stand there. Take off your coat.'

Clusters of massive testicles in great wild tropical curvatures of colour with penises cascading down them like waterfalls. The canvases leaning overlapping along the walls. By the blackened rusty stove, three steps up to a high dais. Before it an easel holding a full length portrait of the Count. Missing an unfinished arm and a lower leg. The rest of his muscular body wearing only his extremely smooth skin, posed against a deep green flowing drapery. His privates most shockingly prominent not to say bulging out of his blond curling pubic hair. And strewn on the floor water colour drawings of a quite black individual, with uncommonly not to say improbably whopping sexual organs.

'This is where I sleep dear boy.'

A wide quilt covered bed stacked with brightly coloured pillows. Upon which Lois throws her great heavy duffel coat. And then sits to pull off her green sweater. A long sleeved tight pink garment underneath.

'You have a lot of pictures of naked men.'

'They are not naked men. Studies, dear boy. Studies of the male nude.'

A table with a jar of marmalade and half a loaf of bread. A fish skeleton on a plate. In a corner by a small window a sink stacked full of dishes. Lois putting out her chest as she arose again. Pressing her hands down across her backside.

'Thank god I've not broken bones. That's all I'd need on top of everything else.'

She crosses to open the door of the stove. Pushing in long pieces of black turf as smoke poured out. And as she slams it closed, a grey sleek cat jumps miaowing up on the table. Lois waving it off and lifting her arms to scratch.

'Have you got bugs madam.'

'Stop calling me that.'

'Well you call me dear boy.'

'Well then I shall stop. And I have not got bugs. But I should apologize for scratching. It is my woolly long underwear. I must wear at least two pairs. To keep warm when I'm working. This is my outside one I dyed pink. Now let me look at you. Just sit there. Yes. On the stool. Now just turn a little to the left. You have the most exquisite face. Your most perfectly straight nose. And such marvellously large peasant hands.'

'I am not a peasant.'

'Ah but we know that. You are a proper little country gent. With the most magnificent mediaeval profile. Elizabethan. Quite beyond anything one might expect would come out of the Irish countryside. I want you to pose.'

'For a study.'

'My dear boy, you do catch on rather fast, don't you. Of course I shouldn't want to embarrass you. But art demands the elimination of the squeamish little restrictions and conventions society has so barbarously imposed upon us.'

Lois surveying Darcy Dancer, holding her head a little to the side. Putting her hand on her hip and sucking air between her lips. With her duffel coat and the big green sweater off, she had quite surprisingly pronounced breasts. I had, when first confronting her, thought she was entirely without bosoms. And now behind her another bunch of bottles. Which must have once held stout. Each time she steps backwards while surveying me I get quite excited thinking that she might land crashing on her arse again. But just at the last rotten second she notices them. Until suddenly she snapped her fingers.

'I think I have got it. Yes, I have. There is absolutely something Flemish in your face. It must be in your ancestry. Transcending of course the underlying peasant aspect. But that's it. I've found it. Flemish.'

Lois raising her chin. And now this insight it seems sending her stepping way back. Just marvellously far enough this time. To go yet with another almighty crash, falling back into and among the stout bottles. Darcy Dancer putting his hand up squeezing into his cheeks and pressing hard across his mouth to keep it closed. As one's lungs were full to bursting and exploding. Too unbelievable that a lady of her mature age should be so stupidly awkward. Especially to trod on her own drawings and the defenceless black man's cock and testicles. She must be a bloody exhibitionist.

'O my god. Bother and damn. O my god. I think I may really be hurt. But if you laugh again I shall never forgive you.'

Her accent extremely high pitched and nasal. I was naturally thinking it was quite typical of her that she should shout rather exaggeratedly English epithets.

'O pish and pother.'

Which she did really loudly as she fell again trying to get up. Her face quite red. One did for the first time feel a flash of sympathy. For she was really doing her damndest to get back on her feet.

'You fucking little bastard you. I absolutely think your monstrous sense of humour absolutely Irish.'

'I didn't do a thing.'

'Do a thing. Why you're laughing.'

'Only moderately as anyone might with a reasonable sense of humour.'

'And at a poor woman. Well help me up, blast you. I think I am badly injured. I do believe the neck of one of those horrid stout bottles may have penetrated my anus. And it hasn't done my constipation the least bit of good. O god bombs in Bloomsbury were nothing compared to this awful place.'

Darcy Dancer again taking Lois by the armpits. Like

lugging a calf to put her upright once more. Her hand feeling down around her bottom, as she shakes herself.

'Hasn't anyone ever taught you dear boy that it is the height of rudeness to find another's misfortune amusing. And it is totally improper not to show your elders at least that much respect. Well answer me. Hasn't anyone ever taught you that.'

'Please don't shout at me.'

'Well damn you, I shall shout. I am most angry. You seem not to exhibit any regard for the feelings of others. And are you going to pose for me or not.'

'Now.'

'Of course, now.'

'You mean without my clothes.'

'Of course.'

'I hardly know you madam well enough. To pose that way. Besides you haven't given me my cocoa yet.'

'You have your damn nerve, haven't you.'

'On the contrary I am merely being candid as one has always been brought up to be.'

'And who brought you up, your nannie.'

'As a matter of fact, she did.'

Darcy Dancer and Lois in a blazing confrontation of eyeballs. Standing across the loose floorboards flecked with blue, pink, orange, green and grey. And now the sound of rain tapping the skylight. Mr Arland sometimes spoke of what he said would be my indoctrination into the outside world. Beyond the halls, walls and pastures of Andromeda Park. Now I am at large. And after a quick look at the gathering of the Count's party it was alarming to discover how bogus were man's interests and concerns. With everyone, if not prattling on about themselves, then loud voiced expressing their quite pretentious one sided opinions. Clearly most adults with the exception perhaps of Mr Arland and Uncle Willie, were assumed of the most hollow attributes. And it is obvious one must deal with them accordingly.

'Well, what are you waiting for, take off your things. And I shall prepare myself.'

Darcy Dancer standing in his dark serge double breasted

suit. Made by Mr Kaighan as he came with his sample cloths, tapes and chalks to measure me each October. As I must I think, take a pace backwards. Put one's elbow to rest on this white long bookcase crammed with volumes and piled on top with ceramics, bottles of linseed oil and turpentine. Round stove with its crooked chimney pipe going upwards high into the wall where it left a wide smoke stain to the ceiling. Rain now drumming on the glass, coming down in one god awful downpour. Drips dropping into the room. Lois, a hand on her hip puts one leg forward and pushes out her chest. Right in front of my hopefully angelic face. A raindrop landing on my nose.

Faint bells toll lonesome out over the city. And madam whatever her surname is, is taking her pink outer garment by the hem and pulling it up over her head and holding it by the sleeves as it hangs down in front of her. And gives me a long hard stare. I am extremely good at staring back. Even as a baby I could make my nannie Ruby drop her eyes if they too long confronted mine.

'Take off your jacket.'

'It's raining on me.'

'Just step to one side.'

'It is a bit chilly.'

'O don't complain. And look at you. French cuffs and gold cuff links. At your age.'

'I am an imperialist member of the squirearchy and imperialists, madam, dress this way.'

'O we are grand aren't we.'

'Yes I am.'

'And a cheeky little bugger that's what you are. Daring to engage me in a staring match. I can outstare any man. Even while I must grope round to do so.'

'You shan't, I regret to say, outstare me madam. And do be careful of bottles.'

Lois slowly swaying her hips. As I do believe she is attempting something in the nature of a tropical dance. Her eyes I thought averted momentarily as she opens the buttons at the neck of her woolly underwear. Pulling it down around her shoulders and hanging it from her waist. With yet another pale blue sleeveless sweater underneath. Which she pulls up over her head. Leaving her upper part quite naked. Tax her with the matter of perhaps corrupting the morals of a minor. About which I am rather widely read from legal tomes I have referred to while endeavouring to satisfy my passing interest in filthy curiosities. A trace of a smile on her lips. As she thinks this rude ruse will make me avert my eyes. Not so madam. I shall stare you into your grave before I allow my eyes to examine your breasts. Of course one catches sight of them on the upper retina. Mr Arland says images get inverted going through one's lens. Perhaps I should impart to her advice. According to Mr Arland's *Domestic Homoeopathy*. When there is torpor of the bowels and there is the sensation of being paralysed there, take three globules of opium. Obstinate cases require tepid water enema. And last night about this time I was in the arms of Miss von B who is not constipated. And shits she says like a meteor scooting among the stars. Although I supplied this latter description, it was in fact what she was trying to say.

'You are, aren't you, quite stubborn, dear boy.'

'Indeed yes, madam.'

To take a train ride to Dublin. And although a little frightening it is thoroughly exciting to find yet another lady so soon to present herself quite and absolutely from the waist up divested of covering. These are smaller but quite sharply pointed breasts. Not quite so rounded and big as those of Miss von B. But longer nipples. Foxy says those big breasts you see on a lady were not of the best. That it's the small tidy bags that make a good milker over the years. Keep distracting one's mind during this staring. Then suddenly concentrate and with my smouldering gaze strike terror in her. The room is warming. The rain and drip has stopped. Lois is clearly faltering. Any moment now this rank imperialist will panic her to being outstared. Mr Arland will wonder where I am. But for the matter of that I might ask where is he. Since I do believe I may in fact take some time to show this rather over confident pretentious lady a thing or two.

'Do you not like my tits dear boy. You may come and feel them if you wish.'

'I'm quite all right thank you. I am going to outstare you first madam.'

'It's all quite natural dear boy. Your mother had breasts. And I have breasts. And you mustn't look as if you think I'm deranged. And you may call me Lois.'

'Stop talking and looking for excuses to get out of our staring match.'

'Of course dear boy, I can't waste time like this. I'll let you win the staring match just this once. It is essential for the task at hand that you be able to see all of me. Perhaps not quite what your tutor had in mind for you on your tour, I don't suspect. But I'm ready now to paint you. Please. I'm putting more turf in the stove. It should be quite tolerable. Do take off your things.'

Darcy Dancer toying with his buttons in the candlelight. Lois's underwear hanging down over her trousers as she pulls open a drawer and takes out two tapers and lights them by the candle. Now quite brazenly she's pulling down her gentleman's trousers and peeling off her white long woolly underwear. Sinewy long tapering legs. Shiny white shapely and smooth. Her reptile like mouth. Tongue shooting out and licking all over her lips. Like a film Uncle Willie had taken me to once in the town. When a great long black snake came out from behind a rock and a woman charmed it with holy water and kissed it. All the catholics in the audience clapped and cheered. Uncle Willie said under his breath. What awful shit. Show her I can take off my clothes too. Only I have a really wretched hole in my underwear. Which is not in the least imperial. Mr Arland is really going to wonder where on earth I am now. And as I'm nearly without my clothes he'd have a further fit if he knew. This may well serve me as experience for the future. When I may in regalia have to stand for long hours having my portrait painted. Especially with this creature with her brushes in one hand and sketching pad in another, waggingly gyrating her bosoms in a dance. Women lately are always trying to do this to me. Make me naked and

135

nervous. When I'd prefer to be normal and ordinary. The thumping of my heart on my bare chest. And worse, she'll see my penis sticking up at the skylight. Maybe make her faint backwards and go down again in the bottles, or crashing stark naked among her easels and tubes of paint. With bunches of brushes falling on her and sticking up out of her ears and arse maybe. Might even loosen up her bowels.

'That's very good. Climb up now on the dais. I shall do some very swift ink and colour washes of you. Yes, just stand there. Straight, with the left leg flexed just that little bit. And stick it out. No not that. It's not what I'm referring to at all. Although, it is a quite adequate one, if I may say so. It's your arse I refer to. Your right cheek. Yes. Tense it. Yes that's it. Now I'm afraid that that must subside. You have an erection. It simply won't do. It's contrary to the whole flow of line. Please make it go down.'

'I can't, I don't know how.'

'You simply must learn to control yourself. If we're to do any serious work at all. I know my body may excite you. But don't let it.'

'I'm trying not to let it madam.'

'Surely if you are so good at staring matches you can learn that discipline at least.'

'I don't think I can. No one has ever asked me to do this before.'

'Well I'm asking you now. So please make an effort. Ignore my nakedness. Think of something which is non stimulating. Look at my cat Fergus there. If he stimulates you, neutered as the poor creature is, you are then really evil minded. Commerce is the only really obscene thing. But dear boy for you to get an erection just as I am about to make masterpieces is an insult to the whole creative concept.'

'This kind of art is new to me.'

'Well let's hope you're learning something then. Ah yes, that's a good boy, I see it is going down. That's very good. Very good. Now just hold it like that. There's a real pet. O you are being very jolly good.'

'Thank you madam.'

'Alright now. I'm nearly there. If you would only just sub-side it that little bit more. O drat. It's going up again. You're ruining the whole line.'

'Well madam when you start to talk about it, it seems right away to go up again.'

'Well damn it, make it go down. Just look around you. And I hope to god you're not homosexually inclined. See. All those other nice calm penises. I was nude in front of them too. And yet not one of them erected. Don't you think if they were able to do it. That you too can. Try.'

'Yes. I shall.'

'I suppose you think I'm eccentric.'

'No.'

'Well I am. I have long ago forsaken all things bourgeois. Ah now, you are trying. It's coming down nicely. Don't shift your leg like that.'

'It itches me madam.'

'I work in instantaneous strokes. Your moving faults the tension of the line. Of course nobody understands. I love the way your foreskin comes down over your penis like the closed petals of a flower. Imagine that they cut such a beautiful thing off in the silly interests of hygiene. And o god, there you go, up again.'

'Well it's you madam drawing my attention to it every time when you say things like that.'

'Well there's simply nothing else for it. I shall just have to put down my brushes and wank you off then. That's all there is to it. Or else I simply can't go on. Or do you have an objection.'

'I guess not madam if it furthers the cause of art.'

'You are a rather clever little one, you know. Far more astute than you let on. Got the touch of the devil about you. But please don't take this as an overture. Or assume for one second that one is enjoying having to do this. What are those bruises on your neck.'

'O nothing.'

'And while I'm doing this you're not to touch me.'

'I wasn't intending to.'

'Well, just in case you might think of doing so I'm telling you to keep your hands to yourself if you don't mind. My goodness I can see you really are jolly well erected aren't you. And quite considerably endowed. A pity it ruins the line. And such nicely ripened testicles too. It's the imbalance created by the blatantly horizontal I can't stand. That's where art stops and obscenity begins. When something juts out like this. I'm not being too ungentle am I.'

'O no you're fine.'

'And please, if you don't mind, warn me when you're ejaculating. I'd prefer to swallow it, rather than have it go all over my floor. Dirty filthy as it already may be. Stale sperm can make such an awful smell.'

'I wish madam you wouldn't go on talking while we're doing this.'

'Well I'm not making love to you you know. Be sure of that.'

'Yes I am and thank you.'

'For god's sake don't thank me. And since we are rather getting to know one another better don't you think it's time you called me by my christian name at least. If you don't like Lois, my second christian name is Euphemia. And I do hope you're not going to be a long time coming. It's quite tiring on the arm.'

Lois with flecks of dandruff in the hair parting mid way down her scalp. The streaks of blonde and brown and the wiry strands of grey all drawn back and a brown shoelace tying up a plaited pigtail wound in a bun at the back of her head. From which a bit of blue ribbon hangs down. Get nearly killed going to a bog to learn about life. And now I am getting very first hand information in this grown up lady's studio with my prick being pulled by her hand. If poor old Foxy could see me now. Up here on exhibition. Like the time he told me of the titled lady judge who went squeezing all the balls of all bulls at the fair. Her hands are strong. Stroking in long gentle strokes. Then stops to say she's not making love to me. Uses four fingers and her thumb underneath. Certainly an improper grip for milking a cow. Send the milk missing

the pail. And I could go gushing all over her face. And Mr
Arland's face was quite flushed in the company of the
courtesan. Kept referring to the Count's party as a bash. And
even as he was getting quite tipsy, said we'll have a bash at
that bash. And then as we got round one corner he said
even before I pushed him, 'Let's bash on regardless.' Dublin
so dark dreary and dank. One has got to be rich. Or be hungry
like this woman. Who was as we walked here, popping chunks
of butterscotch in her mouth. Without offering me a piece.
And who now as I try not to groan, is eating me. Could take it
into her head to murder me by biting it. Foxy said you fast
bleed to death. Be twitching around on this floor knocking
over more of her bottles in my death throes. And who now
would care, or be torn with sadness. Or light up torches for
my funeral. Or beat drums. Or lay me to dusty rest in the
vaults of the Thormonds. Please god even though I am an
atheist protestant take care of my sisters. Send Sexton to
heaven where he so dearly wants to go. And where he hopes
to have his first rest from his long lifetime of religious duty.
Tending roses and kneeling at the feet of his adored Blessed
Virgin Mother. Over the garden wall I once heard him say to
Crooks that never once did his prick ever trouble his con-
science, as it did many the blackguard he knew. And Crooks
said that when he was active his own prick sure troubled a lot
of sheep. And he told him of the farmer across the lake who
kept devout and unsoiled by women but that in this holy state
he wore nearly all the wool off the arses of his ewes. And
Sexton said at least it wasn't as bad as having a woman with
her gab wear all the flesh off your ears. For the sake of art I am
sucked. Pleasure coming just like one waits for pain to strike.
When the town dentist with his evil looking instruments was
looming all over me, his smile widening as he descended upon
my mouth and plunged his drill whirring into my tooth. I
must soon say goodnight. And get me out of here. This lady's
breathing comes strongly down her nose and right at this
moment she's in a complete frenzy as my head goes back
hollering. Pump my personality into her. Loosen her bowels.
As she is bent forward bosoms hanging from her chest, nude

all the way down to her pair of white shoes. Stopped holding her hand over her mouth. And rather sloping in her quarters. She goes rushing to spit in the sink. With the knobs of her spine showing down her back. Her bottom trembling, she looked so foolish heading across the floor.

Like the
Whole world's
Population was
Pushing

11

'Now perhaps that has made you feel better. I do feel it was necessary. You do understand what I mean. Don't you.'

'Yes.'

'Alright now. Are you alright.'

'Yes.'

'You look rather pale. And please don't look at me like that. You do suddenly make me feel quite embarrassed.'

'I rather don't feel too good as a matter of fact.'

'Perhaps you'd like me to stop. Or shall I do one quick one. Using a cerulean and pink wash. Catch you full frontal. You have no idea how exciting this is. You simply can't know.'

'Can I go home.'

'You don't want to go right now, do you. Just when I'm going to enunciate especially your nice swirling little curls just above your penis. O dear me. You little rogue. Despite your not feeling well, you are erecting again. You're simply exasperating. Well there is nothing for it. If you refuse to co-operate then I'm going to bed. Do you refuse to cooperate. Do you.'

'I have tried just as hard as I can.'

'Well your trying hard it appears simply hasn't made it soft enough. Will you blow out the candles dear boy. And put some more turf into the stove. Rotten old spongy stuff wet as it is burns so quickly, it will have me near penniless.'

'What about my cocoa.'

'O god, you're not really asking for it are you.'

'I would rather like some, and thank you very ecstatically much.'

'Well you very ecstatically can't. I have just enough milk for tea in the morning.'

'Isn't it rather rude to invite someone to have something that you have not got.'

'Don't make silly remarks like that. You are an imperialist, you get lots of cocoa. And I'm getting in where it's warm and cosy.'

Darcy Dancer shivering. Stepping down off the dais. Reaching towards his clothes draped over an orange crate. Quite wretched when people aren't possessed of the rudiments of hospitality. Uncle Willie said an Englishman would serve you the leather off his old boots if he thought you wouldn't use too much gravy on it.

'I think I shall dress and go. Please, if you don't mind, would you direct me back to the Shelbourne.'

'I hope I'm not frightening you away. You may certainly if you like come and get into bed with me. Shall I give you some gin. But only a smidgen. I have just this little bit.'

'You do not I assure you, frighten me. I've met your sort before.'

'My sort.'

'Yes your sort.'

'What sort is that. Do please tell me.'

'Ladies who think that by merely divesting themselves of their clothing and then behaving in an extraordinary fashion and using vulgar postures and language do then think that a gentleman will oblige them by entering their beds.'

'You little cheeky bastard you. I think perhaps you'd better go back to the Shelbourne then.'

'I shall certainly.'

'Do.'

'Yes, well I am. I'm just getting dressed and would like to use your convenience if you don't mind.'

'As my lavatory is broken, I'm afraid you'll just have to pee in my sink.'

'That's a disgusting suggestion.'

'Then don't pee dear boy.'

Darcy Dancer crossing to the stack of dishes. Staring into the tea leaves, bacon rinds and the whitened crusts of grease. Pissing now where she spat. And I yet may vomit. With my quite ungentlemanly behaviour one is enforced to display. Nurse Ruby once beat me for pissing out the whim room window and down on Crooks who slapped at the drops as he stood shaking a pony skin rug on the front steps. She got into such a state of excitableness when she caught me doubled up with laughter. And my goodness if she could see me now. Cascading my urine in this way. Only I know it is essential that I acquaint myself with the seamier sides of town life. And at least wash some of this muck down the drain.

'Did you do a good little wee wee like a good little boy.'

'I did as a matter of fact.'

'And now you're going.'

'Yes. I am. Goodbye.'

'Don't go. Wait.'

'Why.'

'Well I adore to corrupt totally innocent little boys.'

'Madam I think that a most disagreeable occupation.'

'O do you now. You speak as a mature imperialist I suppose. In your woolly vest.'

'Yes I do. You ought to concern yourself with more profound things. If, as I think you may mean by corrupt that you hope to make me putrid rotten and defiled.'

'I hope to make you no such thing you haughty little boy. Unless you regard your own body as putrid rotten and defiled. I'm presuming of course you find me attractive. I may not be exactly what every man may find beautiful. But in this wretched country, I assure you, I rank easily among the more desirable of creatures. I suppose where you come from you are up sheep most of the time. Well. Are you.'

'You are rude to say that. We do not among the gentry cohabit with sheep. Only peasant bachelor farmers do that.'

'How quaint. And what else do bachelor peasant farmers do in this filthy disgusting awful country where the people are so entirely treacherous.'

'Why are you here then madam.'

'Because I did not think there was any reason why I should be splattered to smithereens by being blown up by bombs in London dear boy. But of course some Irish I find quite charming. The majority, however, are simply steeped in crut. I mean good lord, they ought to be glad a civilized country like England has dominated them for so long.'

'You have not dominated us, madam. We have fought you.'

'Good Lord that doesn't sound like an imperialist speaking.'

'Well I'm not one all the time. That would only be dull and boring.'

'And pray tell dear boy what do you propose to be in the future. And you can stop putting on your shoes you know, you don't have to go.'

'It's quite past my bedtime.'

'You've your whole life to go to bed on time. Indeed here you are. A bed. Get in.'

'Well thank you. It's not that I am unappreciative.'

'I find you awfully haughty. But quite interesting. At least you can stay and talk awhile. The Shelbourne Hotel isn't going to run away. And I'd just love to know what your aspirations are.'

'You may not think them edifying.'

'I am absolutely quite sure I won't dear boy.'

'Well. I should like to continue to be the owner of a large estate as I am now. Although I would prefer if it had many minions indeed to keep the gardens properly in order. And highly respectful old servants. Those who would go about their duties in an efficient way. And not always bother me with nuisances. Then I should like to travel on steamers to far off places and bring back trophies like the feared water buffalo to my trophy room. There in front of the evening fire I would after dinner write accounts of my travels in my journal. And Crooks, my present man would bring me port.'

'Is that all.'

'Yes I think that's all. Aside of course from perhaps attending upon some agricultural duties.'

'Holy Christ almighty, young man, is that how you live now.'

'Yes it is rather. But are you suggesting I expect too much.'

'Dear boy, as one who has socialist sympathies I most

certainly think you expect too much. Don't you know the entire earth is, and has been in upheaval, turmoil, war and revolution.'

'I don't see what, in the least, that has to do with me.'

'Well to say the least, dear boy, you are detached. And clearly an isolationist as well as an imperialist.'

'Isolationist sounds like one of those wretched American words.'

'Well dear boy it certainly applies to you and you sound so homosexual. Do you mind if I ask you a question. Have you ever been buggered.'

'I beg your pardon.'

'Dear boy, have you.'

'Do you mean what that word most rudely suggests.'

'Yes I do. Someone putting his penis up your arsehole.'

'Why are you asking me that.'

'My, your cheeks do redden don't they. Get in bed with me here. I'm merely asking if not a very nice question at least a simple one.'

'My cheeks do not redden. And I have not been buggered. And this is a rather mournful conversation madam. And I think it may be getting entirely disagreeable as well.'

'Buggery is widespread you know. And most normal young men would long since have jumped in here in bed with me. Or are you tired from your activity on the dais.'

'No I am not. But my tutor will be worried as to my whereabouts.'

'Who the devil are you anyway. Some silly young Lord. Are you.'

'I'm sorry to disappoint, but I have no entitlement of any sort. However I do descend from a long line of gentry.'

Lois patting her hand on a red pink patch of quilt, the long sinewy muscle flexing in her arm. As she beckons with her curling finger. Darcy Dancer kicking off his shoes. Breaking an already shortened shoelace. Feet chilled stepping on the rough floorboards. Wooden arches rise from the walls to support the cold darkness above and beyond the glass. Cross over to where she lifts back the bedding. If I had a timepiece

I might even know if I were to be in the arms of two different ladies in the same day. Something to remember my whole life. One responds to those polite. Who kindly invite. Big pipes coming out of the boiler in the corner. A paint stain on her pillow case. And move up against this smooth flesh, which stood in front of me so white. And there was this morning a frost out on the grazing black cattle backs. Push in under these weighty damp wool coverings. A big eared big footed bog trotter out of the soggy bowels of Ireland.

'Now dear boy, isn't that better. Just a minute. What are these things all down your neck.'

'Birth marks.'

'You did not get them at birth dear boy.'

'Then I believe they are bruises.'

'Teeth marks. That's what they are. Someone's teeth. Who gave them to you.'

'Well I rather think that if they are what you say they are then that should in itself make you further disinclined to inquire, being as it is obvious that it is none of your business.'

'I am beginning to think that your morals may be absolutely loose dear boy.'

'And I suppose yours, madam, are not.'

'As a matter of fact dear boy I am extremely choosey as to whom I go to bed with. And I think I should, as an older person who can help you with advice, know who precisely sank their teeth into your neck like that. It could have been some wretched little skivvy. I certainly don't want you putting in me what you put in her. Although I'd hardly believe you have at your age put it up anybody.'

'Well I have as a matter of fact.'

'I think you're fibbing.'

'I'm not. I have quite numerous times put it up a lady.'

'Who.'

'That's my business.'

'I don't believe you.'

'Well don't.'

'I don't.'

'I could prove it if I had to.'

'How could you. Certainly I'd imagine you've had your tumbles with scullery maids but not with a mature lady of the world. Those are bites of a rank amateur dear boy.'

'My concubine made those marks, if you must know. And she is a lady of the world.'

'Your concubine. Don't make me laugh.'

'She is in fact a German lady of title. A princess.'

'Did she ever make hats.'

'I think I have told you quite sufficient.'

'I know her. My god dear boy you have been in the arms of a Polish Austrian militarist. And perhaps even a sadist. I do feel I've been absolutely tricked by you.'

'I haven't tricked you.'

'Clearly you've already been corrupted. And were most likely whipped and trampled by high heels. And as recently as last night her awfully big Austrian mouth did that to you. How shameful. Where are you going.'

'I am leaving.'

'Come back here.'

'You have no right to say such things to me.'

'Well you do, my dear boy clearly require moral guidance. Come back to bed. Come back.'

'I'm simply not in the habit of listening to people speak to me in such manner. And I regret my departure madam.'

'Please don't leave. It is quite lonely here alone you know. And I am a nice person really. It just so happens my father was a senior civil servant in the admiralty. And I feel rather strongly about Germans.'

'Well apart from Germans I would quite like to hear of naval matters. What did your father do in the admiralty.'

'He dealt with wrecks on the high seas. Treasure and all sturgeons, porpoises and whales. And I believe even flotsam and jetsam. I could always watch a coronation from a most favoured position overlooking the Mall. My mother's family were all Indian army people. Please don't put on your clothes. Come back into bed. You needn't leave. I'd just like to talk to you. Really I would.'

'Alright but you mustn't question me.'

'I'll make you snuggly and warm. Get in. Nearer. I won't bite you. Ha ha.'

'Why are you divorced.'

'Because my husband took up with boys. And absolutely delighted to shove his penis in their arseholes.'

'And I suppose that was very sad for you.'

'Sad, dear boy is not the word. The word is pittance. Which is how one describes my alimony. Of course at the time he was very junior at the admiralty. One wouldn't have minded as much had the boys been refined, shall we say. But they were these rough hewn lower sorts that he absolutely delighted to bugger. Navvies, butchers, porters, dockers. It was all quite sordid.'

'But I thought you were a socialist, madam.'

'I hope that's not meant to be funny. O God and now I just think what's to become of my life. My art. Does any one give a damn. I've sold three pictures in four months. I sometimes lose all possible hope. O I do. I really do.'

'Please, you mustn't cry.'

'I'm sorry, I don't want to cry. Really I don't. Not in front of a mere boy. My only little comfort all these wretched months has been the BBC third programme. I can't believe what's come over me. I suppose I should have known.'

'Known what, madam.'

'Known from my husband's christian names, Basil and Cecil. And that he'd been at a wretched not quite first rank public school. What to expect.'

'What did you expect madam.'

'I never could be absolutely sure. Till one evening I unexpectedly came home from visiting my ailing father. Poor dear man. He was in fact dying. O why does a young man like you want to hear this. You don't do you.'

'No. I don't.'

'Well blast you anyway.'

'I'm only joking, please do tell me. It's absolutely all so riveting.'

'Don't you trifle with me.'

'I'm not. Please.'

'Well I was going to tell you. That Basil and I had this dear little mews house. Just behind Sloane Square. This was of course just after he'd been to sea. And long before I moved to Bloomsbury. I did have dear friends there. We drank in the Museum pub. Of course none of this means a damn thing to you, does it.'

'Well it's not exactly as if I know these places. I've never been abroad.'

'Well anyway we had thick carpeting on the stairs. And as I came up to the bedroom Basil was actually stuck up this boy who was, calm as you please, can you believe it, looking and leering at our wedding picture on the dresser. Had the wretched boy been erected I could have felt he was at least having some sexual thrill looking at us standing under the crossed swords of our naval honour guard. But no, he seemed to be leering at my husband's fellow officers. As if he were our social equal. I picked up the first piece of bogus wedding gift statuary I could lay my hands on and threw it at them. It missed and quite appropriately I thought, smashed our wedding picture.'

'How mournful for you.'

'I can still hear that awful boy's words. Ere ere you, control your missus will ya. O God. And I was even pregnant then. Now I've got nobody. I want someone to love and someone to love me. Just somebody to be with in the world. Is that too much to ask. Is it. O how would you know.'

A massive pounding and hammering on the door. Lois sitting back up on her elbow, her hand reaching across to cover Darcy Dancer's mouth. And her breasts, nipples at attention, sticking out over the quilt. The voice down there shouting.

'I know you're in there.'

'Madam, what's that.'

'Dear boy, don't move, don't make a sound. While I blow out the candles.'

The door rattling and banging. The glass trembling in the skylight. The grey cat scurrying across the floor and leaping up on top of the bookcase and knocking a bottle to the floor. A stink of turpentine.

'Open up. Open up or I'll break the fucking door down. You've got some little squirt in there. I'll kill him.'

Lois's muscles stiffening. And I feel at my shoulders the soft edge of her bosom and her heart beating nearly as fast as mine. Requiring one to inquire.

'Is that person referring to a squirt talking about me.'

'O no. He doesn't know what he's talking about. This sometimes happens. I was telling you. Drunks.'

The sound of kicks. Foxy said there was nothing as good as a swift uppercut of a boot for opening up an entrance into anything.

'I'll get that little squirt if I have to break the fucking door down. Are you opening it.'

'He is referring to me.'

'Hush, dear boy.'

A crash, grumblings and curses. Another crash. Milk bottles. Over which feet are fortunately tripping. And from the sounds. Something tells me I ought to be up and perhaps elsewhere.

'O my god, dear boy. He has broken in. Get under the bed. Immediately.'

Darcy Dancer out of the bed clothes like a frog. Pushing and squeezing a shoulder against the small gap between springs and floorboards.

'There's no room.'

'Then get under the drapery. There behind the dais. It's over the chair.'

Darcy Dancer feeling his way crouching across the mid-room darkness. More thumping thunderous noises and vituperations on the stairs. As I nearly come a cropper putting a foot straight into my shoe. Knew soon as I saw the new moon through the glass on the train that there'd soon be ill luck ahead. From the feel of this drapery, it was hanging in the back of the Count's portrait. Lois had just wrapped her hand tightly around my penis as I was right in the middle of the unanimous declaration of the thirteen united states of America, memorized for Mr Arland. That all men are created equal, with certain unalienable rights. And that among them is life, liberty and the pursuit of happiness. Each latter one of which I'm going to lose by the sound of things. As one wraps up in and under this dusty musty bolt of cloth over this chair. The last time I did huddling like this with Foxy, matters were mournful indeed. And these feet are coming pounding awfully heavy in a toe crushing manner up the stairs.

'Open this door.'

'It's open.'

'Where the fuck is the little cunt. And give me some light.'

'What do you mean by breaking in here like this. Get out. I won't give you light. I shall instead inform the police.'

'Shut your fucking gob woman, or I'll shut it for you. Even in darkness I'll get the little cunt.'

'There is no other person here but me. And I would be awfully appreciative if you would vacate the premises. In less euphemistic words, get out.'

'I will in a tinker's tit get out. I've fucked you before and I'll fuck you again.'

'How dare you assume rights over me. You're clearly drunk.'

'You're fucking well right I'm drunk. I'm laggards. The Bug came in a winner at twenty to one. And I've had twenty bottles of stout. Would I come humping an old whorer like you if I wasn't drunk. And give me some light before I puncture a halo around your head with a Polish nine millimetre Parabellum.'

'You do have, along with your extremely poor manners, the most amazingly unpleasant command of English.'

'You'll have obsequies in Gaelic and a poor funeral to attend when I catch this fucker. Lights. And quick.'

Lois striking a match. The reddish gloom and shadows. Her trembling hand lighting a candle. To bathe faint yellow on this gentleman. Whom I last saw roaring his declarations from the Count O'Biottus's chaise longue. And who now with an awful thud lays a big black flat sided pistol next to Lois's paint daubed pallet on a small round table. As she lights another candle. Five big buttons down the gunman's open macintosh. A stub of a cigarette sending smoke up between his cupped fingers. The knot of a tie just peeking out over the rim of his mustard coloured sweater with a strand of its wool thread unravelling on the floor. His feet flat apart. A great broad domed forehead.

'Don't you bring guns in here.'

'Sure it's only me old equalizer. But it's quieter to knock both your heads off with a fist than it is to blow them off with a gun. Now get him out from under them bed covers or maybe I will start shooting.'

'O god, are you mad.'

'My mental happiness hasn't been that good lately and you might say I'm not too far from it.'

'He's not in here. These are my knees sticking up the covers. You awful RAC people.'

'Get the initials right at least, can't you you awful pommie.'

'AI or RA it's all the same to me. Well look around why don't you then. Under the dishes in the sink. Do you see him. Do you see anybody. Hiding behind the paintings. Or even under that drape there. And you have audacity to come breaking down my door.'

Lois putting her fingers to her temples. The gunman picking up the black pistol, holding it up to the candle light.

'And with a lethal weapon.'

'It's only me semiautomatic emblazoned with the Polish eagle. But with a muzzle velocity of one thousand one hundred and fifty feet per second it puts a nice tiny hole in you. Sure I'd have to shoot you straight in the head if I was to remind you I meant it.'

'You have no prerogatives. No right whatever, to come transgressing upon my private life in this manner. And stop waving that gun.'

'Every nancy boy in Dublin said you fucking well went off with some school kid. And that's the fact of the matter.'

'Please don't continue to use that language with me. And I'll thank you to go. And come back when you are in a better frame.'

'I'm in the frame for a fuck.'

'Well fuck someone else why don't you.'

'Because I'm going to fuck you that's why.'

'That is rape. O God. Tiresome. You're just full of romance and charm aren't you. And stop taking off your clothes.'

'I've got a horn on me that would whip a donkey out of a bog and he leaping in it.'

'Well take your horn then and whip a donkey as you put it, out of a bog. But do it far away from me please. I'm simply too tired and exhausted. I've had a most difficult day.'

'I'll give you romance. Drag you out of here and fuck you up and down the steps of the Freemasons Hall. Sure the whole place is painted with pricks and balls. Take a look at these live jumping ones now for a start. I'll impale you upon the spire of my passion. Can't you see I'm dying for it.'

'Well die. But please cover yourself.'

'I'm going to cover you.'

'O God please. I do beg of you don't. If you have the least sense of decorum as a gentleman. Don't please.'

'Sure look at it. With its very veins bursting.'

'O the horridness of it all. Not tonight. Just not tonight. I've had the most sad news. Can't you see I've been crying.'

'You weren't complaining a few days ago with me fucking well freezing posing on that platform up there. Saying I had a pair of balls on me like melons.'

'That was in the cause of art.'

'Well this bloody horn on me now is in the cause of architecture. It would hold a skyscraper up in an earthquake. And it would give you all the good news you'd need, if you'd only open up your legs and listen. You'd be laughing.'

'O how I hate you Irish. Hate you. Why don't you go and do this to your wife.'

'Because the poor old woman with her belly nine times risen has had enough suffering at my hands already.'

'I'll bet she has.'

'Come on now. Look at it there, like a branch in a storm trembling.'

'You look at it. I want to go to sleep.'

'You weren't so fucking reluctant last week. When I

bulled you in the alley when you couldn't wait to get back here.'

'You mean you couldn't wait.'

'Have you had the little squirt up you already and he went home to his mammy.'

'I don't know who or what you are talking about. I just wish that you could respect a lady's wishes and go. That's all I wish. Nothing else.'

'Move over in the bed.'

'No I shall not. I am English. English. Do you understand. Treat your Irish wife like this. But not me.'

'I said move over. I'm out to fuck the English one way or the other. And make Ireland unsafe for the Sassanach.'

'It's the wrong time of the month if you must know.'

'Well as I'm marching over the border in the morning, it's the right fucking time of the night for me.'

'You're crass. Barbaric. O God. Stop trying to push it in my face.'

'When I was reading gas meters around Dublin I gave many an overeager housewife a black eye with this.'

'Well my gas as it happens has been cut off.'

'Sure I'll have it reconnected. And when the state's taken over and I'm president I'll give you enough gas you could boil the Liffey. Come on give it a good suck.'

'I shall not. Give it to your good Catholic wife to suck.'

'Come on now leave the religion out of it. And take out your gleaming Protestant dentures.'

'No no.'

'Come on now. Do it for a devout agnostic.'

'You're a devout pig. Get it out of my face.'

Darcy Dancer shivering. Under the cold musty damp folds of this deep dark green drape. Knees and elbows on the hard floor. Hold my face sideways to peek out. That man's muscles bulging in his legs and arms. Has curly kinky hair. Came in with a fedora on and took it off. Only gentlemanly thing he's done. If I were only that peasant jester in the funny stories Miss von B tells me. Who was always able to escape from whatever dire difficulties befell him. And revenge himself on nasty people. Grab this man's gun. Shoot him. Just as he's groaning. Pushing it in Lois's mouth. Rain rapping on the skylight. Drips hitting me in the middle of the back. Soaking right through. If I did not come to have cocoa, I could be asleep, cosy snug and warm back in the Shelbourne. O my goodness. I've farted. Made the gunman turn his head. And put his chin up to look at the ceiling. Must have got bopped himself with a raindrop. Just hope my smell doesn't pervade the room. And lead to my most utterly terrifying discovery. Be drilled full of holes. As an imperialist. And just earlier this evening Mr Arland had discussed how the King of Great Britain had with repeated injuries and usurpations, established an absolute tyranny over the thirteen American states. Must stop shivering and shaking the drapes. Till some miracle delivers me out of here alive. Could try to pull on my shoes while his back is turned. Get over all that broken glass down the stairs. Not even a bullet could catch me once I get going. The grunts and moans coming from the bed. Has it pushed deep down into her throat. Could be choking her. She does do such an awful amount of talking anyway. Just get across this floor without making a sound. Go slowly on all fours. Under this drape. Looking like a green baby hippopotamus. Get to the gun on the table. I hope before he gets there first. And bang bang. Mr Arland will find me in the morgue we passed. Those gates an omen of death. Start appearing like my mother does as an apparition to Crooks and Sexton.

'True sons of Ireland, enemies of the British Vampire. Ireland integral is Ireland free.'

This gunman must be very politically minded yelling at a time like this. And making all sorts of rude groaning noises and then shouting up the Republic. Sitting there across Lois's chest. And he'd surely kill an aristocratic feudalist like me. Time it just right and I could in the middle of his orgasm get up and run like hell. Then he might kill poor Lois. Who looks bulgy eyed and gasping with her head propped back against the wall. Her eyes staring open. His thank god closed. Just move further out.

Lois from the bed waving Darcy Dancer back. Alright.

Whatever you say. And at the moment it's not much. Twice tonight she's had a penis in the mouth. Jaws must be tired. Mine I think is even bigger than his. And the same measurements as Foxy's. Who said that size was a lot but not everything. Almost seems as if she's having an operation. This gunman isn't so enormous but his arm muscles look awfully strong. Flexing pressing the wall above Lois's face. An evening newspaper sticking up out of the pocket of his macintosh thrown on the table. He's groaning more and more. O God please stop him turning around. It's the last chance I'll have to run for it. Why does she keep waving me back. Hear the bells, one here and one there, ringing out again in the city. The sounds of which Mr Arland said he had learned to recognize. And always listened to even if he were tipsy after a Trinity hop. When he would lie sadly back in his college room in his bed. In regret. For if the girl he had invited to the dance was too pretty, others would win her away from him. He said it is wise to keep women secretly. So that other men don't know. Poor Mr Arland. Wants so much to find a girl of his very own. Said ladies preferred men of beautiful brawn than those with brains. Unless you had a big income and estates. And all he'd been was a scholar who latined grace at college commons. As he did so elegantly those evenings we dined at Andromeda Park. Per christum, dominum, nostrum. And scholars always raced each other in college commons to say grace as rapidly and accurately as possible. And Mr Arland could make me laugh he was so fast. If only the sun would come out in his life. And the birds sing. Instead of the sounds of this gunman groaning and squirming about. Suffer little children to come unto me. Sexton said God said that. And that the almighty took mercy on the young before all others. If I were a Catholic maybe God would get me out of here. Foxy said the whole country was night and day asking God for favours. And you'd never get a chance to slip your own in. Especially if they had any old uncles or aunts to die to leave them a bit of land, they'd say dear Jesus would you ever strike the fuckers dead. And all I want is to be back in bed in the Shelbourne. And not here with this lady's cheeks billowed out. He's really shoving in and out of her mouth. Her eyes popping. She's motioning me to come out. To stand up. And maybe run. Or grab up the gilt frame and tiptoe to clonk him. To be continued next week. It said at the end of one of the films in the town cinema when Uncle Willie took me on my birthday. Gunman's hands going down lower now on the wall. Could push that long sharp piece of broken glass there through him. Be blood running all over. And dripping down this woman who has tried to protect me. The garda would find her with a dead man. But there is a big mahogany curtain rail. And beyond the steamy train window there was a new moon deep far away in the sky across some back gardens of a country village. Now crisis and predicament befall me. Something out in the planets can set one's life awry. If you see the new moon through glass. Even Mr Arland admits this is true. And so it was for him, when he first left college to go out into the world. He saw the new moon through a third class porthole crossing the Irish sea. And promptly had all his luggage stolen by a fellow overnight inmate of a cheap boarding house room in London. The thief left only an extra pair of shoes he missed seeing under his bed and it was all the belongings he had when he reached Paris. And he went to Pigalle to sell them. Meeting a man who said he'd like to try them on for size. Who when he got about twenty yards away, stepped into an alley and disappeared. Mr Arland said that he did not often cry. But he stood there at the foot of Rue Steinkerque on this spring sunny Paris Sunday overlooked high up by the alabaster radiance of the church of Du Sacré Coeur and the tears just streamed down his face.

Darcy Dancer his head slowly emerging from the green drapery. Getting carefully to his knees and on one silent bare foot at a time standing up. Good lord one's penis is sticking out. Made constantly to stand by my most lewd mind. Just slip the curtain rings off this big long pole. And noiselessly this yoke should do the trick. If I get room enough to get a good enough swing. She's waving me back. And I've got to go forward. And do it fast. Just like he's really pumping it into her mouth now.

Darcy Dancer gladiator, with his eight foot mahogany pole held two handed across his chest. Tiptoeing forward on his bare feet. Nearly losing my balance with Lois's eyes popping out of her head. Which in her extremely limiting circumstances she is trying to shake back and forth. Waving her hand around his arse to tell me to go away. When I've got only this one chance to stun him with just one good belt of this yoke. A hammer like Foxy uses would be better to sink into his head. But if I can sweep this around in a big enough arc it should do the job. If dear god I don't miss. He won't know what hit him. The white skin of both Lois's elbows pointing at me, putting her hands over her eyes. As death gets close you want to live longer and longer. And maybe as old as twenty eight. This man doesn't seem at all like a member of the Royal Automobile Club. As he gyrates groaning. Wish him no permanent harm. As Foxy used to say to the bull when it broke the fence. But I'll break your fucking beast's back end. And I must bust this head good and proper. Sweep this piece of timber in its wide arc over the colours of this quilt to land it thudding and cracking on the back of this curly headed skull. And peace be with you and with thy spirit.

'O God, God. You've killed him. You stupid silly little boy. Why didn't you wait, as I tried to tell you, till he was asleep. He always falls into a dead sleep. And you'd have had plenty of time to get out. You must have fractured his skull. O God there's blood.'

'I'm sorry.'

'Sorry. While my life is a wreck. You're sorry. Of course it can mean little to you. But he does have the biggest balls in Dublin. I'll never get him to pose again if he thinks someone is waiting to batter his head like that. Well get out. Go. Fast as you can.'

'Is there much blood.'

'Don't worry about blood, go.'

'I haven't killed him, have I.'

'If you have, I shall direct those authorities who may be interested in who did, to the Shelbourne Hotel. Is that right.'

'Yes madam. But I did it in your defence, doesn't that

help. Isn't that allowed. I mean it's fair if a gentleman's trying to rape you.'

'And your name.'

'Reginald Darcy Dancer Thormond Kildare.'

'Good god. I know your father. And you with that goose stepping whorer. Who gave those bites. Who went to work for him. Just go. He groaned. He's still breathing. Get your clothes on.'

Darcy Dancer stuffing socks into pockets. Pulling, tugging and diving into his clothes. And pushing his tie with its tiny mauve dots on a deep purple background into a coat pocket.

'I wish madam. I wish.'

'You wish. Yes.'

'That you did not know who I am.'

'You won't be wishing anything if you don't get out.'

'Goodbye. Shall I ever see you again.'

'No you won't. Goodbye.'

Darcy Dancer walking out the open landing door. Sweetly sick smell of decay. A dustbin at the top of the stairs. Go down two at a time. And step gingerly over these bottles and broken glass at the bottom. Lock hanging broken on the door. Chill wind and rain blowing in. Gather my coat around me. I'd better trot or better run. Down and out this alley. Turn right. Along this greyest of greyest streets. Till I come somewhere to the hospital. Where faint lights show. In there the dying and nearly dead. Go left. Till I reach that Church. House of God up the alley. Where went poor Mr Arland's shoes in Paris. On some ignoble person's feet. The coffee smell. Rush back all the rest of the way to the Shelbourne. From where I never did get any cocoa.

> In this
> Big wicked
> City
> Of Dublin

12

The lobby of the Shelbourne this Sunday morning. Step outside under a fresh blue sky, the sun pink through the branches of the trees in St Stephen's Green. And I came back into the warmth to see Mr Arland looking awfully sleepy disembarking from the lift. Crossing to where I stood watching and listening to an irate wife berate her husband for dropping a heavy bag right on her toe. Had she not been so fat she could have hopped about in pain. Mr Arland bowing to me and the doorman handing him a message.

'Well Kildare, this is from your father.'

'What does he want.'

'That's not the tone in which to inquire.'

'Well I can't feel that whatever the communication is that it will do me any good.'

'O dear Kildare. You are being needlessly negatory. You are to be at an address not far from here at noon.'

Much of the night long I lay thinking the garda might burst in the door to arrest me. Or the gunman with a bandaged head to shoot me. Finally woke in my bed my left eye opening first. The tumble of thick crimson lace covered eiderdown made me think it was a big blood covered wave. Pitching and tossing a raft upon which I sat with an enormous naked woman. Who kept grabbing at me with long hideous leathery claws. Till I began seeing across the room and out my window to the grey green purple hills of the Dublin mountains.

Sheltered from the wind one could feel the sun's warmth on one's face as we walked along the street. Till we were nearly run down by two horsecabs racing around the corner. Mr Arland said it was probably a Dubliners' friendly chariot race. That traditionally on Saturday night drunken bets were made on contests conducted on even drunker Sunday mornings. Now down this Dawson Street. At the end of its vista under clean new clouds, the iron fence of Trinity College and the University rooftops beyond the trees. Mr Arland's eyes glowing bright and his walk jaunty.

'Kildare I've never told anyone this, but I one night stole all the ripe tomatoes out of the Provost's greenhouse.'

'Oooo naughty sir.'

'Well I was an impecunious scholar, quite starving at the time. And nearly killed myself climbing over the walls. I did however upon my receiving my first income have sent to the Provost a basket of tomatoes from a reputable greengrocer.'

And entering this place of worship. A tall chilly vestibule. Names and legends on marble plaques up high on the walls. March straight up to the very top pews. The name Arland on a brass plate. The service just begun. These few parishioners. Mr Arland whispering.

'Kildare, there is nothing quite so empty as a protestant church in Dublin except one outside Dublin.'

The party last night only a short distance away from these voices so devoutly singing. Mr Arland joins them with gusto. Makes me feel quite awful, an out and out sinner, in this religious atmosphere. Anyone with the least perception looking at me could easily tell I've been steeped in filth and morbid corruption. And I even have another erection. With the voice of this visiting English vicar intoning.

'Almighty God, upholder of purity, fountain of all goodness, we humbly beseech thee to bless our gracious King and all the Royal family. Imbue them with thy holy spirit, enrich them with thy heavenly grace, prosper them with all happiness.'

Mr Arland with his hands resting before him on the pew. Had such a look of relief on his face pushing in my door this morning in his dressing gown and slippers to see me gnawing through a bacon rasher couched thickly on a buttery bit of toast and sipping my tea. And I must now whisper to him. Especially following some of the political statements last night.

'I say sir, does this reverend gentleman not know he is in Ireland. Should he not bless instead our gracious leader, the Taoiseach.'

'Kildare. We shall have politics later following service.'

During the further hymn singing Mr Arland's voice could loudly be heard lingering on the notes as the other voices had ended. Now the reverend's words reverberating from the rafters.

'Good Lord deliver us from all sedition, privy conspiracy and rebellion. Strengthen us in righteousness, give thy servant our most gracious King and Governor grace to execute justice and to maintain truth.'

And the man I battered from behind last night. Said he was heading over the border this morning and may now instead be looking for me. Mr Arland wondering why I keep turning around. Terror awful as it is does at least put a liveliness in one's step. Like it did when my sisters chased me making growling noises which made me go all the faster. The gunman said he would take the government over. Must be persons like him who made Uncle Willie say, ah we may be a country deprived of its totality by the British but it is them Irish gobshites as come in from the country and stand around in their bad taste in the highest government circles that we should be deprived of.

The church bell ringing. Sexton always blessed himself at that sound, no matter what the hour. And when the bell in the tower at Andromeda Park would toll, he would tell me to make the sign of the cross so no one could say then I was a heathen. And here I now stand a fornicator. Reading what I see written there on the side of the altar nave in gold lettering.

> The Right Hon. Theosphilus
> Lord Newtown of Newtown Butler
> Bequeath to the Poor of St Ann's
> Parish Thirteen Pounds Per Annum
> to be Distributed in Bread at
> Five shillings each week.

The organist playing Handel. His organ concerto. All lighthearted and thrilling. The parishioners leaving, so clean and perfumed smelling. The wax polished balcony. Unlike the damp mouldering chapels in the country with flakes of plaster dropping from the ceiling on one's shoulders and the smell of urine scented tweed. And the whole congregation stinking of horse piss. And maybe even moss growing out of people's ears. Down this side aisle, another plaque. Dedicated to a man who took part in the defence of T.C.D. in 1916 and was mentioned in dispatches.

'Well Kildare, you may not politically but do you feel spiritually improved.'

'No sir.'

'O well, at least God cannot complain we did not attend upon him.'

In the breezy street outside, Mr Arland gave a little bow to an elderly lady who lifted her lorgnette to regard and smile at him. And then looking at his watch, said we had just enough time to walk around a couple of streets. Which kept me looking at every fedora I saw atop a macintosh coming along. And I thought we passed the doorway which led upwards to last night's party. But Mr Arland said nothing. Nor I thought should I. Even though I should like to know what happened with that awfully curvacious lady actress. And we stood at the top of Grafton Street and crossed over to the park. Mr Arland looking up at the granite memorial arch. And reading out to me.

'Fortissimis Suis Militibus Hoc Monumentum Eblana Dedicavit MCMVII. An opportunity for you Kildare. To translate. Or is it a little early in the day for that.'

'Yes. I think it is sir.'

'You sound somewhat blue Kildare. Did anything happen. Was everything all right last night.'

'Yes sir.'

'I was rather remiss to let you attend.'

'I did though bully you sir.'

'Yes you did, Kildare.'

Mr Arland quacked at the ducks on the pond and later, as

we passed by the entrance of the Shelbourne he dropped coins into the hands of the tinker women squatting in position with their babes in arms on the empty Sunday morning pavement. He seemed so cheerful. And as he left me just outside the gate of the strange little cemetery he said was for Huguenots, he even rubbed his hands together and rose up on his toes. Telling me to take my third turning to the left. He would meet me back at the hotel for tea. And walking now, words kept going through my mind again and again. No greater anger hath any man but that. And then words came to finish it. That he belt another into insensibility with a curtain railing upon the back of the head. And as more of these distressing phrases and thoughts scratched at my brain I murmured to them. I'm awfully sorry but I'm not going to let you in. And I was able to smile remembering apropos of nothing at all, one of Mr Arland's comments about tipping.

'The secret is Kildare, how to keep your charm and still remain a mean stingy son of a bitch.'

The door. Painted dark green. A brass number and a polished gleaming brass plate with a name blurred beyond reading. A dark haired girl in black with a white lace apron and lace cap. A big curl falling over her forehead and into one blue eye and her reddened hand brushing it aside. Black and white marble tiled hall. Colder than cool. A brass stand of canes and umbrellas. An ivory handled one I recognize as my father's. A crystal chandelier in the ceiling. A side table with a silver dish. And two big keys resting on a pair of gloves.

'Are you the gentlemen was come to see Mr Kildare.'

'Yes. I am.'

So strange to hear my name and the name of my father. As if he lived here. Within these grey walls. In this strange big gloomy house. A large painting over the stairs of rocks and cliffs and cattle grazing under the glowering sky. And further up. As one looks along the rising carpeted stairs with each step held by shiny brass rods. And the gleaming mahogany banister. To see a woman. Tall with brown hair and thin angular face. In a long white flowing gown, retreating quickly back out of my sight. As the blood rushed to my face. And the servant girl with a nod of her head.

'Come this way sir with me now.'

Up the soft steps. Smells of cooking. Lamb if I'm not mistaken, and mint sauce. My father's most favourite meal was roast with Yorkshire pudding. But Catherine could never make the pudding. Try as she did. The soggy messes arriving which my father ordered returned to the kitchen. Where Crooks said it always meant a bowl or two smashed as Catherine wailed that no one appreciated her.

Top of the landing we turned and walked forward to a door. Past a tiny painting. Two horses abreast in a race. Called Andromeda Beating Adolphus. Which last I saw hanging on the wall just outside my mother's bedroom. The girl knocking.

'Come in.'

My father's voice. And the girl turning the ebony knob and ushering me into this blue tinted drawing room with a roaring turf fire. On the white marble mantelpiece the clock tinkling the hour of noon. Its enamelled roman numeralled face surrounded by ormolu flowers birds and cherubs. And its little pictures at which I often looked, as it sat chiming in the north east parlour of Andromeda Park. My father seated in a chair. His monocle glinting. Behind him a tall window facing out on an iron balustrade over the street. The sweet aroma of Irish whiskey. A pair of reading glasses resting across a folded newspaper. Great double white doors opening back into another room with a window facing out to the backs of other shadowy Georgian buildings. The door closing behind me. Sunlight suddenly spreading over the faded carpet.

'So you're on time you little bastard. You're getting to be a big bastard. Saw you last night. Behaving boisterously. Pushing Mr Arland out of the Shelbourne entrance. Stand or sit.'

'Stand.'

'Now you listen to me you little bugger. You're sleeping with Miss von B.'

'I beg your pardon.'

'Don't beg my pardon. You're sleeping with Miss von B. You little bastard. Don't come the hound with me. I'd send her packing only she's keeping the roof of that place on.'

'Which you've been taking off all these many years.'

'What. Speak to me in that fashion.'

'It is the way you are speaking to me.'

'And what's more, until you attain the age of twenty one, it's the way I'll go on speaking. It is in fact the case. You are sleeping with her.'

'It is not. And I am not.'

'Useless to deny. I have it on good authority.'

'On whose authority.'

'Never mind whose. Can't have that sort of goings on.'

'Crooks has told you one of his silly imagined stories I suppose.'

'Never mind who told me. In any case it is the duty of any member of the staff to inform me of irregularities in the household. Especially regarding fornication. And so you shall be taken away. And continue your further education without the benefit of the lady's bed.'

'You stole egg cutters. Wedgwood, Meissen. You even stole my mother's toilet service. And that clock there. You are a dirty slimy Catholic. You gamble. You sell off our hay and breeding stock.'

The sunshine growing even brighter on the carpet. My father raising his fist and then bringing it down not with a crash but with his knuckles whitening as he pressed it against the top of the mellow faded mahogany table beside him. Which on its single stem and tripod legs tipped over spilling his glass of whiskey on the floor splattering his newspaper and spectacles. The various tiny globules would make them difficult to focus through. If anyone were using them watching me. Standing here. In front of this mean nasty man. Being sentenced. For the very deed my father has many times done.

'You little bastard. You confounded little Protestant bastard. What do you know about running a farm. You still need your arse wiped. I'll get up from this chair and smash your face if I hear anything more like that out of you. You tell Mr Arland I want to see him. By six tonight. Go on. Get out of here.'

'I have heard it said that you yourself have cohabited with members of the household staff.'

'Get out of here you little bastard before I throw you out.'

Cheeks deeply reddened on Darcy Dancer's father's face. The vein in his neck swelling blue straining tight against his white stiff collar, a black tie with small red polka dots and a blue striped shirt. A crimson waistcoat with brass hunt buttons. Thought I heard the floorboards squeak with someone standing outside the door. And the door the opposite end of the hall closing just as I came out. To be back now once more in the world all alone.

Darcy Dancer feeling the smooth banister under his palm. Servant girl in the front hall, waiting at the foot of the stairs. Her red hands turning over one another against her lace apron. Stands back from me afraid to come too close. Hurries ahead to open the door. Step out now. Hear everything shut behind me. No cocoa last night. And today I thought I had been invited for lunch. If you want to make a lasting impression in the hunting field the most heinous thing to do is to let your horse stand on a hound. The howling he sets up has everyone looking at you. As I feel eyes are on me as I walk away along this street. Just as I watched my father once in the garden of Andromeda Park, looking at the last of the autumn flowers. He pulled one and then plucked the petals away one by one. The month of October. When the spiders weave their gossamer across the tip top blades of grass when the meadows become all a white waving sea of sparkling threads. In a big bowl full of hatred can you ever find a spoonful of love. Or put the petals of a flower back together again. Maybe instead I should intercede with some saint. As Foxy says everyone does. To ask god for your favour. To make my father dead.

Darcy Dancer walking along this street. Head down, hands plunged in pockets. Feet kicking ahead of him. Past these tall red bricked houses. Turn and go into a large square. Its centre all full of trees. Over there an entrance open it says to a museum. Through the iron gate. The lawns so green. The glass swing doors and a style which clicks me in. Look up. The massive horns of this great elk. And a stuffed Irish wolfhound, even bigger than Kern and Olav. Under glass, the tiny skeleton of a mouse. Like one which used to come right up on my bedside table at Andromeda Park and eat the remains of my porridge oats stuck to the side of my bowl and noisily bang back and forth over my spoon. Called him porky he was so fat. And these thin little bones are all he was underneath. And as I look down my hands are trembling. All my whole entire body feels cold. How long now will I have dismal days. Could be all through the years till I am the age of twenty one. Commit suicide. Hang myself with a bridle from a rafter in the stables. Or jump on a sword. Maybe it would be better to die more slowly. And swallow deadly nightshade. Or cast myself into the cold deep waters of the Lough and be eaten away by the giant vicious pike.

Darcy Dancer wandering back out again on the street and woeful through the afternoon. Turning right and left. Passing these broken windows. Gaping fanlights over the open doorways. Grimy tattered curtains hanging down inside. A three legged dog with one eye, hopping along the gutter. The blackened red haunting buildings. This tenement street. A line of people behind a small coffin held on shoulders. Women on a stoop. Their hands on the black twisted railings. The voice of one coming across the cold air.

'Ah the little darling girl was only nine autumns old, her mother poor creature she's never out of black with all the dying.'

Ragged barefoot children lined along the kerbstones watching other children following the cortège neatly dressed. Take my feet away. Ghosts and ghosts are in there behind the panes. Secret within the walls of old red brick. Stalk through halls and up and down stairs they mumble. And they live. Cackling as they jump from the side of your eyes just when you think you see them. In this their city. All over here they roam. Their minds wear windows for eyes. The chimney tops are their ears. The slates their hair. Ghosts, ghosts watching. Watching as one moves by.

Darcy Dancer walked to the big grey granite blocks along the Liffey quays. Back up past the bridge Mr Arland and I trundled over last night. And all along that route, past Trinity College and its tall strong railings and along to my father's club and past the little animal carvings on its stonework that I used to watch as a tiny boy. And even some long time ago Mr Arland in one of his rare heart to hearts said it would be useful for you Kildare, in order that you should know what to avoid, to acquire a knowledge of the worldly vices, of women, gambling, drinking and smoking. And now. A lover. And where is love. Disappeared like hoots of an owl. Means something for other people. And nothing for me.

The sky a darker greyer blue up this street to the Shelbourne. Just past tea time. The lobby flourishing inside with afternoon people. Gay and noisy. Turn right into the high ceilinged smoky lounge. The clink of cups. The din of chatter. The tall coated majestic waiters, trays aloft in their hands. As I look over the heads of people. To see for Mr Arland. Not in the middle. Nor there in those big sofas by the windows. Not in either corner. O my God if he's not here. Or doesn't come soon. Or never comes. That would be just doom.

Darcy Dancer, a frowning face turning away. Till suddenly right at one's immediate side. A tugging. And laughter. Of a girl. To look and there nearly beneath my elbow, the blonde head and not that much further down the white alabaster bosoms of the actress. As these two temptations swell out of her pink low cut dress. And Mr Arland's fingers let go of my coat.

'Kildare, you're awfully blind.'

'My goodness, I didn't see you. I was looking back there.'

'And of course, we are here. Come sit. Have tea. And Clarissa, may I present to you Reginald Kildare, whose more intimate friends refer to him as Darcy Dancer.'

'And I hope I can too, Darcy Dancer.'

'Kildare, this is Clarissa.'

'How do you do.'

'Well for a start I'm on my third cup of tea with your tutor. Who has so kindly invited me to partake of. And I hear so much about you. That you're very clever. Lazy at Latin. But a brilliant and brave horseman. And you're going to be quite important some day. Not that you are not already but you know what I mean.'

'I think, ma'am, Mr Arland is somewhat biased in my favour.'

'Now Kildare what alternative have I but to be biased in your favour when you work so little and I teach you so hard. And now what would you like in the way of sandwiches. How about a smoked salmon, eh.'

'That would be very nice, thank you.'

'And I being the lady present, Clarissa will pour you tea. And then I shall of course only be too delighted to ladle you salmon or cakes, or to comfortingly hold either of your hands. Or indeed mop your brow should it urgently be required and I had the necessary mop.'

The skin so soft on her long white magic fingers of this actress. The blue of a gem stone sparkling on her knuckle. Never before in my entire knowledge have I ever heard Mr Arland utter the word eh. Something has distinctly changed. Even his crossed leg has his foot gigging somewhat up and down. A movement he told me no gentleman ever makes. Since it might be deemed he had just nervously peed in his pants. And Mr Arland's shirt changed from the one he wore this morning. Even his tie would give an appearance that its wearer might be at the race track. His hair brushed shining back along his temples. Shoe tips just this side of gleaming. And not a single speck of darkness under a fingernail. And his shoulder is but a hair's breadth away from Clarissa. And as she leans forward to pour, her bosoms make me gulp.

'And Darcy Dancer, you don't mind do you, if I call you that.'

'No.'

'Then I shall ask you Darcy Dancer, how would you like your tea, weak or strong.'

'Weak please, thank you.'

'Ah sensibilities. The certain sign of sensibilities. Weak tea. I have mine strong. But then I have no sensibilities. All I am is too noisy, too loud, and in the politest of places I show too much flesh. Isn't it awful. And everyone is afraid of knowing me. Isn't that true Mr Arland. I like calling you Mr Arland. It does something to make our tea together more serious and profound. Not something silly and nonsensical. Here you are Darcy Dancer. Do you take milk.'

'A little please.'

'And of course, as always after awful wars, there's a shortage of sugar.'

'I don't take any thank you.'

'Ah another sign. Of a young man intent upon grave but noble destinies. Maybe even guiding big nations. O dear but they're all such a bore really, big nations. The horrid despicable things they do to the little nations. But then I was never any good at politics. They say don't they, leave politics to men and leave famous men to beautiful women. And of course the women will do worse things to the men than nations do to nations. Or do they say that. Or is it that I'm just saying it. God I think I will say anything. Even though I am most respectably from Rathgar. And poor Mr Arland, Darcy, he's just been so absolutely good and patient tolerating me. He is as I'm sure you already know, a treasure. Yes that's exactly what he is. A real true treasure. And I adore him.'

The blood coming to Mr Arland's cheeks. His eyes blinking and his lower lip moving back and forth over his upper. All the silvery greys in the blonde blonde of Clarissa's hair. Her melodious voice, a tiny girl's, full of sap and juice. And like my mother's, the pure white white skin of her face. Unwrinkled even when she frowns and smiles. Eyes of greeny grey flecked with brown, dancing and darting as she speaks. And we had tea all the way till nearly six o'clock. I had four cups, two big buttery pieces of toast coated with bramble jam and three cream cakes. People now in the lounge taking their sherry and whiskey. Talk of shooting and hunting fixtures.

And I nearly forgot all my woe and what my father said. With Clarissa leaning forward, bosoms aflow to put her hand gently on my knee. And as she did whenever she laughed really hard, putting back her head and then all of her cascading forward. Then a moment later her other hand would move over a fraction of the inch of faded flowered pillow of the couch and grasp Mr Arland's. And I thought, that at least upon this day, when so many ill moments pursued me from last night. That not all was bleak and miserable. I told Mr Arland my father would be pleased to see him as soon as possible. And at least by six o'clock. Which sent Mr Arland jumping to his feet.

'Then good gracious Kildare, you should have told me, it's nearly that time now.'

'I'm sorry sir. I have I'm afraid been just rather happily daydreaming here.'

'Darcy Dancer, what a nice thing to say. That I set you with all my silly chatter to daydreaming.'

'O no ma'am, you are a most interesting person. I mean only that you really set me to pleasantly thinking.'

'Ah that is more flattering.'

Mr Arland brushing away his crumbs. As I rose to say I would repair now to my room. And I requested permission of Mr Arland to attend the cinema. The one which we passed in the narrow street up to St Stephen's Green. Where a film of the wild wild west was playing.

'Of course you may, Kildare.'

When I bowed, Clarissa offered up her hand. And as much as I wanted to sink my kisses upon her flesh and go osculating up her arm, I merely brushed her metacarples lightly with my lips. And turned back to look as I left. To see Mr Arland standing over her and I could tell she was shaking her head yes to him. I rose upwards in the lift with an awful feeling. That I might not ever see Mr Arland again. Stood looking out my window. And prayed. That Mr Arland would not be disappointed in love. That this actress would not now ever again take out her breast in a public place. For that would, more than anything, certainly mortify Mr Arland. Who tried all these months to gain the notice of Baptista Consuelo. And got nothing but a look down her nose at him. As she sat so high and haughty on her horse. And I hear. Even now and so far away. Westwards. Over the bog lands. And further out across the gently rolling winter bare hills. The huntsman speaking to hounds. Horizons all around us. The huntsman shouting. Find him. Cheering the pack forward. Down on hillsides. Nostrils steaming, hooves thumping and thundering. Charlie is the fox. Puss is the hare. Try up old fellows try. Cool moist winds on the face. The warmth of horse between your thighs. The horn's slow mournful wail of the covert drawing blank. Has Mr Arland found a vixen. Be killed instead of killing. Or a goddess ungodly come to him. To give life to his life. To go on living. Never have death. Through the tears in my eyes. My mother. Ankles so slender. Gold pin closing the silks around her throat. The still still way she lay. So dead. To leave woe.

> And her
> Blood bleeding
> Red
>
> When
> The sky was
> Blazing blue

13

Mr Arland knocking early on my door in the morning. And saying neither sad nor glad that he would await me in the lobby. And that we must hurry. I quickly brushed my hair in order to warm up my brain and found a long grey strand. Clearly turned that way from all my recent cares. It was all twisted and I plucked it out.

The lobby this morning full of traffic. Of business men arriving and country squires departing. Mr Arland being very businesslike checking through our hotel bill. Wouldn't tell me how much it was as I tried to look but said it was substantial. We called at gentlemen's outfitters the top of Grafton Street. Where Mr Arland said he obtained his silk Trinity ties. And where a most agreeable shop assistant officiated over my purchase of shirts socks and underwear. And we stepped back out on the street.

'And what did my father say to you.'

'Kildare, it would do no good to tell you.'

'You are no longer my tutor.'

'That's correct.'

'What will you do.'

'Find a teaching post I suppose.'

'Will you like that.'

'Not really.'

'Isn't there something else you could do.'

'Yes. But I probably won't.'

'Why.'

'O I don't know. There's much to recommend merely remaining a stick in the mud.'

'Sir, this is one of the saddest days in my life.'

'Come Kildare, buck up.'

'I can't sir jump up and down in joy and be jolly.'

'I know you can't Kildare. I know you can't.'

We were passing the cinema where last night I saw the cowboy film with everyone being shot off horses and gentlemen in saloons downing whiskeys while pulling out their guns and between the briefest of insults blasting each other to death. Well pardner if you don't reckon to get yourn head shot clean off you'd all better vamoose. Any normal person would be exhausted losing their tempers so often on the brink of death. And most of the film was quite utterly silly. But they were amazing good horsemen. And following some amusing cartoons and at the end of a travelogue concerning a trip to Mexico I went by myself to have supper. In the cinema's cosy café upstairs. Upholstered seats and little lamps on the tables. Five different teas you could order on the menu. Among which were The Tasty, The Savoury and The Epicure. All consisting of tea, bread and butter but with the variation of eggs boiled, fried or poached and with either tomato, sausage or bacon. The girl who served me had a big freckled cheeked country face and spied from behind a cupboard watching me eat. To rush out smiling the instant I finished anything on my plate, asking would I be wanting more. Before I could say no, with my mouth still full, she said sure you'll have another helping. Rushing away and returning with more sausage, tomato, poached egg, tea, bread, jam and butter. Out of politeness for her hospitality I kept on eating as best as I spiritually could. Till I was physically gorged groaning. But I knew she knew I was from the country, and out of that comradeship she was only trying to give me the best of service and hospitality. As well as clearly depriving her employers of a profit.

Ten thirty by the blue dial of Trinity's clock. As we crossed this wide street and went by the big grey bank. The clanging roaring trams. The street aswarm with bicycles. Big rumbling horse carts stacked with barrels. Replenishing Mr Arland said, the empty cellars of the pubs following the weekend. And getting ready for Monday night which would leave them even emptier. The pavements astir with expressionless faces on their way. A blond young man on the bridge holding out a tin cup and stoically turning the handle of a street organ. Who had also stood there as a young boy through Mr Arland's undergraduate years. Past an ice cream parlour of cold faces seated inside the windows. And further on under the gloomy granite portico of the post office. Where we turned down a street called Henry. To buy me a suitcase and two blue blankets. And with all my new supplies packed in, we took a train.

In the empty chill first class carriage, Mr Arland spoke of Clarissa's friend Rashers Ronald who, aided and abetted by the actress, was in feverish hot racing pursuit to marry a very fat, dyed blonde lady widow who owned four pubs, an eighty acre farm, two newsagents and a tobacconist's shop. From the latter of which Rashers was already collecting a daily ration of twenty free cigarettes of a brand nicely named Mr Arland said Passing Clouds.

In a drizzling rain, six stations down the track, a motor car met us. To take us further cross country several miles from this town and up a winding drive to a big stone country house. From which as we mounted its wide bleak steps, I swore instantly to run away. Mr Arland I thought had moisture in his eyes as he shook my hand in this large barren cold front hall. He said he'd just been to put in a good word with a master he knew. And I felt a shuddering in my breast and globules in my own eyes hearing the motor car door shut, the engine rev and the wheels move away over the pebbles. Two small boys carrying my bags took me back through a long passage and up stone winding stairs into a long dormitory. The day now darkening out the windows. Parklands and fields. A lake. Over which I could see the distant slow progress of swans flying. And as I stood, my bags stacked next to a mattress doubled back on the bed another larger boy my size came up to me.

'You are in our form. I've come to present the compliments of Supreme number one. What's your name.'

'Kildare.'

'And your christian name.'

'Reginald.'

'Reggie.'

'I'm afraid I do not want to be called that.'

'Alright then. Kildare. Well Kildare, you look a good sort. Who would you like to challenge for supremacy. There are those ranking from one down to twenty seven.'

'No one.'

'Well then you shall be everyone's slave.'

'I shall not be anyone's slave.'

'O well we shall see about that. Unless you challenge for supremacy you are at the bottom of the ladder. Where have you been before this.'

'That is my business.'

'You are, aren't you, a rather cheeky fellow. Especially coming brand new here. I am second in supreme here. That is how we rank each other. With a number. First second and so on. There's a mediocre chap Jones from Wales. You could I think just pop him one straight in the kisser and you would then be fourth in supreme.'

'I would like nothing better than to be nothing in supreme here.'

'O it is like that is it. Come come now. You are being a most tedious fellow you know. I think you may be nervous in your new surroundings. Are you anyone who matters.'

'What do you mean by that.'

'O I mean does your father have a title or own estates. The usual sort of thing. It helps you know if you are of the right sort. Are you the right sort.'

'Don't be impertinent.'

'Ah you are of the most brazen sort. Dear me. Don't be impertinent. You know that is a misdemeanour to speak to me like that. You're not a potato digger are you. Or a boggie. Or a shopkeeper's son.'

'I said don't be impertinent.'

'And what Reggie are you going to do about it if I am.'

'I shall sock your jaw off in quick fashion.'

'Ah you challenge me to supremacy.'

'I challenge you to nothing. I will merely do as I have just said if you continue along with your stupid little childish game.'

'Well let me warn you. I am the sixth best fighter in this whole school. But you are a spunky. My name is Purejoy. And of course as you prefer I shall call you Kildare. But Kildare if you want my honest opinion, I think you are very much a type usually referred to as a curmudgeonly fellow. If you are scholarly enough to be familiar with the word. And perhaps should be left to your own sad devices. And miss out completely on all the goodies that the influential top members of this school are in the habit of enjoying. Including, of course, having your own private personal room and slave. O well maybe you've been sent down from another school for being similar to how you are now. But if you have any brains at all, you will change your tune.'

'Goodbye.'

'Certainly, goodbye. But you may be wishing all too soon that you had said something quite else.'

Darcy Dancer sat by the mattress. Looking again out on the fields as darkness fell. Until the lights of the dormitory were switched on. As somewhat smaller boys charged in. And whispered putting books back in lockers. At the sound of what seemed an evening dinner gong, they charged out again. Another boy came in and said he was delegated to escort me. And that until a better name was allowed him by Supreme number one I would have to address him as Stupid.

'Have you a christian name.'

'Yes. But that too has been changed.'

'To what.'

'Awfully.'

Down into a hall, lighted with brass chandeliers. Long refectory tables. A young woman serving soup. Stares at me. And stares again when I stare back. Chunks of leathery beef floating in thin brown gravy. Lemonade and tea to drink. Awfully Stupid sitting next to me. Being awfully loud slurping up his food. Purejoy at a distant corner table turned round once to look. With other heads boisterous and noisy turning with him. No doubt to rain retribution upon me for my reluctant attitude. To become a big bully with them. By midnight tonight I will be miles away. Wear three pairs of socks and all my six pairs of underwear. Head out cross country in the opposite direction from the new moon. Awfully Stupid nervously next to me nudging my elbow.

'I say, Kildare, they are rather looking at you, aren't they.'

'So it seems.'

'They call themselves the Presidium at that table. For infractions of their rules they conduct courts. You must be careful not to offend them.'

The serving girl still staring each time she comes to our table. Now when I look at her she casts her eyes down as she stands waiting with dinner ended. The clattering of dishes and shuffling of chairs and the silence as two masters from a high table file out. Followed by the bigger boys of the Presidium. Purejoy central among them. Who with three others now turned again to regard me with rather sickly grins as they passed. I stood next to Stupid who throughout the meal as I left food on my plate asked my permission to scrape it off on to his. I also gave him my entire pudding. Which seemed nothing more than stale bread chunks soaked in warm milk. Of which latter I could get plenty from some cow in a pasture tonight.

'Stupid. Why not use your middle name for you. Do you have one.'

'Yes.'

'What.'

'Kelly.'

'It's not very original. But we'll call you that then. At least it's much better than Awfully Stupid.'

'I hope no one finds out you're not calling me Awfully Stupid.'

'Don't worry if they do. They'll have to account to me.'

'But they can be wretched. They always travel together. And have bodyguards. Supreme number one two and three conduct attic torture after lights out. They push red hot pins into your skin. If you cry out they later shove your head under water in the tub. And if they think your bottom is awfully attractive they bugger you.'

A bell tolling eight. Darcy Dancer with Awfully Stupid in

the library. As this boy whisperingly showed a play he had written and kept secretly hidden stuck up underneath a library table. Another boy entering as Awfully Stupid tucked his manuscript up under his sweater.

'Are you Kildare.'

'Yes.'

'God I've been looking all over school for you. Follow me. Mr Michael wants to speak with you in his study.'

Following this boy out to the front hall. And up the main flight of stairs and along to the end of another corridor. Stone flagged, chill and Gothic. The boy asking if I played cricket or rugger. And said nothing further when I said no. He left as I knocked. Come in. A small sitting room. Warm inside. A turf fire blazing in the grate. Mullioned windows left and right of the chimneypiece. Books on opposing walls from floor to ceiling. This gentleman with long black wavy hair and sad brown eyes in a grey tweed suit. An insignia on his blue tie just like one I've seen Mr Arland wear. Bag of golf clubs in the corner. He puts a hand out. To shake rather softly mine.

'Please. Sit down. It's all very strange for you I'm sure. This institutional life. I understand you've not had the doubtful pleasure of being in a school before.'

'No sir.'

'Well I'm sorry we've temporarily had to put you among smaller boys. But we weren't quite expecting to have you so soon. Indeed we were only expecting you for an interview. However. We'll get it all sorted out. Mr Arland is an old friend of mine. Speaks very highly of you. I'm not exactly headmaster but I'm senior enough perhaps to be able to do some things which may make your stay here more comfortable. Wretchedly cold out in the dormitories for a start I know. Please don't continue to stand. Do sit.'

'Thank you. But I'd just like to stand sir. I've been sitting rather much already today.'

'By all means, then. I suppose you're well used to big old gloomy places like this. From what Mr Arland tells me.'

'Yes sir.'

'Well both he and I were together nearly Trinity's entire golf team. He's always been a somewhat shy retiring fellow. But a cracking good golfer. Easily ranked among the very best. He's very sad no longer to be tutoring you. But I suppose you already know that.'

'Yes sir.'

'Tell you what. I think we might make things here a lot easier for you. School's chock full of a lot of little ruffians. And a few but very few, rather tough types. Not to worry. We have to get used to you just as you have to get used to us. But I might just be able to see to it that you have no hard passage to row. But no favouritism you understand.'

'Thank you sir, but really it isn't necessary.'

'Well I'm not sure you may not find it so. It is not as if you have come out of some other school. You know going through the mill. The hard knocks, and all that sort of thing. What.'

'Well one does, merely by living a country life come by hard knocks, sir.'

'Ha ha I'll bet you do by jove. Mr Arland said you chase the fox.'

'Yes.'

'Well plenty of hard knocks in that pursuit.'

'I agree sir.'

'We've had scarlet coats through here a number of times. Had to fetch a man rolled on by his horse to hospital with two broken legs. Awful sight he was too. But the defiant gentleman was trying to fight us away and be lifted back up on his horse.'

'Remounting is essential sir in order to ensure your nerve is not lost.'

'Good lord, what about the man's legs.'

'You can always ride without legs but not without nerve, sir. At least if you have even a little bit of legs left.'

'Well anyway. Legs or not, you seem well able to take care of yourself. And you know where to come. Find me here most Monday and Thursday evenings. Just knock. And Mr Arland tells me, you do a little reading.'

'Not really as much as I should sir.'

'Well you're welcome to these shelves any time.'

'Thank you sir.'

'And tell me, not that I want to pry into your relationship with Mr Arland, but you do know who Mr Arland's father is.'

'No sir.'

'Ah. Well that is not, that question, let me hasten to say, indicative in any way that you should know.'

'I know his father is an aristocrat sir. But that is all I know.'

'O well that's enough. We could all do with being more aristocratic. Not really that it is finally any spiritually decisive factor in living a better life. But it materially helps to get one going. Course it can sometimes hinder one to keep going. So. Good to have you with us, Kildare. Goodnight.'

Back through the corridors. Hear my footfalls echo. Men make that sound going to the scaffold. Sound of voices elsewhere. Portraits on the walls. Scent of turf smoke. Organ music. Get back fast now to plan. Would pack what I could in a pillow case, if it weren't so white. Best fill a sweater, tie the sleeves closed, break an ashplant out of a hedgerow. And carry my woolly possessions suspended over my shoulder. That just sounded like a scream. Followed by piercing laughter. Getting educated like this must be a barbaric experience.

Darcy Dancer entering the dormitory. Faint yellow light. My bed down the far end. Past all these others. Must pass so many beds undetected. Two boys giggling and shoving. Stand aside for me to civilly walk by. As if I might bite them if they did not. The girl who served soup. Something about her face nearly familiar. Standing at the side of my own bed. Smoothing down the blankets with the palms of her hands. Awfully Stupid sitting there. Clad in green pyjamas and pink socks. Jumps up as I arrive. Everybody's eyes in this place are like those of a frightened animal. And this girl. Even as she leaves. Grey sweater peeking out at the throat and sleeves from underneath a blue overall. I cannot think why she would stare at me so. Just as I find I stare back. Each time rather more wanting to look in her eyes.

'I can call you Kildare. Can't I.'

'Yes Kelly.'

'Please. They were seen earlier. And I hear they are still lurking around. You must address me properly.'

'Who were seen.'

'The Presidium members of course.'

'I don't in the least care if they are around Kelly.'

'You should you know. Last term a boy got hung up by his wrists and ankles for two hours from an attic rafter. And there are even much worse things than that.'

'What.'

'I'll tell you later I think.'

'Why not now.'

'Well. I think it's so sinful.'

'What is sinful.'

'They make you masturbate while they all watch and you've got to do it three times in quick succession in order to be let off a beating or hanging.'

Darcy Dancer opening suitcases. Lights out. Boys going back and forth to the wash room with towels toothbrushes and toothpaste. Blackness on the windows. Someone passing down there with a lantern. Fog outside. The new moon would be long set now. Be such a black black night. Awfully Stupid does really seem awfully stupid. But harmless. Sitting as he does, his face wretched with anxiety, cracking the knuckles of his fist again and again. Licking his lips. As he thinks up some new question. Then scratching his head. Then frowning. Before finally leaning forward to speak.

'Are you fearless, Kildare.'

'No. I have fears, Kelly.'

'You don't seem to.'

'Well I do. But bullies don't frighten me. Fear can be quite good for you. It makes you watch out.'

'O you're so absolutely right, you really are. I'm bloody well watching out all the time.'

'That's jolly good then Kelly.'

'You know I wish you were going to stay here next to me. I really do. I hardly have any real friends. I really am all alone down here in this corner now. That was Dunster's bed. He got pneumonia. And it wasn't long after he got the tub treatment too. I think that's what gave it to him. But you'll probably get your own room soon. Wish I had one. Even though locks aren't allowed. I'd lock it right up. They hate me because I'm a shopkeeper's son. Only they won't admit. But so are some of them. I come from County Kildare the same as your name. Where do you come from.'

'Kelly I think it is time for you to go to sleep. And conserve your energy for your fight against your torturers.'

'It's no joke Kildare, the way you make it sound. What are you doing. Putting on all those layers of underclothing.'

'Just underwear, I'm easily chilled at night. Doctor's orders.'

'O.'

'Goodnight Kelly.'

'Goodnight Kildare.'

An owl hoot. Some whispering. Stare up at this ceiling. Till all is sleeping. And a dog barking. Somewhere far out there in the darkness. Be sheep dogs chasing me cross country. If only I had Kern and Olav. They would merely snap their necks one by one. As they did with any dog venturing into Andromeda Park. How many miles will I have to go. Without boots my feet will get awfully wet. But they slow you down when you have to run. From farmers bulls and dogs. Poor old little Kelly. Sat there tonight the side of his bed as if he were in prison. Awaiting execution in the morning. He'd be absolutely no use out roughing it. Terrified of shadows. Chewing his fingernails and cracking his knuckles the way he constantly does. And now his bed squealing as he tosses and turns.

Silence growing in the dormitory. Whispers hushing. Only a snuffle and a cough here and there. But that was a whimper. A torch light flashing in the door and down the beds. Must be a master. Checking the inmates. See if any have escaped. Just wait perhaps a little longer. This morning Mr Arland said, just as we went by that alley down which Lois took me, that we were all in our own little ways on a treadmill but that he hastened to add that it was prudent to consider one's position there fortunate. But my monotonous presence here clearly will be unblest. If only I had had time to reconnoitre the ground floor. Should have ate more of my supper. Feel gnawing pangs of hunger now. Even stuffed as I was in the Grafton Cinema Café. Kelly would conclude I was permanently departing if I inquired of him where stores are kept. Kitchens just in back beyond the dining hall. Borrow a bit of bread cheese and butter. The more butter the better. None served at supper. Poor old Kelly there just releasing a snore. Only grown up thing he seems able to do. Nannie nannie, some other little boy has just cried out. Shadows. The end of the dormitory. One two three four. And now five. Tiptoeing. Creaking. Coming down this end. Best to appear asleep.

Figures stopping at Darcy Dancer's bed. Two moving up one side, two the other. One standing at the foot. And a hand reaching. Pushing Darcy Dancer on the shoulder.

'Kildare. Wake up. We are the Presidium. I am the spokesman. We have come to invite you to an inquisition.'

'What inquisition.'

'Your inquisition. Get up. And come with us.'

'I won't get up and come with you.'

'You will if we make you.'

'Well then try and make me.'

'There are five of us. And one of you. Don't be so daft now to challenge us.'

'I don't care how many.'

'Keep your voice down. I suppose you plan to shout and wake everyone up. A cowardly call for help. Is that it.'

'No.'

'Well then. We see you've made a friend of Awfully Stupid there. To start with that's awfully stupid of both of you. At least Awfully Stupid is not that stupid that he would refuse to come. Are you Awfully Stupid.'

'No Supreme number one.'

'We of course, Kildare, will merely take Awfully Stupid in your place, if that's the kind of thing you prefer. We'll let you listen to his agonizing screams through the ceiling. Awfully Stupid has the most god awful scream you can imagine. Ah

that's better. You are getting up. We thought you would not
want harm to befall your new little friend. You may put on
socks trousers and jacket. But no shoes. For silence sake.
There is much stealthy creeping to be done.'

Darcy Dancer, preceded by two in front and followed by
three behind, walking out the dormitory door. Turning left
into a small corridor. And up three steps into another. Under
an archway to a landing. And up a tiny narrow staircase.
Another door. Opening into a water closet. A ladder being
brought in. The door closed. And latch secured. The suspended electric light bulb pulled aside by a string.

'You see Kildare. We post a guard here during daytimes.
Should someone want to use the water closet he then soon
hears within the unpleasant sound of yawking and even viler
sounds should such be necessary to defer further inquiry.'

The spokesman climbing the ladder rungs up to the top
and pushing open a small wooden cover in the ceiling. Darcy
Dancer signalled to follow. And the last member of the
Presidium tugging up the ladder and closing back the tiny
trapdoor. Candles lit. Vast rafters across the ceiling. Sound
of dripping water into a great tank. Dusty wood wormy floors
covered with little black beads of mouse dung. Stack of newspapers and magazines. In a circle, boxes draped with black
cloth. Each with a numeral. One to seven. A chair with a high
back emblazoned with a red skull and bones.

'Now Kildare. You sir, shall be there placed in the middle.
So the inquisition may begin.'

'I'll stand where I am.'

'O dear you are difficult. How many pairs of underwear
are you wearing.'

'None of your business.'

'Strange. Indeed if not even suspicious. Were you expecting us and wanted to keep warm. Surely you are not that cold
here. Now the purpose of this convening is to find out
exactly why, when given a friendly invitation to challenge for
a place in supremacy among us and maybe even become one
of us, you are instead defying us.'

'I'm not defying anybody.'

'You rejected Supreme number two's overtures this very afternoon. We want to know why.'

'I just don't want to join anything.'

'I regret we do not accept that as sufficient reason.'

'It's my reason. I'm not a joiner.'

'O. What a pity. You are then a lone wolf are you. We still don't think that sufficient.'

'I think it is.'

'Well we unanimously don't Kildare. Now. Your full name is Reginald Darcy Dancer Thormond Kildare. Is that not correct.'

'Incorrect.'

'Of course we already know it is correct. You have, have you not, rather barrelled your name up. It's all right the Darcy but the Thormond and the Dancer. That's all a bit much.'

'My name is Reginald Darcy Thormond Dancer Kildare. And not Dancer Thormond.'

'O. Good gracious. And dear me. But I believe that such a slight variation as that is referred to in legal circles as being de minimis.'

'You don't, do you, Kildare know what that means.'

'It means to be of a significance so small as to be deserving of no remedy.'

'Dear me, you are a clever sort. But anyway one could be forgiven for getting names like yours a little mixed up. Now tell us, what do you know of the death of the Viscount Horatio Nelson. He is you see our patron, absent in death of course. Our members learn everything there is to know about the noble admiral's life. And it is the required duty of any of our members to once each term climb to the top of Nelson's pillar in Dublin.'

'I know little of him and care less and would not climb a mouse's back in his honour.'

'Ah just as Supreme number two has mournfully reported to us. You are cheeky, irreverent but spunky. And handy with words aren't you. What if we were to tell you that we cannot tolerate such remarks.'

'Don't.'

'Don't. O dear. Kildare, if you are not merely chancing your arm, you are for someone so recently arrived very much assured. But as you have yet to prove yourself to us you are not entitled to such haughty behaviour.'

'I shall be as haughty as I damn well please.'

'You mean that you are asking us to employ methods sanctioned by the Presidium and usually reserved for boys in lower forms, to make you see the light. I mean come come don't for heaven's sake try to make seeming shocking cads of us. We want to give you every chance. We want only to have a trim well run ship. And avoid floggings. We all benefit that way. Things are then conducted in a predictable manner. There are our circle wanks. A prize for those who can come off first. We have, as well, for those desiring, our own personal female slut. You would wouldn't you Kildare like to know what it's like to fuck a female. Or if one has made close friends with a boy of a lower form and you wish to have shall we say further and better particulars of his attractions. Well. Nothing could be simpler. Your privacy is ensured. Doesn't that make sense to you.'

'If you're finished I should now like to return to my bed.'

'We are not finished, not by a long chalk. Is that not so Supreme number two.'

'Quite so Supreme number one.'

'And so, Kildare, imagine, here you are. Totally at our mercy. And you choose to continue to behave like this. O well. I think the time has come to show you who is boss. And I hereby direct as empowered under the Presidium that the sanctions be imposed for infractions under the syllabus of punishments as constituted. Take his arms and legs Supreme two three four five.'

'Touch me and each of you will regret it in turn.'

'Grab him.'

'Let go of me.'

'Hold him, for god's sake, hold him.'

'Christ he's strong.'

'Hold him, get his head in a lock. Get him down, down.'

'Bloody hell, don't let him loose, knocking over the candles.'

'Get him, the fucking bastard.'

'O Christ, where the hell is everyone.'

'I've got him.'

'No you haven't, you've got me you stupid bastard.'

'A newspaper is alight.'

'Put it out you sod.'

'I can't while this fucking Kildare is loose.'

'I've got him.'

'You've got me again, you sod.'

Crunching splintering timber. Of feet plunging through the worm eaten floorboards. A box sent bouncing. And one last candle sent flickering out. The smell of burning. And brightness once more. Of the pile of newspapers alight. And a box as well. Allowing all to see once again in this attic darkness. The milling bodies, grabbing twisting tugging and tumbling one on top of the other.

'Something's burning.'

'Of course it is you stupid sod, put it out.'

'Good lord somebody, there really is a fire, it's going.'

'Get this wretched Kildare first, get him.'

'Eeeeke. Who's got me. Someone's got my balls.'

'No need to scream about it.'

'The ruddy wretch, stop him, he's pulling my balls off.'

'A randy devil like you will soon grow another pair.'

'Voices down, you awful dumb ninnies, you'll wake the dead.'

'Well the place is ruddy well burning down, and that will ruddy well roast the dead.'

'This is what it must have been like for Nelson at the battle of Trafalgar.'

'Stop. This is Supreme number one speaking. Stop. I order it. The ruddy fire's spreading. Let him go. Put the fire out. Put it out for god's sake.'

'There's nothing to put it out with.'

'Use jackets, anything.'

'Good lord. The school is on fire. It's ruddy well on fire. It ruddy well is.'

'Let's then get the ruddy hell out of here.'

'Get water out of the tank.'

'How, you stupid wretch.'

'Climb in. Overflow it or something.'

'You overflow it. I'm not drowning in there.'

'We can't let the whole school burn down.'

In the orange licking light, Supreme number three, climbing up and over the sides of the tank. Splashing in the water. Supreme number two coughing and eyes smarting.

'That's no fucking good. It's not reaching the fire.'

'Break the pipe.'

'You can't.'

'Well you can't get water like that.'

'O God. The fumes. This is awful. I can't breathe.'

'Raise the alarm.'

'Shut up, I'm giving commands. Quick all grab the pipe. Come on Kildare. You're in this too. Break it. Altogether. When I count to three. One. Two. Three. Heave. Christ.'

The pipe wrenched from its join at the foot of the tank. Water shooting out in a jet across the attic floor, and splashing up against a joist supporting the roof.

'Good God all that's going to do is flood the entire school.'

'Let's get out of here. And anyone who breathes a word about this will answer to the Presidium.'

'Look at it, the flames are spreading right along those dead ivy leaves. Right down the whole attic. There won't even be a Presidium if you don't get out of here fast.'

The trapdoor to the water closet pulled open. A whoosh of air coming in along with the electric light. Flames suddenly waxing brighter. Feverish hands grabbing. Count the silhouette of heads. Five figures crouched. The ladder lowered down. Supreme number one clambering into this much sought after aperture. To take an instantly ill appreciated precedence in exiting.

'I say Supreme number one, that's not awfully exemplary, leaving the rest of us behind. Certainly not in the spirit of Nelson who would be the last to leave his sinking ship.'

'Shut up number three, this is a ruddy burning school not

a ruddy ship. Besides with you stupidly soaking wet and diving in the water tank, I have to be at the bottom of the ladder first to count to make sure no one else has followed your feeble minded example and is left behind drowning.'

'You liar.'

'That's a challenge.'

'You bet it is.'

'Shush. Good lord listen. It's roaring. The fire is beginning to roar. Isn't that marvellous how it can do that.'

'It may be marvellous Supreme number five but upon my great grand aunt Queen Victoria, I am, gentlemen, not remaining to listen but am about to say toodle ooo. And upon decamping out of here where it's already beginning to piss down from the ceiling I'm going to watch this conflagration from the front ruddy lawn in relative ruddy comfort.'

'Come back here number four.'

'Fuck you number one.'

'By god, you sod I'll see you flogged before the main mast.'

'Well I'll see you, my good man, barbecued before the school assembly.'

'Someone's got to yell fire. Quickly. We must rouse the school.'

'Come on number two, and Kildare, get down.'

Darcy Dancer helping to guide Supreme number two clutching at the rungs. His eyes blinking and blinded by smoke. As these two last escapees descend spluttering and choking. Supreme number three holding the ladder at the bottom while shaking his head sidewards to dislodge water out of his ears. His soaked clothes clinging and a puddle collecting at his feet. Supreme number two wiping his eyes with a handkerchief.

'I'll say one thing for you, Kildare, you're quite sporting. Thank you.'

'No reason to abandon someone just because his closest colleagues do.'

'Yes, well thank you again. I won't, I promise forget it. But God they're all gone. Leave the ladder. And we had better not stand here on ceremony.'

'Fire. Fire. Fire. Fire.'

A voice shouting down the halls. Supreme number two running with one hand holding up his trousers. He trips and falls flat on his face just as the lights come on. And promptly go off again as I feel my way along this wall to retrace steps down the tiny narrow staircase. Take deep clean breaths of air. The sound of more running feet echoing. Ahead a bit of light. Move along this corridor. Here's the archway and landing. Down three steps. Turn right. A door slamming. Shouts of fire now. Everywhere. Just time to get into this dormitory before anyone sees me. And let out my own little shout.

'Fire. The school is on fire.'

Darcy Dancer as the light switches on. Running down the centre aisle between the grey tubular iron framed beds. Pulling on again his jacket just removed. And all these heads pop up from their pillows. And start to stare with blinking and rubbed eyes.

'Where. Where.'

With Awfully Stupid, most alert of all sitting up on his elbows. A deep frown on his singularly pasty unattractive face.

'Kildare, is there really a fire.'

'Yes.'

'O my goodness. I must save my chocolate fudge.'

Awfully Stupid jumping out of bed. Rummaging in his locker. As a scream emits further up the dormitory room.

'Look at that Kildare. What's happened. The ceiling, the water is pouring down out of the ceiling over there.'

'By jove, so it is, Kelly. How observant of you.'

'Look, the plaster's coming away, it really is pouring. And good lord right down on Pratt's bed, and he's still asleep poor sod.'

A master at the entrance of the dormitory in long white night cap. Tightening the belt of his dressing gown. A blanket clutched and pulled over his shoulders. Holding an arm out. Halting the first of the eagerly departing. And shouting down the line of beds.

'Remember your drill, remember your drill. File out now,

in an orderly fashion boys. To the left to the end of the corridor and down the kitchen stairs. Quickly. The school I regret to say is on fire. Leave belongings behind. But no need to panic. In orderly fashion now. Quick march. That's it. Count you. As you go. Thirteen fourteen fifteen.'

Darcy Dancer, pushing many stockinged feet into his shoes. Painfully squeezing my metacarples into where they won't fit with all these woolly layers. Awfully Stupid's eyes bulging. A tin flowered box under his arm.

'O dear Kildare, there really is a fire.'

'Of course there is, can't you see everyone is leaving.'

'I want to stay with you. Why are you putting on all those clothes and things.'

'Because in the two or so hours it takes to watch the school burn down to the ground, it's going to be awfully cold outside.'

'You're so right, you're so absolutely right Kildare.'

'Come on don't dawdle.'

Darcy Dancer pushing Awfully Stupid in front of him. The master as they approach counting them twenty six and twenty seven.

'You're the new boy. That should be all of you. Go quickly now. Catch the others up. Good grief that groaning sound is that the ceiling.'

'Yes sir.'

'Why it's about to come down. Good lord it is coming down.'

The master, Darcy Dancer and Awfully Stupid all taking a step backwards. A cat scurrying past in the hall. Clearly everyone's making a run for it. Lights grow strangely bright. As a great massive span of white dripping plaster, bellied downwards, yawns, creaks and cracks. Breaking and splintering from laths and joists. To plummet on beds, lockers and across the aisle. Thunderously followed by volumes of water pouring down on the rubble. The master putting his hands up to the sides of his face.

'O my god. We're ruined. O my god. Go on boys, go on. Out with you.'

A master standing now in front of each little group ranged over the soggy lawn. Lights on in all the school windows. Flames shooting from the roof of the north wing, reddening the smoke ascending into a descending fog. Bell ringing. Boys in pyjamas trembling in the chill. Older boys and members of the Presidium rushing in and out and up and down the front steps. Carrying portraiture. Others lugging chairs. Some unsportingly grinning. A little voice piping up behind one.

'This is jolly good fun.'

'Ruddy right but wish the flames would spread faster and keep us warmer.'

Motor car lights coming out along a road. An old man hobbling in big black boots and overcoat and carrying a pail of water towards the entrance. A cheer going up. A master pushing the old gentleman back with his pail. And a boo erupting. Awfully Stupid giving me a blow by blow description as he chews insanely on his cubes of delicious smelling chocolate fudge without offering me one.

'That's old Conners, the cricket pitch groundsman, and they won't let him go in to fight the fire.'

'He'd hardly get anywhere with merely a bucket of water, Kelly.'

'Goodness Kildare, I guess you are so absolutely right, he wouldn't would he. Look. The flames. The slates are falling through and the flames are coming right out. Right over our dormitory nearly reaching our beds.'

'It's not very good for the school, is it Kelly.'

'I should say not Kildare, I should certainly say not. Look the headmaster. He hasn't combed his hair. Getting up on the steps. He must be going to make an announcement.'

'All right attention everybody. Attention now. Cease the idle chatter. Now I want all of you. To listen carefully. There's a long night ahead of us. And a cold one. Some of you may of course not have seen a school burn down before.'

'Ha ha.'

'But I don't think there is any question but that many of you have not wanted to see one burn down.'

'Ha ha ha.'

'Alright cease the laughter. We are presently awaiting the arrival of the town fire brigade. Meanwhile our own school fire apparatus is being employed. We may be able to confine the fire to the north wing. In such case you boys from the north wing will double up. And I want no larking. We will serve a hot drink soon from the kitchens.'

'Hear hear.'

'Cease those remarks. All of you are to stay where you are until instructed to do otherwise. And on no account is anyone to re-enter the school. That is all. Except that a full investigation is to be carried out. As to the cause of the fire. I want any of you with any information to come to me and disclose such.'

'Kildare do you think someone started the fire deliberately.'

'I'm sure I don't know Kelly.'

'Gosh that would be really not nice.'

'No Kelly it would not be nice at all if someone did set the school alight.'

'Someone must have done it.'

'Kelly who is that girl who made my bed.'

'O she is called Slut. Out of her hearing of course. The Presidium members take turns with her on a mattress they have behind the water tank in the attic. She's quite kindly you know. She was put up the pole by a big landowner. And was sent to do penance in a convent after she had a baby. The Presidium are always snatching feels of her. And pushing her up the ladder into the attic. She sometimes slaps them. But mostly she giggles. Goodness that's where the fire is. Right where the Presidium meets. Was that where they were holding your inquisition, Kildare.'

'O no, we held that quietly in the library.'

A long file of boys moving off. Circling now around the school, heading on the gravel path, for the back kitchen. Sound of a sputtering motor vehicle. Must be the school's personal fire engine. Lights fading and then brightening as the beams cut through the foggy darkness out across the park land. Its ancient wheels pulling to a stop at the front steps. Part of it painted red. Three men kitted out in long rubber coats unwinding a hose. Running up the wide grey entrance of the school. One carrying an axe. A moment later all coming back out again to say the hose won't reach. The engine pumping water. Pointing the hose nozzle at the north wing. Driblets coming out as rain begins to fall. A cheer rising from all the assembled pyjama clad sneezing and shivering boys. Seems appropriate at this juncture that one should now just slowly slip away. And ask this stingy Kelly for some of his fudge.

'Where are you going Kildare.'

'To relieve myself Kelly. And might I ask you to have a piece of fudge.'

'Certainly you may. But only a little piece.'

'Let me have the box so I may choose something suitably small.'

'Hey where are you going Kildare with my box.'

'I'll bring it back. In just a moment. Don't panic.'

Darcy Dancer crossing over the soft mossy lawn. And further out into the wide wide darkness. Look back at the lines of assembled heads. The fire's flames licking from the roof top up into the falling rain. Shouts and arguments as staff members assisted by older boys continue to lug out paintings and furniture. Mr Arland's kind friend in a pair of boots and covered sensibly in a sou'wester. Directing the traffic of objets d'art. Had I hidden under the bed till all were gone from the dormitory, they might think I had perished in the flames. Then in my own living flesh I'd be off now in the world and be entirely somebody else. Except there would have to be a black charred skeleton left. If bones don't burn. With perhaps only Mr Arland to mourn my departure. And maybe Miss von B too. And Uncle Willie. And now as I vault this stud rail fence. Clutch niggardly Kelly's box of chocolate fudge tightly. That woman's face. Staring at me making my bed and serving the soup. Seen her before. Down in the kitchens of Andromeda Park. She was a girl then. During my mother's life. When the household's senior members had their own servants to serve them under the big vaulted ceiling of the staff dining room. Closed up now all these years. Remember her on the stairs. And heaving big platters to table. When I sat with Crooks, Norah, Sheila and Kitty. She had then big mounds of glossy black hair. Rosy cheeks and blue eyes. Face all pale and thin now. Her hair all dull and greasy. Climb over this stone wall. The rain coming down in buckets. If it puts out the fire, it will also fatally warp all the school's antiques. Uncle Willie said to me once. That if ever I should come upon hard times that I should go to him. And instead here I am. On this lake shore. Tripping over the stones. Hear the long beep of a plover. Go around till I can cut again back across fields. O god now I'm trodding in bottoms. Squelch of water. Coming up the sides of my shoes. Feet already wet. Must reach dry land. Over this ditch. Got to jump. Sexton said there may be a little water on top but it can be six feet deep in mud underneath. What's that. A massive shadow. Moving. Big white curly head. Two horns nicely curving down. On a Hereford bull. Dear God. Although I don't believe in you, here is an opportunity for you to prove to me you exist. If you will just not let that beast come after me, trapped as I am here on all fours on the edge of this bank.

Darcy Dancer holding his breath. The bull slowly turning to sniff in the shadows. And the welcome sound. Of ripping grass again. The behemoth grazing. And another shadow seems like a heifer nudging beside him. Much better that he jumps on her than he wastes time chasing me. Dead tree leaves thank god, underfoot. Feels like dry land. Bat flitting overhead. A cottage. Just get closer. Creeping up this mound of grass. The white washed wall around this dim lighted window. Peer inside. A table, dresser full of dishes. A pail. May be full of milk. To wash down Kelly's rather excellent chocolate fudge I borrowed. And chew now at this very moment so gratefully. Like the cottage out in the bog lands. With the bog woman and blind bog man. Dog sleeping in front of the fire. Good lord. There they are. The inhabitants. Kneeling praying. A statue candle lit with its heart burning red. And the dog. Its head rising. Getting up to bark and run. Right at this window. If they catch me a Protestant sneaking around their yard. But they won't now that I'm running. To get at least five miles away. Briars tearing my jacket. Get through this hedge. Charge up this hill. Right to the top. Feel warm now. The mist shifting. Making faint shadows of trees below. And beyond. Way back there. The red glow in the sky. So many young chaps' future education going up in smoke. And a handy beacon to keep me straight in my direction. Which is I pray, truly westerly. And just hope I don't come to a bog. And sink. Down deep in brown blackness.

> Be found
> Centuries later
> Petrified

14

Darcy Dancer stretching out his stiff limbs. This third damp morning. And the sound of clapping wings. Two pigeons speeding out of the branches over my head and disappearing off into the faint lighted fog. Aching now after all the endless hedges, climbing stuck gates, sliding down ditches and skirting bogs with the snipe in a whirr of wings shooting up in the dark. During these chill and slowly starving past two days. To always and always at all costs keep hunching forward.

Rub my eyes. Hands immovable with cold. Massage my joints. The dried scabs of blood all over my scratches. Mud down the side of my face. Where I've used the ground as a pillow. Near a ditch and gurgling water. Under the red berries of a hawthorn tree. And Kelly's fudge box abandoned there in the tall grass and its contents deposited not unsweetly in one's belly.

Get up. Slowly take a feel to see if my ears are still on. The shape of my back in the pile of the hay. Searched for dark hours to find cocks in a field. To make sure that a farmer wouldn't have beasts loose there to come sniffling and trampling me in the night. Kept my side and back warm. Beads of sweat coming off my sweater. Right over my heart. Steam rising out the top of that cock of hay. Be somewhere rotting within. Just as one wishes the fog would lift, it's lifting. The sky covered by purple cloud all the way to the horizon. A bright golden crack opening there full of the sun. My blue leather diary still in my jacket pocket. Written nothing in it over all these horrendous days. Curled now with damp and ink stains running blotting between the pages. Suppose if I had a pencil. I'd write rudely in the appropriate empty space. O shit. Being as I am presently suffering from torpor of the bowel. And need I think to refer to Mr Arland's homoeopathy book for a suitable remedy.

Darcy Dancer bending to cup hands to drink water. And wading through the tall grass to pick a palm full of bramble berries. Tasting unsweet and decayed. But at least one has had breakfast. And again last night I had a dream of being at sea. Where I've never been. On a great liner sinking. All of us first class male passengers in our evening clothed finery. Going down in the ocean's icy waters. Like gentlemen.

A shadow over there. Rusty broken roof of an old hay barn. Next to a high broken brick wall. Beyond the hill through trees, chimneys of a big house. Roof slates gone. Windows broken and walls crumbling. And all around as I stand here, silvery drops of dew hanging off every blade of grass. Miles and miles I've gone. And with just a few hours on Molly or Petunia I'd be home. Singing down into Molly's ears. She always kept in step with a tune. And changed stride to the rhythm of each new song I'd sing. Then go high stepping indeed if I sang It's a Long Way to Tipperary. Got to be somewhere now. If I haven't gone totally wrong with the hopeless muddle of road signs. Every one twisted or bent by the locals in the wrong direction. Some instinct tells you which way to go. Even when it means getting your feet all the way up to your knees covered in mud. Forearms soaked through. Tripped and fell over a tree root last night. Landed elbows deep in the turf. To just narrowly miss a nice man size deep puddle of water.

Climb to high ground. White mists hovering in the dells. Where as evening falls and you descend to the low lie of land, you feel the icy chill growing on your face. The sun rising warmer and bright now. The big purple cloud moving west. Grey landscape poking up out of the grass's greeny green. When the sky opens blue and wide as it does now, it often freezes. A vixen barked last night. Always means frost is coming. And I'll be dead. With my three pounds ten shillings in my pocket. And only my unexpurgated diary to tell people how shameful I am. And I should write down where I should be buried. Where the Thormonds are.

Sound of a donkey braying. And a beast roaring. Right bloody well behind me. Made me rush onwards. To promptly plummet straight down the steep side of a drainage ditch. After finding in the afternoon that I had for many hours been going in the wrong direction. Shouted out of a field to an old grey haired black shawled woman fetching her water. Gave her a fright. She took one look at me. And pointed. That the town I wanted was that way. I tarried thinking I might ask her for some scalding tea, fat rashers and a half a dozen fried eggs accompanied by a finale of soda bread, butter and damson jam. Then she turned to see me waiting. And made lickety split back to her cottage. Water bouncing out of her pail on her long black garb. Could hear both halves of her door slamming shut and bolts being drawn. I must look an awful sight. And not in the least resembling gentry. More like a common sort, dreg of society, low fellow and vagabond. Blamed for starting the school fire. O dear, one does not want to be treated that way ever again. Flail and strike at them. Defeat them all. One by one. No matter what they try. Boot in their balls. And tell the Viscount Nelson up on his pillar in Dublin that he can get stuffed.

Sun growing red. A thatched cottage three fields away. Smoke out of the chimney. In there all cosy. If I knocked and said all I want is to drink the cream off your morning's milking and an hour warming beside your fire. And get lead pellets from a shotgun instead. Got to keep moving. Stop shivering. Take another drink. From this stream flowing here. With its dark green water cress. Chew some for further breakfast. Find a poor man's cow tame enough to stand still. And have a drink of warm milk with another fist full of bramble berries. That would take away this cold pain all down my throat and rumbling in my belly. In the thick fog of yesterday. I went mooing with my hand out towards this grazing cow. Absolutely as friendly as I could be. She looked up with her suspicious big brown eyes. At my every step closer she backed further away. Even when I said in my best bovine accent, look my lady I am not going to harm you. Can't you see. I merely want like one of your calves a friendly drink out of your udders. Don't you understand. Mooooooo. Moooooo. Damn dumb insolent beast went shaking her head at me. And then hooking her hostile horns from side to side. As much as to say don't you dare touch my teats. Her bag swinging creamily swollen full between her legs. And the big foolish stupid thing continuing to back further and further away, head down and snorting steam out of her nostrils. Now one understood Foxy and how he'd flash out with a kick at the likes of her. Or land an old beast a belt of a heavy thorn stick across the haunch. Sheer starving anger made me chase her. Lunging forward, blocking her this way and that. Her long pink teats wagging running, her hooves digging churning deeply in the turf. Me skidding after her, arms astretch through the whorls of mist and smack bang into the roars of a farmer. Twine around his black coat, his eyes blazing in his red weathered toothless face. Erupting with growls of what are you doing. Go on out of that. And I did. Pronto as they said in the stupid cowboy film one recently saw. And he swung his pitchfork whooshing over my ducking head. And I took a flying leap through a thankfully near gap in the hedge, rending my trouser leg wide open and my skin as well from hip to knee with a barb of wire. Later tripping and tearing my trousers right down through the cuff with this flapping out behind like a flag. As I covered ground in the most indecent hurry for some time. All the while thinking I was the chased fox followed by baying hounds. Which, speak of the devil, or just hounds in general, I do believe I just then thought I heard, somewhere there, over the hill and brightly on to a scent. And indeed. That. The huntsman's horn. Urging them on. O my god they could come this way and think I'm a lowly sneaky bog fellow or worse riff raff scum. And set upon me. With hunt members threatening me with their whips. Driving me before them. Of course, no silly such thing could ever happen to a Thormond. But dear god, soiled and cold, one does get awfully low in spirits with one's tired limbs carrying an empty belly.

Crouch running to climb the top of this hill. Across the distant landscape. The galloping scarlet coats blazingly blatant, their red against the green. The blood's up. Boiling. Find him. If they did and it was me. Torn to ribbons in a thrice. Wouldn't even be my fly buttons left. All found later as black specks in the dog dung back at the kennels. With maybe a tooth or two of mine glinting out bright white. The screams and the shouts and whooping and yelling round me during the kill. Rip him up. O god I will never again hunt the poor ruddy fox. And again speak of the devil. There the ruddy fellow is, the very canny canine himself, loping casually as you please along beside that copse of ash trees. In a near one of which has just landed a magpie, shaking his black and white plumage. Letting me know the sight of him is bad luck. O no. But o yes. Ah. His mate thank god. Has just arrived alighting on a branch just over his head. And whoops. She lets fall a load of white shit right on the shiny black dome of her husband below. To my double good luck for the first time in days.

The sterns of the hounds wagging white with their heads to ground, descending the side of another hill only a field away. Now got to move. Or they'll hunt me. Followed on horseback by the mean hardbitten faces, purple jowls jangling. Lips curled in lust. Pounding down upon me. And good lord I may stink of fox. Trying as I did to crawl into one's hole my first awful night. If they lost the scent and pick up mine. Feet please go faster. Find me somewhere soon a big Protestant tree. To climb up. And don't leave me aground forever streaking along all these barren Catholic hedgerows.

Darcy Dancer, clothes flying in ribbons. Stretching legs fore and aft. Over this lumpy pasture. Heart pounding in chest. Lungs hoarse with the cold air. The baying hounds. Closer and closer. O my god there goes that ruddy twisty fox again. Out to save his brush. Steering the hounds in a circle and the ruddy foxy fellow must be following me and now is deucedly detouring ahead cleverly shifting the entire mob of his domesticated pursuers to scenting a poor old escaped schoolboy like me.

The fox leaping the stream. Pausing on the other side to grin from ear to ear and backward all the way down his throat. Knowing that I'm now the victim. With the hooves pounding. And a huntsman and Master coming up over the brow of the hill. And Mr Fox scampering off. Leaving it to me to give his pursuers yet another merry burst of chase. With the ditch to leap. Easily nine feet across and nine feet down and which I'll never get over. And in whose murky slime I may drown if I try. Goodness. Here they come. Got to slip down the side. And hide. Dear me. I've been seen. How shall I present myself. As a fellow fox hunter from a neighbouring hunt. I say chaps, that fox has given you some very pretty sport, ran a fine line there. O dear. That statement sounds so utterly forced. Coming as it must from way down in these squelching boggy climes here. And especially when made to participators in such an elegant hunt as the Moonhound Mad Hatters. Maybe it's just safer to just crouch among the dying stalks of weeds by this bank. Try not to be noticed and certainly not known.

'I say, it is someone. Huntsman come here. There is some nuisance minded fellow who has headed the fox. Brazen cheek and nerve. Who are you down there. Speak up. Or I shall dismount and come give you a few swipes of whip. Poaching are you. You scruffy young wretch. Who are you damn it. Speak up.'

'I am nobody sir.'

'You are damn well someone to turn our fox off his line. Get yourself on your way before I get down and give you a blazing good hiding.'

'I'm a member of the hunt.'

'You uncouth fellow, how dare you try to take the mickey out of me. Hunt member be damned.'

'I'm a hunt supporter too.'

'A hunt supporter, are you. A bloody layabout thief is more likely. Ruin a day's sport. You deserve a good thumping. Get up out of that ditch.'

Another scarlet coat thundering up. The horse's nostrils exploding twin barrels of steam. Copper gleam of hunting horn hanging from the huntsman's neck.

'What's the difficulty here Master.'

'This fellow deliberately interfered with the fox.'

'I did not.'

'You blasted well did. Huntsman, you go on. I'll attend to this young ruffian. Now you. Get up. And be damn quick about it. And move off out of here.'

Darcy Dancer climbing back up the bank. Clutching clumps of grass to pull himself forward to the top. The Master manoeuvring his horse near and raising the whip. Bringing it down across Darcy Dancer's shoulders. Felt like a feather through all my pairs of underwear. And he's raising his arm again. Whoever this big bully thinks he is.

'How dare you strike me.'

'Get on with you. And don't you attempt to ape my accent you peasant cur. Get on. Or I'll give you another one across your face for your trouble.'

Darcy Dancer on his feet. Suddenly throwing both his arms up in the air. Right under the head of this horse shying upwards, front legs pawing at the sky. The Master straining back tightly gripping the reins. And Darcy Dancer reaching and grabbing the Master's whip and yanking it with one great pull out of his hand. The massive chestnut gelding elevating near vertical. High up on its hind legs. The Master losing the reins and tumbling off in a somersault over the tail. Landing on top of his head, his cap visor crushed down on his nose. And a yellow pair of braces hitched to his breeches across his pink tunic under his red coat. The horse galloping away back firing kicks and farts over the pasture. Darcy that Dancer chasing after him. Up the hill and down again into the corner of the field. To grab the reins as he began to graze.

The Master just on his feet standing. As I come cantering over the rise. High and haughty in the saddle. Wave an arm to signal my departure to this Master now bloody nosed and limping. And no doubt desperately trying to gather some measure of speed towards me. Before remaining right where he is insanely enraged. Even have his leather cylindrical port case. Hope it is still full of a good vintage of that dark liquid.

'Get down from my horse. Come back here. You scoundrel. You villain.'

My two muddy cow flop spattered feet firmly planted in the stirrup irons. Pop open and back the leather cap. Pull out the bottle. And feel the welcome sting of this fortified wine warming down my throat. Plunge a couple of heels hard into this gelding's flanks. Giddy yap you steed. Hope you have plenty of go left in you. Because you're going to run run whether you have or not. Down this hill at the full gallop. And leave there plonk in the meadow that poor florid faced Master, angered gasping out of his wretched mind. Foxy said testicles withered on old men. And I hope that pompous bully's may have already dropped off. Wagging his one arm in the air as if the other were broke. And imagine. Screaming. Would you ever believe such indubitable bloody optimism. For me to get off his horse. With life suddenly again all so ruddy wonderful.

'How dare you drink my port. Dismount I say, you low cunt you. You shan't get out of this field.'

Darcy Dancer rounding this strong willing chestnut gelding. Turn him on a six pence. Face all sixteen hands high of him squarely into that even taller impenetrable bank of briars. Show this Master a thing or two about making a hole in a hedge. High enough up so no one else can follow. Foxy Slattery is able to go between two molecules so I'm going to bust between two atoms. Gather you together nicely now. Giddy bloody yap. Up you sod. Jump. Tear these ruddy bramble tops asunder. Soar through and over. And none by god will come in our wake. Nicely done. You good hot and steamy chap. Snugly under me. With your owner well knocked out of his haughtiness back there. Be in an awful evil temper if he has a broken arm as well. Need to see the bonesetter. The Jolly Straightener they call him. Practises all over the countryside. Gets you on a couch and as you lie there, he circles you some distance away sizing up the fracture. And each time around helps himself to a generous swig of whiskey. To yet come round again and say, oh it's a nasty one, a real bad one that, ah bad enough indeed to make your poor wife a widow. Or deprive a mother of her son. Hope the Jolly Straightener scares the Master. As he does everybody, stiff. But his genius for fixing fractures brings many to him from miles around. To have busted collarbones to broken arses mended. All my limbs thank god through these last three days are still sound. And pray now I'll never be identified. With all the mud on my face that Master could never know it was me. Take a look back. Goodness. Some straggling cowards have caught the Huntsman up. Standing round him now the middle of the field. Taking his instruction. Planning their campaign of urgent pursuit. Well you bastards. I'll tell you one little thing. I would indeed be entirely delighted if you tried. But you'll never catch me.

'Away my four footed friend. Away.'

Darcy that Dancer with a length of white thorn ripped from a tree. Landing swishing thwacks on the quarters of this steed. Head stretched forward galloping. Straining at the bit. Foam breaking from his mouth. Hooves pounding slapping the dried tall sharp pointed stalks of rushes. Flying over ditches. Up hillocks, down the other side. Slam splashing through the cow pats. Scooping out the turf to catapult it back into the sky. Crashing through the withered bracken and fern. Past the tall rusty dock weeds, brushing off their winter brown leaves of seed. Blue green of the grass growing fat up this double bank. Whoopee. Leap. And plunge straight down. Horse's belly asplash in the stream. And up the other side. You stout hearted fellow. Sloshing through this bog. To high firm ground. On all your bloody fours. Make the wind whistle. I know this country now. Fly your ears like wings. Keep west. Scare the pheasants up. Towards those rising wooded lands ahead. The rooks and jackdaws. From tree tops. In their cloaks of black shiny feathers calling me. Like a dream. That all fox hunters have. To meet one's end in the sport one loves so well. With a busted neck I could get vaulting this monstrous fallen beech. Up. Up. Good boy. Thank god. So many times thanked today. And not that far now in miles. Past the white grey bark of these beech. That old stone bridge there on the road. Where Foxy told me a man called Pulling Tom always stood. Without much brains. Who each evening if he wasn't in the bushes yanking his prick was instead scratching and scratching his head. Because he said he was thinking. And he'd be asked what he was thinking. And he said he was thinking he was scratching his head. And that Master now should be without wits. Imagine. Left miles out in the middle of nowhere. With a total stranger taking away your horse. How utterly humiliating. Not to say profoundly irritating and inconvenient in the extreme. But indeed, for such a foul ignoble person, so splendidly well deserved.

Darcy high in his stirrups. Head crouched streamlined over this blue beribboned mount's plaited mane. Cantering into the woods ahead. Towards a path both Foxy and I know straight through an overgrown old avenue of lime trees. A short cut to the other side of the forest. And get there without an overhanging branch sweeping me off. And what's that. Just behind that great oak. One black and one white tail swishing. My goodness. Two riderless horses tethered. Giddy yap. Fast. Down between these limes. And good gracious. Something scarlet. Dead ahead. Dear me. Two chaps writhing one upon another in the grass. Quite the usual thing of course. Two hunt members in a fight. But the one underneath. Has a lady's loose long blonde hair. And on top, between the uplifted knobs of a pair of knees, is a gentleman's exposed bottom sticking out from under his redcoat. With his very face now upturned to regard me with consternation. And wearing the features of none other than the Mental Marquis. With my recent diet of wild damsons and rose hips, perhaps I'm seeing things. With me thundering down upon him and the person over which he presently somewhat indiscreetly presides. But my god, the clarity of reality. Even as I head straight at them his bare bottom is still going up and down between the lady's parted naked legs. Her black garmented arms around his back. Her boots and breeches strewn beside her. O my goodness. Got to jump clean over them. And clear the upraised top of the perspiring Marquis's balding skull not to mention the twin mounds of the unbelievably unbecoming hairy cheeks of his arse. If they've only got the sense to lie low. Down there in the rather moist grass beneath these flying hooves. Up. Over. Banging myself in the branches. Nearly smacked by a big one. Looming and brushing back the hair of my head. Still can't believe the absolutely unmistakeable. Even when one's eyesight gets so fantastic at such times. As I look down and back flying over. To see facing straight up. The smooth creamy skinned face. The long brown lashes across eyes closed and now flashing open, in the lids widening back from their blue blue cold colour. Teeth sparkling athwart a blood red mouth agape in groaning rapture. Baptista Consuelo.

Bursting forth in sunlight out the end of the lime avenue. Darcy Dancer raging down the side of a great gentle sloping meadow. Head down low to the side of the steed's steaming neck. The big bellowing lungs nearly sound bursting. That pair back there will never dare to tell their tale. And if I do the hunt will have my trail. Between these ancient parkland oaks and especially straight through this flock of hysterically bleating and rapidly scattering sheep. Which no one will thank me for disturbing and putting to rout. Up. My boyo. Over this white iron fence. Down this entrance drive. Hooves clattering on the stony road. Lickity split, sparks flying. Past the front of this country house. In order that one may get between two points the fastest and not have to negotiate an entire lake. Past the great gloomy ivy covered elevation of this mansion. Standing in its velvet aprons of grass. That indeed I'm indenting deeply right across their ruddy front lawn. Where the five spinster sisters live. Called Rose, Camellia, Iris, Pansy and Marigold. Famed for their copious lashings of fortified wines and tubs full of butter melting hard boiled eggs at their splendid lawn meets. And known widely over the countryside as the bunch of flowers. Just hope one of their dear kindly number quietly sipping her port in some window bay after lunch isn't watching. And such refreshment get choked back in her throat in a fright or more likely in umbrage as I go streaking by their polished windows, pounding over their tonsured paddocks. Leaving holes as big as turnips. O my goodness, there indeed in the window is regrettably one of their dear number and I do believe she has elevated her lorgnette to look with concern upon this trespassing marauding horseman. Who madam, I assure you, will be pronto gone if only this steed's heart holds out. Just this little bit longer. Poor wretch it must be beating at its limit. Thumping deep down there in his chest. So sad sometimes that the most ill bred of people own the best bred of horses. At least the momentum left will take me blazing through this ruddy stable yard now. Much asplattering. Scattering and even cowering the barking dogs. Chickens and geese flying in all directions. And a shout from the men.

'Hey where are you going.'

'To the races.'

'Ah jesus, will you look at that. Your man's in the Grand National.'

Darcy that jumper just clearing the top of the farmyard gate with the gelding's hooves clipping the iron and clattering its hinge and rocking its pinion in its spud stone. Pounding along a road between stone walls. Up over another gate. Five barred and wooden and merely splintering the top rung. With the tall woods beyond now. Past the old plantation of oaks. No sign of pursuers. In any event, if they ever reached the lime avenue at all they will have had to return to render medical assistance having trampled Baptista and the Marquis into a broken bunch of bones. So I shall walk this good horse. Give him a well earned breather. And what a sight back there those two. Rolling enthralled and pumping one upon the other. Saw the very flecks of colour in Baptista Consuelo's sapphire eyes. Totally utterly calm. As they flashed open and closed. The whites so white. As if a horse or anything jumping over her in such displayed position was an everyday occurrence. As indeed it rather might be. With the good seat the Mental Marquis was displaying in riding her. Bare of arse. With her own as I remember quite amply big. Along with her mouth which had referred to Miss von B in such distressing words. And poor Mr Arland who in every kind of inclemency, wasted all his hours and hours of time. To plead his cause. With nosegays on her doorstep. And maybe even dreaming of inviting some major philharmonic orchestra to play her a symphony from right outside her house in the middle of the road. But at last he seems to have come upon his own reward.

'That's it, you fellow. Going well. Stride on. Let us gallop again now westwards into the wind rising.'

Darcy holding his arse horizontal, elbows flying from his chest. Reins shortened in my hands warming on this stout brave chestnut gelding's neck. All kinds of lust in the hunting field when the blood's up. Leading one must suppose to all kind of later disgust and disgrace. Like the randy Major who when not busy starving, whipping and being horrid to his servants, mounts stable girls any time his blood is even moderately flowing. Before hunts, after hunts, between hunts, and indeed anywhere near or far from stables and especially at night. But never on hunts. When it might impede the pursuit of the fox. Foxy went there robbing. And twice saw from the Major's stable loft the Major himself grabbing these likely lasses by the ears. Dragging down their breeches. As they pleaded for mercy. Plunging his big veined prick between their legs. As they sobbed for release. And if they were totally uncooperative he would twist their hearing appendages quite extremely. Holding their heads down in the straw. Poor girls yowling in pain. Desperately landing out with kicks. At the Major's testicles. Which he protected by a steel covering till he was absolutely sure it was safe to leave them dangling. Which according to Foxy was never.

Darcy Dancer, his tatters gently flying. Cheeks flushed with blood. Torn spattered and disreputable. Finally triumphantly cantering up this hill. Breeze cool at the top. Which I haven't felt for days now being so cold. All the splendid wild gallop I've had. Blood boiling. Makes the soul soar. So sweetly bright across the wild green. And there. Across two valleys. Under a sky such plaintive blue. Peeking up out of the trees. The great castle. No longer with the Count inside with metronome ticking taking his long demonstration leaps. And all that edifice's many many stones, windows and turrets. Standing through the centuries. Grey white in the sun. Dismount right here. Good old chap.

Steaming so absolutely soaked with sweat. Scratched and bleeding. Deserves a pat. And a long time munching grass. Tie up his bridle. Give him a good swat to run away from here.

'There you go now my good fellow, trot off to nibble meadow.'

Walk on my own two feet now. Down through these familiar fields. Of Thormondstown. Across by the end of the lake. The wind stunted beeches. The fawn grasses standing still up from the water. Two white swans sail on its brilliant black blue. The woods and paths of Andromeda Park one knows by every step. Back there the pace was fair, and the hounds hunting well. Till I came along. As the fox. Unwilling to yield up my life. And give insuperable pleasure to those pursuing me. Licking their chops as the baying pack lacerates my body to bits. Giving an orgasm to hunt members shiveringly thrilling in their saddles. As I suffer a nice ghastly termination to one's existence here on earth.

Darcy Dancer stepping out across this meadow. Sloping down towards fields rising gently again. Criss crossed by their bumpy stone grey walls. Less than a mile to go. Sound of saws sawing in the wood. Somewhere on my land. And I heard back there the thundering crash of a tree. Hawk takes off silently. From behind the shelter of this wall stopping the wind. Leaves a half finished meal of a mouse. Shape of flattened grass where a beast lay in the night. And I see two large shaggy heads. Coming. At speed. Legs outstretched. Ears flapping. Barks booming. Tails swaying in the wind. Hair flying. Kern and Olav. Straight at me. Caught my scent from many hills away on the wind. Hello my lovelies. My two big powerful friends. You bounce and leap about me now. And your big scraggly heads know that no amount of mud upon my face. No tatters no matter how much torn in my dress. No scruffiness however foul. Would ever deceive you. Jumping up high. Paws over my shoulders. Big massive tongues licking my face. To soothe warm and clean. And let me know. That where I stand upon this land, surrounded by their big hairy faithful bodies. Escaped from artists, gunmen, bullies, schools, farmers, hunts and hounds. That finally thank god I'm home. And not left. As the fox is left. Fighting for life amid the hounds. To be rendered just a bit of steam.

    Rising from
    The grass
    Where last
    He was known

15

Darcy Dancer crossing the gravel as rain begins to fall. The wind rising. And the clouds scudding grey. Kern and Olav with their big black cold moist noses wagging tails smacking me either side. Climb the steps. The front great door of Andromeda Park locked. Bang the knocker and pull the bell. Till the minutes pass. And the door comes finally scraping and squealing open. Crooks in one of my father's blue velvet smoking jackets and slippers. His collar open and his tie hanging loose. And his crossed eyes, one looking nearly north now the other entirely south. With soup stains as usual all over him.

'Lord save us, Master Reginald. I was about to get the shotgun to inquire of your business. What has happened to you.'

'I have been in a manner of speaking out hunting. Horse ran off with me.'

'Surely you're maimed. Without hunting jacket, breeches and boots.'

'I am in fact, quite in one solid piece. And do believe I am just in time for tea. And are you to keep me out here Crooks.'

'Begging your pardon Master Reginald. Welcome home. I was only telling Catherine this minute ago in the kitchen that you'd be knocking over the opposition like nine pins in the rugger scrum. Well it's a most commendable school that has its own pack of hounds.'

Darcy Dancer entering the front hall. To see the disappearing black shadow of a back and a bowler hat. Heading away down towards the schoolroom. Stand here. Watched by the centuries of Thormonds on the walls. In their robes and rich raiment. Wondering what on earth in rags the cat dragged in. To their great grand sanctum. And who should now sidle over and so earnestly toast his bottom with the dying embers of their fire.

'Who goes there, Crooks.'

'It's the agent, Master Reginald. He was only the while ago paying off some of the men.'

'Tell him in future not to wear his hat in this house. Most inappropriate behaviour.'

'Very well Master Reginald.'

'Where is Miss von B.'

'Taking tea in the north parlour. Will you be joining her.'

'Yes as a matter of fact. I shall.'

'Master Reginald, I don't wish to be impertinent but is there something wrong.'

'Perhaps. Fetch tea. If you will please.'

'Won't you want a wash and brush up. And to get out of, forgive me for saying, those rags.'

'Presently.'

'With all due respect Master Reginald, it would, if one did not know you as well as I do, be hard now to tell who you were.'

'That is quite understandable but it also can have its advantages. Now would you mind awfully Crooks, please doing as you are told.'

'Very good.'

Darcy Dancer watching Crooks depart. Everything of his clothes too big for him. His accent seems to be slipping as well. Sounds one second like a minister of foreign affairs and the next like the true treacherous bog man he is. At least the grand staircase hasn't yet collapsed. And everything seems as it was before. Miss von B must have been having a most leisured pleasured time. Keeping the servants' bells tingling and taking her big hot baths after a day's hunting. Quietly turn the door knob to the north east parlour. Tiptoe in. To the welcome warmth. The couch pulled round. Facing the fire. Her hair gleaming straight back in a bun behind her head. Greeny tweed jacket across her shoulders. Over the chimneypiece, the clock shape on the wall tinted a shade lighter where that enamelled timepiece stood which my father has now chiming back in Dublin. A thrush chirping its evening song in the first darkness just out the window. The floorboard creaking. The head turning around. A book closing. Miss von B jumping up. Tea cup, and a spoon tingling against a saucer. Her hand clutching at her breast.

'Ach du grosser Gott. It is you.'

'No it isn't me. But there is quite a strong resemblance underneath my rather tattered garments, my entangled hair, my mud, my cuts and various unpleasant spatterings. I suppose you want to tell me I am bringing muck in on the carpet.'

'Yes. You are bringing awfully filthy muck in on the carpet. What has happened. That you are like this. You are scratched. All over you.'

'You are shocked to see me.'

'But of course I am. You are supposed to be miles away somewhere else. Of course I am shocked.'

'I should like please, to have an immediate large thick, deeply buttered slice of that barmbrack I do believe I see situated on that distinctly early Meissen plate there on the tray.'

'Of course of course. But my goodness, first you must change your clothes.'

'No I shan't.'

'But of course you cannot take tea like that.'

'I can. And I shall. Take tea. Just like this. Which for reasons of my own I prefer to do. And Crooks is presently bringing me a cup. And I see you are using my mother's very best tea service. And what's left of the best silverware. I may also, should the fancy take me, even dance about the room. La de da de da de dee.'

Darcy executing a series of minor midget grand jetés. To come round the sofa in front of the big crackling glowing logs. Miss von B nervously reaching to slice the barmbrack. Cutting neatly through all the colourful flecks of dried fruit. Her bracelet falling down her wrist and her diamond ring catching red flashes of the fire. Her hands trembling as she buttered it.

'The agent was in here.'

'Yes. He was here. Just popped in as you say.'

'About what.'

'O it was nothing. But come. You must sit.'

'Don't you think it will matter now that my muddy garments may soil the couch.'

'Please of course not.'

'You usually do mind so much.'

'What is wrong with you. What has happened.'

'I have run away from school.'

'But you have just but gone.'

'Yes. I have just but gone. But I did not choose to like it. Therefore I did just but go. What are you reading there.'

Crooks knocking. Shuffling in. Sporting now his shoes. On both his reluctantly moving feet. His collar closed and the knot of his black tie neatly tightened. At tea time my mother always required the whole household to be especially on their toes. As it was she said the very most important time of day. When even the tower bell was rung. To announce and summon those darjeeling or lapsang suchong minded guests from their various suites. For a reawakening of the spirit when the aftermath of lunch produced drowsiness. And the soul required just the mildest bit of stirring. Being as it was that reflective time midway before one must preside over a long many coursed dinner, and precede that by one's early evening bath, the laying on of powders and scent, the hair coiffed and the dilemma of choosing gowns and the jewels with which to be adorned.

'There you are Master Reginald. Brought you a fresh pot. Bramble jam in the saucer. Fresh whipped cream in the bowl. And more toast. Will there be anything else.'

'Thank you Crooks. Close the shutters. Light the mantel candles. And I think that will be all. Except you can draw me my bath.'

'In the copper.'

'Yes in the copper.'

A smile on Darcy Dancer's muddy face. With his cheeks

fat with chewing. Trouser split down from my thigh and over my knee. The whole naked side of my scratched leg. Blotted with great bruises. Like the sky so often is. Blackened by a cloud floating across the bright blue. Welcome soothing red heat blasting out of these logs blazing. Darkness fallen. Wind blowing. Rain taps on the panes. Upon the graves of the dead. And I did not die lonely out there under that sky. Beyond these shutters banging closed. When you have no roof, no walls, no tea and no scrumptious other thing. Each night a long long night. Clutching oneself. Asking when will dawn ever make the black darkness be over. And my feet, hands, knees, arms and back be no longer cold. All glowing now. With tea.

'You haven't madam shown the least inclination towards embracing me. Am I so disreputable and soiled looking.'

'Well you might at least not bring the bog into the drawing room.'

'Ah that is precisely how I thought you might feel. Despite your superficial display of tolerance.'

Miss von B, her tweed jacket taken from her shoulders. The title of her book. Called *Priests and People in Ireland*. And leaning herself back now. Cushioned, as I am in the swan's down. The shoulders puffed up in her pleated grey wool dress. Making them unpleasantly broad. Perhaps she really is a sadist. With thonged whips. To lash bare flesh. Her bosoms only a reaching hand away. She inwardly winces each time I move. Or turns to stare a moment, drawing her lips tight as she did when in one single gulp I took my cup and drank it held with my soiled torn hand. I did however at first try not to cram the entire piece of barmbrack in my mouth. Only hungrily snapped off most of it but even that last little piece did not stay long in my fingers. And as I rammed it in it made her further tense. Till I thought she may have been pleased when I chewing so vigorously, bit my tongue.

'O fuck.'

'Serves you so right. To stuff your mouth.'

First Crooks leaves me on the doorstep. Then find the agent using the hall as if it were a train station. Now Miss von

B behaving in a most certainly shirty manner. Life does somehow allow one unhappiness to beget yet another. Start tumbling down all over you. One merely must then simply seek the nearest soothing comfort at hand. And enfold oneself there. Shift backwards into this swan's down softness. Watch with concealed enjoyment as she shrivels in distaste as each big lump of cake hardened mud is dislodged from me crumbling on the floor.

'Madam, are you a sadist.'

'What do you mean.'

'Are you in favour of cruelty. And of wiping certain races out.'

'If I think you are suggesting what I think you are suggesting, I should slap your face.'

'I'm merely inquiring.'

'And I am merely telling you I will slap your face should you ask such a question again.'

'O well perhaps that answers me.'

'Where have you been. To whom have you been talking.'

'No one in particular.'

'My god you should come back looking like that. And asking me such questions.'

'We have my good madam, been ratted upon.'

'What do you mean.'

'Someone of the household has well and truly snitched. My father has accused me of fornicating with you.'

'And what is fornicating.'

'It is, to use a vulgar but better known term, what is popularly referred to as fucking.'

'Grosser Gott.'

'Quite.'

'You I hope have said it is untrue of course.'

'Of course, that's what I immediately said. Totally untrue. Absolutely the most filthy and disgusting kind of fiction.'

'O god, how sad life can get so immediately after a moment when it was perhaps beautiful even if only for the shortest of time.'

'Have you madam fucked many others. Or put another

way, how many others have you fucked. Has my father been one of them.'

The blood leaving Miss von B's face. Tightens her finger about the handle of her tea cup. One wants to be so mean to her. To make her cry. And sob. And be defenceless and begging for help. Instead of being back here as she's been so comfortably these past miserable days.

'You are again I think in your most unpleasant mood. But I will answer your question. As to fucking. And that is what you mean. Yes.'

'Yes, it is.'

'I have, to use the phrase, fucked my share. Not your father. Nor anyone I did not respect. And certain things have happened to me. That I will not discuss at this time.'

'You have been raped, madam.'

'I have warned you, I shall slap your face. If you ask such questions again. What has become of you. Why are you like this. Sitting there, in rags. Like you were a tramp. You make me so angry.'

Miss von B standing. Putting her long angular fingers to brush back a strand of hair loose at her temple. A crumb on her wool dress tweezed between two fingers and put on her saucer. Lifts her tweed coat over her arm. Turns and places her book on the hunt table. She abruptly leaves. In what one would term a huff. Rather banging the door which shook the window panes. And Crooks took an unseemly delay to appear after I rang. Approaching me across the parlour floor using a bowing motion. As if he were a water pump.

'You called Master Reginald.'

'Yes Crooks. Decant our best laid bottle of Chateau Margaux. As well as that of our most ancient Chateau d'Yquem. Tell Catherine to prepare a roast side of beef. Rare. And not burned to a cinder. Nor perfectly raw either. And together with suitable gravy, choicest of spuds, selected sprouts, I want served an immortal meal.'

'I shall, of course, Master Reginald, as the available ingredients might allow do precisely as you instruct. For two.'

'For two.'

Following three more cups of tea and barmbrack and four slices of toast slathered in bramble jam I repaired to my room. To disrobe. To find most of me in my dressing mirror quite white except where the bruises were quite blue. The rain now blowing in gusts outside. And proceeded with some dispatch skipping over the rattling floorboards to bathe with all my scratches stinging. Could feel the smooth copper of the bath replenishing my blood. Making me quite chipper. Dressing for dinner. Till Crooks knocked. To announce that Miss von B sent her regrets and would not be joining me. In this my celebration of my most astonishing homecoming. Calling for my silk shirt removed from its protective tissues to stop it gathering dust. And also in view of the mournful news. Told me by Norah as she brought me towels from the kitchen oven. And said through the door. That the mighty and wilfully spirited Thunder and Lightning had been kicked to death when put to cover a young mare. Another blow fallen. Another revenue gone. About the only damn use that such news can be, is to older gentlemen to make them specially mindful of the antics of young ladies. But never mind. Distinctly more pleasant hours are upon me. My bath bringing out my embedded thorns and I squeezed and pinched away the pus. And as I descended the beech grove stairs heading for the library for a sherry before the fire, Crooks was backing his way with a tray out the door.

'Ah Master Reginald, it's a transformation.'

'Thank you Crooks.'

'But Master Reginald can I ask now, has anything happened that would make you curt with me.'

'Curt. I don't believe I have been curt Crooks.'

'Ah it's only that I'm mindful that there's been rumoured changes are coming.'

'What changes.'

'It's not my place to remark upon them Master Reginald.'

'Well you are making a damn good start if you don't mind my saying.'

'Now. That's the curtness I mean. Ah I'm getting on now.

There are not many years left me. Sure what do they do with old butlers but shed them. Like a dog's winter hairs in summer. And send them with their tray into the grave. And they don't know the good servant's gone till they're sitting in all their splendour waiting in the drawing room. Wondering what's holding up the refreshment after dingling the bell down the kitchen hall. And if it's me they're calling I'd be coming only that I'm gone. And with luck be up there serving God instead.'

'You're being most dramatic this evening Crooks. Do you think god prefers his sherry medium, dry or sweet.'

'Ah now, not to be impertinent, but that's blaspheming, Master Reginald. How would I know how almighty god prefers his sherry.'

'I'm sure some good butler must know Crooks. Surely god would not be without one who'd maybe been in ducal employ. And I think we are all quite conscious that certain good servants may go unappreciated. However, do let me point out. That not many of us may look to heaven as a place where we may continue our valued service on earth.'

'Ah well now some of us may not be wanting to go bowing and scraping continuously hereafter in the after life. Me own legs for a start wouldn't stand it.'

Crooks went mumbling off. I tarried in the hall. Looking up at my Thormond ancestors. To see in the faint light if their previous critical view of me had now changed since I was to put it mildly really decked out for dinner. But no expression seemed particularly approving. Indeed they appeared nearly more bored than usual. And in a moment Crooks was back again letting the side down in his slippers, the heels of which were clacking more loudly than ever. He put a plate of cut soda bread adorned with smoked salmon on a library side table. Miss von B was actually standing nearly in behind the door and I had closed it before noticing her. First catching upon my nostrils the immediate soft light sweetness of her perfume. No question but the time has come to be at my most gallant. Administer one's every charm. And sport the lady's every possibly courteous entitlement.

'Ah your highness, how pleasantly agreeable to see you. You have decided to join me.'

'Yes.'

'Why.'

Miss von B stepping towards Darcy Dancer in five long slow leisurely strides. Her whole beautifully undulating loveliness stopping in the candle light. The blonde long body rather more than apparent in her form flattering pale purple dress. And I do believe I may just be that fraction taller now. With all the leg stretching one has recently been doing. I was holding the neck of the sherry decanter. Prior to inquiring if madam would, as she frequently did, have hers pale medium. And wham. Good god. Stars. Absolutely like the ones one saw sparkling out there when the great bowl of black sky cleared one night over me. Nearly dropped the sherry. Rocked as I was back on my heels. With the stinging feel of her palm and fingers, right across my face, making the most frightful ringing in my ear.

'That is why. To slap your face.'

'My god I mean to say, look here.'

'You look here. And next time, don't you ever dare to address me in such manner as you did during tea.'

Miss von B in three or maybe slightly more steps. Vanished from the library. With the door slamming once more. Hardly the thing to do in a mansion which merely by brushing against a wall could bring the entire roof down. And leave me here covered in rubble. With nothing now whatever to celebrate. Sipping sherry. Nibbling salmon. And dear me, why should I care about another cursed thing. Except to preserve my own sweet life. Towards the destiny which the better of my past best ancestors ordain.

> And avoid
> Forever
> These
> Damnably difficult
> Women

16

'Shall I remove this setting Master Reginald.'

'No Crooks.'

'It's a grand roast of beef, Master Reginald, fetched this evening by urgent bicycle from the butcher's for your delectation.'

'That's most agreeable Crooks.'

'And done to a rare turn.'

'Most agreeable.'

Candelabra and sconces all lit. The fire roaring up the chimney. The wine crystal sparkling. Darcy Dancer seated end of the gleamingly polished mahogany. The chill blue colours of the onion pattern Meissen. Norah lugging in the covered dishes. Set by the hearth on the brass warming table. Crooks pouring my glass full of deep red softly fuming claret. A nice cool crack of breeze coming up between these two floor boards. Always means that less than arctic conditions are prevailing in the dining room.

Deliberately I delayed each course. Hoping Miss von B would reappear. Till Norah trying to catch her breath said that her Royal Highness was taking supper in her room. Somewhat mournfully I awaited Crooks to pour my lonely enjoyed Chateau d'Yquem. Knowing that madam especially would appreciate the noble rot of its rich textured pale goldenness softly sliding down the side of the glass rim and its musky heady scents wafting up the nostrils. And instead now she would I suppose, following her supper, be somewhere perusing another anti Catholic volume in the household. In her pale purple gown. By the library fire, or her legs wrapped in a rug in the chillier drawing room or parlour. Or perhaps even freezing her tits off waltzing by herself in the ballroom. As indeed I noticed before she slapped me that she was rather thinly covered there. And the welcome bosom swelling sight of her, did I thought, even make me feel a little dizzy, before as well as after her striking me. And I do indeed feel that way right now.

'Master Reginald, is there something wrong.'

'Well as a matter of fact Crooks I think I may be feeling rather heady.'

'It's that d'Yquem, the great accumulated golden overtones from sublime sauterne, would, with enough of it, put your brains pleasantly swirling. Sure it's the very mummified death of the grape you're drinking there.'

'Well I do believe my brain is, as a matter of fact swirling, or else the table is swaying.'

'Now would I fetch up a bit of our best brandy, it would bring you around in no time. There's a bottle in the cellar lain there since the middle ages for just such a moment as this.'

'I think, thank you Crooks, that I shall make do with d'Yquem. O god.'

'Good lord save us, Master Reginald.'

Darcy Dancer pitching forward. Face banging the table. To slowly keel over sidewards and fall to the floor with a room shaking thud.

'Master Reginald, can you hear me. Can you hear me. Are you all right. Norah, fetch Miss von B.'

Crooks walking stumbling upwards backwards, his hands caught under each arm of Darcy Dancer. Could feel his big fingernails digging into me. Hear all their voices. Out there beyond me in the dark. Even thought in my unconsciousness that a rake of an ancestor on the staircase wall winked at me. Miss von B in a big grey sweater over her gown. Had me by a leg. And Norah with her lace cap knocked askew, her hair loose was carrying the other. Could smell her rather strongly. Mixed with the clean sweet scent of Miss von B. But as the direction of the hall breeze changed, both ladies' essences were promptly drowned by the close up smell of Crooks. As he grunted, huffed and puffed shifting me up the beech grove stairs. And along the hall to my room. Backing through the door and loading me all black attired and silk shirted, flat out on my bed.

'Now ladies perhaps a gent should undress the poor young master. Leave it to a gent.'

'Crooks I am perfectly capable of undressing Master Darcy.'

'Ah well, would it be right and proper.'

'I am in fact quite a very capable nurse.'

'Very good then madam. Far be it for me to interfere.'

'Norah fetch me a hot bowl of water. And a thermometer.'

'What is a thermometer madam.'

'O dear then get hot bottles for the bed. And towels to wrap them in. And build a fire.'

'Very good madam. But is he dead.'

'No. But he will be if you do not quickly attend to what you have been asked.'

'O dear god, he was such a nice poor lad.'

Gales outside the bedroom window. Darcy Dancer's black black hair aswirl on the pillow. Some strands still entwined. From his cross country adventure. Miss von B leaning over with a cool compress. Touching it upon the fevered brow and the hot burning cheeks. Feel the touches one feels. Outside one's head. And inside like a big hand ahold of one's whole brain. Lifting me away out of my body. I was up there on top of spy glass hill. And it was summer again and Crooks had put together a picnic to have by the lake. And as I watched his old bent figure pack it on the float I felt somehow that that dear old strange fellow had not betrayed me.

Three days Darcy Dancer lay abed. In feverish semi consciousness. The gales blowing. Baskets of turf fetched to burn to keep the sparks from flying. Miss von B the morning after the collapse in the dining room, brought the doctor. Driving my mother's phaeton with Petunia like a whirlwind it was said, out and back along the drive. And he came then each morning smiling with his little case and stethoscope. Making cheery quips to Norah and Miss von B while he made me, half awake, roll my eyes, and cough with his stethoscope over my chest. A wooden stick pressed down my tongue as he looked down my throat by torch light. And late afternoon of that third day I saw Miss von B's anxious face. And Norah at her shoulder. My head felt so tight. My lungs full of rumbling and trying to catch my breath. Norah's hands entwined. And her eyes looking up to heaven as she mumblingly prayed and then whispered.

'The poor lad's dying isn't he. He's dying. Jesus Mary and Joseph. The poor lad's dying.'

Till I drifted off. And then heard whispers.

'It's the crisis now. It's the crisis.'

The tower bell rang. I thought all had been summoned to my room for tea. As I lay hot and swirling in dreams. Down at the foot of my bed. All hovering. As each now comes in. One by one. I'm dying. Sexton there. His head looming over the others. He had placed on my dresser a plaster statue of his Blessed Virgin, a special candle burning in a red glass in front of her. My sisters. Where are they. They loved me. There. That must be Beatrice Blossom in the corner of the room. And then it was Catherine the cook. Her one big old hand wiping itself across her apron, and a big ladle held in her other. Shaking her head sadly back and forth. I'm dying. Going down under the waves of sleep. Head Groom Slattery. Foxy furtively behind his shoulder. A smile ready to burst out on his face. Thought his eyes were looking around the room for something to rob. Now they were all filing in. As the first who came walked out. I'm already dead. They're just viewing the body. The silver hair of Edna Annie. Eyes sunk so deep in her head. Her great ancient purple veins under her parchment flesh. Yet soft as her bony hand touches against my cheek. Her words. Ah god love the little man put so soon out there now to rest under the lonely sky. Long before his time. Sure god in his mercy to a good little Protestant gentleman like that will give him the peace to die a good christian. Luke the groom. His ear now well healed but badly bent over at the scar where Foxy had nearly bitten it off. Norah and Sheila brushing at their uniforms and too terrified to come closer. My mother's two friends the clerics. So elegantly so darkly approaching. Both blessing me with prayers. Edna

Annie feeling her rosary beads through her hands saying the two parsons assembled together should do a power of good in heaven even with the unfortunate blasphemy of one being an Episcopalian. And voices. Please now. Time to go. Ah one last look. While he lives. Darcy Dancer. And Uncle Willie. The only one with tears in his eyes. And Miss von B stood there on the bedroom carpet. With all the other dark shadows gone. Her body all golden. Her belly softly round. Bosoms swelling full and fruity. Her arms raised from her sides. To welcome me into her embrace. And as I moved towards her I was walking on a road. Out there way beyond west of Thormondstown. Bordered by shrubbery trees. Marching with an ash plant through the boggy lands of the countryside. A cottage thatch ahead at the end of a path. An old woman in her shawl approaching. A farm labourer in his loose black old coat leaning by the side of the fence. Who doffed his cap to me. And I said, with no one in particular in mind to say it to. To hear me. And understand. That I am a member, perhaps presently in poor standing, of the landed gentry. I really am. And that I am possessed still, of all my gentility. Despite the depredations to my estates. And would not soon nor never be descending to the very last resort. That poor common dreadful state of being native. In rags, penury and ignorance. With big dirty fingernails. And clumsy boorish mind. And that still, the country women curtsy and the men remove their caps. As I pass by and go further. And there on the road ahead. Miss von B. A true real aristocrat. Glittering in diamonds. Her body waiting. Getting closer. Our nakednesses nearly in embrace. My arms widening to weave around her. And squeeze and squeeze. Nothing is there.

That evening it was said all over the household that a miracle had happened. That out of all the praying and right from the very sheer brink of death the very life of Darcy Dancer had been restored. The doctor came, ruddy cheeked and smiling as usual. To listen to lungs, spy down throats and read thermometers. And to say yes that the gentleman was indeed on the way to recovery. He came again next morning. Bright cheery and inquiring from Miss von B of the hunting.

Said there was the greatest story ever told in years going round the countryside. And he was sorry she hadn't yet heard it for it was not a story could be repeated by a gentleman to a lady.

Frost white out on the meadows. The air stilled under the sky once more after four days of blowing. Darcy Dancer sitting up clear eyed in bed. Sexton had brought bunches of tiny wild flowers he'd picked. And together with Miss von B placed and arranged them on my bedside and dresser tables. And then after my nourishing broth the next morning I even nipped out of bed to look out the window. At the sound of wheels over the pebbles. Luke the groom holding as Miss von B climbed in my mother's phaeton, called the High Crane Neck for its elegant curvatures. She looked so smart in her tweeds and bowler seated there atop. And her blonde hair peeking swelling out in a bun over her ears as she delivered a light flick of the whip over Petunia's quarters. To go off trotting away, perched so neatly upon the swan like springs. And indeed I had a little flutter of the heart. Till suddenly there were the boards creaking and there was Sexton himself standing at the foot of my bed. The great tall dark patched one eyed hulk of him. Cap under his arm. Hands joined in prayer. His hair greasier and blacker than ever. As if I were already this long time dead and he were praying for the repose of my immortal soul. And the Latin words mumbling out of him.

'Good lord Sexton. Look at me. I'm alive. Here by the window.'

'I was just praying in thanks for your safe deliverance from final darkness. Ah god Master Darcy, sine dubio it's like the time you were rescued from the bog. That last afternoon there I thought we would be bringing you beyond to the sods. Or if there's any suitable room left, be stacking you in with the rest of the Thormonds. And no sadness should that be, close with the unfaded beauty of your mother. Antoinette Delia Darcy Darcy. Wonderful woman. Ah god excuse me. Can't stop a tear or two at the mention of her very name. But sure the whole lot of us in this house will all be going that way soon. So fast there won't be them ones left to bury the others. How are you now.'

'I am feeling much better thank you, Sexton. But surely one can't say that you are exactly expostulating the most cheerful of views.'

'Views born in the bitterness of life they are. But I'm glad to hear that you're feeling better. It was as near a wake as ever I've seen. With the lot of them wailing down there in the kitchens you'd think you'd been already put cold out there under the meadow.'

'That is in its way complimentary Sexton. They could have been laughing and rejoicing.'

'Ah never Master Darcy. Sure like your mother they worship the ground you walk on. And speaking of walking I'm glad you're up doing it. Because let me tell you. The sooner you're about the estate the better. The depredations. The depredations would make you reel with consternation. That filthy little cur the agent. And there'll be others in on it with him. The looting and banditry. What's he doing but selling them fifty tall straight oaks. Planted by your great great grandfather and aged by the centuries. Majestic they are. Standing there in adoration of the great majesty above. Who gave them the ground in which to grow. The sacrilegiousness. It's sickening. Never mind the tuppence ha'penny that shrewd snake in the grass says he's not getting. O he's getting it alright. And it will be more than tuppence ha'penny he'll be keeping for himself. Be damned if it isn't.'

'You mustn't upset yourself Sexton. It is making you unduly red in the face.'

'Well I won't stand idly by and stomach that vulgar treatment of nature's beauty. Never mind the scurrilous wholesale robbery done thereby. I was up over there and told them there'd be repercussions. I told them. And six of them great majestic oaks down already. In the garden out there I can hear them up beyond, poor trees, screaming in agony on the ground.'

'O Sexton, you do get distressed don't you.'

'Well Master Darcy, I've spent nearly all my years with

the growing living things and the beauties of God. And sure in this country where treachery and deceit were invented, and where if the crowd of them could find any semblance of beauty not doing a soul any harm, they'd have an axe to it in an instant swinging it lashing in every blessed direction till not a sacred contour of its beauty was left.'

'Well perhaps Sexton we can at least change to another mournful subject. Thunder and Lightning is no more.'

'Pulverized he was by that mare. All his power beat out in seconds. In the hounds' belly now, every bit but the biggest bones of him. And speaking about hounds. And mentioning hunts. Ah god there tells a story. Mournful and disgraceful enough too. Didn't some tinker rascal who could jump a horse over the moon and thread four hooves through the eye of a needle, steal off with the master's horse, over a parish or two there beyond. And the whole hunt after him. The cowards and all. Coming out of their saddles, busting their heads on branches. And now rumour has it. And a filthy disgusting rumour it is too. That the entire lot of them pursuing the villain went cascading down that old lime avenue over there and other side of Thormondstown. The foul demeaning stories coming out of there. Slandering that lovely blue eyed beauty. Haven't I said she's a distant relation of the Thormonds. Haven't I told you that.'

'You've told me that, I believe Sexton.'

'Well slurring her name they are. All over the countryside. Licking their lips. Whispering. Disseminating the most unspeakable of the unspeakable. I wouldn't repeat it. Never never in a million years would I repeat it.'

'Repeat what Sexton.'

'What them rabble rousers of them mad bloody hatters, or cappers, or natters or whatever they call them bloody selves. Are saying.'

'What for heaven's sake Sexton are they saying.'

'That she was compromised. Compromised I'm telling you. Besmirched.'

'Dear me. What a dastardly business. But how. How could anyone compromise such an elegant young lady, Sexton.'

'Well in not more than two dozen words now. I'll tell you how. Didn't the entire hunt chasing this rascal come upon her and that Mental Marquis. In the middle of the lime avenue. With every last horse having to jump the pair of them stark naked together entwined on the grass. That's what they're saying. With the hounds, the fox, the huntsman, whipper in, and the Master looking for his horse, all thundering over them. Ah god I hate to have to use such an expression but next they'll be saying that the fox ran up the poor girl's hole.'

'O dear what a bother isn't it Sexton.'

'Well let me tell you Master Darcy if a one of them comes repeating that story to my face they'll get a fist in the gob for their trouble. Ruining the girl's pure virgin name, that's what the gossipy swine are doing. Tongues never still. Wagging and wagging. In one shopkeeper's ear and out to a dozen others. And in a thrice don't they have the whole story all over Ireland.'

Under the sheets to muffle my sounds I did laugh rather heartily the moment Sexton stepped back out again into the hall. Indeed I nearly kicked the bottom of the bed out. And finally did. With Miss von B bringing me beef tea, tucking it all back in again. Although kindly she was continuing to be distant. I did dizzily recall the intimacy of her rolling me over upon my stomach and intruding a cold thermometer into where I thought it was quite indiscreet in front of Norah. But Miss von B as I groaned my reluctance insisted that it was the only proper place to take a temperature. It seemed a long time before she pulled it out again, reading it in front of the wall sconces brought up from the dining room. One admired her lack of squeamishness. For two more days when I wasn't feeling like an overly cosseted baby, I felt like a long piece of overly boiled cabbage. As the household rallied about leaving me with little peace. In with breakfast. Out with lunch. Back with tea. And flowers and visitors and tidbits in between. But there are times when it requires just too much energy to protest.

Saturday morning. With a red dawn and this day growing

crisp and sunny. In a long mauve dressing gown with chocolate brown borders and facings, Darcy Dancer sitting by his
fire. Sporting these, my mother's racing colours. While
suitably and contentedly reading *Priests and People in Ireland*.
Of the low morality rampant in the Mecklenburg Street area
of Dublin. Ladies of ill fame. Children kidnapped into vice.
And in which volume it frequently appeared that Catholics
did behave quite disgracefully. Of course one is always glad to
be Protestant. But there are times when one is extremely glad.
However I read with much interest of the Discalced Carmel-
ites and how these gentlemen had established an oratory in
honour of the divine child, Jesus of Prague, in whose devotion
wonderful graces might be obtained. And I must confess,
just for the novelty of it I prayed as one heard Sexton praying,
to this Jesus of Prague to bring me back my strength. As every
time I went now to pee or move my bowels, my legs were
deucedly weak under me. And while I sat absorbed earnestly
praying I heard the floor board squeak. And perceived from
an eye. Miss von B at the door ajar. As she peeked in.

'Please. Madam. Please. Come in.'

Miss von B in her brown hunting coat and white breeches.
One gloved hand holding the glove of the other. The blonde
buns of hair caught by a net either side of her head. And the
red mark of her bowler striped across her brow. Her cheeks
ruddy. Her riding boots black and so gleaming. Her bosoms
swell up beneath her dark brown sweater and a gold pin stuck
in the silk stock at her throat.

'Ah I do not want to disturb you. Each time I come. There
is already someone here. How are you.'

'I am feeling immeasurably improved today. Thank you.
You have been out exercising.'

'Yes. We went a long ride around the lake. We were lost
but behind Kern and Olav I found my way again. And I am
pleased to see you so much better.'

'I shall be up and about by Monday.'

'No. You must not. I do not think the doctor would allow
that.'

'I must. To stop them taking away our trees.'

'You are still so thin, pale. You take too much responsibility. What matter a few trees. There are thousand and thousand.'

'I want nothing further to leave this place, not a branch, piece of straw or blade of grass.'

'And of course, what does it matter if they take a few bits of wood. They pay something. It would be more important if they pay nothing and they take your cattle, your land, or even the beauty from your face.'

'They are indeed madam already taking these things. And more often than not, paying nothing.'

'Ah my poor darling. There is but one thing that is important, that no one can ever take your good manners from you.'

'Miss von B. I thank you for saying that. Undeserved as I fear it may be. And especially in the light of my recent life. I do appreciate it. I think I am at a cross roads. And which way I turn may indeed be the direction of my whole destiny.'

'Ah you are far too young to speak so. Life it comes. Bang. It knock you a little this way. Bang. It knock you a little bit the other way. And the direction you go. Well you are lucky if it is not backwards.'

'Or bang, it could madam, flatten one altogether.'

'Yes, it does do that too. But then we must get up again.'

'I am going to get up and go away from here.'

'Come come. In this house, as I say so often to you, this is where your life will be. You are sitting reading, so comfortably your book. Where it tell you how to bribe a saint and about the sin, priests and beggars everywhere. What could make a good Protestant gentleman happier. And you can as you will do, read just like that into your old age.'

'My father will come. We shall argue. I know.'

'How do you know he will come. When he did not come when I. Ah perhaps I should not say.'

'Say what.'

'O please, let us forget. It was nothing.'

'It is something. You said my father did not come. When I was dying. That's what you meant.'

'He may not have got the cable. Plus as you know, you did not die.'

'Yes, plus, I do know. But he will. He will come as soon as I stop the agent from selling the trees.'

'Too many rashers of bacon for you at breakfast, that is what the matter is. You are getting your oats. Feeling them I mean. With your appetite back.'

'I am I must admit rather deeply at this moment feeling my oats. And further for a long time now I have in fact been thinking. That things may not remain the same as one had expected they might. Especially now that Mr Arland has left.'

'I did myself too become much fond of Mr Arland.'

'O dear, I do desperately miss him. We did have some rather nice evenings together. One does not want to be unseemly and sentimental. But I cannot imagine my future here now. Andromeda Park is rather just a big old rambling monument to antiquity. And I do believe I've outgrown it.'

'Come come. What is this. First no one is to take away a blade of grass. And now you speak of going away. And leave altogether. Ah I think you are just a little low after your sickness.'

'The best part of my indisposition I suppose has been that you are now speaking friendly to me again. And that madam, is making me distinctly more content.'

'Ah little man sometimes you are so sweet.'

'Why madam do you stay here.'

'Because there is plenty to eat.'

'I see.'

'Ah but I am half joking of course. I stay because I like it. At first I did not like you. But now I like you. And I like to live in the country. It is somewhere very pleasant. When you have nowhere. Of course I miss the mountains. The snow. The skiing. The crisp cold air. And the white everywhere. But then here there is the hunting. And such beauty over the fields. The crazy people who hunt. Who give me a laugh. Like imbeciles when the fox run out, they all shout and scream which way he went. So I shout too.'

'Of course madam that is quite incorrect. To point to the

line the fox has taken you must put your horse in that direction, take off your hat and hold it out in front of you.'

'But of course which of them could do that, each with a bottle of whiskey in them before breakfast they don't know where they point.'

'Please madam, come closer. I do like that coat on you. And you know don't you that I have been very much wanting these days to put my arms around you. And hold you.'

'Ah ha. How do you say, you are randy.'

'That is not madam a ladylike term.'

'Ah but it is what you are.'

'Please don't make light of my feelings. It's not usually customary for me to express myself in this candid fashion concerning one's deeper emotions. You wouldn't would you, think it was disagreeable if I could just rest my head against your bosom.'

'I will perhaps if you are a good boy, come back later tonight. And hold your hand.'

'Now.'

'No. Anyone could come in. Why do you take such a risk. When your father is suspicious already and you have run away from school.'

'Well then we must do all we can do right now. Otherwise everything is going to be too late.'

'Ah a relief to hear someone is in a rush. That is welcome for a change.'

'Are you going to the next meet of the hunt.'

'Yes.'

'I shall join you.'

'But you are not to do so. You are to stay as the doctor says, indoor for some time yet. And certainly not to hunt. So many are out who are all so stupidly dangerous.'

'Ah madam in hunting there are but two words about safety. Should this in the least concern you, the words are. Don't hunt.'

Sunday the sun outside was momentarily shining bright as heaven, as Sexton would say, and feeling much stronger, I walked through the house. Even to the spick and span ballroom. The parquet all waxed and gleaming. Where I felt it might be time for me to hold a grand party. Invite everyone of note from all over the countryside excluding only the very meanest. Unless they were especially of significance. No point in cutting off one's social nose just to stick to one's principles. And let them drink the cellars clean. Then before I decamp, pile straw in some quantity in the front hall and set to it a match and burn the whole ruddy place down just as the local peasantry have been threatening to do for centuries.

Darcy Dancer passing down the hall to the schoolroom. On the wall the old barometer newly cleaned. Its brass polished and hung back up again where it had not been for years. Its gilt doves surmounting its dial nestled in gilt oak boughs. Makes one feel you know the mystery of what's happening out across the skies. And its rectangular mirror flanked by thermometers. Reading as usual rather cool interior temperatures and the weather pointer pointing as it always did between variable and rain. Everywhere one sees the work of Miss von B. Her constant improvements are the only things that give one hope for the future.

From out of the back of the library clock Darcy Dancer fetched the key to the gunroom. To unlock the big heavy iron barred door to that windowless chamber and therein choose from the mahogany rack of firearms my grandfather's best shotgun. To polish and wipe clean its barrels of dust. Fill my gunbelt with a dozen cartridges. Just as Crooks pushed open the door.

'Begging your pardon Master Reginald. I wasn't sure that it was your footsteps I heard on the floor below in the wine cellar. You're shooting.'

'Yes Crooks, thought a few snipe wouldn't come amiss.'

'There should be plenty down in the bottoms. You'll lock up well now Master Reginald. It wouldn't do if any unauthorized person should have access in here. It's this arsenal that keeps them having a second thought who would be contemplating getting past Kern and Olav with a mind to trespass in this house. And that scoundrel Foxy Slattery has been at the door with a chisel more than once.'

After lunch in my room and following a brief walk in the orchard and garden and through the farmyard where there seemed still fewer pigs and chickens in evidence, I returned with my legs decidedly springier and feeling quite refreshed. Went to take tea by the fire in the north east front parlour. Miss von B who said she had finally given up smoking and now had to occupy her mind, was seated with a local newspaper which was blotched and wet and brought personally for her by Luke all the way on his bicycle from the town in a miracle of speed and dispatch when an English ladies' fashion magazine he'd been sent to collect didn't arrive. The presence of a newspaper was in fact quite unprecedented. As my grandfather, who did not believe in modern communications, maintained that you could by human voice and ear, get enough news of anything that mattered within five miles of Andromeda Park to last you a lifetime and he would therefore have no newspaper or radio in his house. Much to the irritation of my father, my mother inherited this same principle. And now Miss von B totally hidden behind newsprint, was laughing. Rather uproariously I thought. And crossing and recrossing her legs most provocatively under her clinging grey wool dress. Perhaps she needs to take one hell of a hearty pee.

'Would you mind awfully pouring me some more tea.'

'Ah I am sorry.'

'What has you so damned amused.'

'Here, you should read. It is always of course, just like I say. The whole place is nuts.'

Miss von B's finger pointing to the headline across the entire top of the page. Which I hold up between my two nervous hands. As one certainly does not know what and who, and especially including one's self, will be the latest news these days.

SACRILEGIOUS ROBBERY

On Friday evening last, the Parish church near Thormondstown was broken into and robbed of vestments and a cask of the finest old Marsala Altar Wine. The empty cask was later found in the chapel graveyard. The Police are seeking to interview a man they think can help them in their further inquiries.

The man in question was seen by a witness who described him as 'laggards drunk' and who was spreadeagled on a memorial stone not far from the cask, singing 'It's A Long Way To Tipperary' in a riotous manner, considering the vicinity. Witness thought that in the interests of keeping the peace he should inquire as to what such person was doing on the grave stone. As the witness who wishes to remain anonymous, more closely approached, he was at first aghast to see that it was a priest who was there prostrated and he immediately suspected that the reverend gentleman was delirious as a result of foul play. However as he inquired of the prone figure as to whether he could be of assistance to him, he was met with shouts and arm waving and loudly told to F off. Realizing this was not the language of a man of god he attempted to ascertain the identity of the stretched out form and thought he recognized the face of a person he had seen upon occasion in the district who had a reputation of a violent nature. This impression was immediately reinforced with the prone figure becoming quickly erect and with further use of obscene language and threats witness thereupon realized the fruitlessness of pursuing further pacification.

However the witness in beating a quick retreat, was then without provocation attacked, taking upon his face a swipe of a fist and his backside sustaining a kick of a boot. Witness said that in the circumstances he was forced to run every which way hopping over the gravestones for his very life, and as a consequence went down into a hole involuntarily disturbing and desecrating the dead and badly twisting both ankles where he lay incapacitated till dawn. The fact that his pursuer was in priestly robes and spouting filthy language left him with a very bad taste in his mouth.

The garda should like the assistance of anyone who

might have knowledge of the incident to help them in pursuing their further investigation.

I did think that Miss von B as she took the paper back again and slowly read aloud certain passages that she was rather making much of it all in ridiculing our simple country ways.

'They are so funny.'

'Well I'm glad you think so.'

'Ah but you must forgive one. Imagine two broken ankles he gets falling into someone's grave.'

'They were sprained as a matter of fact. And how would you like it if someone trampled your skeleton.'

'O dear you are so serious sometimes.'

But in any event I was quite certainly serious about the way Miss von B's grey wool dress looked quite stunning with a very large thick leather belt and a big brass buckle tightening it snug around her. And I did not really mind her being so amused. And must confess my penis was painfully hard as I stared with great excitement at the way her girth made her waist so slender and her hips and bosoms swell so splendidly out. To use Miss von B's unladylike word I was indeed randy. Even as I managed to change the subject of rural indiscretion to discussing my pedigree. As Miss von B had been previously leafing through the vellum volume describing it.

'I am at least agreeably surprised by the Thormonds and the Darcys. But nowhere can I find the name Dancer.'

She of course quite cleverly ruined all the compliments by stating that so much Irish ancestry had been compromised by parlour and scullery maids, grooms, gardeners and game-keepers. And that it could hardly be discerned by appearance as to who was mistress and master and who was servant or menial. I don't know what on earth she thought we gentry did all the time, if indeed we had any free from our presum-ably constant putting it up our various female staff. I mean we really didn't sit around all day as I only just happen to be doing with damn big erections. Or indeed, having the lady of the house get it put up her by stablemen, cowherds and shepherds. Her whole aspersion began to be quite heinous. Especially as to most of us being English, Jews or Danes and that the fine blood of those races had been horribly diluted by that of the native peasant Gael. I was quite alabaster faced with anger. I mean to say, one's pedigree gives one confidence to keep others in their place. She did however finally smile in the firelight and say I was singularly possessed of an amazing resemblance to Uncle Willie. Whose most attractive eyes were further apart than my father's and who also had my upper class jaw and cheekbones.

'Ah yes, all is not completely lost. You have at least, the good bone structure.'

That late evening following supper in my room, and when Crooks had left my hot drink by my bedside, Miss von B came. She had quite marvellously and magically repaired my suit and darned so beautifully my socks worn in my cross country escape. But I of course despite my penis bulging in my trousers, could not help immediately resuming defence of my ancestry. The whole damn issue had already ruined my enjoyment of the rather tasty boiled bacon and cabbage and buttered spuds Catherine had dished up. But as I was about to let her have a socially redeeming salvo or two, she opened before me a black leather album embossed with a coat of arms and full of photographs.

'I brought this for you to see.'

Bending close by me her soft grey breast touched my cheek. I couldn't just grab her as I dearly wanted at that moment or I'd muck up her album. As her fingers turned the black sheets of pages of pictures of her when she was a little girl. With the castles and palaces where she grew up. And in front of which, festooned in furs in the winter snows, she sat in a horse drawn sled. Of course it was quite grandly embellished and there was a coronet obvious on the sled's lantern lights which she did not allude to. In other pictures she was on skis, big boots on her feet. And then there she was in a hay meadow in front of a hunting lodge with balconies growing flowers. Smiling in her native costume. A bonnet on her head and holding a big scythe.

'All the colours you cannot see were in the meadow and also in my frock.'

As each page turned she grew bigger. Then there were pictures of her with other girls, her bare arms crossed. And in one, she sat in the long grass on a hillside overlooking a castle. She said she was angry at that moment. She would not say why. Nor when I asked, was she entirely forthcoming as to whose particular castle it was. But it was suitably impressively imposing sitting there with numerous turrets and battlements. And then on the castle terrace she sat a smiling jolly looking girl. Who seemed she might enjoy a good joke and play tricks on you and not nearly be so solemn as she seems now.

'And here we are for the boar hunting.'

A photograph in a valley on an edge of forest with great white capped mountains rising out of the steep wooded hillsides all around. Gentlemen in breeches and boots and others in short leather trousers with staves and their hats with brushes sticking out. She showed me her robust grandfather with a great moustache and big watch chain across his chest. I thought he looked quite an ordinary chap as a matter of fact. And another sadder one of her walking along a country road in a black dress and a coat tied half way closed and her long tresses over her shoulders. Which she said fell reaching all the way down to her bottom.

'The week before this picture was taken, the handsome Count to whom I was betrothed had while skiing disappeared forever in an avalanche of snow. In my face you can see the end of the world.'

And that, by my reckoning anyway, was three poor gentlemen of whom she was clearly enamoured gone to their doom. She was clearly such a nice girl. Although in the picture she was only seventeen, she seemed quite grown up. Behind her all in black as well, was her favourite aunt called Mafalda.

'She did my dear lovely aunt die six months later of consumption. Her husband, he was dead but a year later of grief.'

'You have haven't you madam, had much sorrow in your life.'

'Ah but when you expect little else, it is then just life.'

'I do think I live in quite as grand a house as some of those you have lived in.'

'Ha ha.'

'I do think so, madam. I really do. Especially when you include our ballroom.'

'This. Just look. This is my uncle's castle. Andromeda Park you could fit into the drawing room and sit on the chimneytop and not be able to touch my uncle's chandeliers. And besides inside there is beauty and elegance. Not like here, where everything is ruin. There everything it was polished, spotless. Gold leaf, it was simply everywhere. Pearl, marble. Not like this, rotting boards, damp crumbling plaster, pipes that you do not know where they go or what will come out of them.'

'I rather take that amiss you know.'

'Ah you poor little peasant, you get so upset when I point out to you that there are far grander places out in the rest of the world. You have never for instance been in a palace. Have you. Come now. Have you.'

'Of course I have, as you well know. I've been in the great castle.'

'Nothing. Absolutely mere nothing. A palace is so much more splendid. With long long halls of mirrors. Ceilings of mirrors.'

'Well, when our ballroom shutters are closed they are inside painted gold.

'You do not paint gold. It is with a hammer you make it into like a leaf.'

'Well we did have mirrors in our own dining room ceiling. My grandfather had them put there. So he might by casting his eyes upwards peer down upon the ladies' bosoms and the only reason they were taken away was because the hot dishes from the kitchens fogged them over which angered him when he couldn't see the ladies' décolletage and he had them removed.'

Miss von B and I went on and on about our various lists of embellishments. I nearly punchéd her when she just laughed in a superior manner when I told her of the vine my grandfather had trained to grow from the greenhouse through a hole in his bedroom wall so that he could eat grapes in bed. I thought it a jolly good damn idea even though the grapes never ripened. And then she spoke of all manner of architectural accoutrements, formal gardens and water works. I did somehow think that she was rather putting it on. Assuming graces to which she was not entitled. With her princes, princesses, dukes, duchesses, counts and I may as well say it, cunts and their seemingly endless castles and palaces to which she was privy. In order that I should feel that Andromeda Park was not quite grand enough. Nor my blood royal blue. However I made it quite clear that the Thormonds had not descended to squalor and we could easily claim to be a minor dynasty with a standing in society quite assured. And for many miles about one was still accustomed to locals giving way on the roads. Fortunately, when finished viewing her album we only kept on earnestly discussing that kind of thing for another few hours till perhaps well past midnight. And I was nearly hoarse. When she finally said.

'You take it all so seriously. I am not saying you do not live here in some refinement.'

'You are. If you are not directly saying we have descended to squalor then you most certainly infer a distinct lack of stylishness.'

'Ah. In that, there is far more than a lack. There is none.'

'What. How dare you. My sisters are ladies of rank and my mother bought her better things from the very leading London shops across the water. And I say damn you.'

'Ha ha. You sweet little man. Do not upset your lovely dark curls or your vivid marvellous eyes. What matter is it, a little lack of as you say, stylishness.'

And I did so want to kiss her. To put my lips on her soft smooth skin. O god I was nearly dying to. Utterly mad to. And to undo that belt around her waist. And then replace it with my arms squeezing her tight. Her slight aloofness these past few days was most irritating. Not to say inciting to sheer blatant lust. And I felt she might be heeding the attentions of other men. Some perhaps as odious as the agent with whom she admitted she sat for more than just the cursory moment in the parlour.

'Are you not going to allow me to touch you.'

'No.'

'Why.'

'It is that time of the month when ladies don't.'

'But you would otherwise.'

'Ah, who knows.'

'Are you no longer in love with me.'

'Love. My god. Love.'

'Yes. Love. Or are you now frightened that we may be spied upon.'

'Love. That is such a silly word.'

'Why.'

'Because love is a future and what future is there. For me. For you. Ladies must think always of the future. Her beauty is her future. It is that which makes men want you. When it is gone all is but beautiful memories. You must then have things which replace the attentions of men. It is most important.'

'Like doing embroidery you mean.'

'Yes.'

'You will always be beautiful. My mother was. And I could hire you forever. Then you could go and sit with Edna Annie down in the laundry and do embroidery. It's warm there mostly.'

'You want a sock in the jaw.'

'No please.'

'Anyway you would not want me around forever, I assure you. As every little lady in the countryside is beaucoup busy counting your acres, your horses and grooms. Even already I notice how they are riding at your back at every hunt. Keeping close and following you like the hounds do the fox. Just waiting for the moment when she can toss her head and attract your eye and procure you.'

'Your English madam has improved marvellously but procure, I think is hardly the word.'

'Ah perhaps the word is then conquer, snare, make a grab. Catch you. I practise my English. But two hours every day is not enough. And I will need to be expert to find another job.'

'Are we now discussing the down to earth probability that you and I shall be departing soon.'

'I think so, yes. I mean but a day or so ago you were gone.'

'But I am here. And I may be deeply in love with you.'

'You would be certain if you were.'

'Well perhaps I yet will be. When I've thought extensively enough about it. But I could be already. Other men are attempting to befriend you I suppose.'

'Ah of course, there are always men. Who are maybe bored trying putting it up the sheep. There is the Major, the agent, Murphy the farmer. There is hardly a shortage. Even the Mental Marquis.'

'You are sometimes a little brutally blunt madam. But what did the Marquis do.'

'O he let me know when he saw my long magnificent legs that how do you say, that he fancies me.'

'That does not become you to brag like that.'

'Ah you are angry.'

'He fancies Baptista.'

'Dumb minded little bitch.'

'Well she may be quite stupid in brains but the Marquis it would appear was quite happily content to ravish that part of her body not containing them. The whole of the Moonhound Mad Hatters hunt came upon them in the woods. Stark naked on top of one another.'

'I do not believe it.'

'It is absolutely true, ask Sexton.'

'Ah then who was on top. Baptista or the Marquis.'

'The Marquis as a matter of fact. And you may think it's all a joke but there are many witnesses should there be any doubt as to the accuracy of the matter.'

'How very unsporting. The Marquis crushing such a small girl into the grass. And how indiscreet of the Marquis in front of people. But how typical of the little bitch. To choose to open her legs in such a theatrical place where the hunt would find them. And how very inclement and how very unfastidious to know no better than to be on the wet ground. It serves her right.'

'And now madam, it is you who is angry.'

'Certainly not. But the hunting field is not the proper situation for the parting of a lady's lower limbs other than upon her saddle. And even then it is not preferable for her to be mounted astride.'

'Do you not agree that their blood, madam, must have been up. Or if they were leisurely doing gates together, I do believe they may have grown rather familiar. And then as often happens in our mild wintry countryside, a lady and gentleman so delegated, are pausing also to build back up walls, with the lady bending over and her behind flattened by tight breeches, does thereby give a gentleman the opportunity to take an unpremeditated fancy and that the parties then promptly, even in the deep mud, disrobe, and there entangled go splashing and sloshing.'

'Sweet one I do wish the time of the month for me were different and then I would have you do more than to pull my leg.'

'Madam honestly I do not pull your limb as enchanting as that should be to do. Quite seriously often when one is jumping a wall in chasing a backtracking fox one does find that there, sheltering in the lee of the boulders, there are pumping pairs of nude bottomed hunt members absolutely lust embroiled out of their minds and crazed with a lasciviousness that would be hard to believe.'

'And how would you Master Kildare, like if I should give you a nice bath before you try to tell me any more tall stories. If you do not mind the little smell the water has of dead mice who rot in the water tank.'

'Dead mice tend to sweeten the water madam. But do you really mean that madam. You will give me a bath.'

'Yes I do really mean that. But do not let your eyes pop out.'

'They are not popping out. But that would be most cordially splendid of you. And I do really most marvellously appreciate your so beautifully refurbishing my suit. You are, aren't you, a really clever lady. You really are.'

'Well really. Then you really come. And really flattery will get you far. And really right into the bath which really I shall as you say really draw for you. Which really stinks of dead mice.'

'You mustn't madam. I can't help it if I really get excited.'

'But ah I really like it when you do. I really do.'

'And I shall never say that word again.'

'Unless of course you are. Really excited.'

Darcy Dancer in his mother's racing colours. Behind this bathroom door firmly locked. Candles burning in the chill steam rising from the copper. Disrobing before Miss von B. Was throbbingly thrilling. It really was. To have one's penis stand up towards the ceiling pointing at her belt buckle. It felt distinctly ticklish, for want of a better word to use. And I do believe Miss von B was casting brief admiring looks at it. As I made it twitch up and down. She seemed to take such instant open hearted interest in such things. As often she would remark quite casually upon the enormity of Thunder and Lightning's engorged penis when we had occasion to be together near that now sadly departed stallion. Who got an erection immediately any lady came within sniffing distance. Madam also had a certain fearlessness which was devilishly attractive. That she might do whatever I might saucily off the top of my head suggest to her.

'Would you grab it madam. Please.'

'Ah you are always so in readiness with that, are you not.'

'It is I think merely the gush of blood to that part due to the bathroom chill.'

'It is just as I say, your randiness. And you are twitching it.'

'But your merely taking hold of it might calm it down.'

'You devil.'

Although my penis kept mightily rigid I pretended that

one was not in the least excited. After all one had posed this way for artists. But I was most embarrassed just as I, while lifting my leg to climb into the bath, without warning, hopelessly unintentionally but loudly and at length, farted. One bang followed about four others. And in utter anguished mortification I lowered myself to nearly drowning in the water and watched as she sniffed and then brought her finger pinching both her nostrils closed.

'Peewewew.'

'I do, my god, madam apologize. Honestly. I really do. It just came out.'

'Ah but I really think at least you did it with a certain aristocratic charm. That is what matters my darling. My Darcy. My Dancer. It was just perhaps a trifle too big a bang for it to be royal but it was aristocratic enough.'

'I do thank you for letting me off so easily. You could have pretended to be quite offended and I wouldn't have in the least blamed you.'

'Such things my dear darling are the real music of love. And often such tunes play long after the kisses have stopped.'

'My goodness that is madam an awfully nice turn of phrase. You really are a one. Aren't you. O dear that word again.'

Miss von B had with her a most elegant pedicure outfit in a black crocodile case, vaguely resembling one belonging to my mother. Pearl handled silver little instruments. Each with a coronet on the handle. Which did appear to be that of a Duke. But one has had enough of that thorny subject and that's when I think I expanded my chest in order to present a muscular image to her which exertion put pressure on my belly and made me break wind. Serves me jolly right for showing off. I should have been enough content to enthrall Miss von B with my elevated penis. As the tip top of it was now doing as a periscope, lying back in these hot waters. Miss von B leaning over me smiling. Taking each of my hands in hers and with my wrist over the edge of the bath resting on a towel as she clipped my nails one by one. Pushing back the skin to show, she said, a little bit of moon. Then filing each gently round. Such divine deliciousness of the pressure of her fingertips on mine. Then taking each foot up over the side of the bath. And from each toe the nail was trimmed. She had rather to struggle a bit to cut my main ones.

'Like elephant tusk these are.'

'But that's what we Irish use to dig our potatoes with.'

Miss von B flicked bath water in my face and then frowned and made a mock funny expression with her mouth. It was quite damn easy to keep her amused in fact. And the muscles flexed along her forearm and the white neat scar there. She's so absolutely right. They were indeed rather long and thick. Resting my head back against the soft slipperiness of the copper I could see Miss von B was really putting her all into pressing together the scissor handles. And when she leaned back on her heels to take a much needed rest she was more than somewhat impressed with the Thormond coat of arms emblazoned on the bath. At least it was a little evidence of our ancestral haughtiness that one must not lightly overlook. One did not want to resurrect our social fencing match but I thought it was as well that it was made known especially in view of her coronet on her pedicure instruments.

'Ah I shall agree my sweet fellow it is quite haughty. And of course it has the simplicity of those escutcheons which carry the most ancient distinctions.'

Quite obviously one must accept that one is the product of one's antecedents and Miss von B had previously rather made one feel rather socially less esteemed. So her observation certainly made me feel much much better. Although good god, with one so lazily warm in the bath, I was feeling so damn good anyway. Recovered from death. Clonking the gunman and nearly committing my first murder. A temporary horse thief and highwayman. But then one must suppose that everyone really is trying to knock or demean you somehow. And whatever it is one may profess to be. How pleasant for a change, to have a little social flattery. So many have so little of anything. Like poor Lois. All she wanted she said, was someone to love and love her. And good lord, it seems that simply everyone is running around looking for that. Makes for such a ruddy mêlée. With people bumping indiscreetly into each other all over the place.

'And now shall we wash your hair.'

'Yes please, indeed do.'

'And we hope we shall not get too much of Edna Annie's strong soap in your eyes.'

'Madam when you were in Dublin, what was your life like.'

'It was work. It was sometimes funny, sometimes sad and sometimes highly irritating. Now just put back your head.'

'When was it irritating.'

'When these women come in for their hats who think they are the cat's whiskers. Now close your eyes.'

'Surely that must have been unpleasant, having social inferiors in a position to command you about.'

'O perhaps. How is one to mind about such things. If you want their money, then you must give them what they want. And you cannot then pretend to be better than them.'

'And did you have gentlemen friends.'

'Ah but that is none of your business. Back again with your pretty head please.'

'I am merely inquiring about your life. In which, if you don't mind my saying, it is not in the least unusual, considering our relationship, that I should take an interest.'

'Ah well then. My life. I shall speak of. But not the gentlemen in it. For there is a rule which women are unwise to break. And that is to talk of men to other men. There were of course parties. Every night. They bring back drink from the pub. Everyone becoming drunk. So boring. They sing, then they argue. Then they fight. Then they wash off the blood, shake hands. And drink again. And then fight. Night after night it is like that.'

'Dear me.'

'The next afternoon they meet in the pub to talk of the night before. Of how much they drink, about who was fighting, about how many teeth knocked out or fingers broken. It is like a race they are in. Who has drunk the most. Who slaps his wife the hardest. It is like a club. Which the members have joined so that they all go to hell together. They are all so proud of the hangover they say that morning they wake up with. Like it was a halo. How they give their wife a fist in the gob. Or they say a boot in the hole if she protest that they broke down the front door to get in the house. So many such simple sad little people. Who read the gas meter. Who own a shop. Who have maybe some business. Or uncle who leave them money. And there is a crazy lady artist always inviting them to her studio to paint their privates.'

'Are these people not what one calls Bohemians.'

'Bohemians. Ha ha. They say they are poets when they are pigs. Pee everywhere and shit anywhere. They are imbeciles. They say they write books. When they only sharpen pencils and pull corks out of bottles of stout. Their moments of glory are when they can find someone they can insult.'

'You do madam, don't you, rather paint an unpretty picture.'

'Well perhaps it might only have been like that on Saturdays, Sundays, Mondays, Tuesdays, Wednesdays and Fridays.'

'What about Thursday.'

'They sleep that day.'

Miss von B rinsing Darcy Dancer's hair. Pouring glasses of mouse tainted chilly water out of the tap. Sweeping back the wet locks from my forehead. Kissing me moistly on the brow. And just staring down at me peeping up out of the bath. I did not let her kiss me on the mouth for fear of my disease and she kissed me on the neck shoulders and bosoms. Then soaped me all over with Edna Annie's nearly dissolved big bar of yellow soap. That that ancient lady made every month down in her laundry. Who was now said to be beyond a century in age but could still see a wren at a hundred yards or hear a pin drop at fifty.

'Now my darling. Keep your head up out of the water.'

'Madam, I do hope you never grow old.'

'Ah but I shall. Isn't it sad.'

'Yes.'

Miss von B's hand pushed up over me. Making big hills of

suds on the water. As I arched up my back for her to make suds all over my privates as she whispered.

'Ah my darling my past might be unhappy but this, this is all so very exciting.'

Her hand pressed over my mouth when my moaning suddenly turned to screaming. In what must have been a death defying tumult, furore, fuss bother and frenzy of a thunderstorm of the emotions as I writhed in certain ecstasy. Nearly I do believe flapping like a fish out of water. Clearly Miss von B was a past master at this kind of pleasure giving. But I did not want to sound too desperately thankful, feeling as I was rather like a libertine in my licentious life. But my god it did feel so awfully utterly good.

'Ah my little one it is like a gushing fountain.'

And the warm waters. Her soft soothing touches of fingers and hands. The smooth wondrous skin of her throat. The velvet pink lips parting across her teeth as she smiled. And the tiniest of golden little hairs on her flesh. Who could care a tinker's curse about the low morality rampant across Ireland. Or of Lois painting privates. Or of hunt members taking each other by the ears or arse and entangling goodo upon the grass all over the ruddy countryside. Where one in spite of sighting the fox, was quite liable to be compelled at almost any time to rein up and shout, hark, what new wantonness do I perceive with rear cheeks naked in yonder copse. To make the innocent stars dance in consternation.

> And the
> Fox
> Run
> In shame

17

Stars afloat in the deep black sky. The night grown cold. From bathroom to bedroom shivering we went. Over the rattling floorboards. Miss von B drying, powdering and pampering me and now tucking me up in bed as I grabbed, felt and squeezed her in a playful manner.

'There you are now like a good boy. My special, my most dear little bog trotter, as you say.'

'Madam, when you call me such things there is nothing about you that I can love. I am at least as much of an aristocrat as you are. Because I don't believe you enjoy any distinctions to which I may not be entitled myself.'

'O my goodness we are again once more back on this battleground.'

'Only because of your slightingly unnecessary reference to me. Anyway, I don't care about the chimneytop of Andromeda Park not touching your uncle's chandeliers. I am equally as aristocratic as any.'

'Ah my sweet, my potato digger. Do you even know what an aristocrat is.'

'Of course I do.'

'Well then what is an aristocrat.'

'An aristocrat is one who drinks wine with dinner in a large dining room and is served by a butler and who plays billiards and into whose windows others not so distinguished want to look and see how they live.'

'Good lord, how easy then it is to be one.'

'Well there are also large paintings on the wall of his ancestors. And much carpeting and beautiful furniture throughout the house.'

'You can buy them at many auctions.'

'But then you cannot madam buy the proper accent with

which such people speak in such surroundings. And they never shout angrily except at other equals and never at servants whom they do not beat or strike save only in the dire necessity of discipline.'

'My sweet boy where have you been all these years.'

'I have been right here living as a member of the gentry and I am fully aware of aristocratic behaviour. Not the least of which is that they associate only with the proper people.'

'And who my sweet are they.'

'They are listed in the appropriate volumes dealing with such matters in order that impostors may be readily shown to be just that. They know the correct thing to say at the proper time. Nor do they get things all arsy versy as the common people do. And they have a fondness for books and all the finer things. Like birds' eggs or butterfly collecting. They also generate their own electricity. And they simply know that they are better than other people.'

'Ha, eggs, butterflies, personal electricity, don't sock the servants. Plenty stink of dead mice too. And they practise I suppose looking down their noses in the mirror in the morning. And up the arse in the evening.'

'Well why not. And do be careful for just think of all the mouse water you have drunk out of the tap. And also just remember madam how Baptista insulted you. She was looking down her nose.'

'And she, my little sweet is certainly not an aristocrat. But perhaps it is aristocratic to hunt to the hounds. Is it not.'

'Yes. Of course it is. And to have one's clothing made by the best tailors and boots by the best bootmakers and shotguns from the best gunsmiths. And your house should stand surrounded by ample parklands.'

'Ah do they belch and fart.'

'Upon occasion, yes.'

'And they come out stinky peewewew.'

'Upon occasion, yes.'

'Ah I see now how quite simple it is to be an aristocrat. Do they pee in people's parlours or on their front porches.'

'You may madam go on and on like that if you like. But it simply does not in the least alter my description of a true aristocrat.'

'What about their souls, my little darling.'

'You do not need a soul if you are really an aristocrat.'

'Ah that is the only thing you have said which is truly aristocratic.'

'Well madam do you not also agree that they pursue a policy of being the richest, the mightiest. And upon whom all others look in envy.'

'Of course yes. That is how they are haughty.'

'And also you will agree that they will sometimes not answer questions put to them and will look in other directions until the person asking such questions of them has sheepishly retreated.'

'O come, my god, enough. Let us continue the battle in the morning. And for now let us say you are the most arsy versy randy little aristocrat there is.'

Miss von B kissing me on the brow and sat there holding my hand till I went most contentedly to sleep. Waking momentarily in darkness to hear the friendly little scratching of my mouse devouring his crumbs. By the moonlight the branches of the trees all white. Frost settling on the grass. All is so blissful to be so deeply in love. To want hands you want to touch you to touch. With words said you know you both will say. And lips and eyes and all their colours there swirling in the mists of the new wonders that come in every embrace. And of course Miss von B did see me peeing off the front steps one evening.

Black as I woke. To lie thinking. Of the chilly morning. So warm in under the covers. And now standing aristocratically peeing into my suitably emblazoned chamber pot, a faint light was slowly pinkly brightening in the window. The wind risen and long patches of blue between the sky's clouds gliding from the west. Where Uncle Willie said the great Atlantic ocean made them the grey they were. I rang for Crooks. And miraculously he was knocking with a tray of tea in a thrice.

'Good morning Master Reginald. I trust you had a good night.'

One does not know quite at this early dawn how to aristocratically reply to what might in its casual statement hide quite saucy implications. But in the interests of not disturbing the recent pleasant tenor of household activities, best to reply in a like manner.

'Thank you Crooks, yes. Indeed I had a splendid night. I feel quite chipper.'

'That is good news. I'll leave the tray here. And while the sun's not up yet just let me stir the fire with a blow of the bellows and I'll have a blaze out of these embers in a moment.'

'Lay out my shooting clothes please, Crooks.'

'You are not I hope intending to proceed to the outdoors Master Reginald.'

'I am as a matter of fact proceeding to the outdoors, Crooks.'

'The doctor will not like the sound of that. He said you came through that pneumonia hanging by a thread of life.'

'Ah but now Crooks can't you see I hang by a string.'

'Ah you may be that bit stronger but not fit for the rigours of shooting. Will I be drawing your bath Master Reginald.'

Another remark of which one must be wary. If good lord my every activity is monitored. And my most marvellous bath had the ruddy household fighting each other at the keyhole to behold the doings beyond the door.

'No not this morning Crooks, had one last night.'

'Ah well it was a good long deep one you must have had too. Reading my bible I could hear the drain gurgling.'

'I beg your pardon Crooks.'

'There's not much Master Reginald that one misses in a house like this. Human it is. You learn to know its groans. You can hear it sigh. Hear it weep. You would even know if it ever erupted in ecstasy.'

'I do hope Crooks that you are referring only to the house's structural proclivities and not those of its human inhabitants.'

'Ah isn't one thing nearly the same as the other. I often

recall to mind the evening I heard Her Royal Highness our housekeeper, singing there in the ballroom. The marvel of that voice nearly made the whole building throb with life.'

One did not relish prodding further into Crooks's musical appreciation or concerning from where he was spying on that particular evening or indeed the wide all encompassing custodial chores he would appear to have taken on. But quite pleasant to hear aristocratic reference being made to a member of one's household staff. Miss von B did however, more than once hint of her suspicion that Crooks was spying upon her undressing which I'm sure accounts for his improved good relations with her. And not surprising when Crooks knows that Foxy and I nearly broke our necks doing it. And certainly how could it much matter now when the poor old fossil has already once seen her stark raving nude.

'Have you any special desires for supper or shall I refer myself to Her Royal Highness.'

'Her Royal Highness, Crooks.'

'Thank you, master Reginald.'

In a double edition of my woollies that Crooks laid out I dressed rather rapidly to be about my business. But I did indeed recall that evening of aria. Prior to dinner and just before drinks were to be served in the library. I thought at first it was a new lease of life that my father's gramophone had taken on. Till I realized the sound was coming from the ballroom. To whose door I tiptoed thinking, o god who now has gone bonkers. And pushing the door ajar I saw Miss von B. In a long white flowing gown, a candlestick in her hand, her arms held out. In the centre of the ballroom floor. Her head held back and singing with such lyric feeling and compassion. Her whole marvellous body alight with such shimmering beauty that I began to shake and tremble. Goose pimples galore all over and my hair standing up on the back of my neck. Had to loose the door knob I held in my hand because it began to rattle too. There I stood in the darkness transfixed. And a little frightened as well. The candle light throwing shadows upwards across the side of her face. But of course I was rather shamed not only by my having an erection during such a culturally magic moment but also that I had spied in this manner on what was another's most intimate reverie. And then she moved, the candle fluttering, to glide silently in circles till the candle blew out.

Darcy Dancer proceeding down the beech grove stairs. Rooks squawking out there in the tree tops. And with my grandfather's best Purdey gun from the gunroom, I came round the corner in the half light out across the hall. Norah taking ashes from the grate. And jumping up in a fright. As I came upon her silently on the rug Miss von B had just resurrected from the attic floor hall. To then quickly regain her senses with a little smile and her usual little nod of her head. When you're nearly dead it must make people become a little wide eyed to see you abroad alive again.

'Good morning, you did give me a start there, Master Reginald. 'Tis good to see you, sir.'

'Good morning, thank you Norah. And how are you keeping.'

'Middling sir, only middling.'

'O well, that's better than poorly, isn't it.'

'It is sir, yes.'

Rather disturbing enlargement one thought one noticed of Norah's belly. Or else she is simply getting rapidly and deucedly fat. She has when one really looks, quite an extremely pretty face. Big brown eyes. Freckles on forehead nose and cheeks. Ample bosomed and trim strong legs. Which I must confess I have upon occasion turned to watch disappearing down a hall or ascending a stair. Good lord, I hope not yet another pregnancy in this house. That's the trouble with wet weather. Causes so much hanging about getting up to mischiefs. If the remaining last of the useful servants start having babies it will be a damn nonsensical nuisance. With priests and nuns clammering about to find out who did it. And perhaps why. Will certainly not increase the household's day to day agreeableness. Seems one hardly gets down the stairs and out the ruddy front door. Before more tribulations unfold.

Darcy Dancer on the front steps. Taking in deep cold

sweet lungfuls of air. Kern and Olav happily pushing and shoving their big heads at me. Then growling in jealousy at each other. And pending parturition makes one distastefully recall. My father's tufts of lighter hair high on his cheek bones. His chomping hunting boots, the crops and whips and horse equipages piled at the front entrance of the house. And the mysterious pregnancies that began to appear among the household staff. With suspicions forthrightly cast upon the grooms but whispers had it said it was my father. And a story going round the countryside that while he was out and about on his horse that he never hesitated inquiring after any likely girl he might see. For whom an immediate staff opening was provided at Andromeda Park. Then too there was the story of the pretty girl, the daughter of the gombeen man at a crossroads some miles away who sold groceries and various and sundry divers manufactured articles and one night my father aseat on his horse had watched her through the lighted window behind the counter of the shop and on a pretext that he was lost and needed directing in the dark he took her off into a wood the other side of the road. Her bald father later came to discuss with my father behind locked doors of the rent room. And was even once received in the north east parlour. And there were whispers about the consequences for years and that a little boy was growing up in Dublin who was a Kildare.

'Ahoy there a moment Master Reginald.'

Sexton coasting around the rhododendrons on his bicycle. Wheels grinding over the pebbles. Like waiting for my breakfast tray in the morning to arrive from the kitchen. Hearing it coming and coming in the early silence. Along the halls, up stairs and then finally arriving with a knock on my door. As Sexton squeaks to a stop. On his two wheeled vehicle he said once belonged to a Protestant Bishop.

'Ah you look alive and well. And doing some shooting Master Darcy.'

'O just a bang or two at a few pigeon or snipe.'

'Good day for it. Try over there in the little bit of bog the corner of the field the other side of spy glass hill. There's always a bird or two lurking which later could nicely tickle the palate.'

Drops of moisture descending Sexton's cheek from under his eye patch. He wipes them away with a big knuckle of his fist.

'And are they Sexton, still up there in the oak plantation.'

'O they're still there. And will be at them trees. Till all fifty are gone. Sharpening that big cross cut saw every morning like a razor. And by evening they'd have it so dull it wouldn't cut butter. Three horses pulling the logs out to the road and two pulling them into town. And the gombeen man ought to be taught a lesson. Sure didn't one of the barbarians working for him come upon a pair of rare antique inkstands. Hidden innocent they were for years in an old walled up space in an architectural masterpiece of a mansion the land commission were knocking down in honour of the greater glory of peasant Ireland. O god weren't they ormolu mounted of the most refined taste imaginable. In the true genuine regency style. And with the same sledge hammer this barbarian was using on the building, he smashed the innocent things to smithereens with a stupidity nulli secundus. You wouldn't mind now if he even had the decency to avail of the dignity of a judge's gavel to wreak his havoc on such sacred things. And the likes of that gombeen man who employs him wouldn't know the difference between a Louis the Sixteenth style chaperone sofa and a cast iron bucket in the Adam style that he'd sit his own naturalistically coloured arse into. Forgive me using such words. But coarse doings call for coarse language. And down through the ages it's the lovers of beauty are vilified and the wielders of violence are sanctified. Ah but it's grand to see you there on the steps. In front of your own great house. And with your acres out there ready to take the tread of your boot and the air feel the shock of your gun.'

Sexton of course delayed me with his flowery rhetoric for some considerable time. Relaying his plans for the gardens in spring, and for the laying out and planting of masterly embellishments and vistas and grand ornamental flower beds.

However he could finally sense that I was impatient to be off and touching me gently on the arm he smiled as he always did.

'Ah I delay you and I must myself go about my business but now you go with the blessing of the Blessed Virgin Mother, and bag a few birds.'

Darcy Dancer crossing the frosty cobbles of the farmyard. Snorts and stampings in the stables. The whinnies of Molly and Petunia. Who smell me near. Luke mucking out. Forking up the big brown lumps of dung matted with yellow straw and shovelling it into his barrow. At least someone is working. But I suppose I shall have to spout a few hackneyed words to pass the time of day.

'Good morning to you sir. It's grand to see you up and about.'

'Thank you Luke. It's a chilly draughty old morning.'

''Tis that sir.'

'Gives one a mind to thank god for inventing fire.'

'Ah now you've said it, sir. On these winter days you need the little bit of hell the lord puts flaming in a grate.'

'Is Foxy about.'

'He does be about. But always on the move you might say. Like you might see him. And then you don't. Sure the nights they haven't an idea where to look for him. And I haven't clapped eyes on him this long time now. But try above beyond there where he had a mind to hauling some of them potatoes if there's any left not rotten to be put in the cellars.'

'Thank you Luke.'

'And it's a grand morning for a bit of shooting.'

Darcy Dancer proceeding into the farm tunnel. An arm encircling his gun. In this gloomy light walking over the wet cobbles and the damp dripping down the walls. All the years ago now this was built. All the backs bent with digging. All the stones lifted and placed by hand. The hours, days and years of work. Just so as Uncle Willie said, the likes of me could stand at my library and drawing room windows and look out on the undisturbed green gentleness above. And not have my view or mind discomforted by the movement of those who by their big handed hard toil, kept such gentry so agreeably rich and mildly pleased in comfort. Now walk past the stone where Foxy and I came out that night. And the entrance to the subterranean passage down steps where the big rats go scurrying. All the way to the dusty tombs. And all the silly rumour of jewels said to be hidden somewhere out there. That they were supposed secreted away from thieves. But really that they were concealed from my father by my mother. And Uncle Willie said laughingly that if ever I were in dire need he would perhaps give me a map and shovel to go digging. But it was a strange way he said it. Which was not laughing at all. In my delirious sleep I saw my mother. Appear at the foot of my bed in her evening gown. Just as I was allowed to look at her before some grand evening when she sometimes would come to the nursery and kiss me in bed. The diamond necklace around her throat and sparkling in pendants from her ears and bracelets over the white soft kid skin covering her arms to the elbows and glittering too with diamonds. And certainly one does not know now of the whereabouts of such gems. Perhaps there are monstrous massive Thormond or Darcy riches. A cache of gold, pearls, emeralds and rubies. With which I could buy back all our lands again. But like the end of every rainbow I ran to with my sisters, all I ever found was misty rain drops.

Darcy Dancer coming out of the tunnel. Hands up shielding from the sunlight. Ahead the old iron fence and stile and a cattle grid across the road. Air sweet in one's nostrils. The sky swept bright. A magpie so black and gleaming white on the branch of that tree. Without its mate. Hope to god that doesn't foretell a spot of ill ruddy luck. Coming too damn soon after quite a goodly batch of it. Interspersed I must frankly admit with some highly agreeable moments indeed. At the tender delicious hands of Miss von B. What a really good useful woman she is. To suddenly make the whole world falling in on one become a world of stunning bliss. She and I could get on awfully well together. She would have her permanent employ. Lots of embroidery to do when she got old like Edna Annie. And once one had absolute proof of her titles we could then perhaps elevate her accordingly. Ah a heron flies there. The big slow flapping wings. The long neck. A lonely bird. Sailing down the wind to the boggy shore of the lake. Dear me one was so tempted this morning to rush to Miss von B's bedroom. Jump in under the covers beside her. Push my hands up under her bosoms and then try to join them together around her waist. Squeeze and feel her. And now I am equally tempted to blast these pigeons popping all over out of the trees. Only it would give warning of my approach.

Darcy Dancer, the brown and green flecks of colour in his tweeds. Boots up over his stockings, stepping lightly. Deer stalker set square on his head. Hear the sound of the saw. Makes one's feet hurry to save every chip of wood. Were Mr Arland here he could have written one of his marvellously threatening letters. You rogues desist. Or something to that effect. And I must try to convey the distinct or indistinct appearance of a landowner who does not intend to be trifled with. And is capable of giving a good account of himself to anyone attempting to get too tiresomely tricky or impertinent. Pop them with a fisticuff or two on the jowls. Use footwork. To avoid them grabbing me. Some of these workmen are deucedly strong and can lift the weight of a weanling as they would a kitten. And just over there, and when I was just a tiny boy. Sean the arm, he was called, because of all his strength, went sawing a branch high up an oak broken in a storm. And sawed it off under himself to go crashing down swinging into a tree where he was impaled by the spoke of a broken branch going right through his heart and out of his back. Just like one of my grandfather's butterflies in his trays stacked in the back of the cupboards in the ballroom.

Darcy Dancer moving up along the edge of parkland. And past a wild growth of rhododendrons. Approaching the grove of tall straight oaks. Where they grew on a gently rising ground. Wheel ruts criss crossing the mud. Three draught horses and a big heavy cart. A ramp and poles. A man smoking a cigarette. Wearing a grey weather beaten trilby hat. And long black coat. Two men with long staves levering a log towards the cart ramp. Two men at the foot of an oak. Each on the end of a great long saw. Their backs and shoulders swaying back and forth. At the foot of this majestic tree. Two great oaks already with branches smashed and their long boughs prostrate on the ground. And now another one nearly sawn half way through. As Sexton says. You can hear the screaming.

'Stop that. Stop that sawing at once. And get off this land.'

'Now who in heaven's name might you be. As if I didn't know.'

'I am the owner of this land.'

'Ah I didn't know that now is that so.'

'That is so.'

'Is it the son of the house himself who would be telling me to stop sawing and to get off this land.'

'Yes.'

'Ah me is it. Sure I've bought these trees. And having bought them, I will saw them down. And having sawn them down I'll take them away. And not a soul will stop me.'

'You'll get back your money you paid.'

'I will not have my money back. I'll have me trees, that's what I'll have.'

'You'll have a sudden stream of swan shot tickling your bloody damn nose my good man.'

'What. What are you about at all. Threaten me. With a firearm. You damn buckeen. I'll put you across me knee and give your pelt a good hiding with the palm of me hand.'

Bang. All five men ducking. And just above your sixth man's grey trilby, a branch severed cleanly from the tree. And falling crashing upon his head. Aside from crushing his already battered hat it made his knees buckle. As he angrily tried to knock it away with his arm.

'What are you mad. Kill me is it. You madman. Fire at me. I'll have the guards.'

'You'll have yourself, your tools, men, horses and cart off my land or the next barrel will, I regret to say, travel close enough to save you shaving your whiskers off for a lifetime.'

'It's assault with a deadly weapon. Grevious bodily harm

and attempted murder. Sean, Billy, Mick you saw by god what happened.'

'And if you have to be told again to clear off you'll see more of what will happen. And not one more piece of insolence out of you.'

'By Jesus, what are you Darcy Thormond Kildares coming to. Raising little maniacs. I'll report this to the guards. You can bet on that. I'll have you in the courts. And put in prison. You can bet on that too.'

'Shut up you gombeen bastard. And get off my land.'

'I'll shut up alright but you haven't heard the end of this don't you worry. You'll hear from me.'

'And if I do I'll come and blow your fucking head off.'

'Hear him. There are witnesses here. I know my rights. I have it in writing, I've got it down in black and white with the agent. And no buckeen is going to deprive me of my rights. You wouldn't be that bold without a gun.'

Somewhere high above the oak tree tops a crow was squawking. And the bright blue of sky was closing over with clouds. The smell of gun powder out on the air. Foxy said it was always good to use the word fucking in your threats. Then they always fucking well knew.

> That you
> Fucking well
> Meant it

18

With black darkness closing down on a rain-swept countryside, Crooks this day later came with the message into the front parlour where Miss von B and I were taking tea. Following a game just played of chess. In which I literally crushed her. By casually abiding her overconfident reckless attacks during the middle game and then exercising a blistering positional cross fire of my bishops with a knight and castle overseeing the plunging blade of my queen into the heart of her king.

'Master Reginald. There are two gentlemen from the Garda Siochana in the hall. I did say that I did not know whether you were receiving but they say it regards urgent and serious matters.'

'Show them in Crooks. And do fetch some whiskey.'

'Very good Master Reginald.'

Two uniformed damp looking guards. Hats in hands. One had to dip his head to walk in the door. And the other nearly to turn sideways. Both massive apparitions standing there in the shadows. Who nod greeting. And to which one must present one's very best dazzling entitlements.

'Guards, allow me to present you to Her Royal Highness.'

'Sorry your majesty to disturb you at your tea.'

'It is quite all right.'

'Now guards do please. Come in. Sit down.'

'We'll stand for the moment. As you never know that what we might have to say may not be welcome. And I'll get to the point. We have had a complaint of a serious nature from a certain timber merchant. And I'm sure you know now to what I refer. He claims this morning that sometime in the vicinity of ten o'clock, that you let fly a shot gun at him while he was in pursuit of his lawful right cutting down some trees.'

'Please, gentlemen, sit. Ah. Crooks. Good. Now will you gentlemen have a drink.'

'Not while on duty. There are a couple of very serious matters. The first concerns yourself and is a serious charge. Discharge of a firearm in a fashion so as to endanger life.'

'Well as a matter of fact, it was all a complete reflex action and horrid accident. I in fact was shooting a pigeon. That happened to be flying out over this gentleman's head. Quite high above it you know. They're the devil in the summer with our oats and barley. The sight of one instantly put me in mind to shoot it. But I do think I rather gave him a fright when it knocked a branch out of the tree which fell on him. For which I was very sorry.'

'The timber merchant said nothing about a pigeon. If you don't mind now, we'll take that statement down.'

The sergeant, his cap tucked under an arm as he held open his notebook. While Miss von B miraculously captivated both of them with utterly devastating smiles. A good bit of scribbling was done. With the sergeant requesting me to pause until his pencil caught up. Of course one spouted out a lot of old rubbish. Of a quality however, which did not make the guards look too foolish pretending to believe it. Yes. I was of course, telling them to vacate my lands. Of which I was the absolute freehold owner in trust perhaps. But still no one has a right to take property without my leave. Yes all guns in the household were properly licensed. And indeed if either of the guards enjoyed a shoot now and again. Do please let me know. Plenty of snipe down on the edge of the bog, pheasant, plover, duck. Anything in fact a sporting man likes to see on the wing ripe and ready for later delectation and needing only to be blasted out of the sky.

'Now Mr Kildare, we'll give you the benefit of the doubt. That there was no threatening language up there at the time of the discharge of the firearm which was in every way unintentional. But it wouldn't do for the good look of things for persons who live in big houses using firearms on persons who live in small houses.'

'I quite understand Sergeant.'

'But sure you're bound to hear great exaggeration. But we're duty bound to listen to both sides of a story. Your man says he has rights, and if he has the courts of course are waiting to uphold them. And in a similar fashion the courts is the proper place if a man is trespassing and doing damage on a man's land. So we don't want to hear any more of shot guns just letting fly in pursuit of a pigeon and then just happening to blow a branch off just above your man's head.'

'Of course guard. No one would dream of doing such a thing deliberately.'

'Well now to the other matter and then we'll go off duty. And maybe a bit of that whiskey will do the trick to kill the chill on the wet way back in the darkness to the station. It's every bit a cold journey.'

'And what is the further difficulty guard.'

'Ah well now it involves a personality that you might say has become familiar to all of us over the years. Now we are aware that Foxy Slattery is an employee upon the estate. And we have reason to believe he can help in our inquiries. First regarding a sacrilegious theft of wine and other divine divers artefacts including priestly vestments and the wearing of same with the intention of impersonating the clergy.'

'But Foxy is most devout and I am sure would never do anything so unfortunate.'

'Well he left his fingerprints all over the face of a witness to such act. And occasioned him actual bodily harm as well. And further. In regard to the unlawful taking of a horse, the property of a Master of Foxhounds. And again occasioning that gentleman actual bodily harm. And connected with that incident. There is the damage done to property in the act of trespass and being in charge of a horse in a dangerous manner.'

'Good lord, how heinous.'

'Which also involved charging the same horse at two dismounted members of the hunt and then jumping over their heads. Particulars of this latter matter are still being pursued as witnesses have been reluctant to come forward.'

'Upon my word. How irredeemably wretched. And

especially to thieve clerical clothing. Dreadful. But Foxy has impeccable references.'

'No need to get alarmed now Mr Kildare. Sure the reverend Father in question is a humane man. Not to say a cultured gentleman of the very highest order and indeed is an habitué of this very house.'

'Yes indeed he is, and a noted collector of fine art.'

'Well he would not be pressing charges. And we are likely to consider that in the case of a person with too much drink taken that they might in such a state, on occasion, behave in a bizarre manner. And not be meaning in the least to impersonate a member of the clergy. And we are proceeding upon that assumption. He could be let off with a caution and small fine. But it is the Father's robes, tailor made in Paris of the greatest kind of cloth and blessed by the Pope, that we want to recover. And we would earnestly solicit the help of all here in so doing.'

'O dear. What a botheration for you gentlemen. But I'm sure Foxy would not impersonate a priest.'

'Well the witness on interview said and I'm quoting now, that the culprit shouted that he was setting off in the direction of the town to hear midnight confession and that no one, and forgiving your presence your majesty, would effing well stop him. He then suggested to the witness that he should kneel behind a gravestone and he'd start by listening to the dirty old deeds of his black old soul. Or words to that effect. Now if that is not impersonating a priest I don't know what is.'

Following two glasses of whiskey each, and a comment or two about the low price of cattle, Miss von B and I conducted the guards in a quick tour of the salon, dining room and library. While both of us made suitable descriptive remarks upon the furnishings, architecture and embellishments. All of which they seemed to appreciate as they appraised the gold velour, green damask, embossed bindings, chamfered square supports and cabriole legs. With Her Royal Highness pointing out highlights and distinguishing marks. The only difficulty occurring when the heavier of the two guards put his foot crashing through two floorboards, and grabbing a drape for safety, brought both it and the curtain rail down on top of his head. Causing what one can only describe as a brief moment of consternation, especially as he wildly threw his arms about attempting to unearth himself from the confines of the extremely dusty drape.

'Ah god now, I'm very sorry I did that.'

'That's quite all right guard. One likes to know where a possible extensive dilapidation is brooding and your departure briefly downwards, although giving you a fright does also give us a jolly good hint as to an area that needs repairing.'

Of course one also knew that such minor embarrassments would have a way of absolving one from major prosecution. And back on the terra firma quality of the front hall tiles it was apparent that the guards were quite satisfied that they had successfully conducted their business and with all kinds of cheery words to the princess from whom they hardly ever removed their eyes, they departed down the front steps to their bicycles.

'Cheerio now.'

'Cheerio.'

Watching their red tiny back lights go disappearing round the rhododendrons along the drive, both Miss von B and I stood willingly chilled and battered by the little moistures out of the black above. Certainly it was, with the number of accusations flying round advisable to at least see them off in some style. And Foxy wearing the elegant Father's best Sunday cassock, soutane and biretta, could be out somewhere right now in the fields trying to convert my Protestant cattle to being papish minded in preparation for heading to a good Catholic abattoir.

'O dear madam, the eyes of the world are upon us.'

'Ah you handled it very well. I was very impressed.'

'Were you really.'

'Yes. You perhaps here and there might have been a little too enthusiastic in your outrageous lies. But it was not bad.'

It was staff tea time so arm in arm we carelessly danced together across the tiles. She was so splendid reeling off her descriptions of furnishings to the guards. Of the bombe front of a drawer. And they ooed and ahhed as she pointed to a George Fourth silver mounted fluted glass mustard pot on the dining room table. As Miss von B recited a litany of its characteristics.

'You will perhaps notice its simple but attractive plain reeded rim and also notice especially the shell thumb piece to the flat cover.'

'Ah now your majesty that would do as a great yoke for mustard on any man's table.'

There in the echoing front hall in the sight of one's glum faced ancestors on the wall I grabbed up close to Miss von B and she turned to nibble me on the neck. And with indecent swiftness one's trousers were sticking out frontally as I hugged and kissed her.

'Madam I do so adore you sometimes.'

'Ah only sometimes.'

'Yes. Other times you cause me considerable discomfort. About my pedigree especially.'

'Ah you should not worry. I will whenever you should require, be glad to give you a social recommendation.'

'Now that's exactly the demeaning kind of thing I mean. You can make one feel such an awful commoner.'

'But surely, isn't that what you are.'

'You're just angry because you can't bear losing to me at chess.'

'I would much prefer to lose at chess than I would at love. And at love I have lost so many times.'

'But it is only at chess you lose to me. And if I were assured that I would not again be slapped in the face I would suggest that this evening might be appropriate for us to imbibe the claret and d' Yquem still on the sideboard.'

'Of course you will, my sweet, not be slapped if you behave and perhaps later I will teach you to jitterbug.'

Dressing for dinner I chose a purple silk hanky for my breast pocket and brushed my hair to a sheen. And made the best neat bow I possibly could of my tie. She seemed to have a courage did Miss von B. And that she would take risks despite her zealously careful ways about the house. Although she still complained that the dust, smears of hands and marks everywhere did get her down. And they even appeared on the few places where she had scraped, prepared and painted herself. I tried to reason with her that it gave it a natural ageing effect.

'Ah my god. This place is too much naturally aged already.'

To her, I was dying to make love. Looking upon her face even beautiful when distorted through my wine glass. We had trifle pudding to end our most marvellously pleasant supper. Crooks clean shirted although noisily slippered was only really clumsy once. Dropping and then trodding in the butter which of course Miss von B insisted we all clean up. Can you imagine. Gentry on their knees. I could see she was aggrieved that Crooks was of course traipsing this grease all the way back and forth cross eyed into the pantry. But he did at least try hard to avoid further disaster by two handedly laying down the remaining plates. This also got at Miss von B but she was most good to hold her tongue. Poor old Crooks had so obviously made such an effort. With most of the more conspicuous of his frontal stains removed from his livery. Norah too, with her belly bulging pronounced in her white apron, was rushing attentive to our every little table need. And except for a bat flying round the dining room and a resounding crash of glass in the pantry, the whole meal was carried off without a hitch. Even though it was just cold slices of beef in hot gravy with boiled cabbage and potatoes. Which of course required one to indulge in lofty conversation in order to elevate the elegance of the fare.

'I do so like the lyricism in Mozart's bassoon concerto in A major, don't you madam.'

'Yes. I do. But it is in B flat major.'

Of course that was immediately the kind of thing which reminded one of eating potatoes and cabbage again. However with port we repaired to the ballroom and opening the doors through to the library we listened to the gramophone. Miss von B leading me through the most god awful gyrations. It was surely fast and best described as a leg busting gavotte sending limbs out every which bloody way. And I must confess I soon steered reluctant Miss von B from these maniac paroxysms towards honeymoon bridge on the fur on the floor in front of the firelight in the library. I was feeling so pleasant and physically improved that I could not really give too much of a damn of what damn key Mozart was composing in nor indeed concerning my privileges and distinctions previously so dearly and bitterly debated. And I had much fun in F major when Miss von B lost also at cards. And I made much of it while pointing haughtily with my finger.

'Now madam, would you mind just standing over there close to tears.'

And in fact she did do that very thing. Proceeding, her shoulders hunched over to the chimneypiece. Bending her head slowly into her hands and good lord releasing suddenly a cascade of sobs which made me jump up so fast and rush to her that I knocked over a side table stacked with tomes on lineage. To take her as best I could in a comforting embrace, which seemed to make her sob even louder. I was really getting scared. Saying, what's the matter, please tell me and was nearly in tears myself, when she then burst into laughter.

'Why you absolute dirty rotter to do that. I feel quite that you have made an absolute fool of me.'

I was in fact now standing there in actual tears of rage. And I gave her a good damn sock of my fist right on the shoulder. And she convulsed in laughter even harder. Till I really let her have a thundering hard punch on her thigh when she smacked me back with a bone painful blow to my own shoulder and sooner than soon we were grabbing, pulling, tripping, wrestling and crashing all over the place. God she is strong. Every time I thought I had her pinned down she twisted right up again out of my grasp. And threw me over. And she didn't appear to be in the least concerned with the upheaval of pillows and crashing furniture. But I finally managed to get her in a scissor grip with my legs. And although she agreed to give up she had me bloody well twisted by my fingers and demanded I surrender first. And not being a ruddy bounder I naturally consented.

'You are being absolutely unladylike madam fighting like a man.'

'But of course what would you expect, for me to fight like a woman. You would then have your eyes scratched out.'

'That is a most chilling thing to say.'

'Ah but perhaps I should suggest some warmer way of expending our energy that we ought really to try. But I think it must wait till a little later. Just in case there are inquisitive eyes and ears still awake.'

I was quite flushed in the face and I was amazed at her sudden indifference to her appearance and getting her dress mussed. And I brushed her off especially about the bosoms. And the white brilliance of her teeth as she smiled. We picked up the books and replaced other disturbed furnishings. Put logs on the fire and I lay my head back on her lap sitting on the floor. And just looking up into her eyes. The wind rattling outside. The crackling fire. So wonderful to have this conspiracy of love between us. Even if it was sometimes breached when we actually tried to kill each other in a fight, to only be, in just a matter of seconds later enraptured in writhing passion, flesh to flesh embraced. Our smells making one fume. If one could get that hot on such an extremely cool evening. And if too, of course she had let go of my badly twisted fingers. And climbing up the stairs her hair loosed from her combs and falling down her back I was going to ask her. Of what would happen if we ever had a baby. And if our love made another born, would it change anything between us. Then reaching the landing I couldn't summon my voice to speak such words. And instead I asked, had all the war, all the death, destruction, made matters of who was better and more esteemed than another, any different. As when her shoes were worn through and broken and her clothes thread-bare and she had no butter bacon or eggs. Did not the lack of such things then make her feel all dismally the same as everyone else. And did that make her feel glad and relieved that her elegances and superiorities need no longer trouble her.

'Ah my grand fellow. You have got everything so arsey

versy. My elegancies, they have never troubled me. But in matters of distinctions nothing changes. No cannon, no bomb is enough to shatter rank. But even if everybody suffers, your own suffering does not seem less. And there are always those for whom superiorities are dearly and bitterly important. Who still care so much about their privileges and distinctions. Either gained or lost. Either hoped for or disappointed. And they would wear their crowns and medals on their deathbeds. It is sadly an unchanging fact of life. That everyone does like to feel esteemed in the eyes of everybody else. No matter who they are.'

'Even a king.'

'Of course, even a king. He feels important in the eyes of God.'

'I am an atheist.'

'Only because you are nobody important. Except to me.'

We parted kissing. And I said I will return quickly. And as she tapped me on the tip of my nose with her finger she said, and I hope quietly and discreetly. And I checked every direction and especially for sounds on the staircases before proceeding in darkness in pyjamas, slippers and dressing gown, to Miss von B's room. And who minds being no one important if I am important to her. Lock the door behind me as I enter into her pleasant smells.

'Hello my little potato digger.'

'I'm not speaking to you if that is the attitude you are adopting.'

'But it is my term of endearment for you. Then I shall call you my prince.'

'Yes, I do far prefer that.'

The candle burning on her dresser and moonlight coming in the window. Her riding clothes neatly laid over a chair. Not like my room where everything was strewn until someone else picked it up. And the top of her pair of boots crowned with her bowler. And together we will have many more hunting days soon. I may even keep my own pack of hounds. Jog the jolly doggies up and down dale. For the greater glory of their fine fettle. Invite only those with the proper social credentials who were also consummate masters of equitation to join one. Then as M.F.H. with her royal blonde beauteous highness just behind me, we would together set the entire hunting world astir with great rampages across the pastures of Thormondstown. Show those select few, sport of such majesty and magnificence that all would gladly die in satisfied joy following the close of day as they took their final sips of after dinner port. And of course I would have the field obey me as slaves. And any gentleman who mounted a lady or even pulled down their breeches to examine her bruises and scratches would be banned. Till next hunting season. Vets of course would come fully equipped with the necessary splints and bandages and would have handy their amputation knives. But be forbidden to fight with these. Especially with another of this profession as was frequently the case, due to their conflicting opinions given various clients on their ailing horses for whose costly demise one vet promptly blamed the other. So much squalor permeates the hunting field these days perpetrated by those who would attempt to make hunting history by their signally bizarre behaviour. Ruffians most odious. Of course anyone with the gall to even mildly flaunt my wishes in the field would succeed in making me immediately take the hounds home. But for those of the true spirit I would indeed provide such wild blood inspiring sporting gaiety that nothing in anyone's life would succeed in vying with it.

'And what my prince have you so intently on your mind that you should stand there like that.'

'I am going to form my own pack of hounds.'

'Ah, in your scarlet coat you will be master.'

'Yes as a matter of fact.'

'My prince. My master. How sad. I did so like you as my dear little bog trotter.'

Instead of taking off my pyjamas I just wish I had enough self discipline to deny my randy desperation and to just turn in my slippers and depart when she makes fun of me so. But dear me she is so attractive as she lies waiting there for me in bed. Her eyes look out, just looking. Somewhere there in the dark. The side of her face in moonlight and her smile just smiling. As I fold my pyjamas and gown, both in my mother's racing colours which really I shouldn't keep on wearing. And certainly not as I take a hurdle in Miss von B's direction. Tingling all over. As one might do in the roar of hooves in a point to point race. Crashing over and through the willow branches of the jumps. Turf and leather flying. To be a haughty winner. Just as one seems to be so awfully proud standing here barefoot and rudely pointing one's penis. And I must confess I did dally there centre carpet wanting her to see and I hope to admire it because the thought of her looking at it really made it glow. Lit up like a bicycle lamp. And her smile got bigger. She winked and pulled an edge of the bed-covers back. Her hand bringing out the yard stick which to my absolute astonishment was the same one Mr Arland used in the schoolroom. Good god she is going to hit me. Just like her previous slap. And I am indeed stepping right back the hell out of here.

'Ah my darling. Ah my dear little darling. It is your rudder. Your weathercock. I am only going to measure. Not to strike you.'

'Well thank god for that. I honestly thought you were going to give me a thwack. And you do, you know at times, really confuse me so that I hardly know what to expect next.'

'Ah but this time. All is different. Come up close now.'

'I won't actually. Not till you absolutely promise this isn't just a trick.'

'It is not believe me. We shall see how many inches long it is. I promise. No trick.'

'You promise.'

'But of course my sweet. Once we have your measurement then when I make for you your social recommendation we will put how long it is and I will sign it. Hold still. My it is very stuck up and extremely upper class, according to both the width and the length. Ah you see, that is how long it is. Clearly you qualify for the *Almanach de Gotha*. Alright get me paper.'

Of course how was one to know Miss von B was again only

joking. She is so very good at pretending. But damn. I did stupidly get her a piece of Andromeda Park notepaper. Upon which she drew an extremely risqué silhouette of one's personal part thereon. Writing in big letters underneath. BOGTROTTER. Which when showing it to me she laughingly pulled away.

'But my sweet do you not now know that with this important paper you may enter the very best of social circles.'

I promptly pushed the offending document right up into her face. Promptly starting another fight. Grabbing her hands. As she strove again exerting all her strength to throw me over. But this time I had her half trapped under the thick pile of bedcovers and she just suddenly gave up and I fell an easy winner on top. To then climb in bed beside her. That wonderful feeling of feeling her touching all up and down me. And we kissed each other everywhere. Rolling about locking and unlocking our arms. I adored the way her head arched back on the pillow and the sinews stretched along her throat out to her shoulders as her jaw opened and her head turned back and forth and a frown came above her eyes as she groaned. One cannot imagine this activity ever being called impurity. As Foxy said it was preached from every altar in Ireland. Sins of the flesh. And hers so smooth on her long stemmed body. Beneath me. That I entwine open armed. Once full of hunger. Once fleeing saving her life. Her voice quiet and soft. When telling her tales of fear. Without a sorrow. Or regret. You want so much to live. When all around you want you to die. She speaks with her greyest, her bluest her greenest of eyes. Press lips on the soft cheeks. See her now. As I will last remember her. If ever I go away. And no longer can gather up. All her white tall body. Her bones. Her eyes. Lay with them held. By every soft pressure of flesh. If this makes me a sinner. Here I am then god. Blackened in joy under your celestial blue.

'What my darling, what is that.'

'It's I think a carriage. On the drive.'

'Who could it be.'

'No one this time of night. It's gone past to the servants'

entrance. It could be Luke or anyone coming back from the pub.'

'O god you are so sweet. That you have made love for me beautiful once more. That our bodies should touch so natural and just be as they should. If only you were not so young.'

'I am lord of the manor madam.'

'But you are young too.'

'I am a man.'

'Yes. O well. Perhaps I shall just take some young hours of your life and in exchange I shall give you the rest of mine.'

'Would you.'

'No I would not. For nothing can win my sweet in a race against age. This is all we can ever have. It is not wise to seek more. But I would be so proud to walk at your side. If we were together in life. But we have, even for such a short a time, we have lived. What more can there be but to just make it as long as we can. There was the swallow bird who last summer fly in my window. He sit up there on the big brass curtain rod. And all his family, they sit all seven out on the drain along the roof making a white path shitting down the wall. And first when he come in, his little breast was beating in such fear as to how he could get out again. And his terror was so sad. But he swoop and swerve. His flight so brave. Till he find the space to fly free. And then he was gone. And he, that swift graceful bird, my little sweet, is what I think of whenever I think of you.'

Sleep coming. Quietly to my eyes. Miss von B and I. Side by side. Rest my head back across her outstretched arm. The sweet smell up in under her hair. When the whole world goes and fades away. Right up into the little plaster trio of feathers in each cornice of the room. If I lie absolutely still Miss von B may not chuck me out till morning. And may just let me fly around like the swallow under her covers. One has had rather a fine day. I might even record all the details in my diary just as my great grandfather did for the sake of his heirs. And perhaps even make as he did some philosophical observations. Except not even once did he make a saucy comment. Seemed only to care for hunting, shooting and fishing. Or in the case of the agricultural, of making improvements. Which he would do by periodically convening the estate workers to make known information recently obtained by scientists. Which he said thus put the knowledge of an educated class at the disposal of a class who derived little information from reading. He had his own remedies for cattle disease. With all kinds of mixtures either boiled or cold. Of oil, turpentine, sulphur, permanganate of potash. And gave his annual address to the tenantry, servants and staff of the estate. When he spoke of his great delight. To go in and out among you, not as a stranger but an old familiar friend. And he would end by saying. I trust that with god's help I shall not be found an unworthy descendant of the old stock. And be assured it is my most earnest desire to promote the well being of my tenantry and to deserve in my own person their respect and attachment.

Feel Miss von B's toe wiggling against mine. Probably to appreciate the splendid pedicure she gave me. Tasted milk out of her breast. The lush salty silky sweetness between her legs. The gunman I clonked on the head and if he never woke up. I'm a murderer. Be accused as an arsonist. If the school burned all the way to the ground. In any event Awfully Stupid is certainly never going to be stupid enough again to let someone walk away with his box of fudge. Even when they swear hysterically on three stacks of bibles that they'll bring it back in just a moment. The sounds. The corridors of that school. The feet. That walk. So lonely along a hall. And get louder and louder as they approach.

'Mein Gott, who's at the door.'

'Open this.'

'O my darling who is it. Who is out there.'

'This is Reginald Kildare. And you have madam, I believe that little bastard in there with you. Do you agree. Or must I have this door broken down to see for myself.'

'No. You do not have to break it down. No. You do not have to.'

'And I'll see you, you little bastard, first thing in the morning in the library.'

The footsteps walking away. And my great grandfather's words. That the prosperous state of the tenantry was due to a just and considerate agent which had added to the reputation of a noble name handed down through a long line of ancestors and had placed him on high vantage ground. And he trusted that by such esteem he should do his duty to all who stood before him. And I had dreamt that I had made an annual address to the staff. As they all stood stark naked in the front hall applauding me with huzzas. As I stammered out some feeble apology for my erection. Now I must begin saying something to Miss von B. Whose tight grip on my arm is squeezing even tighter. And from her there came just a strange little sound. Like an animal out in the dark woods when a predator tears life from them and they let out their squeal of death. And Miss von B sat up. In the moonlight so pale and white. Her splendid breasts shadowly trembling on her chest. Upon the softness I so cherished to lay my cheek. Hands now to her eyes making fists at the side of her face. Which shook each time she brought her arms up and the breath stuttered into her lungs. Her whole back bending and shaking as she sobbed. Her voice. Begging. O please please please, don't let it happen. I beg of you don't let it happen. Please please please. And I did not have to tell her to stand over there close to tears. The whole of her. Inside and out. Weeping. Anguish pleading in her eyes. And I listened. My own deepest sorrow stirring.

And
I loved
Her

19

As a bright orange dawn broke I crept from between the covers and tiptoed out. Leaving Miss von B finally asleep, her breathing making a strange high pitched sound like a singing bird. In my room, under my chilly blankets, I stared out the corner of the window at a now snow threatening sky till Crooks brought me tea. His crossed eyes as ever made it rather more than impossible to discern what expression he was wearing and what on earth was going on in his mind.

'There are the two boiled eggs this morning, Master Reginald. To keep your pecker up.'

Of course one could make no other comment than thank you. And I applied one of the more common egg cutters of an inferior nature kept in the kitchen. Decapitating the brown shell to dig out silver spoonfuls of the deep orange yolk swimming in melted butter.

The sun suddenly blazing golden white on my bedroom wall. And the beads of moisture on the blue tinted glass window panes hung like strings of diamonds. Through the night with the foxes barking, I was held clutched by her. Her body and bosoms pressed warm on my back. She wakened again and again from her sleep to clutch me even tighter. Her whispering voice all hoarse from crying. You're not gone. And other words in German I could not decipher. Our tall candle now a stump and nearly burnt out. I wanted so much to tell her that everything was going to be alright. She seemed so exhausted. Her eyes swollen and red. But magically, still so tenderly attractive. Her dress she wore was black and hung on a hanger inside her cupboard door which had opened in the night. And I thought it was a ghost. With a whole face of eyes and fountainy head of hair.

Darcy Dancer descending the main staircase this morning. Someone's feet departing from the front hall. Where the fire was blazing. And somewhere outside a faint roar of a cow for its calf. I had gone into the whim room for a brief think. Kept seeing Miss von B hanging suspended, hung by her neck. Her eyes popping and tongue hanging out. And indeed I opened the whim room window to look down to see that her body wasn't already thrown there lying broken and lifeless on the front steps.

Passing the dining room door I thought I heard a noise. And peeked in. Sheila with a tray just departing pushing through to the pantry. My father in a brown shooting tweed sitting at the head of the table presiding over a dish of rashers and eggs. A bottle standing near by which said Powers Gold Label. And a half full glass of whiskey next to his cup and saucer of tea. A great bunch of household keys on a plate and the wine cellar book open beside him. And as I stepped back to leave and close the door, I winced at the sound of his voice.

'Who gave you the damn leave to drink these wines.'

'They are the property of this house and therefore mine.'

'Like blasted hell they are. What do you think you are running, a private whorehouse here. Shut that door. Damn you. And who do you think you are to contravene my orders and interfere in the affairs of running this estate. Burning down a school. Shooting shot guns at people. And think you're squire here. Well I'll bloody well squire you, you little bastard.'

'Why don't you shut up. You thief.'

Amazing how few words one has to use to gain one's desired effect. As this odious person pushing his chair back slowly gets up. Crumpling his napkin in his fist. I could of course just wait till he lunges and slam the door shut in his face. Have the concussion of the entire monstrously heavy mahogany swinging on its hinges stop him in his tracks.

'You little bastard, I've had just about all I shall take from that insolent mouth of yours.'

Most amazing thing, his flies are open. As he strides, hunched forward. Approaching me with the napkin clutched in his hand. Although I moved away along by the sideboard I was horrified I was not immediately making my hasty departure. But in fact it appeared he was just judiciously closing the door from which I had just as judiciously stepped aside. He then turned and crossed to the pantry door and bolted it. Returning now to confront me across the gleaming surface of the table. Including the silver mounted fluted glass mustard pot. Which I may yet have to use flinging it and its contents at his head as he stands there so deliberately holding back his coat as he unbuckles and removes his gun belt.

'I'm going to teach you a lesson.'

His lips drawn in a mean tight line, approaching me around the table as I back away. And I don't know how on earth he did it so accurately. But the first swipe he took at me with the belt came whizzing around and caught him right across his own face which paled. A hissing noise coming out of his mouth with his eagerness to land a blow on me. I merely pulled out the chairs from under the table to impede him. He slapped and pushed at them. And while jumping one he stumbled to a fall breaking a brace between a chair's legs. I kept moving gracefully. Not even bothering to stop to open a door.

'You damn little cunt you. I'll flail you alive.'

Darcy Dancer dodging left and right. The swishes of belt landing everywhere. Just a matter of a discomforting but safe distance behind me. And once wrapping around a decanter neck to snap it off the side table to land it thumping on the floor. Round and round the table one went. The candelabra crashed over and candles flying. His thin red veined face getting redder. As I dragged one chair behind me as my adversary tried to extend the lashes of his belt past the obstacle and I raced bumping and crashing it down one end of the table and up the other.

'If I ever catch you, you little bastard, I'll kill you.'

Stopped in front of the chimneypiece, more objets d'art were sent from their repose to their desecration as he struck out trying to reach me across the table. The seats fallen out of nearly all the chairs. Over one of which this crazed madman crashed straight into the sideboard. Everything trembled as it was sent back against the wall. And the massive painting of the Irish Wolfhound, Prince of Errold, the great great grandfather of Kern and Olav, crashed down. The bottom edge of the giant frame breaking an array of Meissen vegetable dishes and crushing the silver tea service recently put sparkling there by Miss von B. And just as my pursuer stopped and was estimating the pawn shop value of these drastically cheapened items, a sympathetic vibration also brought crashing down another monstrous painting of one of my mother's uncles, a founder member of the Kildare Street Club. One did not mind this latter loss. A tiresome looking chap anyway. Especially the supercilious manner in which he appeared to gloat down in his dress colonel's uniform. And one thing had become absolutely apparent in one's life. That even despite my recent bed ridden state and all my other shortcomings, and even the boggish demeanour Miss von B says I display in peeing off the front steps, that at least there were few if any persons abroad anywhere now capable of catching me on foot, wheels or horseback.

'I'll bloody your bloody head yet.'

'You will like bloody hell.'

'You little bastard. Fucking christ.'

Happily and exactly upon these latter two hissed words, he put his foot through another section of flooring previously opened up by the heavy member of the Garda Siochana. And indeed even penetrated the ceiling below. Landing on one knee while the other completely disappeared beyond floor level. And as he tried to pull up his foot he pitched forward right on his face. His monocle dropping out of his eye and rolling in a circle into the hole.

'Fucking damn christ you little bastard I am going to get you if it's the last bloody damn thing I do on earth.'

I nearly collapsed backwards laughing. For I had just taken the drape still hanging half off where someone had attempted to put it back up and I threw the dusty heavy brocaded folds right over him. Lashing out as he was now at everything. And distinctly getting out of breath.

'There you are you stupid bully find your way out of that.'

Darcy Dancer leaning in close to shout his words into the rising dust and shape changing drape. And suddenly to try to jump back as he felt his ankle caught by a big strong hand. Upending his leg. And then a thumb and finger sinking deep into the side of my neck. As we grappled and crashed back again into the sideboard, knocking off another decanter or two and scattering the broken pieces of dishes among the salt and sugar grains under foot. Mixed with the greasy fare of the breakfast plate now off the table. Lowering my head I butted him. And twisted free of his hand. He fell backwards, holding on to the table and catching his breath. The sound of his angrily hissing voice. Silenced when I opened and slammed shut the door of the dining room. In the hall my hand going up to my face, wet and cool as I ran. My fingers covered crimson. Blood pouring in a cascade. On my chest and pumping knees. As I raced up the grand staircase.

Miss von B hysterical as she saw me. Coming into her room. Throwing myself in her arms. There beside her bed. Packing her luggage. And I felt my own few tears between her sobs. She cleaned the wound. A deep gouge down my cheek. And covered it with gauze and bandage. Which went right round my head and under my nose. Her photograph album open on top of a neat stack of her clothes on the floor. Two pictures removed from their mounts. One of her as a tiny child and another I had not seen before. Of her side faced and laughing. Her hair shortened in curls at the side of her head.

'I want you to have these please of me.'

And on that morning, grown grey and cold again after a sunny sun, the pictures in my hands, I begged her not to go. That this was my house if she would but wait. But then I knew and could understand. What she meant when she said the drums were beating. That throughout the household were furtive frightened looks. From Norah and Sheila, rushing past just nodding their silent heads. And Crooks quickly exiting from rooms and Catherine the cook working behind a closed kitchen door that was usually always open. The breakages still left in the dining room. Crooks's crossed eyes seemed now heaven and hellwards turned instead of in their usual east and west directions. And Miss von B said I should have careful stitches in my face. But I would not let her have the doctor summoned. That I was quite content to be scarred for life. And then I heard her voice. Down in the north east parlour. Shouting. As I was descending the grand staircase.

'Haven't you done enough to the poor boy. To cut and disfigure his face. When he has only been recently out of his sick bed. You brute.'

And I could not hear what he said. But it was something that made Miss von B shout all the louder.

'How dare you, how dare you say such things to me.'

By the time I got to the north east parlour door, Miss von B was opening it and slamming it behind her. Tears again welling in her eyes. Her face and neck all flushed red above the edge of her grey sweater and string of pearls. Her hand reaching out for my arm.

'Come. We both shall go. Leave this place. I will take you away with me.'

And the parlour door opening behind us. And there he was in the same brown tweed with its faint line of red squares. His monocle back in his eye. Miss von B her arm around my shoulder standing together in the middle of the hall. Under my every important ancestor's eye.

'And Miss von B I will have you arrested for kidnapping.'

'And you squander this boy's birthright.'

'It is none of your damn business what I do. And the quicker you can get the hell out of here the better.'

'I shall go. I shall go instantly. I am packed. You need not worry.'

'Damn good riddance to you too.'

The door slammed. My stupid so called father gone back into the parlour. Miss von B and I went to her room. All the work she'd done mending and fixing, dusting and cleaning. And I tightened some leather straps around her bags. Of this woman. Who'd stopped the whole place from completely tumbling down. If only I could see Uncle Willie to ask his advice. Or even Sexton. Who regrettably imparted even more dismal news when I came across him in his potting shed. Separating out bulbs.

'Ah Master Darcy, now, it's a pretty kettle of fish. None of my business. What goes on in the big house. It's not for the humble likes of me to comment upon. But they've got the guards alerted to keep an eye out at the station and around the roads. Sure now the disgraceful accusation is that it was yourself who took the master's horse that led the gallop into the gossip concerning that poor innocent girl.'

Crooks was standing on the front steps as Luke came up the hill from the farmyard with the float. Miss von B in a long grey wool coat, a dark blue boubouska tied around her head. She seemed so suddenly really scared that she could be accused of kidnapping.

At the station, we waited for the train. Under the eggshell blue of a cold evening sky. Tiny clusters of clouds grey and underlined in pink. The sun setting. The trees' branches so stark. The fields a faded green in the dying light. And two great swans coming overhead, their wings beating their white powerful strokes.

'Look swans. Flying together. I hope that's like us.'

'I too my sweet, hope they are like us. Flying together.'

And chugging around the turning a little faster than usual came the train. Thundering and blowing and hissing steam into the station. Kern and Olav had run behind us on the drive out to the gates. And they sat really looking sad as we went down the road. Miss von B said to say goodbye to Sexton. And Crooks in parting clearly had tears in his twisted eyes. Luke looked all solemn and furtive. And all the way taking me back, to my every desperately cheerful comment he would say, ah now you've said it. Till I said nothing at all. And Miss von B with her four bags. None of which were awfully grand. Or marked with coronets. But I had made them at least secure with the big leather straps I tightened around each. And helped stack them over her head in the carriage. Silk stockings on her legs. Which curved she said in the true manner of an aristocrat. And as her skirt lifted getting her into the carriage, a gentleman already in the compartment was falling all over himself to help her in too. I was quite ready to punch him. But with my bandage attracting so much attention I thought best not to attract any more.

I held her gloved hand in each of mine, feeling through the thin kid skin the heat of her fingers. I was now going to say goodbye. My face looking up at hers as she leaned forward and down out of the compartment window. The wind and fresh air of the drive had brought a new freshness to her skin and colour to her cheeks. And it may have been the evening light but something seemed lost in her eyes. As if they looked over my shoulder and far away into the past. Or even remembering how she found me unaristocratically peeing that night off the front steps of Andromeda Park. But maybe it was because she had said goodbye on other trains. Even sadder than this. And all now that would be left of her would be the smell of pine and lavender she used in her cupboards and drawers.

'My sweet, my sweet, my sweet. Just kiss me.'

In the scent of turf smoke to put my lips upraised towards hers. And feel the softness of their flesh. And suddenly the train was gone. I couldn't somehow believe it. That I would see its lights going away down the tracks. And leave everywhere I looked so empty. Hearing the engine growing fainter now. Puffing and chugging and pulling. To roll. Big steel wheels clicking and clacking on this track. Out of this grey station to go past the miles of empty winter countryside. Over which the hounds give tongue. The scent taken. Watching from a hillside. Their distant white specks running across the low land of a valley. As they did one day. When Miss von B and I were gaily hunting. Standing with all the horses sending up a cloud of steam so that we all vanished from sight. Till away we went again. Over the beige rushes against the green. Find him. Run. Flying. Out under the scattered clouds. Gallop thundering on the endless green. Find him.

> For he
> Discourses
> Somewhere

20

      The carriage lamps lit as darkness fell. I had Luke take me round the country roads beyond the village. To delay returning to Andromeda Park. Petunia knowing her unerring way over the winding lanes. Passing the graveyard and church where Foxy had committed his sacrilege. And then the entrance gates and the curve of the rhododendron lined drive up to my mother's elegant clerical friend's little grey Georgian house. Whose sallow freckled face I remembered so quietly serene when once he talked of his travels abroad before the war. To hear opera in the strange distant romantic cities of Europe. And faintly recall my mother leaning forward like a bird to pour him tea and before he would reach for his cup he would always press his handkerchief further up under his silk cuff.

      The shadowy trees go by. And the looming hills and walls. A moon alight behind the clouds. Smoke rising from a cottage chimney and mists settling on the great rusty black bogs. Across which the train now takes her. So that I may never see her again. I looked up at the window of the pub where Mr Arland had stayed. A lace curtain there. Nearly discern him standing just beyond its secret whiteness. The loneliness he must have suffered all those months. Pining for a lady whose ample backside would readily bare itself to open up her legs for anyone rich and titled. And whose grey stone house we also passed. What are her activities now. Having so conspicuously degraded herself. With me to thank for her downfall. Or even triumph. If ever she becomes a marchioness.

      Cold windy and pitch black as we came in the back farm gate of Andromeda Park. Went splashing through the puddles and pounding over the broken branches and leaves collected on the road. As the float stopped at the steps,

Crooks was standing at the south east parlour window. Not used since my mother's death. And full of damp sofas stacked with pillows and faded prints of the hunt all over the walls. Then Crooks was opening the door and looking extremely concerned judging by his frown.

'Master Reginald, I'm glad to see you. The guards were here. Looking for you. Did you see them.'

'No. We came in by the back road.'

'Thank our merciful saviour for that. I said you'd gone by the train up to Dublin for a few days. Which I thought was as well. As something told me by their attitude that, and god forbid such a thing, that they wanted to take you into custody. I told them it was that cur Foxy who did whatever they thought you did.'

'Where's my father.'

'He's down below with the agent in the rent room. And if you will be preferring to dine alone, I'll take you up some hot supper whenever you're ready. I wouldn't let it be known where you were to anybody calling.'

'Thank you Crooks. I'll dine in my room. And I do appreciate what you've done.'

'Well master Reginald, I wouldn't be much of a gentleman's gentleman if I didn't look after one's master's business as well as I would look after my own.'

I supped behind my locked door and waited till just before dawn. And the household still. My father retired to the north west corner of the house over the ballroom. I dressed with two big thick pairs of boot socks, two woolly vests, cricket shirt and dark blue sweater under my shooting coat. And got my boots from the front hall. To go out into the world. Starting in the darkness of the morning. To make my triumphant fortune. And come back again to be master of this house.

But I fell down the whole flight of stairs. To the stone paving of the servants' corridor. Without breaking any bones and no one stirred. Edna Annie and Catherine still snoring asleep. Finding a candlestick, I lit it to go flickering tiptoe into the warm kitchen. Returning into the long cold hall with a bag full of cheese, butter and bread. Catherine now groaning nightmarishly asleep in her cell. Blow out this candle. Go past the old rent room. Its maps and map table. The door with two bullet holes. And its outside hall and stairway sealed up with brick. Where years ago the tenantry formed a line out the door to pay their tithes. The agent still attending at the round green leather topped table with its index drawers and pedestal cupboard to pay the men. Sexton said it was a chamber of misery.

Go out now that door. Past the steps and stairway to the schoolroom up and down which I often rushed. To hungrily steal goodies from under Catherine's very nose. And share these with Mr Arland who as he chewed so pleasantly told me not to be rude and thieving. Where would he be now. Happy I hope in full employ. Attending theatre and opera with his lovely actress.

Darcy Dancer pulling back the great bolt. Open quietly this scraping big old portal. Through which so many lives have come and gone to toil and live in these cavernous damp rooms. Close it. And leave behind sleeping. Those souls working towards the end of their days. Down beyond the sunlight shut out high up by the wet dripping stone wall holding back the earth from the rusty barred windows. Catherine maybe will retire to her farm. And Crooks find another situation. And then. Just as it was doing before Miss von B came, all above in this house will moulder and tumble in a heap.

The grass frosty under foot. Makes one shiver. But must go. Never turn back. Forward. Through this iron gate and climb up over where the farm tunnel goes under. Shrouded in the shrubbery there, the old jam house. Head out past the cemetery. Its ivy leaves and great yew tree. Out to these lands. Where I know every copse, hill, and pasture. If I say goodbye. Can the dead hear you. Or listen as I say I stinking well can't stand it any more. To be told what to do. And I'm getting the stinking god damn hell out of here.

Darcy Dancer sliding sidewards down the steep side of an

incline. Bending to squeeze under a giant bough of a tree. Sown by a great great grandfather. Who was friends with the curator of Kew Gardens in England. And who planted all these strange trees. And o my god, the cold cold air. Feel it in the cut on my face. Made bleed again by my fall. Each step now crushing the whiteness underfoot. Fog again out on the sky. Keep tripping over the lumps of frozen cow dung. As I follow. Poor Miss von B. If only she gave him a good clout in the face when he had her on the carpet this morning. Her breasts so swelling in her grey sweater. I wanted to throw myself on my knees and clasp her round the thighs and just hold her. And I must go on. And in the morning chase after her train. Could I lie up hidden in the old game larder till full light. But without any hay or straw it would be so cold. Head now in that direction. That will take me somewhere. Safe from guards and make my headway cross country. Find the fastest way to Dublin. But travelling, each time one looks up, there are always more fields, hedges and hills ahead. The nights running from school I kept the moon at my back. And still did not know where the hell I was going. Except now I go away from home. Running from everything. Come back in a few months, when my fortune is made. And even before next hunting season has arrived, be again the lord and master of Andromeda Park.

Darcy Dancer trudging up the hill. Past this monstrous branched tree. Upon which I did lie on its great extending bough in summertime just staring up into the leaves and hiding from my dear sister Beatrice Blossom. Who got so jealous when she saw me pee standing, when she had to squat. And beyond across the parkland shadows, there stands the grove of oaks. To be mutilated again I'm sure, any day. And through the copse on the other side of the sheltery field. And five more stone throws away. Against a wall, the old disused pump house. Abandoned now to cattle. Where in its cool shade they escape the flies in summer. And where was kept their stock of hay for winter foddering. Go in there. To sleep. Be nearly like a little house with its leaded windows. Rest cosy and warm till daylight.

Darcy Dancer standing on the frost hardened mud at the entrance door. Lifting to dislodge it open. Something blocking behind it. A stone. Push harder. Reach in a hand to heave it out of the way. And close it again to keep out the fog and cold. The sweet smelling warmth of the hay.

'Who's that. Another step. And I'll fucking well send this hammer in me hand fucking well through your skull.'

'Foxy.'

'Who's that.'

'It's me.'

'What are you doing atall.'

'I'm looking for a place to sleep.'

'Sure haven't you got your bed beyond back there in the big house. What gave you the idea to come up here.'

'I'm leaving. Perhaps forever. I'm now a criminal on the run. With the guards after me. Just like you.'

'Don't be daft since when was gentry ever criminals. What's that on your head.'

'It's a bandage. I got a cut.'

'Ah you'd want to rub a bit of dirt into that, that's where the cure is, in the handful of sweet soil. But sure are you crazy to be going off. What's the matter with you. For the likes of you to be sleeping rough. When you were dying there only a few days ago. Sure you only just arrived back from school.'

'Are you hungry Foxy. I've got some food.'

'Well I can always do with a bite to eat. Although it's not yet time for me breakfast.'

'Is this where you've been staying.'

'I am for the time being. While the guards are looking for me. And while my father has been in his bed for a while groaning after I landed him a blow of this hammer.'

'You're always doing that Foxy.'

'And me father and some others like him are always deserving it too. Did you read about me in the newspaper.'

'Yes.'

'Ah that's all a cod. I have the account here in me pocket. They haven't got any of them facts straight. Don't listen to any of them lies. Sure wasn't I having an old dig between the juicy legs of the good Father's housekeeper's daughter. That old bag gave birth to her eighteen winters ago and has been saying round the countryside ever since that it's her niece from Dublin. It was the daughter. Herself one lovely bit o' lass, who told me where the sherry was.'

'It said in the newspaper Old Marsala.'

'Now I don't know the bloody difference. But it would come every bit as close to making you feel in your head the same as sherry does. She gave me the key to the sacristy. I was invited. Now that old bag says I've put her daughter in the family way four months gone. Demanding I take her up the aisle and put a wedding ring on her finger. With the eegit guards thinking I'm guilty of robbing.'

'But you were in the curate's robes.'

'I'm in them this very second, can't you see up here. And warm as a hand up a cow's arse they are too. Ah but that's another cod. The daughter's doing entirely. Didn't she say she wanted to see what it was like to get it from a priest. Sure what harm is there in that. To put on an old cassock. And even though I couldn't get the white collar around me neck to make me look the real part, I was suitable enough for her when I took out me prick. And that had a white collar of skin around it I'm telling you. I fucked her all over the sacristy. Sure she was consuming the sherry as well. Wanted me to do her on the altar. I told her to fucking well go on out of that and get some manners on her, that I wasn't going to commit sacrilege. And I never broke into any ould church. And I wasn't doing her where we might leave clues up in front of the tabernacle. I did her at the side altar instead. Where not so much attention is paid. And that eegit. Inquiring what I was doing on the gravestone. I was taking my fucking ease was what I was doing. After a good hump. Couldn't he fucking well hear me singing. And then the old hag the mother has three of them at the dance hall attacking me for what she says I did to the daughter in the family way. I took a few knocks but I beat and belted and kicked the bejesus out of all three. Put two of them lying in the hospital. And the other in church praying I don't come after him to belt him again. Bring up now some of that cheese.'

'It's warm up here.'

'Sure it's as fine as the big house. I'm back and forth there when there's a need. They think they have me locked out. Come up from under the slab in the pig curing room where I took you. And have nearly everything brought back here except the kitchen stove. Hid in here behind this old bit of straw. Crock from the kitchen, only borrowed mind. To keep the food in or the rats will get at it. Be another month before foddering up here in these fields. And I hear tell plenty about you. Shagging the kraut herself.'

'You're not to speak in that fashion of her.'

'Ah you're a bit sweet on her. Sure I don't care. I don't mean to be disrespectful like. O but god be praised hasn't she got the greatest body now on her. It's the rare time when I wouldn't mind being gentlemen gentry like yourself. That such as the likes of her would give me a tumble. I speak with respect now. But they're on to you. So I hear in the yard.'

'Someone snitched on me.'

'Sure it's the agent. Don't you know that. Fancies her, he does. Slathering after her like a lapdog at every meeting of the hunt. And making up to her, rolling his eyes and tipping his hat and begging her pardon from one end of the big house to the other. Sure I've seen the crafty piece of work at it. And you wouldn't blame him for that I'm telling you if you ever clapped eyes on the wife he's got. With her face like the innards of the gears in the old mowing machine. Sure he cottoned on to it all going on between the two of yez from that stupid eegit Crooks with his big stupid mouth mumbling about the house. And sure I hear tell the agent's buying your land. Has a mind himself to be the big boss in the big house. Maybe even have her ladyship kept on as the housekeeper. Live like a Protestant. Set up himself and the ugly wife like a king and queen over all these acres. A grand bit of cheese this. What I'm telling you is gospel. Did you ever hear tell of me lie to you. Sure he's busy taking over the whole place. Selling the trees and buying the ground they stand in.'

'He will not. No one will. It's mine.'

'Well I don't know a thing about that now, but if it's yours you'd better soon start minding it. And where now are you going.'

'I don't know yet. Maybe Dublin.'

'Stay out of that place. The gurriers there would carve you up with knives and have you raw for breakfast. Sure you wouldn't be crazy enough now to step out forever and be gone. Do yourself a permanent mischief. That's daft. A roof, one of the biggest anywhere, over your head. Them gardens. And anything you want flowing to your mouth with the snap of your fingers or yank of a bell. With the grass growing, the beasts grazing and calves popping out of cows all over the place. You'd be daft and all. And meaning no disrespect now, but haven't you got a fuck laid on now like hot water in the pipes. You wouldn't get me out of there with the likes of that kind of living, I'm telling you. Sure your father for a start won't be around forever. Don't go abandoning anything that's a bit of use to your comfort. I've learned a bit. Me now, my whole life is discomfort. And I wouldn't know a bit of differ. But you now, gentry, who has to kow tow to nobody. And here you don't know where you're going or what you're doing.'

'I could get work on a farm.'

'What kind of place would give you a job. They'd take one look at your hands and know you weren't suited. But maybe you could try a stable at one of them big stud farms. You'd know plenty enough about horses. And what I taught you. But you'd be daft. With your own stables right here. But never mind me telling you. All I've got is lumps on me head, busts in me arms and scars all over me body. With kicks as well in the shins from them old ewes when I'd shove it up them. And two black eyes you can't see on me. But I'll tell you one bloody thing. At least it wasn't me like the guards and everyone are saying it was who ran off with the master's horse over there and led the hunt thundering down on that old bald bastard the Marquis digging it in there between the legs of that blonde bloody raring to go bitch. I would have loved to have seen that. To put among my memories. The like of that hunting mob over there now is doing their nut now to catch whoever it was.'

'It was me.'

'Go on. You're codding.'

'I'm not.'

'Ah god then, you're well on your way. And the faster your legs go, the better. That mean bunch are out to hang by the neck the one who did that. Sure you're well able for Dublin then. But mind now how you go out on your own. Cover up who you are with a tall story. Told once you'll believe it yourself. Rob only just before dawn and pass the time of day to everyone you see now on the roads like there wasn't a bother on you. You'd be as well now not letting them know you're gentry. Sure it's no extra trouble to call them sir. And you won't come to any harm. And mind, let me tell you something. You're the only one who's ever treated me decent and I won't forget it. And I'll even tell you something else you should know. But I won't.'

By the first chill light of a grey still dawn, Foxy Slattery at the old pump house door, took leave of me. As I stood on the thickening frost and backed away over the stiffened mud and cow flop. He stood there ecclesiastically with his serious suspicious face. As if he were thinking of how to rob you while keeping on good terms. His black priestly garment stuck with hay and straw. His face all scars. And he suddenly beckoned me back. Lifted my bandage to look at my cut.

'Ah it's only an old scratch on you. Sure pull this thing off and let the healing air and sun to it.'

Foxy seemed sad to see me go. As I reached the old wall, climbing over it, I turned to look back. In the doorway, a lonely figure. Still see him at the door. Then as I came to the top of the hill, he was gone and the door was closed. And I heard mewing sounds and calls. Four swans flying overhead in formation. They go south. I go east. Out to the world. Maybe even across the high seas. And I know what Foxy wanted to tell me. Something you can easily tell. From just a warm smile and glow in someone's eyes. That my father is Uncle Willie. Who stood that day by the mound of mud. Head wet with rain. Eyes dropping his tears. Upon the sods.

> Burying
> The beauty
> Of my
> Mother

21

That late morning, to pass down a sloping field making foot tracks on the moist meadow to the bank of a stream. Cup my hands to drink the water. Big grey rat jumps off a log. Swims away like a fish. Distant wheels hammering on the road.

Darcy Dancer clutching the moss, climbing up to await a boy trotting closer with his donkey and cart. Hitching a ride up and down hills along the meandering byway. Without a word spoken. Save growls and grunts at the big eared shaggy little beast whose tiny hooves pecked away the miles. And when I said thanks at a fork in the road the boy gave me his nod.

That evening nearing the outskirts of a town. A suspicious Garda Siochana looked at me twice. And the third time he turned I had already disappeared over a wall by a hospital. And ran like the devil through a graveyard. Whose tombstones just sitting outside the hospital windows must make the sickly want to recover. When I offered it, Foxy would take nothing of my money of six pounds, thirteen shillings and eight pence. And now I adhere to his advice. To pass the time of day with strangers. With a remark on the weather. But make yourself scarce when you see the law.

Darcy Dancer in gloves, boots and Aran Islander's hat. These two chillier days proceeding cross country. Last night as I stood still a badger walked right between my legs. And passing once two farmers standing scratching their heads surveying the innards of an automobile. As its wires showered out sparks and its exhaust exploded smoke. And along with the time of day I proffered my help.

'Ah me young lad it's not help we need. Sure you'd have a horse pull a plough a mile before you'd get this yoke to roll a foot down a hill. Mechanical failure is a fatal disease rampant across Ireland. And if you were needing to get somewhere you'd be better off with a pair of legs.'

And somehow one was comforted by this farmer's words. For all I carried with me were my idle hopes. And the cut on my face still sore but at last healing. As I went now in circles with road signs twisted pointing every way but the right way. Meeting farmers driving their cattle to and from milking. Or cows loose grazing the long acre of ditches and hedges bordering the road. Or straying sheep and lambs scattering ahead of me. And the world, each step I took, was a green place under the sky. Waiting till the sun might shine. Or trying to catch a hare supposed to be slow running downhill. Who left me spreadeagled empty handed flat on my face. To look up and see two farmers standing near by in a field. And recall the words of Sexton.

'Ah there's a way an Irishman stands in a field that you would know by the manner of how he stood that he was buying land and for that you'd know who was selling.'

And the third day following the bank of a river along a railroad track I ventured into a town. Mid morning coming to a bridge and a woman passed with a basketful of groceries. And dropped a potato on the path. I picked it up. And she nervously looked around over both her shoulders. And when I smilingly put it back in her basket she whispered.

'Ah I am grateful to you. Would you like to come home with me.'

A side street terraced with villas with little front gardens. One called Ivy another St Kevin's. Statues of Sexton's Blessed Virgin inside over the doorway. Two little chill smudged faced children across the street watching us entering. A narrow long hall.

'Ah you're a good looking likely lad. Would you like the smoke of a cigarette.'

One got extremely uneasy as she began to behave in a rather strange manner. Licking her lips and suddenly shoving me up against the wall to kiss me. In the middle of her assault she stopped to bless herself as the Angelus rang. Then asked would I come say the rosary with her in the bedroom. And that she'd give me a pound to dig her garden out back. I simply don't know how I managed it but between her prayers to the holy ghost and her tugging at my fly buttons and trying to stick her tongue down my throat, I suggested gently that a plate full of bread and butter and a pot of tea would be welcome. But seated comfortably in the tiny kitchen and my teeth clamped in the middle of my first slice of bread, she leaped on me. We fell backwards on the floor. Her denture came out. She was panting saying let's do it the way they do it in the films. Wrestling out of her arms I grabbed for my bag and the thickest slice of buttered bread and ran out the back door. And chased by her I had to crash through ruddy shrubbery and climb up over a tall wall at the bottom of the garden. Losing my gloves and dropping on the other side into the yard of an abattoir.

Darcy Dancer nights lying awake above a pub in a room like Mr Arland's must have been. Found a job within a minute of my escape. And now daily heading to work. My hands raw and blistered. Blood on my clothes. With the religious maniac's house just the other side of the wall. The round pleasant faced butcher paid me three and six pence my first afternoon. And seven shillings a day for sweeping, cleaning, washing and carrying beef entrails out of his abattoir. Each night returning to a suspicious lady publican watching me from the cold dining room door as I ate. Wondering perhaps if I were a tinker. With just my old battered bag slung over my shoulder and no gentlemanly luggage. And then at the end of the week must have thought I was a spiv when I took out my pound notes to pay. But breakfasts, with the landlady out of sight, I swept up the bacon, eggs, tea, jam, butter, with one's elegancies totally deteriorating as I licked my plates clean. To be finally seen one morning.

'Is that the kind of manners you were taught at home.'

'They are madam. And were yours as good, you would mind your own business.'

'You can vacate you can.'

So much for back chat. People, it would appear are highly unappreciative of a clever turn of phrase. But worse that same day the religious maniac was up on the other side of the wall staring down at me. Would have had to be standing on a ladder. Seemed the whole damn country wanted to look at me for one reason or another. Sending me on my way next day to another town.

Money nearly all but spent, I slept huddling in hay barns. And warming on sheltery hillsides in any sunshine of the morning. Legs stiff and tired. Gloves lost. And even stuck my hands into freshly plopped hot cow dung. Foxy said that it was a great fast way to get the knuckles warm. Let the muck dry on you like a pair of mittens. And a better fit than you'd ever get from a pair you'd buy. But I looked bad enough already without appearing as some stinking handed monster. And washed and further chilled my hands in the first stream I came to.

The worst were the dogs running out from farmyards and growling round one's legs. Or barking through gates. And then the weariness. With every time one looked up. The never ending fields hedges hills and bogs ahead. East south east. Losing track of the days. Each night colder. Ever growing hungrier. And then from a hillside saw a hunt in the distance. The scarlet coats passing amid the trees. Saw the start. The run. The hounds in full cry. And the death. And I moved off to be gone nearly hiding and feeling like a criminal. Striding up hills I remembered the strong silky fleshed mountain climbing thighs of Miss von B. Muscles swelling back strongly from her knees. And I dreamt of the light play of her fingers over my arms, shoulders and up and down my back. O my god. The comfort. Peace. The sinking of my own lips softly upon her mouth. And am I soon going to die. Shivering now. On the verge of tears.

Felt some little cheer as I stood looking at a road sign. A village called Prosperous. First uplifting word one had seen all these days and lonely nights. Driven by the wet winds. The damp now chill through to my back. And in the first light of dawn hitching another lift southwards on a cart. A farmer with two monstrous sows. Warming myself standing between them, honking snorting and grunting.

The farmer gave me a shilling helping him drive his pigs up a back alley into a butcher's. And this latter fat chap with his bloodied apron when I asked for work, hired me for four more shillings. And I felt now so at home to lug out guts and sweep and hose down the reddened cobbles and carry boxes of bones. The shed steaming with cattle entrails freshly dead. Pigs squealing. Beasts kicking and mooing. A hammer landing between their eyes. A groan and sigh flopping to their knees and falling over on their sides. The butcher slitting their throats cutting open their bellies and winching up the carcass. Who now and again would chat with me.

'Well now me lad I am pleased with your work. Not idle a second. Where are you from with an accent the like of that that anyone would think you was English gentry.'

'I am the son of a butler, sir, who is in service in a big house and it was required of me to speak grandly.'

'Is that a fact, now. Did they have grand goings on in the big house.'

'Yes they did.'

'And I suppose ladies dressed in finery.'

'Yes and gentlemen with violins and harps played and everyone danced in a big golden ballroom.'

'Fancy that now, fancy that. Sure it's a long way then for you to be here in this up to your knees in guts.'

'I don't mind sir.'

'Would you like a situation here. Teach you a bit of butchering. A lively lad like yourself, would be well able for the job.'

'I am very grateful to you sir. And for your kindness. But I would sir, prefer to work with horses.'

'Ah well I can't help you there.'

'Would you know of anywhere.'

'Well lad your best bet now, is to head for the Curragh. That's your man. They've got horses aplenty all over the place. But you look that bit shook to me you do. Come home now with me till you get a good feed.'

The kindly butcher's wife gave me tea. In the kitchen of their snug little house. As much as I could eat of bacon and eggs. Till I went back out on the road. Foolishly saying when they asked me to stay that I had a place to sleep. But first having an altogether jolly time making the butcher beat his fist on his knee telling them stories of the big mansion. Of the gowns and tiaras of the ladies. And that my father was called Bonkers.

'Bonkers is it. That's a funny enough name if you don't mind me saying.'

'Yes Bonkers. And although I do not want to speak disrespectfully he is very tottery. Always spilling soup on the floor and then slipping on it. He once tipped gravy all over the head of a very grand titled red haired lady till her tresses were quite brown. She jumped up with shock of course. Knocked the entire contents of a bowl of cabbage into the lap of the Protestant bishop. Naturally the scalding vegetable in his lap made him jump too and upend the potato tureen out of another servant's hands.'

One wondered if the butcher would break his knee pounding it with his fist laughing as he did. And rain was falling as I went out up the dark lane. Past these little cottage houses. In each the glow of a fire inside through the curtains. Turf smoke rising up into the night and the breeze wafting down its sweet smell. A dog curled up whimpering in a doorway. Who growled as I walked past. Who'd serve as only a canapé for Kern or Olav. If they snapped their big jaws on him.

Reaching the shadowy road winding into the blackness beyond the town, I shivered. With my heart thumping. Keep my legs moving. Find a barn to sleep. Feel as I felt that night when I collapsed at dinner. My bowels may at any moment move. Find a spot by a wall. Won't be as there is at Andromeda Park, a lavatory knob to flush. Just sticking up by one's hand from the mahogany seat. Yank upwards and the great flushing gushings come to wash all the turds away. To leave the porcelain clean. Where words said. Dent and Hellyer, Red Lion Square. And now the cold night wind freezes my bottom. And my bowels won't move.

Darcy Dancer hunched up, hat pulled down around the ears. Head in the direction the butcher told me. Look back at a sound. See a blaze of light in the sky. An engine of a motor car approaching. Two beams of lights blinding my eyes. The long heavy vehicle shaking the road. Roaring past and cutting shadows up against a black sky through the trees ahead. The silver bark of their tall looming shapes. An oasis in there behind these great high stone walls. Where there could be some friendly understanding Protestant fellow squire who would welcome a cold lonely member of the gentry temporarily bereft on the road.

An archway over a great gate flanked by lodges. Escutcheon carved in stone. Wish I could go in there. Down that long long drive. Under the big old trees. Thump a knocker on the castle door. A kindly butler comes shuffling. My good fellow I'm lost on the road. Do you mind if I just pop in. Join his lordship for a nightcap in front of the library fire. In the butler's eyes, a glowing sign of recognition. Ah. Upon my word sir. If it isn't one of the Darcy Thormonds. Do by all means come in. By jolly jove Bitters I shall, yes. And what sir can I get you to drink. Whiskey please. Very good sir. O that's far too much. O no, that's alright, I'll drink it, save you pouring it back into the bottle. Thank you Bitters. You're most welcome sir and I'm sorry his Lordship has retired but he hopes you will make yourself entirely at home. Thank you profusely Bitters, indeed I shall. What time will you breakfast in the morning sir. Ten, please. Very good, would you like the usual six eggs sunnyside, with the usual ham slabs, pucks of tomatoes, heaps of sausages, buckets of tea and bowls full of honey and marmalades. Thank you, yes Bitters, the usual. And along with your hot cocoa what selection of books would you like by your bedside from the library sir. O Marco Polo will do, and perhaps that awfully interesting chap Darwin who says we're just a bunch of ruddy bloody chimps might not come amiss.

Darcy Dancer backing slowly away from the great gates. To turn and walk now along this high stone wall with the tall tapering branches of the trees arching out over the road ahead. Growing from their deep roots in their ancient park lands. O my god, where am I going. In this ceaseless rain. And a gale rising. Further and further away from the apron of gravel over which I have on wheels and hooves come into and gone from Andromeda Park. The place where for all its dilapidations did at least keep the harsh physical strife of life to a minimum in its great rooms and halls. Thought I heard the big canine lungs of a wolfhound bark. Don't let me die. Miss von B. Please. If I could only know where you are tonight. Right now this moment. Your long soft body. Clutched so closely to mine. Your voice panting your cries in my ear. Remember everything about you but your feet. And O my god. Now other men may have you. Flesh to your flesh. Where mine once touched. And Uncle Willie said ladies find it so awfully difficult to be faithful. When any prick in proximity will do.

Darcy Dancer following the high estate wall turning away inland off the road. Cross this ditch. Push through these shrubbery beech. Save for the motor car not one person, cart or bicycle has passed me all this way. Along all these miles of empty road. The whole countryside locked up. Behind doors and shutters. Afeared of goblins and fairies. And tinkers too. Passed the tiny shell of one of their tents. Embers of a fire glowing outside. Sealing themselves away for the night. Warm and snug with the bugs beetles and lice. Foxy said what harm is it for a few of them little creatures to be crawling on you. Sure aren't them living things just like yourself. Nurse Ruby said fairies were angels Lucifer cast out of heaven. Saw one the other night on horseback galloping up over the moonlit fields as I looked out of a hayshed. Fairies come and steal. Take away the old people. A farmer's wife milking a cow in a doorway jumped up when she saw my head peeking at her over the wall. She ran screaming back to her cottage her boots splattering mud up all over her frock. After a good swig of warm milk from her pail I heard her shouting blue murder for Sean. And I decamped rather rapidly. Disappearing like the fastest fairy who ever lived.

Darcy Dancer proceeding through the dense shrubbery along this wall. Tramping further and further. Nowhere to climb over. And find some hay to sleep in for the night. Rain keeps falling. Wet through hat and hair to my scalp. Feel so weak. So numb. Face hot. Heart thumping. Should have stayed in the town. In the butcher's house. Or spent seven shillings and six pence for a room. Can't walk any more. Lost out here now, so far from the road. Soon sink covered in the brown stale slime of some bog. Can't go on. Because I'm dying. Death comes slowly up sleepily from one's toes. Tells you. Who seeks me. Beseeches my presence. Knows where I am. Follows me in my big black footsteps. Up these stone stairs. Yes right here. Where you are in your broken hearted sorrow. Where no one seeks you. Beseeches your presence. Knows where you are. Dying alone. Beyond this big iron gate in the wall. Squealing on its hinges. And like the sound of my dear beloved wolfhounds. O God I am in delirium. And it's Christmas eve. An avenue of yew trees. Choir voices. In this place to die. My body stretched on this soft moss. Miss von B. You too were very very sad. Weren't you. Made me so full of pain to watch. Like you were that night in bed. Your back bent in sadness. When I left your arms. Your eyes swollen up big and red. To make you wear a veil. Black lace tucked in under your black silk stock pinned by your gold and diamond pin. Please come to my funeral. If ever I'm found. No address. Nor my name. Just my love words written in my diary. And a flat little snowdrop flower I pressed. To remember you by. Is all I can say. All I can send. To wherever you are. And if they bring me back. To bury me. Even lonely out under the meadows of Andromeda Park. By the tall ancient boughed trees. Will you come all black and elegant. Tears streaming from your eyes.

Will you
My lady

22

Sunlight streaming over the wall and through the bars of a gate. A cassocked figure leaning over the form of Darcy Dancer curled and crouched on the mossy grass. The black sleeved hand gently pushing on a shoulder.

'Come now. Can you hear me. Wake up now. Wake up. Who are you. What are you doing here. Please speak. Can you hear me.'

Darcy Dancer groaning. Tuck in his arms and legs. Further away from the chill. But yes. I hear and see the sun in my eyes. Which way is it to heaven. I know that's the way I'm walking now. Miss von B watched me go. She was just at my funeral. Wore her bowler she wears to hunt. So sad, she was nearly carried. By the elbows. Crooks on one side, Sexton on the other. Holding her. Her feet dragging. Sobs racking her. My coffin borne on the shoulders of the grooms. Slide down. Dead and done. In my grave. Held the bars of a gate as I died. Begging God not to let me. Yet like this. It's so quiet just to be asleep. Till morning. Wake in time for Mr Arland. Coming down the hall now to the schoolroom. Books tucked up under his arm. His smile. Greet him. Just as he said I was once. A plutocrat in the pluperfect. His small admonitions. Young persons Kildare, should conduct themselves discreetly. And Mr Arland, please sir, is there anything indiscreet in the promiscuous exercises of etymological parsing. Don't try to be funny, Kildare. Please sir, I am being absolutely serious and I am so glad that you were able to get to my funeral. You look so smartly turned out too. And hello Clarissa. What a very stylish looking couple you and Mr Arland make. So nice of you both to come all this way on the train. And be so smilingly happy, happy together. Waiting to wed. Soon. Soon. How sad then, you must on such a splendid note, attend my obsequies. Yes it is rather a pity. Who said that. Uncommonly rude thing. I shall damn you sir demand satisfaction and climb right up out of my coffin. If someone, who is unnecessarily holding same will just let go of my shoulder. Let go. Is that you Sexton, did you hear me. Do please stop pushing on my shoulder.

'Now. Now. You're alright. Can you hear me. Who are you.'

That sunny cold Christmas morning three dark figures carrying Darcy Dancer by legs and arms along a gravel path. A fourth cassocked figure opening a heavy door. Into a stone flagged hall. And down a long corridor. Through cooking and waxy smells. And into a small vaulted white ceilinged room. A dim red glowing filament of an electric bulb burning straight above my head.

For six days Darcy Dancer laid abed. Face pressed in a creaking pillow and dark hair sticking out from thick mauve blankets. A thin faced man calling twice a day leaning over to put his hand on my brow. Quietly asking questions. As all these men in black and some with collars, come and go. Making me horrified to think that heaven might really be a Roman Catholic place after all.

'Who are you young man. What is your name. Where do your parents live. You can understand me can't you. You understand what I am saying. Can you write. You have been very sick. We need to know who you are. Do you speak Romany. Are you a travelling person. You have nothing to fear from us.'

For four more days I watched the light fade to darkness out the tall narrow pane of window. And then send a bright shaft across my little cell as breakfast came in the morning. Brought by a woman in a white uniform who had my first evening put hot soup on a spoon between my lips. The granite stone arch of this ceiling. Squeaking pallet under my back. Other faces come. They look. Nod, whisper and go away. And then two more tall priestly gentlemen in black.

'I think father, the young man may have been struck dumb. Or suffered amnesia or such. He may require the treatment of a hospital. He was ranting something when found but hasn't spoken since. He could quite possibly be retarded as well. I don't suppose the disgraceful diary in his pocket means anything. The truth of the Daring Dancer's activities. He could have found it. But he's recovering well and is much stronger.'

'Shall we see how he is again in the morning. Wouldn't do now anyway to move him.'

Mornings, afternoons and evenings, there were choir voices singing. Chanting. So peaceful. The sound comes. A bell rings. Feet pass to and fro in the corridor under long webs of vaulted criss crossed ceilings and gothic arches. When lights were out one listened to the gales outside lashing rain against the panes of glass. The world seemed kept away. And the plainsong made me feel I was floating while I was dying. All through the grey days. Turned dark in my heart. Unable to speak. To these ecclesiastic gentlemen. Who seemed so calm civil and kind. Planning each night to say something and then in the cold light of day a stillness would stay my lips. Watching as I would the sunny pink of the rare sun coming in over my shoulder and warmly bathing the wall. Where a Christ is nailed on a cross. Just above a table and chair. As now this morning the door opens. And a tall cassocked figure steps in.

'My name is Father Damian. It is I who found you out there against the wall. Now can't you tell me how you got there. You've been here nearly a fortnight now. We would like to know who you are. So that we can help find or contact your parents or next of kin. Surely someone is missing you. You do speak. We know. Someone heard you last night in your sleep. And indeed you were mumbling when I found you. But we shan't force you. But it would help us if you tried. Perhaps in your own good time. As the robin builds its nest. Have you run away from somewhere. Have you been in an institution. Do you speak Irish. No. Well I'm sure we won't get anywhere trying you in Latin or Greek. But I'll be back again. In the meantime you're not to worry. We shall take care of you here. You understand that don't you. Good.

Well we can get a lot out of you anyway with yes and no. Yes. Good.'

The white uniformed lady who no longer had to push the bed pan under me twice a day, now smilingly helped me hobble on my first trip out into the hall. To make my way in overlarge slippers and faded white pyjamas and dressing gown thirty paces down the flagstone corridor. To a damp water closet with a cistern high up which dripped water down on my back as I sat. Till finally I got warmly dressed again. In my own clothes now cleaned and ironed and my diary back in my pocket. When I was put in a massive kitchen and given potatoes to peel and eggs to break each dawn into a great cauldron. I could with astonishing dexterity break one in each hand but of course did lose many shells in the mass of yolks. Father Damian came.

'Good morning. Hard at work. You look much better. You're feeling that way are you. Good. I think we might try to get you out and about a bit. And perhaps there won't be so much shell then in the scrambled egg. Would you like to do some gardening. Good. Just let me know if you do not feel up to it.'

Darcy Dancer with an old man they called Deaners. Raking up the leaves and scuffling the winter weeds away between the pebbles. And often in dereliction of one's duties sitting long moments on a garden bench in the fragrant fresh air and rare sunlight. Cheerful chirps of birds. Living on their wings. Here in these walled gardens. Perching over the gravel paths. In their winter darkened feathers. And the jackdaw who daily took a leisurely drink out of a roof gutter, went high flying beyond the turrets of this large building. With its big halls. Thick walls. And bells tolling. Where now at dawn before work began I attended at mass. Shuffling chilled from my bed into the chapel across a courtyard. Kneeling in the rear of all these black gowned figures filling the pews. An organ playing. Their voices singing Latin. And my soothed mind full of Miss von B and where could she be. In the big town of Dublin. With each week now passing. To await yet another. Feeling at least my strength returning if not my courage.

Grunting to Deaners who never stopped asking me a lot of foolish questions. Was I out of the looney bin. Did I come from the land. And why didn't I get a move on me just sitting there on my backside while he was doing all the sweeping up of the rotted leaves and spreading all the manure.

Then a wet old morning pushing a barrow of cut branches down the gravel path to where I'd dump them on top of the manure heap and where, when no one was looking I could squat day dreaming a leisurely hour or so hidden by the shrubbery and trees, my back suddenly stiffened and my pace quickened and I was altogether, albeit momentarily, a very energetic gardener's helper indeed. For there right behind me came the voice of Father Damian.

'Well now. We've been watching you.'

As one stops in one's tracks. O my goodness. Here it comes. They're going to fling me out. Shirking at work. Three helpings at meals. And putting lumps of clay in Deaners' hat when he took it off. And laughing like a drain when he put it back on.

'Young man you work with great intelligence. Now run and fetch me this list of books from the library. There's a good lad.'

I was blissfully thunderstruck. And perfectly willing to be thought mentally capable. And now my afternoons were spent working in the library. Stacking and carrying books. Or when the librarian's absence permitted, plopping myself behind a partition to most pleasantly and soothingly read these splendid tomes. Till a week later I sat on the verge of tears. Deaners at lunch saying that he heard tell they were on to me and that it was my last morning of gardening. And I saw once more the wet and winter cold stretching cross country. Instead of enjoying early mass and the murmuring prayers and the thundering organ sounds. And when Father Damian came in. I was ready to vocally beg there and then for another chance. Till a great smile across his face.

'Now my boy. You are. Aren't you. Finally going to speak to me. You're an educated lad. And dare I say it, clearly of good background. I have recommended that you be entirely relieved of your gardening duties and that you be permanently assigned to the library and that you be permitted to attend classes here.'

'Please sir.'

'Ah good lord, at last. At last.'

'Sir.'

'Call me Father.'

'Father. I am a runaway orphan.'

'I see.'

'I'm from the west. My father while he lived was a butler.'

'So that explains this elegant voice. You are a rather surprising discovery. To turn up on Christmas morning. However we won't read anything into that coincidence. You are clearly a young man of ability. We can do something for you here. But we should have to certainly make an effort to find those who as your next of kin may be responsible for you.'

'There are none sir.'

'I see. Are you Catholic.'

'No sir.'

'That's a bit awkward. But doesn't seem to prevent your devoutness at chapel. Well. That's between ourselves. And we won't press the matter further. But we must have information in order to seek permission from those in authority that we can provide for your further education. It's not often one comes upon a young man whose aura and carriage gives promise of, how shall we say it. Future importance, perhaps.'

Promoted to cataloguing books in the library one now not only had a measure of authority but even a proprietory interest when sorting and restacking the shelves of dusty volumes. One also graduated to the end of a table in the large dining hall. With a group of young novices in training for the priesthood. Two of whom distinctly of peasant farming origins, constantly made snide remarks and behaved at every opportunity towards me in their most unpleasant ways.

'What has our pukka boy there been up to today.'

I sat through meals in my secular attire silently looking down at my place. Just thankful to ruddy god that one had food three times a day and a warm place to sleep. With days now peacefully spent with much reading and scholarship in the library. The librarian with his massively thick spectacles seemed so often occupied with some vast work he was writing on the influence of the Old Testament on Gaelic literature that I indeed enjoyed a rather majestic privacy. Till one evening meal in the emptying dining hall. Just as I was leaving table. The more unpleasant of the two unpleasant clerics stopped in front of me. Who had so often passed his sour smirking asides in my direction. Just as I had often gritted my teeth instead of popping him a fist in his sneering face. And now he took his forbidden half smoked cigarette out of his mouth and threw it on the wide wooden scrubbed boards at my feet. To then lift his foot and with the sole of his shoe grind it into a small round smudge of ash and tobacco.

'Clean that up pukka.'

'No.'

'Do as you are told, you phony snot. Or I'll lay about you.'

'No.'

'So you are daring me. Come lads. Pukka is daring me. You are aren't you. Pukka.'

'Yes. I am. And I shall probably punch your face for you should you touch my person.'

The cleric's muscles tightening across his cheeks, his teeth clenching in his jaw. His face grown white. A sickly smile slowly spreading on his lips. Staring at Darcy Dancer's eyes staring back. The dishes clattering being collected from the distant tables. And the sound of my final evening chore when I worked in the kitchen. The barrels filled with leftover food being carted away out to the pigs.

'I think we can settle this sudden display of bravery from our snooty pukka, outside. Is that right pukka.'

'Yes.'

'Well then outside. Have you heard that now lads. He's challenging me. Imagine. Pukka is challenging me. What about it lads. Any wagers as to how long he'll last.'

'Why don't you leave him alone Healy. He's done nothing to you.'

'He's said he'll break my face. That's what pukka has said. In his pukka phony English accent. And I'll be damned if a son of some butler's bloody well going to tell me that.'

Rearing in my face, acrimony. When each day now I attended vespers. Then following dinner, had my cherished solitary long reads in my cell. Poring over dictionaries I had from the library. Of quotations. Of English proverbs and of English etymology. No longer a vagabond. With somewhere finally to be content. And even fencing with a Latin epigram or two with Father Damian.

The gathering from the table pushing back chairs and standing. With a noise of doom. Healy leading the way trooping out of the dining hall. Along down a wide vaulted corridor lined with paintings of previous presiders over these vast ecclesiastic stacks of stone. Walking one's last mile, one sees now every crack and stain. Turning into another long corridor. Past the narrow stone steps I take up a flight to the library. Now through a narrow dark passage to a door and out into a small walled courtyard. And all the way, behind me Healy's associate whispering.

'Healy is going to break every damn bone in your damn body, you snot. And make you scream for mercy.'

Faint flashes of moonlight high up on the wet stone. And a sprinkle of rain. Healy in the semi darkness turning to stand and wait in the middle of the little concrete yard. The clerics gathered in a black circle. And suddenly confronting Healy, Fitzpatrick, a bushy browed blue eyed big farmer's son who seemed friendly disposed towards me and with whom on the playing field I once hopelessly kicked a soccer ball.

'Let the lad go, Healy. He's been ill. Why don't you fight a bully like yourself for a change.'

'He's challenged me.'

'Well bloody hell I'll challenge you.'

'This is none of your affair Fitzpatrick.'

'It soon damn well might be.'

'Well why don't you stand aside and see for yourself. Pukka has his fists already doubled up.'

Darcy Dancer two fists hanging rigidly down at his sides. The knuckles white. Fitzpatrick stepping back.

'Well then I would just like to see him beat bloody damn hell out of you.'

In the faint light, the rain gently falling. Moon must have a halo tonight. The soft gurgling of the drains. The water pouring down pipes from the massive lead gutters on the great roofs. The two protagonists squaring off the centre of the dark circle. Darcy Dancer holding up his fists. Healy raising up the open palm of his hand.

'Well just look at that now. The great Joe Louis himself. Note how he adheres to the classic rudiments of boxing. The left forward. The right held back in reserve to deliver the knockout when that time comes.'

'Why don't you put up your own fists and fight Healy.'

'I am. I am about to do that right now.'

Healy feinting left and right. Darcy Dancer jumping back. And the cleric just nudging Dancer's nose with a wild swinging right hand that whistled past the eyes. The two circling round. Suddenly a flurry of fists. Lights flashing. And Darcy Dancer facing the concrete. The wet cement growing red with drops of blood.

'You damn bully Healy.'

'He asked for it and now he's got it.'

'That's it, get up, get up pukka. You can do it.'

Darcy Dancer pushing himself slowly to hands and knees. The left leg crouching up. Then the right. Now rising to his feet. Lifting his hands again. And another fist crashing into his face stumbling him backwards. Across the courtyard. The circle of clerics parting. Healy pummelling with both fists. The circle of spectators crowding round as Dancer crashes back into the wall. And falling forward grabbing around Healy to hold on.

'That's it, hold on pukka, hold on.'

Darcy Dancer closing his right arm around the back of Healy's neck. Gripping his right fist with his left. Pulling Healy's head forward and down. Squeezing tight with all one's might. Tighter and tighter. This gruesome hateful head further and further down. Scratching and tugging at me. His breath gasping.

'That's it pukka, that's it. You've got him. In a head lock. Hold on. Hold on.'

'Come on Healy kill him. Don't let him do that to you. Trip him. Pull back.'

Darcy Dancer hauling this head downwards harder. And the two entangled figures fall to the cement. Squeeze tighter. Dig my knee deep up into his guts. And as Foxy says put every living ounce of your energy into it.

'What is going on out here.'

A voice in the doorway. Figures scattering. Authority arrives just as I'm winning. And loosen my grip. To stand up. Across from this still leering face. Lashing another fist at me. And laughter from the doorway.

'That's it Healy, let the ruddy pukka have it. Nobody has come. It's only me.'

'And you. You're bloody well going to get a fist in the face.'

The voice of Fitzpatrick. A skirmish at the doorway. And the phony voice of authority now pleading for mercy. As my lip gets smashed cut over my teeth. Another blow landing on my eye. Sends half the world black. Taste of blood in my mouth. Get just one punch into his belly with all my might. Send his damn reeking breath out of his throat as my knee nearly did along with his dinner. My head like Foxy's getting used to being bludgeoned. Bright sharp pain of fists landing. High on my forehead. Crouch low, knees flexed, step forward. Hide if I can my head behind a shoulder. Cock my right arm right down by my hip. As Foxy showed me once. Swing now with all my almighty strength. Land a fist he'll never forget deep into his ruddy guts.

'Holy Christ.'

'Don't take the Lord's name in vain.'

'Begorra. Did you see that. What an almighty right hook into Healy's belly.'

Healy bending over double. Wobbling. Staggering forward. Nearly falling to his knees. Then falling. His mouth exploding vomit. Someone shouting.

'Get going lads there's someone coming for sure.'

Darcy Dancer standing above this bully propped up on his fours. Before I depart give him something to remember me by. Bring a heel right crushingly down on the back of his hand. Make it a long ruddy time before it tightens itself in a fist again.

'My hand. My hand.'

Healy howling in agony. A blissful sound. And now run. Last behind these figures. Back in through this door. The pounding feet echo down the hall. Just ahead someone trips. Headlong into a plinth and pedestal. Once carrying just these few seconds previously the marble bust of St Ignatius Loyola. Requires a detour with not indifferent haste, out this other door. Across the courtyard. Where I once dug and weeded the rose beds. The quickest way back to my cell. Shove open this heavy oak portal. Hammered together with copper nails turned green. And Christ. Crash into this figure pacing the hall reading his breviary.

'Excuse me father.'

'Damn you. Where do you think you're going.'

'To hell.'

Lights lighting up the windows. A hullabaloo arising. Darcy Dancer racing down through trees. Air colder. Snow beginning to fall. Moon behind the fast moving clouds. White specks on the white stone statues. The stations of the cross. Ghosts looming out here in the trees. The new pale blades of daffodils shoving up in the crush of frost under foot. Eye paining. Ears ringing. Head throbbing. Lips bloody and bruised. Keep running. Till one is finally far away out on the other side of the road. Crossing the frozen dew of the meadows.

> Without
> A single hope
> In the world
> Any more

23

The night spent curled up in the warmth and snugness of a thatched store of hay. And one was not surprised at one's rather sadistic impulse. And indeed rather enjoyed the thought of that bully maimed. And a dream of losing my shoes and coat in a big cinema. Later searching for the lost and found department. Up alleys and along doorless walls. An attractive girl I stopped to ask directions was curt with me. She later returned and apologized. And god even in my dream I seemed so relieved she had. Feeling as I was so awfully gruesomely crushed. Like Healy's hand.

Two more nights were wet with soft moist winds. One sheltering under a leaking lean to. The next huddling under rusted sheets of corrugated iron. Eating raw cabbage and turnips. Then it snowed again. Left tracks behind me in my thieving. The whole damn countryside would soon be on my trail. Tried each big farm I came to. Even enumerated all my gardening skills. And everyone suspiciously viewing my face turned me away.

Till one morning. Coming to the top of a gently rising hill. In the first sunshine for days. I stopped at a large gateway bordered with lawns. A straight avenue down between great arching beech trees. To a house with its windows shining and a gravel drive to its yellow door. Walking trepidatious between these railed fences. Green velvet paddocks. Mares with foals gambolling on the close cropped winter grass. A clocktower entrance to a stable yard. Where a red crinkly haired groom led a horse clattering across the cobbles.

'Begging your pardon sir, but I am inquiring as to there being a position open for a stable lad.'

'Well now I wouldn't know. But there could be. As we

had to kick a little bastard out of here yesterday. You'll have to talk to himself the gaffer, over there by that stable.'

'Thank you.'

Darcy Dancer crossing to a checked coated and capped gent in flared twill breeches and boots. Touching one's forelock. And approaching this figure whose pinched reddened face held a cigarette nodding up and down between his thin lips.

'And what do you want.'

'Sir I would be inquiring as to know if you might be needing the services of a stable lad.'

'Who sent you.'

'I made bold to come myself sir.'

'Who gave you that belt in the eye. And them bruises. We don't want trouble makers around here.'

'I was after having a fall sir.'

'Fell me arse. Looks more like a beating you deserved. I'm just after putting my boot flying into a cur was sent out the gate you just came in. What do you know about horses. Who have you worked with before. Come on. Who.'

'Well sir. Sure I am a butcher's son but I have spent me time in the stables since I was a slip of a gossoon. Serving me time in the big house that was near where my father had his trade. I know a good bit.'

'Lay hand to that fork. We'll see what you know now. Go in there and muck out that box. We'll see what kind of a job you do. Plenty of your type around thinking you know it all. Go on. What are you waiting for. Put your shoulder into it.'

Darcy Dancer entering the box. Laughter in the courtyard as this stallion reared and bucked and sent sparks flying off the wall with lashes of his hind legs. Ears flat back and his great yellow teeth bared to snap off my arm. Love and affection calms the horse. Provided you can administer these before you are bitten, trampled or kicked to death. Meanwhile step back out of harm's way. Murmur quiet peaceful words. There, there now. Easy there. Quietly now. Good old fellow. Blow soft soothing breath up in your nostrils. And put on your head collar. There you are. My big evil fellow. Lead you out. So I won't be killed. While attending to your toiletries.

'Who told you take that horse out of that box.'

'You asked me to clean it sir. And that big fellow not knowing me yet would as soon send me flying over the moon.'

'Well ask first if you can remove a horse out of a box. And stand up straight when you talk to me.'

'Yes sir.'

'You're a little know it all I can tell.'

'I'm sorry sir I didn't understand you the first time. May I be taking the horse out of its box sir.'

'Take him out. And into that box there. And next time you'd better know enough to ask.'

Darcy Dancer shovelling up the matted brown knobs of dung and heaping it in the barrow. Lugging and forking in yellow clean straw from a stack. Shaking it up with the fork. Spreading the golden fibres neatly and evenly across the floor. Heaping it gently up against the walls. And storing that little bit extra in the corners. The gaffer coming to peer in over the half door. And grunting begrudging approval.

'Well you know how to do something anyway. Now there's no quitting here till you're told. You'll sleep up there over that stable. We'll give you a try for a few days. Twelve and six a week and your keep. What's your name.'

'Dancer O'Reilly sir.'

'Named after the great stallion himself I suppose.'

'It's a fact I am sir.'

'Dancer is it. Well I'm Matt. Named after me hard working father. And I've no bloody time for slackers.'

'I'm not a one for slacking sir.'

'Well we'll see about that. Just let me catch you stepping out of line, and you'll hop it from here in a hurry I can tell you.'

The loft room was up a narrow worm eaten wooden ladder. Musty and dusty, a pile of oats in the middle of the floor. Little brick built cubby holes in the walls for chickens to lay their eggs. A wooden bench of a bed with a horsehair mattress. Three old dirty grey blankets smelling of hay and straw. Under which one slept till wakened each morning by a gruff shout of a groom up the steps. Peeling back the damp covers and arising already dressed in the chill darkness. Eyes still glued together in sleep. Pushing cold stale stockinged feet into Father Damian's priestly shoes. Day after exhausting day. To go down into the welcome warmth of the horses below. Their comforting snorts and movements through the night. And now know what the life of Foxy was like. And it would damn soon make you go round biting off ears and smashing heads with hammers.

'Get a move on there's fifteen mares waiting yet.'

My hair and the passing days growing longer. The weather milder. And dust rising in the sunlight forking over the straw. Carrying armfuls of hay. My red chapped hand churning in pails of crushed oats and water. Lugging buckets of warm bran. And the pleasant moments grooming a big old mare who would stretch her head to each side and snort in ecstasy as I brushed her down. And Matt growling when he could find nothing to complain of concerning my work.

'What are you doing standing there, haven't you something to do.'

Felt like shoving my fork up his mean arse. Never a complimentary word from his lips. At night, even as I sat on my bed, I hardly had the strength to pull up the covers. And was already asleep as I slowly lowered my stiff limbs back. Aching in every bone. By days waiting in the basement hall outside the big kitchen of this house, holding cap in hand. Murmuring me country accents. Begorra, bedad, and humbly bending me head. To take my breakfast of porridge oats, tea, bread and dripping. Lunch of bacon potatoes and cabbage. Sitting at the most inferior position of the table to eat. With the other household servants who suspiciously regarded me when I did not bless myself at the sound of the Angelus. With the cook mumbling.

'What have we now, a pagan in our midst.'

Looking up and seeing them all stare. And the cook once correcting me for my table manners. God what bloody inglorious moments. To find servants more full of snobberies than one is oneself. The maids all so self importantly jumping at the dingling sound of their assigned bells, rushing to a grey swing door at the top of the stairs as if it led to heaven. And one called Assumpta looking back over her shoulder at me all snooty and superior.

'Don't you wish now you could come up here.'

But matters distinctly worsened. An officious overbearing butler appropriately called Smears arrived. Who pranced about in a military manner reeling off his previous service in previous castles to previous Earls. And who straight off presided at the head of the table as if he were conducting a symphony. Keeping a long silver skewer by his plate which he tapped for our attention.

'So that lunch may begin, are we all now fully gathered. And you what's your name again. I have difficulty remembering common ones.'

'O'Reilly. Dancer O'Reilly.'

'Do please do me the honour if not the pleasure of sitting straight and take your elbows off the table. Although you have brought in the smell of them you are not out in the stables now. And you, young lady what's your name.'

'Assumpta.'

'You are not to exhibit amusement when I bring another member of the staff to order. Clearly there must be severe changes wrought here. Standards are distinctly slack.'

Five thirty in the morning I started. And the clock bell was tolling eight in the evening when my work was done. With hardly a second through the day when someone didn't have something unpleasantly new for me to do. Saddling and unsaddling. Cleaning tack. Hands now swollen red. Weals across my palms. Cut and blistered by bucket handles. Tumbling in under the blankets and merely a minute later it seemed tomorrow. Never again shall I treat the servants of Andromeda Park in a thoughtless and uncaring manner. Or attempt, as one was inclined to do in particularly shabby ways, to extract from them every last ounce of their daily energy. Not indeed that one could. For if they so wished they could be so jolly clever at avoiding work. Indeed one knew a servant's trick or two oneself.

'Now that I've got you all lined up. Who for the last time, thieved those five bananas.'

The mistress of the house in her persistent stingy mindedness was trying to keep track of every potato and turnip. Not to mention every biscuit and jar of jam. And she finally confronted us as well. But as I was usually out in the yard she seemed to think me unworthy of an accusation. And it was I indeed who did neatly thieve the bananas arrived one morning with peaches and black grapes in a great wicker basket from Smith's of the Green. Later the cook was screaming at Assumpta, who also ruddy liar that she was, had stolen the remaining two herself. While trying to blame everyone else for the disappearance of the entire five. And Smears now went up and down the servants' hall reciting.

'I ain't got no bananas.'

And one morning I was sent for to be given the embarrassing task of lugging baskets full of turf to drawing rooms and bedrooms. Which at first I at least found preferable to having to use a pick to clear away embedded big stones fallen from a wall in a paddock. Or collecting in from a field each day two mares who in their furious hatred of each other nearly kicked themselves as well as me to death. And I was surprised I was quite perversely enjoying dropping turf mould over the carpets as I went galumphing about. Till a bedroom door opened. And the mistress of the house stood there with a hair curling iron in one hand and holding her dressing gown closed in the other, promptly throwing a fit.

'You. It's you is it. Dropping turf all over. And in muddy shoes. You're not to come traipsing through this house in muddy shoes.'

Only for a second or two did one worry about being sacked. One's wages being hardly more than those of a slave. I was however momentarily mortified. But then clearly realized she simply lacked breeding and style to deal properly with servants. To first kindly approach smiling making some comments about the weather, and then to inquire after one's health following which, and then only purely as an indifferent careless afterthought, to mention mud on one's shoes. No damn ruddy wonder poor Irish peasants burned down so many of the sham gentry's mansions. And left standing those belonging to the pure and true aristocracy.

'And see that your hair is combed when next you come indoors. We're not in the habit of tolerating scruffiness here you know.'

My god was I dying to let her have a piece of my mind. But instead pressed on choice wall areas a few blatant grubby hand prints so disliked by Miss von B. These regrettable people were not only known by a most common surname but were also glaringly nouveau riche. And even to be called upon to apply such a term makes one wince. I was of course supplied by Smears with an old pair of shabby slippers to wear. And another morning lugging in the turf baskets to the drawing room, I so longed to just flop down on the sofa. Not only from fatigue but with the persistent irritation of never being able to loiter and leisurely study the vulgarity of this house. With the ruddy grand piano covered with pictures of about a dozen priests and two dozen nuns, interspersed with photographs of what must be their son and daughter on their horses. The furnishings all so clearly contrived to give an appearance of expense. And just as one might have expected, there prominently displayed on a side table, was a copy of the most recent *Tatler and Sketch*. I picked it up. Thumbed the pages filled with photographs of recent hunt balls and other grand and fine happenings. And my god, there they all were. With their toothsome grins and tiaras. Assembled in the great castle hall through which I passed on my way to the Count's dancing lessons. The Master of Foxhounds. Baptista Consuelo. The Mental Marquis. The amputating Vet. The Randy Major. The Slasher sisters. Even three of the bunch of flowers, Rose, Pansy and Marigold. Across whose elegant velvet lawns I wreaked such great hoof steps. The whole hunt. And sundry other layabouts, all having such a radiantly wonderful white tie time. And one particularly large laughing picture of the Mental Marquis and Baptista, captioned.

TWO HUNT MEMBERS TOGETHER EXCHANGING A JOKE

Can you imagine. Having a joke. When those two bare

arsed people had long since had a blatant fuck in the woods. One did feel shocked. And forgetting myself completely, I just sat down. Plonking deep into the soft blue and pink sofa. Not knowing whether to weep or cry foul loudly up to the gods. And not exactly stunned but certainly feeling deeply sorry for myself. Till I turned towards a sound made near the door.

'What is the meaning of this. How dare you.'

I of course now did sit momentarily stunned. Looking up from the glossy pages. The images of the happy faces of the hunt members still before my eyes. And for the moment totally oblivious as to where I was. Till I was looking straight up at this woman's face. The mistress of the house. Glaring at me in a manner which was so demeaningly hostile I was tempted to slap her face. Of the eighty thousand things that came all at once into my mind to say. I selected the one hundred and twelfth. Wrapping my lips around my vowels in all my most haughtiest possible manner. Just as her next words were shouted accompanied by her raised eyebrows rising even higher.

'Stand up at once.'

'Yes ma'am. I'm sorry. I apologize.'

'And don't you use that affected voice with me.'

'I'm after begging your pardon ma'am. Me accent slips betimes. Me ould feet were playing up the very divil with me and I did sit down to take the weight off for a thrice.'

'You were reading that magazine, don't tell me such fibs.'

'Ah I was and all. You have me there ma'am. Twas the great grand things you'd see in them pages that I couldn't tear the sight of me eyes away.'

'Well you'll tear yourself up and out of that sofa I'm telling you now and remove yourself at once.'

'Ah yes ma'am. Fast as me ould legs will hop.'

'And get back to your chores. Don't you let me ever catch you doing such a thing again. The unbelievable nerve. Your dirty filthy clothes on my best damask sofa.'

'I am sorry ma'am to have given trouble. Upon me word now it won't happen again.'

'You're certainly right it won't. You're not to come up into this house again.'

The only thing to do was slink retreating out in the most menial manner possible. Bringing my hand up and down to my forelock. In nervous moments my accent seemed always to slip badly. But also as I so mortified headed out I bumped straight into and fell over a small carved and gilded Adam window stool. Crashing a vase off a nearby giltwood side table. By far the best piece of furnishing in the house. With its veined agate top held elaborately on six fluted tapered legs ending in gadrooned feet. Upon which one had presently bruised one's vertebrae. And from which, O god, also was pouring a goodly amount of discoloured water. Dripping on to the light beige and bright blue and pink colours of the carpet. Which latter was, to say the least, in such excruciatingly bad taste anyway that it could benefit by an extensive dilapidation. The advantage of which was totally lost on madam who was now quite wildly hammering her fists around her head.

'Get out, get out you clumsy oaf. Get out. And don't let me ever catch you setting foot in this house again.'

Assumpta stopped me at the bottom of the stairs, trying to block my way past. Her eyes like saucers and her nosiness driving her crazy.

'A thump from above in the drawing room has sent plaster down off the ceiling into the cook's soup. Was that you did it.'

'I couldn't care less Assumpta if the entire floor descends into the bloody soup. And it was me who did it.'

'Jesus, Mary and Joseph, sure you're not fit loose in a house.'

And this night now passing off to sleep, angrily pulling on my penis. And less angrily thinking thoughts of Miss von B. Her bosoms and all the parts of her beautiful body. Especially the soft silky loveliness between her legs to where I so feveredly wished again to bring my fingers, lips and prick. Were I of full age and out of one's minority I would propose to her marriage. Bring her back to my estate. Sleep my body naked next to hers. Wake with her head next to my head.

Far away from these musty smells. And the tapping of rain on these slates. I will descend the grand staircase at Andromeda Park. Wearing the court dress stored many years in my mother's wardrobe. The whole staff in their best livery. Gathered assembled in the front hall bowing and curtseying as I make my way down the grand stairs and go between them in my black satin breeches and white silk hose. A sovereign's crown perched on my head. With Crooks geared out in blue gold trimmed court vestments announcing my ruddy bloody appearance.

'My Emperors, Lords, Ladies and Squires. The King.'

Honestly thoughts like that make one feel so damn good. To have them every night before going to sleep. There I was. Instead of under the flaking broken plaster of this ceiling I was standing there elevated on the stair as the ball commenced. The orchestra on the landing, its violins, oboes, flutes and harps sweetly making waltz music. And the ballroom pulsating with the latest chic two steps. And I even imagined swirling with Edna Annie who upon my word was done up like a queen.

Of course at meal times Smears now suggested snidely concerning my demotion from turf carrier. That although I had inferred a familiarity with a previous grand household, it was all too evident that when not trained to it, a stable lad simply could not elevate himself to that of a pantry boy. But also these days he had it in for the master and mistress. Who according to him, and I devoutly agreed, were simply not to the manner born. Smears taking this attitude following confronting the mistress in a state of nudity and when, as is customary at such time, a butler remarks that madam was looking her best, Smears got a swat across the cheek for his trouble. Big pompous idiot that he was.

But by god, things came to a head one most absolutely marvellous evening. On the occasion of a large dinner party when forty eight guests were invited. Along with a small string orchestra. Candelabra were lit, and all the staff mobilized with two extra staff called in. Even I in the absolute emergency of the moment was delegated to lugging wines from the cellars and pulling corks. Naturally with one's substantial knowledge, one privately paused to sample these mediocre liquids. With Smears up in the pantry in an absolute dither when he wasn't castigating the socially inferior nature of the guests or bemoaning the shirtyness of the new staff.

'Of course O'Reilly you wouldn't know, but these people are quite honestly the most ordinary lot I think I have ever had to preside over in my career which previously has been exclusively in service to nothing but the best aristocracy hardly any of whom was below the rank of Earl.'

I kept racing to proffer bottles that I urged Smears to taste to make sure that the contents was the wine that the big folks required, my accent later slipping badly, but not overly noticed by a progressively squiffier Smears.

'Smears you absolutely must taste this unremarkable burgundy.'

'I think O'Reilly you are getting far beyond your station, smart lad though you sometimes give an indication of being. I could train you up if you didn't stink of horse piss so much.'

I kept polishing his glass and refilling it for yet another taste. There being plenty of time before the guests got from the drawing to the dining room. Since Mary the cook had blown up the whole oven by mistakenly dripping something which was distinctly not butter fat into a roasting pan. Smears got so absolutely paralytically squiffed while the oven door was screwed back on that he served the sweet directly after the soup which had maids crashing into each other retrieving courses before they were even served. With no main course at all. The master and mistress were fulminating. The former shoving his irate red round face into the pantry.

'God damn it, what's wrong with you.'

There was quite sufficient wrong. For meanwhile Smears had fallen down the whole flight of servants' stairs and although miraculously unhurt he could by now only totter holding his hands out in front of him like a blind man to feel where he was going. And I by god could hardly stand up laughing. It was the most wonderful night. Especially when the electric lights short circuited and the ruddy swing door to the servants' stair flew open with a guest, his flies undone, his penis shifted out, was there nonchalantly peeing right down the servants' staircase. Just as Assumpta and I holding a candle and with a massive cauldron of boiled potatoes were at last heading for the dining room where the guests now, were themselves roaring drunk not having got a morsel to eat for over an hour. And stupid Assumpta not knowing what a prick looked like, was heading half way up the dim lighted stairs and confronted by the guest peeing straight down at her, at least did recognize piss and both she and the potatoes fell backwards tumbling to the bottom of the stairs. God was I laughing. My belly wracked with pain. And I fear, my feet squashing spuds. And with Assumpta hors de combat, Smears squiffed, the master finally came storming right down the stairs shouting and screaming at the top of his lungs and rushing into the kitchen where at that very moment I had eight different bottles of liquors open with Smears and cook tasting each with the uttermost blotto sincerity.

'You damn idiot fools. Where's the bloody roast beef the bloody main course, the creamed damn onions. Don't you know what you are doing.'

Smears reared up nearly as if he was sober but had to lean back and prop himself up with the table. Closing his eyes between his measured delivery of every couple of words.

'I won't take that language from you. When I have long had, prior to coming to this place, the pleasure and privilege of serving the true aristocracy and gentry. And not people who have merely made money.'

'You're sacked. You're drunk, you're sacked.'

Smears in the most strange quasi military manner, marching out the door. And towards me the wrath was suddenly turned. With my hand still wrapped around a bottle of Crème de Menthe. But he thought the better of continuing the tirade. No doubt remembering the plight of his poor starving guests. Who if indeed they had an appetite left at all, certainly now could not care much in their blotto state.

'You. You bring the roast beef up this instant.'

Of course outside of fox hunting and horses there's hardly anything else in this world I know how to do, but at least I do know considerable about proper butlering. To which, would you believe it I had just been promoted. Although Mary the cook, even in her own wobbling inebriated state seemed sceptical about my sudden elevation in the servants' ranks. Murmuring under her breath.

'Ah it serves them right to have a stable lad bringing them their dinners.'

'I beg your pardon, Mary, note my fine grand accent. Sure I'm as good a butler as Smears ever was.'

'Never mind that smart lip you, Dancer O'Reilly. And get these roasts of beef up to them, sure as it is they're all nearly a cinder they'll be carving.'

The two hired in waiters poised to carve. One of whom during the early darkness of the short circuit I saw popping the more valuable and pocket sized pieces of cutlery into his pockets, which must have been specially tailored for the purpose, as the vast number of pieces disappearing hardly made a bulge in his coat. Any moment I waited for him to be anchored to the floor by their enormous weight. Of course the short circuit also in its way saved much more embarrassment not only for ladies who were thinking it so much more romantic in the candlelight but also because it hid momentarily the now totally rebellious and drunken staff from view. Some of the guests were rumoured very important and prominent in government and business circles. Including two inseparable Dublin actors who shouted above everyone else, and inaccurately quoted Shakespeare. And a most unkempt and inappropriately dressed Dublin poet who not only had his shoes off drying his unbelievable stinking feet under the table, but was also spitting over his arm behind him in a genuine effort it seemed to avoid spitting directly on the table. And then arms waving and roaring while the little string orchestra played lightly an operatic piece.

'Ah jasus will you give us a jig instead of that.'

The seemingly honest hired in waiter kept nudging me unpleasantly in the ribs, pointing out the two Dublin actors.

'Look at them will ya look at the pair of them. Sure they'd jump on you as fast as they'd jump on each other.'

The evening temporarily seemed to settle down. Except a very sweaty recovered Assumpta was getting her passing bosom felt by the poet who kept grabbing at it between his yawns and barely disguised insults levelled at his host's nouveau riche attempts to curry favour with the true cultured members of the Irish intelligentsia.

'Ah you're phonys, phonys, the lot of you.'

One did shut him up however serving out a grossly over-cooked slab of roast beef. Upon which he fell like a ravening dog. Gobbling it straight off the plate with the peas as well. One of which flew from his lips and popped neatly down a lady's décolletage. He of course went after it. And she behaved as if she were being raped. Which she was. With the gravy I held over her tipped over the two of them. Astonishingly at first no one appeared to notice the poet wrestling the lady straight to the floor, so busy were they all attempting to impress someone further down the table and all leaning forward to do so. And the poet was at the lady dog style as she tried to escape under the table. Fortunately everyone was of a class who would never mix with one's own otherwise one would be sure to be recognized. And be mortified. As the entire table lifted right up from the floor in front of the ruddy guests' eyes. With cutlery, food and wine sliding off upon those on the downward sloped side. With the poet underneath roaring.

'Come here now till I get that pea.'

> Or you
> Whore
> I'll chase you
> Till kingdom
> Come

24

The débâcle took days to calm down. With Smears barricaded in his room threatening to sue for wrongful dismissal and grevious disparagement of his capabilities in the performance of his profession. And with the extensive repairs required to where the poet had rutted, butted and seemingly pissed his way round the dining room with his shouts of yous is all whores everyone one of yous. And where now white coated I actually was serving the master and mistress these few perilous nights at a singularly gloomy table. As well as bringing food up to a bloody complaining Smears.

'Damn it O'Reilly where's the smoked salmon I requested. You don't think I'm going to eat the same slops as that pair of social upstarts down there.'

I was while devouring plenty of bananas, rather enjoying it all. And one might even venture to say that there was hardly anyone anywhere who could bow and scrape with such menial servitude as I could. Is the tea to your liking madam. Is the toast just right. Of course the mistress was stunned by my seeming transformation from a horse piss soaked stable lad to major domo and there were dangerous moments when both the master and mistress thought I was taking the mickey out of them. But I do believe they revelled so much in being treated with such obedient doormat solicitude that they finally were convinced they merited it.

'That will be sufficient unto our needs of the moment, O'Reilly. We'll ring when requiring you further.'

'Very good madam.'

My brief temporary status really improved my prospects in the big brown eyes of Assumpta. Who with her big bosoms, every groom in the stable yard was panting after. And in our hour and a half free after lunch, I airily took her walking.

While having the dumbest imaginable conversations. With our interests utterly dissimilar. And not even agreeing on the colour of the sky. But she could gab when she got going. Of how we could go as a pair in service, me butlering, she as a lady's maid. She had of course since I was promoted out of the stables, also elevated herself up from kitchen maid. The only dangerous thing about such thoughts was I found myself actually considering the prospect.

'Ah now you'd be answering door to the important people arriving and I would be bringing to her her ladyship's shoes she'd selected.'

Once we got a bit out into the woods my present randy concern for her ample body drove such plans out of one's mind. Especially during our prolonged desperate physical struggles which went on for seeming hours. Until finally I was able to overpower her astonishingly strong flailing arms and legs to trip her down into the wet grass. To do what I could up her dress between her bulging thighs with all her kicking and praying to St John the Baptist over my still thoroughly Protestant shoulder. And as I felt, squeezed and twisted towards naked flesh, came her boring constant refrain.

'Aren't you the blue eyed bold lad now.'

As well as all the time saying would I marry her. After what I was doing. Which was actually ripping her pants in tatters right off her. Or else she'd have the master of the house, the parish priest, her brothers, sisters, uncles from Cavan, and aunts from Mayo who were nuns, all assemble to make me. But despite my endless wrestlings no how could I get my penis in her. And all she'd wide eyed say as I knelt muddy kneed wanking over her.

'What's that funny white stuff coming out of you.'

And then she thoroughly ignored me. When a week previous I had again been demoted out of the house by the arrival of a new butler. And on this Saturday noon. The sun higher, the evening light lengthening. A first hint of spring in the balmy air. And following my ninth week of hiding my wages behind a loose stone in the loft wall, and hearing that Assumpta thought I'd given her a baby by lying on top of her,

I was rather just about to panic and depart altogether when the master's big splendid motor car recently removed from blocks in the garage and newly polished early that morning, came speeding up along the drive. I could see the mistress and a young man step out just as I was collecting from the field the two enemy mares. And Tom the groom acting as chauffeur carried luggage up the steps behind them to the waiting hands of the new butler. A sheepish cowering type who sneaked and lurked around the house digging his fingers in his nose and ears while tabulating the number of bananas I made disappear. And because I regarded him with more than mild displeasure and he regarded Assumpta with more than middling lust, he demanded and was all too eagerly granted the favour of my departure back to the stables.

And late that afternoon all was silent as the rest of the men had gone off to watch a football match. Even left with eighteen boxes to muck out and horses to groom, I was at that second eminently content with the bright chirping songs of the birds in the balmy sunshine. But was, some few seconds later, standing leaning on my fork wondering quite sincerely was it time to flit. However for the sake of another meal and night's sleep, I was about to bend to grip the worn oak handles to push this heaped barrow of straw and dung, when suddenly I felt someone there in the yard looking at me. And I turned to see a figure in riding breeches, cap and boots crossing on the cobble stones in my direction. A face with its jaw dropping about eighteen miles. And making its wearer, Awfully Stupid Kelly, look even more so.

'Kildare. I say, what on earth are you doing here.'

'Working.'

'But you simply can't be working here.'

'I am.'

'As a common stable lad. I simply cannot believe my eyes.'

'And I suppose you live here Kelly.'

'I do as a matter of fact. And good lord, I have only just this moment come back from school. And by the way where is my box of fudge. That you wretchedly ran off with. All of my fudge.'

'I merely borrowed it.'

'You stole it. Deliberately. Bewley's best fudge it was too. I have a good mind to be most angry.'

'I most heartily regret that sad incident Kelly. But I quite honestly promise as soon as circumstances allow to have Bewley's send you another box. I needed your fudge to sustain me in the rigours of my extended cross country journey.'

'That's no excuse to trick me Kildare.'

'No I suppose it isn't.'

'Of course I could somewhat understand your running away when the Presidium put the blame on you for the fire and the flooding. And had you told me, I would have given you my fudge. But crikey, this is indeed a most strange state of affairs. How have you got here.'

'Merely by walking down the drive.'

'But did you know this is where I lived. You haven't have you, come to sponge and steal further from me. I should heartily resent it you know.'

'I assure you Kelly had I known this was where you lived I should have skirted your acres and tried elsewhere to find employment. But as clearly it's all a horrid mistake landing here I would ask that you do not please inform on me.'

'I am not a rat.'

'Well I'm pleased Kelly to hear that.'

'But you must take off those sordid clothes and change into something respectable. I shall invite you into the house and you may then be introduced to my parents in a proper manner.'

'That is awfully kind of you Kelly. But honestly, circumstances being what they are, I do think perhaps it might be more politic for me to remain where I am. Or your head groom will sack me. At this moment I have all those boxes to muck out.'

'But you don't intend do you to stay here as a lowly stable lad. You're from the right sort.'

'Good lord, I wonder.'

'But you are. Why I've even made you an elegant leading character in my most recent play I've written.'

'Well my dear Kelly that's very sporting of you. To feature me like that. I haven't really made any firm plans as it were. But clearly at the moment I'm rather not, what one might term, of the acceptable sort. As you may all too soon hear. Even made a shambles of being a temporary indoor servant. In fact presently I'm banished from your house.'

'My God, you Kildare, a servant.'

'Yes Kelly. Me a servant.'

'You aren't the one then who's been stealing the bananas.'

'I am I regret to say.'

'Thieving other people's property seems to be a habit of yours. Nonetheless I shall help you. Purejoy said although you weren't very matey you were very spunky. Of course everyone in the upper form thought you so attractive that they all wanted to bugger you.'

'I beg your pardon Kelly.'

'It's exactly the truth. They of course think I'm far too plain.'

'O no, not at all Kelly.'

'Well they do, Kildare.'

'Absolute nonsense. I mean I'm not suggesting that you would win a beauty pageant but you are quite presentable.'

'No need Kildare to flatter me. I know I'm not awfully attractive. But at least you in your own way were quite kind to me at school. Although I was aggrieved you stole my fudge, I will not forget your getting me off a beating from the Presidium. But what has happened to bring you to this sorry pass. Have your family been reduced in circumstances. Mr Michael told me you come of very grand ancient landed people indeed. And that you had your own private tutor.'

'Yes, once upon a time, Kelly. But now, however mournful and regrettable it may seem, I am but a mere stable lad.'

'But of course you're not. You mustn't say that. How awfully awful.'

'It is rather, but I fear it is the case.'

'Well Kildare, it's for me to help you if I can. Otherwise circumstances are going to make this a most awful holiday.'

'I'm sorry.'

'O it's not for you to be sorry.'

'Well Kelly, if you could intercede to get me another mattress to sleep on I would be very grateful.'

'But of course I shall Kildare.'

'And I ask only further of you that you do not disclose to anyone who I am. One has already incurred sufficient disfavour. And I did rather contribute to the dismissal of a previous butler.'

'That's no cause to worry Kildare. We're always getting new butlers. We're just really trades people you know, and the butlers who come to us because we can pay more, usually do so from far grander service, and always end up getting drunk and declaring their superiority. Some of them have even angrily broken whole dinner services on the floor. Inevitably they give in their notice or must be sacked. Of course my mother and father do endeavour to keep them in their place. But somehow they never succeed. So you're not to worry in the least.'

'Well I am somewhat relieved to hear that that state of affairs is customary in your household Kelly, nevertheless I should prefer to remain incognito.'

'But it is a disgrace that someone of your social class should be so demeaned like this. I find it most upsetting. I really do. Are you staying in the loft.'

'Yes.'

'Well that really is the limit.'

'The loft's not so bad Kelly.'

'Well I should not like to be flung into a loft. I mean if something like this Kildare happened to me I should not atall take it lying down.'

'Well Kelly I suppose you in fact may be right. It's not actually awfully nice.'

'But it is your own fault, isn't it, Kildare. I mean you ran away from school. Not facing up to things.'

'Yes Kelly I regret to have to agree. But if I am to face up to your further admonishments, I think, that for my own peace of mind, I may have to suggest that you are rather full of shit.'

'Damn it how rude. And how unthoughtful. When I'm doing my best to help.'

'Yes. That was perhaps not nice to say. O dear. I do apologize Kelly.'

'Well this situation is not awfully nice. Especially for me. Have you thought of that. It's distressing Kildare. That's what it is. I could of course think that this is your just deserts for having stolen my fudge.'

'I do again apologize Kelly. I really many a time indeed grieved and was extremely sorry to have done that to you.'

'Well you're forgiven. But that is not the way to behave as I am sure you must know. Anyway as you are in fact working here. You may as well saddle up my horse.'

'Very good sir.'

'And there is no need to be menial about it either Kildare.'

I must confess I was sorely tempted to leave Kelly's cinch loose so that he could that more easily come off on his head and be put upright sticking in the mud. But alas, he is sine dubio my last remaining connection with the civilized world and one has to cherish his existence. I waited till he returned and pretended to be elsewhere out of sight when he shouted for me. And then watched him heading back from the stable yard to the big house. And I was standing on a chair washing a mare's tail when the gaffer appeared just before tea time.

'You're wanted urgently up at the big house. Get lively now. Go on. I'll get Sean to finish that. And you'd be as well to smarten up your appearance.'

Darcy Dancer unbrushed and unscrubbed thumping the knocker on the brass nose of the lion on the front door. Assumpta answering, thinking my presence there a joke. And shoving me back over the threshold. Making her big brown eyes grow bigger.

'Go on with you away. Imagine that you'd be invited to tea. Haven't you been told you're not wanted in here.'

'I am invited to tea. By the young master.'

'Sure I'm not letting the cheeky likes of you past if it was St Joseph himself give you the invitation.'

Darcy Dancer putting his foot forward to stop the

slamming door. And rearing up straight clearing one's throat. The breeze noticeable between my legs. Avail myself now of my ruling class accent.

'I say, stand aside girl and don't presume upon a gentleman to keep him from making his prompt appearance to tea.'

Assumpta reddening in the face, standing shook in her tracks with disbelief. And forgetting to shut the front door as she watched me remove my priestly stable blessed shoes and proceed forward to the drawing room. The wind slamming closed the front door and Assumpta running mumbling towards the kitchen stairs.

'It's O'Reilly behaving out of his mind saying he has been invited to tea with the master and mistress.'

Although the Dublin poet had already indoctrinated them into the custom, raised eyebrows greeted my shoeless feet in the drawing room. The fire in the grate blazing. The red varnish painted on Kelly's mother's fingernails looked as equally false as the smarmy smile frozen on her face. Kelly jumping up and down as if he had peed in his pants. Which judging by the dark stain he in fact might have. His portly balding father wiping his brow with his handkerchief as he put his entirely limp and unpleasantly moist hand in mine.

'Well young Mr Kildare. This is a pretty kettle of fish now to find out you are who you are.'

'I apologize sir, to be without shoes, and do hope you will forgive the rest of my rather unpremeditated appearance.'

Kelly's mother who at first seemed feigning some indisposition now finally made some bodily movements and was at this moment anyway looking surprisingly pretty. Certainly one had a brief moment now to contemplate her features without them wearing a look of repugnance. Her light hair waved back at the sides of her head looked passably elegant in the drawing room light. But her aquiline nose did sniff and her eyebrow frown at my reasty aroma. However she calmed visibly as I sat and pushed my holey stockinged and regretfully much smelly feet out of sight under the tea table. And Kelly's father took the opportunity to clear his throat, obviously finding it diffi-

342

cult to believe this present member of his household staff was plonked on his damask in front of him.

'Are you comfortable there mister Kildare.'

'Yes. Thank you.'

Kelly's father adjusting a lone long strand of hair across his shining pate. My God, after all this time to be addressed in a respectful manner. As if I existed as a human being and were not about to steal or break something. With Kelly's mother and father having obviously tarted themselves up to look their very best in view of the fact, one must suppose, that I have so often seen them at their utter worst. But one certainly doesn't like what one might think is an American style tie he's wearing. And an overly red and far too wide stripe running through the far too smooth fabric of his suit. And Kelly's mother's accent is more than ever oozing with refinement making it so much more obvious and uncomfortable when her every few words are shattered by the undertones of her considerably less graceful vowels. Her lip now trembling a trifle as she raises her chin to further put on the dog.

'Now despite the circumstances. We'd like to treat you as a school friend of Hugh's to tea. We understand you are a Darcy Thormond.'

'Yes, on my mother's side, madam.'

'A very well known racing family. And certainly no need now to address me as madam. Of course had we known who you were everything would have been extremely different. You should have told us you know.'

An altogether too large diamond clip rather garishly adorning a too shiny puce fabric of Kelly's mother's dress. Better worn in a ballroom than at afternoon tea. But then she frequently appeared out in paddocks dressed as one might for a wedding. Nor could one be kindly about their racing colours needlessly blazoned everywhere. However, good lord in my present shabby regalia who am I to talk. Although one is rather enjoying having all the privileges of a commoner while remaining an aristocrat. Yet the house with a few widespread changes in furnishing could easily be made not so painfully obvious that its owner inhabitants were only recently removed from the shop keeping classes. Just rake off the room's overly ornate wallpaper. Get rid of the carpets, chiffoniers, cabinets and secretaire bookcases stuffed with their unread badly chosen titles. And chuck the overly stuffed multi coloured and ornamented sofas out the window. Although one would then face a certain bareness, nevertheless the good advice as to how to achieve at least a decent camouflage in the status they were attempting, might be put into action. But again who am I as a recent stable boy to pass such opinions. Except I damn well know the boundaries inside which people should stay who wish to be acceptable.

'Do please mister Kildare help yourself. As you know we only stand on ceremony in this house when it's absolutely necessary.'

'Thank you. Of course, yes, I do know that.'

The Kellys couldn't be accused of stinginess, at least not above stairs in their own drawing room. And below stairs, with a sleight of hand, one could always remedy the situation. But now tea continued to come in its copious cascades, as Assumpta stared miffed out of her mind watching me intently as she fetched in more hot water for the pot. And through the bow of the polished windows the sky broken in blue with fluffy white clouds undertinged with the pink of a setting sun. The sound of horses pounding the turf in the paddock across the gravel drive. Kelly handing me everything but the kitchen sink from the laden linen napkined tray. He seemed terrified that I might not get enough to eat. And I assuredly left him thoroughly mollified by stuffing myself to the eyebrows. Eight scones buttered inch thick and spoonfuls of honey dripped between the warm soft steaming dough.

'Now young Kildare, as Hugh's father it's incumbent upon me to inform your family as to where you are. And let them know you're safe and healthy.'

'Please Daddy, please. I told you he does not want that. You must not ask him. Please. He merely departed home because he is so fond of horses and wanted to be independent somewhere to learn their finer points.'

'I'm only trying to do what's correct in the circumstances.'

'Well he wants to remain incognito as a stable lad Daddy.'

'We can't have that. I'm not saying we would chuck you out. I'm not saying that at all.'

A blazing fire, and so many goodies close at hand. In one's reversal of role. Sitting here, with the horse chat. The foals. The pedigrees. The yearlings. The racing at Fairyhouse, Phoenix Park and the Curragh. Instead of one's shoes soaking up horse piss and lugging about loads of dung. Kelly seemed quite proud of my presence. In spite of the little bugger having me saddle up his horse. My god, one can see such a different side of people when one's merely a menial. And Matt the head groom changed his carping tune to me in a hurry. But Kelly, I must confess, is not a bad skin. The poor little chap's eyes wide as melons as I defame the ruddy school he still attends.

'Well actually the food is appalling, the bullying sadistically revolting and most of the masters were to my mind thoroughly commonplace, sir.'

'Well we thought Hugh was in the best of hands.'

'Well Daddy, Kildare you know, isn't used to institutional schooling.'

'I see.'

Kelly's parents upon their departure from the drawing room were most plaintive in their assurances that I was welcome now as an old friend of the family. But it had been quickly agreed that now my true identity was known, my continued presence as a gentleman squire at the very bottom of the stable hierarchy might not be conducive to good blood-stock management. And for that evening at least, in my sudden upgrading, nothing was too good for me. Sean the second groom even brought the tatty remnants of my belongings in from my loft room.

During dinner it must have been a fulminating situation down in the kitchens. As I in one of Kelly's borrowed jackets, tie and tight shirt, assumed my full social position. The sneaky new butler's face wore a look of broken jawed disillusionment which I did not lessen as I released a nasally clipped thank you each time he served me. And following weeks of my hard rustling horsehair mattress, that Saturday night, down the hall from Kelly, I flopped, my belly filled, into a most luxurious bed under a pale green eiderdown. Bathing in the adjoining bathroom with scads of hot water and big warm towels draped over the chromium rail.

In the morning Kelly couldn't wait to alert me to breakfast in the dining room and sat across the table watching as I shovelled down six fried eggs, eight pieces of buttered toast, six cups of tea and just about the entire contents of a quarter pound jar of marmalade.

'Alright Kelly, you're counting.'

'I am not, I'm doing no such thing. But Assumpta's been three trips and you've now had six fried eggs, eight pieces of toast and six cups of tea, that is rather a lot you must admit.'

'Well you were urging everything upon me at tea yesterday and dinner last night.'

'That was because I thought you might be hungry. But now I'm thinking that you may be just only greedy.'

'Kelly I know it's your house and I should not want to grieve you, but frankly I have been, as a previous member of the staff, forced to steal sufficient food to stay alive here.'

'I know that must be a damn lie.'

'O dear Kelly, calm down. I'm just pulling your leg. The staff food was absolutely tops.'

'And I should jolly well think so.'

But things were quite amicable when I took final leave. Standing in a dolorifically unacceptable striped trousered suit of Kelly's father and more than somewhat too big for me. But balanced in a manner of speaking by an excruciatingly tight collar adorned by one of Kelly's prep school ties. I looked at least passably neat. And with an extra fiver plus the entirety of my accumulated wages heavy in my pocket, I was playfully entertaining optimistic thoughts while Awfully Stupid's parents performed their relieved dismissal of me in the drawing room. Having of course, repeatedly politely and faintly invited me to stay while I just as repeatedly insisted less faintly that I must depart. And I had concocted the most slavish stream of flattering leavetaking remarks to deliver to my hosts but thought it might simply sound all too reminiscent of my abject menial solicitude during my temporary sojourn as houseboy. But it is amazing the amount of insult one may dispense in the guise of blandishment.

Assumpta suddenly in sobbing tears at their front door. And although one saw her worshipful eyes begging for recognition, I realized one must be firm and keep her in her place. As clearly I now was to her a knight in shining armour. I did feel caddish as the large grand grey gleaming motor car swept up and took us in its warm soft sumptuous interior. Which Kelly said had spent its recent years up on blocks in the garage due to the shortage of petrol. And now out we murmured over the drive and swept along the winding lanes to the train station. Leaving behind blankets lugged up over horses' backs, and the hours of grooming in the dust of hair and scabs. Tom the chauffeur driving and frowning with hostility every time I caught him looking in my direction. Assumpta told me he had proposed to her. And Kelly at my side in the back seat.

'Where Kildare will you be staying in Dublin.'

'At the Shelbourne, Kelly. You ought to look me up now and again.'

'I should like to do that.'

'Do.'

'You know Kildare I do feel rather good to be riding together with you like this. As if somehow it was predestined. O I don't want to sound pompous. But you do know what I mean.'

'Yes I do Kelly. I know exactly what you mean.'

The wheels arriving at the station made the most magnificent pebble crushing sound with everyone turning to watch us. O God what utter amazing ruddy bliss to no longer be a menial. And once more step like a country gent up these steps. To feel extremely chipper on the station platform, being so much socially uplifted by the journey in the great motor car. And Awfully Stupid was extremely bouncy himself as we regarded these other travellers and he stood there legs astride and a little parcel held behind his back.

347

'But what Kildare, will you do in Dublin.'

'I shall Kelly go straight to the tailors and then, the weather permitting, I shall go to the races.'

'What about our most marvellous horse, Tinkers Revenge that will soon be running in the big races.'

'Well he was dead last in his last race, Kelly.'

'But his blood lines go back to the great stallion Dancer. That was only his second race and was only an outing.'

'Well, of course. I shall wager on him. I'm so glad you reminded me. One gets into such a dither Kelly. Been rather a lot happening recently.'

'The odds should be staggeringly good.'

'Well in that case I shall take perhaps a staggering risk.'

'You know Kildare, in my play about you. That's how I've drawn your character. As a chap who would take a risk. Even a suicidal one.'

'Well I'm not sure that quality is exactly native to my character Kelly. Mostly it's rather been with me that I've had no other choice than to be blatantly suicidal.'

'Well I feel that you have the true air of a hero. And I do so admire your seemingly endless nerve.'

'I'm not quite so sure that's particularly flattering Kelly.'

'Well I mean the way you've run away. Fought the Presidium. And have rather taken care of yourself the way you do. I mean imagine, being able to be a stable lad. A butler. And an aristocrat all wrapped up in one.'

'It has however rather taxed my acting ability Kelly. But damn it all, aren't we just as some great playwright or someone said, actors on a stage.'

'O jolly right but you, you're real as well. And I should like to continue to know you into the future.'

'That is very complimentary Kelly, and I must say that I am rather glad to hear of something which elevates rather than deflates these days.'

A breeze gusting across the train tracks. From the west still come the clouds. And just over the wall one sees the elegant motor car parked waiting outside this grey stone station. The choo choo throb of the train. The bud tips pushing out on the flowers. None the worse really after my weeks of work in Kelly's father's stables. Indeed I feel quite improved in strength. And absolutely able for the world.

Darcy Dancer looking down into the smiling face of Kelly from an open window of a first class compartment. What a pity he doesn't have another box of fudge. I could munch contentedly on my journey. The station master blowing his whistle. Waves his green flag. Train doors bang shut.

'Goodbye Kelly, and thank you.'

'Goodbye Kildare. And here. I brought this for you.'

Train moving. Kildare reaching out for the neat little parcel. Take it safely in one's hands. Look back. Kelly waving. The terrace of thatched cottages of this village go by. Take a soft seat. Put my head back on the white head linen. And find a smile from my one fellow passenger who is nicely done up in tweeds. Clank slowly now past a long platform of cattle pens. Cross a river and a canal. Stations named Sallins and Straffan. Rain streaks the glass. Like little stabs one feels in the heart. Never see my sisters again. Nor hear Crooks shuffling through the house. Or Foxy scream oaths at beasts. Or the splendid sight of Miss von B's bottom. Even when those ripe mounds were so snugly held in her white riding breeches as she stood warming in front of the hall fire of Andromeda Park. And that sad man. Good old Sexton. In his potting shed. A half smile in his one eye. Discoursing on the affairs of the world. That one could be dignified by bleakness and solitude. Which helped to conquer the pessimism of each day in the world. And kept the snobbery vanity and insincerity at bay. And above all Master Reginald, you need confidence. And I'll tell you what that is in a hurry. Haven't I read all the great Irish thinkers and metaphysicians from Johannes Scottus Erivgena at the court of Charles the Bald in France right down to the latest from Berkeley. And let me tell you, not one of them knew better than a cow does when she goes to shelter behind a hedge in a winter's gale. And none of them could give you a better definition of confidence than I'm giving you now. It's a pound sterling in your pocket.

Darcy Dancer crossing his legs. The thin white stripes in my trousers. The click clack of a train track. And now open up Kelly's packet. And from its smell it seems. And it is.

Chocolate
Fudge
From
Bewley's

25

As the train rumbled chugging along the brow of the Liffey valley one was feeling as marvellous as one was terrified. On the rich winter green hillsides stood big country houses mournfully grey. The western clouds drizzling out all their rain. One was nearly tempted to travel third class but my sense of dignity overcame my parsimony. And pleasantly, my compartment companion was a most well spoken horse person.

'Do you mind young man if I smoke a cigar.'

'No, indeed, I quite enjoy cigar smoke.'

A damn lie of course. But the gentleman's manner was so agreeable that one was eager to acquiesce to his wishes. He was a member of the Turf Club. Suggested I look him up any time. My god, horses did make friends for one. And we most interestedly discussed hunting, racing and a splendid deed or two of this man's well known thoroughbreds. Until one could see the Wellington Monument peeking up in the sky in the Phoenix Park.

Darcy Dancer at the kerb outside the station. Asserting himself to the forefront of some very lackadaisical country people being archly warned aside by those sporting their tweedy elegance. The rustics with their belongings trussed up with broken straps and string. And mostly looking as if someone had upon their arrival, hammered them senseless with a sledge on the head.

'Are you waiting for a cab.'

'Ah sir you might say we're in no hurry now.'

To a blonde tweedy lady I had to administer a few I beg your pardons before she would await her turn. When a red nosed tinkerish looking Jarvey with a rather scrawny mare pulled up. In my most gentlemanly fashion I ushered these three older country people just behind to proceed ahead of me. But they nodded in eight directions and looked up at the sky in four more as if asking every saint in heaven for assistance and then urged me with their country voices to take the horsecab.

'Ah it's soon enough later for the likes of us.'

Helping me up, they closed the cab door behind me. In their little lonely dark group they seemed so pleased to be left just where they stood. Staring up at the grey clouds. Looking all round them in wonderment. A soft drizzle falling. And one nearly weeps for the love of such folk. So unarmed against the fashions and smartness of the world. And one took not a little comfort from the blonde tweedy lady who was now angrily shrieking.

'Porter, porter get me a cab.'

Darcy Dancer sitting back in the dusty upholstery. Chew a chunk of Kelly's fudge. On a cobble stone road trundle up past this hospital. Turn left at the top. Along this wider avenue. These neat blue painted doors on the buildings. The smell of the big brewery. A fortune must flow out of that for somebody. And as Uncle Willie used to say, wouldn't it put silver spoons in plenty of mouths.

All so drab, so dark and grey. Glad to see the glass canopy of the Shelbourne. At the end of these Sunday empty Dublin streets. With smoke pouring from the chimneys of houses. The twisting narrow alleys. Lone tattered figures hunched in doorways. The odd cyclist whirring by. All with the same solemn, grim jawed pale faces one remembers in this city. Except inside here the reception girl's smiling greeting. Puts me in my same room I had previously staying with Mr Arland.

'My luggage I'm afraid has been misplaced on the train.'

'We'll telephone straight to the station, sir to inquire for you.'

'That is, thank you, awfully good of you.'

Stretched on the bed I lay back in peace. Relieved when they said two hours later that no one answered at the station. My head sunk softly in the pillow. Arm up across my eyes.

Stop the tears. Let them fall and they would overwhelm me. After all these weeks. Stare again at the glass of this shiny window. Purple mountains lie out there beyond the darkness. The flower beds, lawns and little lake of Stephen's Green below. My whole life ahead. With distinctly no money to live it. Where might be Miss von B. Trundling along in the horse-cab looked everywhere turning to see if even that or that shabbily dressed person might be her face. Creases in her soft smooth skin around her mouth when she laughed with her bright teeth. Even gone I can feel her body close. My head tucked in to the side of her neck. Squeezed her shoulders up when she felt tickled. Sleep now. Let her call me bog trotter. Till her laughing heart's content. Sorrow and tears hanging from her face. Bent, as it seems all ladies bend, to cry. When then you do not remember them so soignée, chic and radiant. Her blonde braids wrapped in a crown on her head. Please. Cheer me. In this cold fear. Of all the days now coming. Who shall feed me. Mend my socks. Bake my scones. Or teach me. Mr Arland. Your steady calmness. Firm in all the battles of life. Win against ignoble enemies. Defend the weak who would be vanquished. Exhibit helplessness to those who fear strength. And thereby draw the ugly bully upon your sword. My land. Sprinkled with rainy woe. Pound it with the hooves of a high couraged horse. Run after hounds. Leave behind those who mope.

In a Monday bright sun Darcy Dancer sauntering down Dawson Street. New day in the heart. Gather up one's most iron nerve. Turning left around the corner of Nassau Street. Past Elvery's Emporium of sporting outfitters. Bells jangling. Trams roaring on their shiny tracks. Rooftops and granite buildings of Trinity College across the road. Founded to increase learning and civility. And to banish tumults, barbarism and disorderly living. See the tip top of the glass from the underneath of which poor Mr Arland helped himself illicitly to fruit behind the Provost's house. Dame Street. Banking edifices rearing in splendour. Pass down this boulevard to enter this establishment of saddlery. Blatantly march up to this most dignified elderly assistant. And hope to be greeted. Hope to be welcomed. And hear said. O my dear sir, how can we lay the world at your feet.

'Good morning sir.'

'Good morning.'

'And what can we do for you sir, this morning.'

'Suit.'

'What had you in mind, sir, worsted, tweed, flannel.'

'Tweed.'

'Very good sir, come this way.'

Without a word discourteous or a movement disinterested, in a little cubicle I was measured. My presently most ill fitting togs from Awfully Stupid Kelly's father, the trouser waist of which could easily encompass three of me, now removed and folded. Revealing my most unflattering too light blue and too short ankle sock.

'And something ready to wear sir.'

'Yes as a matter of fact.'

The gentleman assistant and I pored over a sample of tweed patterns and made an appointment for fitting. Nipped out in the old togs to select the new. From a glass enclosed case chose a cap and a cravat rather purplish in colour with pink round dots. In every way quite sporting and resembling a previous favourite tie. Four pairs of wool socks, light grey, dark grey, one black and one navy blue. Four silk shirts. And off the peg, one cavalry twill trousers, one Donegal tweed hacking jacket. Six white linen hankies. When down in the mouth fine fabrics do put a good face on things. With wool, linen and silk. Jollied up in haberdashery. Cut a figure. Steady one's footing. Where one was previously slipping badly. Comport myself now in places where one one gets dinner and party invitations. Not quite appearing like a race course tout but nearly. I must last out. Hoard the very feeble confidence of the remaining pounds in my pocket.

'You have an account with us sir.'

'Yes.'

'May I inquire of the name please.'

'Kildare. Darcy Thormond Dancer Kildare.'

'But of course. Andromeda Park.'

'And please would you in due course send it to the Shelbourne where I am presently in residence.'

'Certainly sir.'

'And you may give these clothes to some deserving person. They were given me when my luggage was misplaced.'

'Of course sir, I had thought the tailoring was by the look of a line or two, not quite paying full due to your figure.'

My next few days one must say were pleasant. Visiting the painting galleries, a tour of the big brewery, theatre in the evening and sometimes, racing permitting, the cinema in the afternoon. Till I returned for my final suit fitting. Brought off with all the suitably pleasant murmurings. Little tuck under the arms, a nip at the waist. And by god with the trouser just further narrowed I would soon cut a swath.

'I think sir, we are going to have you looking your best.'

'Rather.'

And at last this sunnyish balmy day. Walking up and down Grafton Street top to bottom for the fifth time. Sporting my new suit. To take lunch. At Jammet's. Following my second successful day at the races. After numerous abysmal losing ones. Entering through this shadowy little alleyway off Grafton Street. Welcomed. Hand my dark brown trilby to the door man. Just acquired at the hatter's three minutes ago. Sit myself up on this stool. Cool marble counter. Open the racing pages. Study the form. Yesterday won seventeen pounds on the first race. Lost two pounds on each of the next four races. And now just following the purchase of my head garment there was the hatter's rather churlish refusal of credit. Requiring one to distressingly part with cash. But leaving one still in possession of a pound or two.

'Sir.'

'A snipe of champagne please and a dozen oysters.'

Darcy Dancer folding his racing paper. To survey the day's tips. The nostrils assailed by the aromatics of these passing plates lofted to place settings along this counter by these most attentive presiding gastronomic gentlemen. And this face next to me, turning. Looks and looks again. At me I believe. One absolutely hates this kind of inquisitiveness at lunch. Next he'll be wanting to borrow my cutlery. My god. Good Lord. His face. How does one in the middle of one's oysters and champagne as well as an unwelcome inquiring question become awfully scarce.

'I say there, excuse me, but don't I know you. I think I do. Can't place you exactly.'

'I'm sorry, but I do believe you may be confusing me with someone else.'

'No. Not a chance. Served in military intelligence fourteen years. Could pick a certain wog out of a black hole chock a block full of them. Black or white never forget a face. Damn sure I know yours. From somewhere.'

Never has one had to enjoy champagne and oysters less. Having as they have now become my most treasured midday habit. Following my long breakfast of tea, sausages, bacon and ham, hot bath, stroll about the Green. And then a perusement of shop windows. To now have to keep one's face as averted as possible without being blatantly rude. Surely my utterly single minded indifference to him has got to make the ruddy conversation dry up. Or any second I may be chased right out across this room and out the door. Followed by this face. Which as Master of Foxhounds I saw last, full of rage tumbling off arse over spurs down his horse's tail. Ah. That did it. Just hit him nicely in the eye. Nothing like a squirt of lemon to shift his attention.

'Sorry about that.'

'Dammit. Don't mind a bit of lemon in the eye. Just damn mind if I can't recall where I've seen you. By god I do know your face, I know I do. It's either polo or the hunting field I'm damn certain of that.'

'I'm awfully sorry, I can't help you. Don't hunt or play polo. Hardly even associate with those who do. I live as a matter of fact out the end of a peninsula which perhaps you might know called Mizen Head. Quite remote.'

'Well it's bound to come to me, damn it, have a drink. What is it to be.'

'Well as a matter of fact, it's champagne. A snipe.'

'You shoot those do you.'

'Yes as a matter of fact I do.'

'On your peninsula.'

'Yes. On my peninsula.'

'Jolly good. And that's a jolly good drink this time of day.'

Amazing. With this big rotter trying to figure out who one is, one has quaffed now four snipes. Making a full bottle together with three dozen oysters. The Master of Foxhounds is even clapping me on the back. Clicking my vertebrae all down my spine. But never mind, also picking up the back breaking bill.

'And where are you off to my young fellow.'

'Curragh Races.'

'Good show. So am I. Join me in my motor car.'

'Well as a matter of fact.'

'Good let me have the facts.'

Of course my most salient fact was that one was terrified. Weighing as he must obviously do, at least fifteen stone. But my flattery of him in every conceivable way seems to have at least made him forget he remembered me. Till indeed I think he took my buttering him up as an overture of lasting friendship. He could be and probably is an absolutely sadistic pederast.

'My Bentley is just around the corner.'

As now he is positively insisting upon departing in my company. Although clearly one is out of danger of being recognized now, one might next really be running the risk of buggery. He did say between snipes that youth gave the eyes a sparkle. And one must show appreciation to another's flattery. I did rather roll my eyes. Seemed to make all proceed quite nicely. Till I felt his hand pressure my arse as one decamped from one's stool. Heading as we are right to the door. In his generosity to the doorman. Pouring change in his palm. He's dropped about four shillings. Pick this one up. Hand it to him. As one's face turns. To look somewhat upwards at his. And O my god never has recognition struck such a thundering blow. Once again his scarlet coat. His upraised whip. His white gloves. And face bloating red.

'By gad. I know where I remember your face. It's you. You bloody bounder. You. Stole my ruddy horse. And had me thrown. Why you, come back here.'

The doorman in his ministrations to the Master of Foxhounds obviously at first thought we were reciting lines from a stage play. And I must say with the words so out of context of a damn good champagne and oyster lunch, anyone at all would be forgiven for thinking that. Until the doorman saw aghast, the swing door of Jammet's open with such speed that it came loose off its hinges.

'By god would you believe it. That ruddy young scamp. Unseating me from my horse. Accepting my sociability. And sticking me with the blasted enormous bill.'

Of course I could not hear these latter words spoken but dear me imagined them. And it was the Master's fatal mistake to take the seconds he did to reflect to the doorman. Even though the latter's duty was to listen to all sorts of sad tales. I was not long in reaching the passing throngs of Grafton Street. And at some increased speed arriving just a few feet away at the front entrance to Mitchell's granite palace erected for the greater glory of afternoon tea and cakes. Where one awaits the Master to harmlessly pass by. Wiggling in among the stream of early afternoon ladies from Foxrock and Rathgar. Catching my breath in their perfume. Peering out from between their tea bonnets. To this present moment in Grafton Street. So sunny. So silly. When all one can think of is the rather red scar across the Master's nose upon which I remember his cap visor crushing down. Whoosh. Here he is. Charging like a bull in my pursuit. And wham. Crash right smack into the most dearest of little old ladies. Laying flat the poor dear tiny creature cold as a cucumber on the pavement. What a disgrace. Her black straw hat decorated with yellow primroses, flung flying. Alarmed ladies making a protective circle around the dear old prostrate thing. And the Master hulking totally distraught and hysterically apologizing to one suffragette striking at him with her parasol. Just hope he doesn't have the same recognition for voices as he does for faces. As one cries out. Four loudly articulated words. To echo the deepest feelings of these absolutely appalled gathered ladies most of whom are clearly members of the Royal Dublin Society.

> You
> Big
> Stupid
> Oaf

26

Those first weeks in Dublin memorable for living life with what one can only describe as an inscrutable insobrieous insouciance. Unwise however to spend any time longer in the horsey habitat of the Shelbourne. Especially as that very morning one was handed one's first hotel bill. Which one had in the splendour of one's tweed been previously requesting to be put on next month's tab. One did not trouble to even glance down at the long white amended and re-amended sheets of paper. Fearing to gasp at the amount because one had become utterly overwhelmed with extravagance. Of course daily one was awaiting the remedy on the race course. And I found it necessary to rock a little back and forth on my heels while requesting the assistant manager to arrange that my many weeks bill be put on my quarterly tab. And when at his slight hesitation I loftily inquired as to whether there was any difficulty.

'Well, Mr Kildare no, but I am wondering if you perhaps are encountering any.'

'None at all. I'm extremely comfortable thank you.'

'Well as a matter of fact Mr Kildare we were concerned if perhaps some mistake had been made on your bill. You see we usually require some kind of prearrangement for the longer settlement of accounts.'

'Ah. But of course. My bankers are organizing a draft. But you know how we Darcy Thormond Kildares hate to be rushed.'

'There's no rush. Certainly sir. Seeing as your mother's family have been our valued customers over the years. And I think for the moment an exception can be made.'

'I am indeed most appreciative. Funds held up. A death in the family you know.'

'O I'm sorry to hear that sir.'

Then at Leopardstown races. The worst happened. Wiped out. And walked all the way back to Dublin. And not trusting to a future encounter with the Shelbourne's overseers being so successful I piece by piece discreetly removed each item of my newly acquired wardrobe down and around the corner to the Royal Hibernian. To there ensconce in a back snug blue carpeted room. With now an irate Shelbourne management concerned over my whereabouts and not a sou in my pocket with which to even place a bet at the Turf Accountant's in Duke Street. Indeed in such impoverishment one desperately depended upon an hotel's kitchen's hospitality. Even to having the Hibernian's chef daily knock up a sandwich lunch picnic for me to eat in a lonely deckchair in Stephen's Green. However although one had nothing else to complain about in the Hibernian, they could not as I had hoped they might, agree to an arrangement whereby my bill was rendered half yearly. Nor could one insist in view of my still insubstantial amount of luggage. Mostly carried in loose over my arm. But one would now have to distinctly avoid walking in, through or indeed past the Shelbourne or any other of the more horsey environs these days. And not only in case of marauding Masters of Foxhounds.

'Good day sir. Breakfast well.'

'Yes thank you.'

'Have today's *Sporting Herald*.'

'Yes I will, thank you.'

'Put it on the tab sir.'

'Yes, please do.'

With these words exchanged each morning with the hotel porter one did feel as if it were one's own front hall. But instead of out to pastures, one stepped under the glass awning and down steps to the boulevard. Where with motor cars more prevalent one enjoyed the rather pleasant acrid fume. Wonder hourly what to do. Begging was a thought. Stirred each time I walked by the same blond and staring organ grinder on the bridge. Or sauntered constantly daily on the favoured and more socially acceptable streets. Paying special attention to that of Grafton. The delight never waning of walking up one side and down the other. Past the jewellers. Medical instrument suppliers. Cafés. Coffee shops. Then back and forth through Duke and Anne Streets. Up and down Dawson. Somewhere somehow I'm bound to meet Miss von B. Or surely find a party raging. Where one could meet and talk with someone. Or even find a lawyer perhaps. To sue my father.

I did however get myself a cane. From my faithful ever willing to please horse haberdasher in Dame Street. Which instantly cheered me up in my loneliness. And goodness sauntering with it this sunny Wednesday mid afternoon I disported in the peace of College Park to watch the girls play hockey and the gentlemen rugger. Then while contemplating rogering nearly every lady of any reasonable appearance, I nearly ran smack into Lois. Right in the roasting coffee aromas in front of Bewley's Oriental Café on Grafton Street. Just after I had opened an account there and sent off a pound of their best chocolate fudge to Kelly with a quarter pound each of marzipan fondants and oriental jellies. Stood there thinking. For at least one and a half seconds. Before following her. My trouser sticking out like a tent. And Lois in a long knitted white wool coat. A green wool knitted hat popped atop her grey blonde hair. Striding in long mannish strides. Feel just like one of her hoard of sexually frustrated people she said trailed her. Avert my eyes from the many eyes in the passing faces that become more and more familiar each day. In the lobbies. The coffee houses. Everywhere on the street. Now need to run after her. With her walking speed. Down the street. Into Switzer's. Lurked a moment feeling such a pervert in the ladies' corsetry area. My penis throbbing. And Lois discussing with an unfriendly saleslady some undergarment she finally declines to buy.

Then through back streets. Kept swallowing my saliva. Thinking of her bosoms. As she bought vegetables in an old market. And every time I turn a corner. One is ready to meet one's father. Or jump aside out of the arms of the waiting Master of Foxhounds. But my most lowest of low moments followed the last race at Leopardstown. Leaving me ever since so absolutely god awful broke. Winning the first two races. Losing the rest. Then without train fare removing myself so unglamorously all the way back to Dublin on my two feet. Had an intervening glass of water from a reluctant publican in Stillorgan. Who whispered to another customer that it was safer to serve the insane what they wanted. And reaching the lobby of the Hibernian as exhausted as I was stony broke. Not even able to dispense my usual shilling tips to the boot boy or the most solicitous doorman. And now. Like a sex starved maniac I am. Following this Bohemian home. Back by the Hospital. Whoops. Nip into a doorway. As she suddenly turns around. Nip out again. Keep creeping onwards. Wait. Let her go up her alley. And peruse for half an hour in a shaft of warm sunlight this cobbler's window. With a statue of the Blessed Virgin surveying at her feet, a bunch of old warped shoes.

Darcy Dancer rapping on the door. Up between these shadowy walls. Strewn newspapers and patches of grease on the cobbles. The big doors of the warehouse. Heart thumping to knock on this pale green plank marked number four. O my god if the gunman answers. Bang. Bang. Be at least the end of the agony of wondering what's going to happen to me. Feet coming down the stairs.

'Identify yourself please.'

'It's me.'

'I am most certainly not going to open up my door to that remark.'

'Well I was here once before.'

'Nor am I opening it to that remark.'

'Well I'm the imperialist member of the squirearchy.'

'Nor does that remark interest me since I am a fervent socialist.'

'I've come to buy your pictures.'

'Now that is more like it.'

Door opening. Lois stepping back. One hopes bloody hell, not over the milk bottles again.

'It's you. Good god.'

'Yes.'

'I thought I might have seen you. In Grafton Street. Well don't just stand there. Come in. My god have you grown. Or have I shrunk since I last saw you. And when you nearly committed murder.'

'I have been wanting for so long to apologize to you.'

'Don't apologize to me. People are poleaxing people in my bed all the time.'

'Well it was discourteous striking someone from behind like that.'

'Well no matter dear boy. At least you escaped certain death at the hands of a ruthless gunman. And as a matter of fact. It was hardly your fault. Well sit down. Will you have tea.'

'Thank you.'

'And you needn't worry. He's not about at the moment. And if he were. You'd hear it from his own lips. Quite amazing. When he woke up. He was simply ecstatic. He had according to him, when you bashed him, the greatest orgasm of his entire life. While I of course was having my greatest fright. Anyway how nice of you wanting to buy my pictures.'

The big studio. The full length portrait of the Count with his arm and lower leg now all in one piece. A ring of strawberry leaves round his head. The strong smell of turpentine in the warmer spring balmy weather. A north light bathing the stacked canvases. The stove door stuffed open with biscuit wrappings. Dishes crammed in the sink. Penises and balls everywhere. And my own dying to be exercised by that hand now putting a kettle on to boil.

'Well this is a surprise. You of all people. An imperialist. Liking my pictures. And just in time. I'm simply so bored by my impecuniousness. It's so tiresome. Well my dear boy, I don't want to rush you but I have a collector coming, and I would like you to have first choice. Which of my paintings would you like to see.'

Darcy Dancer casually crossing his tweedy legs over his erection. Such a marvellous activity to spend these moments as a connoisseur of art. Sound of a fresh breeze blowing over the skylight. As one stares glued to her bosoms and swelling orbs of her bottom as she bends over revealing her canvases one by one. Then putting out her chest standing at a new swatch by the wall. To unveil art when I'd rather she unveiled her nipples. Her belly. Her crotch.

'No. Can't show you these. They're not worthy. And my integrity would not allow me to sign them. But this dear boy is out of my green fertility period. Note how the penis here is pregnant with movement. And the testicle showing its marvellous spheroid line. It's what one tries for. Tension in total and complete repose. Do you think I've caught it.'

'Yes I do rather.'

I bought six paintings. One for every inch of my erection. And all for the awful staggering total of ninety-six pounds. One of course would have to hang them in a locked room away from prying eyes. Lois seemed not in the least troubled by my not having my cheque book with me. But otherwise she was all business. Showing me her most recent washes of the male nude. And not once even suggesting the removal of my clothes. Or giving even the remotest sign indicating she would welcome my stiff prick loosed into her presence. With its throbbing tension in total and complete repose.

A knock down at the front door. O my god. The gunman. Just when one was on the verge of simply taking out one's penis. Encouraged or not. And Lois jumping up. A hand up to put back her wisp of hair. Loosed each time she bent over. And I planned to make a grab for her. And now instead make an immediate move towards the drapes to hide.

'You needn't worry dear boy. I'm sure it's my collectors. For tea.'

A most baggy suited tweedy couple. One would almost expect wrens to fly out of their sleeves. She with bobbed straight grey hair hanging down around her head. He with a red carnation in his buttonhole. And a bright orange tweed tie. They mounted the stairs spouting a fountain of superlatives. How utterly quaint. How divine. All the way to the door. Through which they come to pause in stony silence at the sight. As I stand for introduction. Nicely embarrassed by

365

my face I just spot in a drawing in which my form is adorned by a rather limp but large erection.

'Ah let me introduce you to a young connoisseur who has just happily bought several of my pictures. Ah now, please, do sit down.'

The couple hardly looking up. Or around. Never mind sitting down. The Professor clearing his throat.

'Are these. These, your pictures.'

'Yes.'

'Well. I think there has been some misunderstanding.'

'O.'

'Well. I think, and I am abundantly sure my wife will agree with me, that this is not what we expected. I mean take that there for example. Indeed that too. They are I regret to say, pornographic. And in the most blatant meaning of that word. If this is a sample of your work. I'm afraid we simply are not interested.'

'I don't mind in the least that you're not. My singularity of purpose can't please everyone. But please do sit and have tea.'

Professor and wife sitting. But one could sense their legs would quick be running. Just as soon as their numbed limbs recovered feeling. Lois pouring water from her kettle into a tea pot. Professor again clearing his throat. A speechless croak came out. Then silence. Then licking his lips, he exploded.

'Artistically they fail, if I may be so blunt as to say so.'

Lois putting down her kettle, wiping her hands. Seemed very slow in her movements. Walking over to the paintings in question. Picking up the offending canvases. Turning with one in each hand hanging down at her sides. Crossing to where the two collectors sat adjoining on their chairs. Lois standing in front of them. And suddenly raising both canvases in an arc outward from her hips. Up over her head. To crash them down on both of theirs. Perforating the canvases and the paintings encircling their necks. As they both now sat with their stunned visages poking up out of the painted pudenda. And not a muscle moving as if they were acquiescing to a time honoured chastisement meted out in Dublin Bohemian circles.

'Forgive me Professor but both you and your wife are philistines.'

I did think perhaps one should depart. As one was already sick with unrequited laughter. And turned to bow back to the victims. Who nodded to my courtesy. Sitting otherwise unmoved and mummified in their shock. But still in the throes of my most appalling randiness and out of eye sight of my stunned fellow collectors I kissed Lois at the top of the stairs. Even put a hand to her bosom. But she was so utterly indifferent that one pretended one was being merely ebulliently theatrical in parting.

'Goodbye Lois.'

'Dear boy. So nice to have a new patron like you. So eclectic in your appreciation. I will have your pictures packed and wrapped ready for your collection. And you must also come back and pose you really must.'

Proceed through the street. Back along in front of the Gaiety Theatre. Pause to go down Grafton. Walk instead straight. Along the Green. After one more fraudulent pretence. In one's descent downwards. A collector of art. Where do all these other people get their money. And me with only a British three penny bit in one's pocket. And the bars on one side of this many sided coin look like those of a debtors' prison. But at least one had an exchange of words with other human beings. And witnessed in action an artistic temperament. Plus had a chocolate coated biscuit. To assist one return in randy madness to one's lonely hotel room. Once more await dinner. Once more lie on one's bed listening to the wireless. Counting the tiny fissures in the ceiling and dreaming of the lovely limbs of Miss von B.

Darcy Dancer walking briskly. Traffic thickening in the streets. The giant guards coming out to take up their evening traffic positions. Their patches of white on the arms of their tunics held up to motor cars piloted by the swarms of bicycles. God, people really do rush when it's time to go home. And now go back up these steps. Into the welcome elegance of the Hibernian. Where I can still eat and run up the bill.

Darcy Dancer collecting his sporting papers from the porter. Tuck them up under an arm. Climb these marble steps. One two. Three four. Routines so essential. Never let the mind begin thinking. Just rekindles one's lust. Take a long leisurely bath. It can so cheer one up. Brush and groom one's hair. Snatch out even one more grey one. Put a white spotted blue hanky in my breast pocket. Instead of my spotted maroon one. Tie my tie knot neatly up into the softness of my silk collar. Wipe shoe tips on the back of my trouser leg.

Darcy Dancer, the satin lining of his tweeds cool against the knees. Chin up and spine straight. Out now down the deeply carpeted hall. Past the brass numbers on the doors of these rooms. To the top of the marble staircase. Descend. Ah. Some people bustling into the lounge do turn to watch. My command performance. Take a sherry before dinner. Ferried to me by the waiter between the little group of chairs. Occupied by so many all so happy in each other's company. Cosseted in the soft pleasing solitude of this sanctum. God. How soon will one be chucked back out into the uncaring world. A vagabond. The thought is so greviously upsetting that I had better step down into the dining room. Sit in my usual little corner the head waiter likes to reserve for me. Not yet knowing I cannot pay my bill. Have trout and spinach tonight. And Chablis. Top off with trifle and vintage port. Ensure all the health giving vitamins. In case one has to make a run for it. With irate managements waving hotel bills in my wake.

Darcy Dancer in his seat. Smiling up to hand back the menu. Settle down now to study the weekly fixtures in one's sporting paper. Show jumping, horse trials, fairs and sales. Look up. People making an awfully loud entrance. One never knows these days when the wrong sort will appear in the right places. And standards just plummet. But over there. In the opposite corner of the room. Clearly some fellow elegants. A man with flowing grey hair sweeping back from an aristocratic countenance. And a woman. She must be stunning. By what one can see of her back. Her arm. Or her gown. Which my god. Miss von B wore in the ballroom the night she lonely sang. And wears now. Sitting there. My heart pumps and pounds. Breath catching agony. Up from the soles of my feet. Right where I look. As she leans forward. Across from this man. Adoring him. Reaching with her hand. Putting hers on top of his as it lifts. And he bends to kiss that skin. Upon which my own mouth has pressed. And my tears have fallen. Until I can't watch. Her running. High up some hill. Further and further away. Get up to go. While her body stays. Taking away her soul. Which laughed so. Out of her eyes. Lay between her thighs. Up in her silken softness. Till now. I reach. Hoping and hungering. For her.

Darcy Dancer leaving the dining room. Chin down. Spine bent. Step back up these few carpeted steps. Treading on the wool woven roses. Go out. Not know where I'm going. Nor care. Why she adored. Walk. On these night time streets. Away through one's crashing dreams. Under lamplight. On the grey speckled blocks of granite. Leave the fence of Trinity. A pub Lincoln's Inn. Big closed back gates of the college. Light in the porter's lodge. Turkish turrets across the street. Down Westland Row. Stone pillars of a church. Iron pillars of a bridge. Train chugging over. Every part of her comes haunting. The slap she gave me in the face. The album of her castles. The ballrooms. The waltzing ladies and gentlemen. Charging at me on her rearing horse. All the way to the moored looming shadowy ships on this black river flowing through this black city.

Darcy Dancer stepping over a chain strung along the quayside. Coal grit blowing over the cobbles. Lonely lights in port holes. Sailors singing. Arms over each others' shoulders weaving out of that pub. And have no friend. And have no love. Turn back. Walk by these vast gloomy walls. Inside through bars in a window. A man shovelling coal. Far down in the dark cavernous interior. A red glow of flames. Footsteps behind me. An arm grabs mine. A voice asking. Grinning in my face with her rotted teeth.

'Do you want a short time for ten bob.'

Shake away from her clutching fingers. Her wide staring

eyes. Pale hollow cheeked face. Run. Pound the pavements. Fly back. Reach my own familiar streets. Up Kildare. Silently slowly along Molesworth. So safe in all its Protestant virtue. On each lamp post these escutcheons. Three castles, a sword and a crown. The Royal Hibernian ahead. She sat inside those drape darkened windows. Chic soignée and so beautiful. Like frost sparkling in moonlight. On the miles of road I walked. And the worst of all. She saw me. And turned away. When her back was bent in sorrow I comforted her. Put my hand on her hair. While her tears were falling. And tonight. Along the quays. Mine fell. In anger bleeding.

> In
> Such
> Painful
> Drops

27

The sunset sent slivers of warm light in my window. The wireless weather report said the days to continue fine. The going good at all the courses. And me penniless. Presented now on two occasions with my hotel bill. The cuts from my vagabond roamings all finally healed to tiny white scars. Finger nails glistening clean. The afternoon maid Bridget making my bed said I ought to go out for some fresh air. And so damn randy was I. Nearly said why didn't she stay for some fresh prick. And I did go out. Down to Trinity to ask for the whereabouts of graduates. But they had no address other than care of Andromeda Park for Mr Arland. Then I stayed further days in my room. Brooding. Cured of loving ever again. Yet scheming to find her. Please let me come back to you. Please. Dazzle her. Whisk her away. From that man so certain of her adoration. And on Sunday. With everyone on the wireless praying. Ventured out. And a third time presented with my bill. As I was devoutly. Avoiding to be evicted.

'The cattle are coming up to market on the Tuesday next. And of course one will settle one's account.'

And Monday. What an awful awful struggle to arise up out of one's bed. From dreams. My own stables. Chock a block with steeplechasers. Great slab muscled marvellous boned springy sinewed animals. Running like wolfhounds. My army of grooms on parade. Each morning as the clock tower tolls eight over the stables. Glockenspiel chiming 'Onward Christian Soldiers', as I appear. In my gleaming leathers. Riding crop thwacking the mahogany of my boot.

Then all too soon. Back in one's penury. Late afternoon. The lobby all abustle. With voices. I say. How jolly good to see you. Come to the ball. Other people's invitations sound so good. So white. Like my mother's were, stuck round her dressing room mirrors. The black glistening bumps of the letters. Bid you come to the big houses with big oak doors. Mirrors in their stately rooms. Miles and miles of lawns to cross under the shadows of the trees. O god. How one so adores that light loveliness of social froth. Gives one's skin such a nice deep glowing social polish. So clearly needed by these two now arriving. Escorted by a taxi driver. Taking from them an endless number of orange ten shilling notes. Their twanging American voices. O gee, o gosh. Is this here place called Ireland.

And a person. With all the graces. Whom one watches. Attired in a kilt. His familiar voice. Going through all kinds of strange postulations at the reception desk. As one peers closer. Would you believe the nerve of the man. Sporting a clearly false handlebar moustache. And an equally phony monocle. Checking into a double room. Major and Mrs Jones. When my god, it is none other than the Mental Marquis. With Baptista Consuelo over there in a sheepskin coat. Pretending to be engrossed patting someone's grey curly poodle on its fluffy head. When both were last seen. With the naked hairy arse of the Marquis planted between Baptista's unclothed flailing legs. As one stares. I must admit. Stunned. But also inspired. By his Lordship's most sickly guilty smile as he looks up from the register. And sees me. Now that I have gained the proximity of his elbow. And one simply takes one's ruddy nerve into one's hands.

'By god your Lordship, how jolly nice to see you.'

'Yes. Rather. How nice, how are you. But you are confusing me with someone else.'

'O I'm jolly fine. I'm Reginald Darcy Thormond Kildare. You do know me I hope.'

'Well if you care to stand on ceremony, it would appear perhaps one could know you. But I've already said once, how are you. To which I can't really delay to hear the answer as I fear I do at this moment find myself in an awfully binding rush you understand. But nice seeing you all the same. Been a damn long day at the races. And must bathe.'

'O yes hasn't it. Marvellous day at the races.'

'I said a damn long day at the races sir, I did not say marvellous.'

'No. Quite. You didn't. But really. I do hope I'm not inconveniencing you. Stopping you and holding you up like this. I really am awfully sorry to do this. Your Lordship. Sorry about that. Damn title keeps coming out. But I wonder. I've had the most unfortunate inconvenience. Also at the races. Lost my ruddy pocket book.'

'O damn poor show.'

'And I wonder. Your Lordship. I mean, Major. Could you lend me a fiver.'

Without one instant's hesitation the Marquis pulling open his sporran. And digging with some nervous rustling into the interior of this black pouch. And with a shake of tassels and a most audible inhale and exhale of breath, producing a fiver. Distastefully holding forward the large white note by the corner in his upraised fingers. One did feel he might at least attempt to slip it to me in a back handed manner. Especially as he is wearing decorations and I think the Military Star of the Order of the Bath. Last time I saw such award was in a reference tome of my grandfather's library. Astonishing how one's recollection is stirred by desperation.

'Now please, do sir, get out of my way.'

Darcy Dancer standing back. Carefully folding this written promise of the Bank of England to pay the bearer on demand five pounds. To now appropriately secrete it in one's waist coat pocket. At least one thing being a menial has profitably taught me. How to gracefully step in to obstruct those in the privileged pursuit of their private pleasures.

The hall porter gathering up three massive leather cases. The Marquis proceeding behind him towards the lift. And Baptista Consuelo her sheepskin coat now over her arm retreating from her close perusement of a Malton print of Dublin on the wall. I turned away at their threesome departure to cool one's flushed face. And met the most strangely appreciative smile across a nearby chap's red haired moustach-ioed visage. Who stood in front of the blazing lobby fire. And whose eyes seemed to twinkle with delight. And whose identity I simply did not at this time wish to remind myself of. Remorseful as I was, nearly having committed the most mortifying act of all my life. But a voice was now confronting me.

'By jove that is one of the most splendid underhanded blackmailing episodes I have ever witnessed in my life. And I've long pursued a career as a gentleman chancer and cad.'

'I beg your pardon sir.'

'Beg my pardon by all means, but come come my good man. You just took a fiver off his Lordship as one might suck a speck of caviar from one's knuckle. Let me introduce myself. The name is Ronald Ronald Ronald. Triple barrelled as you might say. Some anti christs of course would refer to me as Rashers Ronald. I may not be the most successful con man in this town but I'll have you know I am easily the most persistent. That's why I'm so full of admiration. Young chap like you. By God. You're hardly in your late teens. Admirable. Simply admirable. Masterstroke. The timing. Takes one's breath away. His bloody Lordship there. Ruddy blundering idiot. Registering in his most awfully loud voice as Major Jones. When all for miles around know it's him. And upstairs under some unsuspecting eiderdown about to bite off the most delightful piece of crumpet I've seen in a long time. My only criticism is, and mind you it's a mild one. You should have gone for a tenner you know. It's the setting. Always be conscious of the setting. Never underprice yourself in posh environs. Sky's the limit. Of course in ragged circumstances in some flea pit down on the quays things can be conducted quite more humbly when one ventures to secure a half crown from an associate in similar shabby circumstances as one's own. I won't say I could teach you every trick in the book, but turned out the way you are, I could assist you to take your place among the great cads of our time. And please do wipe that state of utter shock off your face. Ruddy marvellous you were. But for your age one would think you trained in the lobby of the Ritz in London before the war. We're chips off the same block my dear chap and we may indeed find the same appropriate alabaster ladies' shoulders to land together on. And cunningly prevent each other from being brushed off. I suggest therefore, we make each other's immediate acquaintance.'

Rashers Ronald spoke between a slight division between his two upper front protruding teeth. And smiled as he turned to greet a passing dowager. Her grey uniformed and leather legginged chauffeur behind her lugging cases, while two poodles cradled in the bends of his arms were licking his cheeks.

'Now my dear boy. Did you see her. Portly perhaps but just the charming side of sixty. Three hundred and twenty acres in County Dublin. Stabling for forty. Absolutely first class grazing well watered and fenced. Four footmen. Six gardeners. Grows the most sweet juicy bloody damn peaches in her greenhouse. Excuse me a moment.'

Rashers borrowing a cigarette from the doorman. Inserting it into a long ivory cigarette holder and placing it lightly between his lips. Doorman striking a match and lighting him up. Standing there in his morning suit, chin up, shoulders back, blowing out a leisurely long cloud of tobacco smoke. And taking from his pocket a pair of spectacles.

'Of course my dear fellow you're wondering why I am so dressed as if one had just retired from a wedding. Fact of the matter is I always adorn in my striped trousers and tail coat of a morning. And find no need even to change as the day or night progresses. Hardly any in their right mind these days will have me at their weddings and few, even at their dinners. But at least I can appear as if I've been there. Also it's useful garb when one encounters some bounder to whom one owes money. One merely turns one's back and blends into the hotel woodwork appearing from the rear at least, as a member of the staff. Now these spectacles. Of course I see perfectly without them. But these are a useful prop. Especially when one wants a dowager to know that one is contemplating her. When one puts them on slowly. If she primps then one immediately knows that one's next step is to introduce oneself. Of course there are people who would cast unkind aspersions. Call me a chancer and fortune hunter. I openly admit to the latter. But in the former category I am a rank amateur in this metropolis. But come. Let us proceed under the auspices of your recently acquired fiver down into the Buttery. For drinkies. And I'm sure you won't mind my momentary impecuniousness which I had hoped would be remedied by the Marquis until you my dear chap beat me so beautifully, so consummately, to it.'

Darcy Dancer following Rashers Ronald through into the lounge. Past the lift. Which appeared to be out of action. The American couple, he in electric blue she in chintz awaiting its rapid repair. While on the staircase Baptista Consuelo was perched on about the sixth marble step. The Mental Marquis on the ninth and the porter apparently collapsed over the weight of their luggage on the twelfth. As I passed by a writing table, Baptista turning her head away towards the wall. One hopes in some modesty for the solemnity of her sins. Rashers bowing to that embarrassed direction. Just as a gasp emits from the watching elderly American couple. The porter's hand making a sudden grasp for the largest of the Marquis's leather cases. Which misses. The luggage breaking open as it falls. With whips, bridles, boots, reins, bits, tumbling out. Not to mention an unbelievable saddle and numnah as well. The porter lunging after the leathers. And promptly dropping the rest of the cases. To trip and tumble down crashing into the Marquis. Both engripped with one another rolling backwards down at Baptista. Who, with an awfully impressive presence of mind, stands into the wall. As they go bumping past head over heels entwined in tack. Rashers running forward to assist.

'My god, Major Jones, are you all right. Please. At least let me undo you from your hunting and chastisement gear.'

'Get away from me you. I mean I do appreciate your solicitude. But damn it man. Do you really have to interfere. Jumping to sadistic conclusions like that.'

Baptista in her dark brown sweater. A long string of pearls

suspended down across the rise of her bosoms so flatteringly pronounced by the tight thick strap she wore just like Miss von B round her waist. Her long blonde hair in the chandelier light flowing gleamingly down over her shoulders. Her cream coloured skirt snugly enfolding the melon ripe amplitude of her otherwise over ample quarters. Strong calves flexing in her silk stockings. And marvellously sensible walking shoes. She looks quite smart and radiantly attractive as much as one hates to admit it. As one must with my new tweed trousers absolutely out like a tent. Standing utterly stiff as she stands up there. Quite unfazed. Indeed, even with a trace of a smile on her lips. Looking down at the Marquis. Whose kilt is up around his neck. With eagerly nosy folk and hotel staff in from the lobby. And others from the lounge rushing to the scene. Gasps at the sight. And a scream from the American lady.

'That guy's got no pants on.'

The Marquis groaning. Disentangling himself from both the porter, reins, bits and bridles in which he was wrapped. And carefully readjusting the strap of his sporran. Rashers like an usher at a wedding reception controlling the impoverished members of the bride's relatives desperate to sink fangs into the free flowing refreshments. The Marquis turning to the gathering.

'Damn you all. Does a crowd really have to collect. Haven't you ever seen anyone fall down a staircase before.'

'Ah but Major Jones. You may take it from Rashers Ronald, that many may have seen a plunge on the stairs. But few have ever had such an opportunity to get such a marvellous eyeful.'

> Of what
> Is up
> Under a
> Kilt

28

Rashers Ronald beaming a great smile. Guiding Darcy Dancer by the elbow. These two gentlemen proceeding forward into the mirrored lounge. Presided over by the ceiling's central dome of glass. Ministering waiters passing quietly between tables with their trays. Rashers bowing to the seemingly unaccompanied ladies of all ages. Seated in their finery. Wrists ablaze with gems.

'Of course my dear chap, and excuse me for whispering but I must keep my voice down. Imagine the Marquis poor devil being exposed like that. Publicly on display. Not only with his bit of blonde fluff but his ruddy pudenda and all. Rum luck. Worse than having one's prick out pissing off the top of Nelson's Pillar during the holy hour. Damn tragedy for the aristocracy. Fortunately this hotel is most elegantly populated. Incident will spread only in the best circles like wildfire over the entire country. But allow me to point out. Seated over there, that's her ladyship. Often referred to as Her Grace the greasemonkey. Her age is quite indeterminate. But her acreage encouragingly is not. Seven hundred and eighty seven statute. Plus salmon banks and two trout lakes. She loves tinkering with the underside of motor cars. Wears out three or four pairs of white flannel overalls and gloves a week. Handbag full of spanners. She always carries a spare exhaust pipe or two in her luggage. Even siphons her wine out of the bottle at dinner. And unless one has one's own rubber tube you don't get a drop. She can sometimes be so tiresomely rural. But her most amiable quality is she takes it both back and front. Awfully useful when two chaps want to have a go at her together. See by your tailoring, you're from the country of course. With no disparagement thereby meant, my good chap.'

'Yes I am as a matter of fact.'

'And where my good chap are you staying in town.'

'Here.'

'What. In the hotel.'

'Yes.'

'Masterly. Absolutely masterly. Dear me you are a professional. If one has to stoop to the wretchedness of plying one's youthful beauty for mere filthy lucre, why not then be damn efficient about it. I'm of course presently at no fixed address. My previous fixed one was down what one can only euphemistically refer to as a beneath lower basement flat. Damn place was more like a mining shaft. Now just stand here a moment, and just let the ladies see us. It does so cheer me up this place. Especially as one does have one's such rapid ups and downs. A recent black gentleman posing as a Prince from the Sudan beat me to that choice dowager there. She my dear chap is just straight forwardly just damn rich. My father was an army General. That's really all my trouble. Damn old fool never made Field Marshal due to several late career reverses on the field of battle. And was merely knighted. Poor sod just fishes and shoots, retired on his pension. Leaving his son a commoner. With not even the helpful courtesy entitlement of being an Honourable. Dooming me to fortune hunting. Which pursuit I must make quite clear, I do try to conduct in as romantic and moral a manner as possible. Now there, in the corner. For God's sake don't stare. But she, the dear girl, buried two husbands, is just in her early fifties. Never know it. Handsome isn't she. Slender and long legged. And where it counts, fleshed nicely fore and aft. And never mind her thin lips, she gives absolutely the most marvellous gamorouche. Has some damn nice thoroughbreds. Has had two winners at Aintree Grand National. Her father, ancient old crusty bugger he is too, manufactures an established industrial commodity. Of his own originating. Amazing considering the only thing ever invented in this country was soda water. Dear girl will fall heir to the ruddy lot. Factory covers six acres of floor space. Must always have your financial facts straight. So many businesses go to the wall these days you've got to be careful. One's beauty doesn't always last you know.

A mature chap like myself is fattening slightly under the jaw-bones as I push into the latter end of my twenty third year. And of course with so many of the less discerning old hag ladies admiring young men's bodies, one has to strike while the rod's hot. If you catch my meaning.'

Darcy Dancer at the top of the stairs. Rashers Ronald at the bottom smiling back up. As I hesitate. Looking down. In fear. Plunging into hell. After the most despicable incident of one's life. Only thing worse than blackmail is not succeeding at it. But now my nobility of person tarnished. Ready for the devil. Feel like a lone chicken at Andromeda Park. After the fox had killed all the others. And the bird perched high up in the rafters of the barn. Waiting for death. As the fox waited sitting below. Till at last this feathered tidbit would fall in frozen terror down into its jaws. Just as I fall. In shallowness and deceit. Planning to perpetrate ignominious shenanigans. In the company of this fellow. So totally abbreviated in his code and conduct. Without scruples. Already claiming me as an accomplice. When I should demur. Depart.

'Do please, my good chap. Proceed to join me. Indeed you must. As I am totally impecuniously unable to cater for myself. You'll find the Buttery this time of day a most suitably charming place.'

Darcy Dancer stepping down the thick carpeted steps. To go below ground into this late afternoon darkness. Where is she now. My Miss von B. In another man's eyes. In his arms. Turn left into shadows full of tinkling glasses. Scents of perfumes. Voices murmuring. Through the shoulders and laughter. Follow Rashers. Right up to the bar.

'Now. Dear me. My friend I must allow you to ask me what it is I am drinking. And from the bottom of my heart I do apologize for the seeming extravagance but I would so like to have my usual champagne. It has become a habit with me. The vitamin C it contains I believe creates a dependency. Or else it's the vitamin D. In any event I failed at applied physiology. O god the sadness sometimes of one's life. With only its very briefest sparks of joy. When one has had a big winner at the races.'

Darcy Dancer ordering a bottle of champagne. Such a nice dry name, Heidsieck. From a bartendering chap who would appear to be momentarily suspicious of me. When I demanded it be put on my hotel bill. Until my suitably haughty demeanour put him at his ease. And he hefts up a two handled silver chalice with panels of gold wire filigree. Clanks in ice. And places the bottle to rest snugly in among the chill cubes. With Rashers lighting another borrowed cigarette in his holder.

'Now my dear chap. You see. Although ice is utterly new to the country, the style of my own wine cooler is not. It is an enlarged replica of the Ardagh Chalice. Had it made by the best of silversmiths as soon as the invention of frigid water came to pass. Most precious thing I possess. Would not part with it for the world. Every time I have stood outside the pawn shop with it, its semi precious blue and red gems have shed silver gilt tears. I simply couldn't do the mean thing. But I do rush on. Who on earth in Dublin are you anyway. Not that one doesn't think you already such a splendid young chancer. Please. Don't object. Just as you are about to do. To that word. Be instead proud of it. Now, my young fine feathered friend who are you.'

'I'd really rather not say.'

'Triumphant. Absolutely triumphant. Precisely as you should. You have said. That you'd really rather not say. The nuance is perfect. One already senses the hint of your debrett entitlement, the rolling endless acres of grazing. The fox hunting. The polo. The bloodstock. The right people left and right.'

'I think you are rather making over much of it. I merely said I'd rather not say who I am.'

'Ah you are touchy my dear chap. But it is the way in which you said it. But then in our line of adventuring mountebankism it is best if one can use the old nom de guerre instead of the old nom de famille and thereby keep the old incognito intact. But between professionals dear chap there should be an exchange of confidences. Especially while the champagne is cooling. Now let me tell you the plans. We shall take our refreshment here till the noise and the people dictate otherwise hoping of course to avoid the doom of closing time. But a bash at which we shall attend should present itself long before that. Ah shall we now fill our glasses. Awaken our senses to this pale golden wine. There. Ah my god, what bliss. Now to my distant future plans. In my fortune hunting you especially will be pleased to hear that I have laid hold of a lady. Whose stout build I did not object to nor from whose full false upper and lower dentures did I cower. Owns the freeholds of three Dublin pubs. Two of them in squalid but good trading positions in North Dublin. She has another pub in the country. The profits from which purchased all the others. Together with her in wedlock we shall convert her eighty acres to a small stud farm. Of course I don't want you to think for one second that I am an unfeeling person. I am not. I would worship the very expensive deep pile carpets the lady walked on. But as recently as this morning I was shirtily refused my daily ration of cigarettes from her tobacconist's shop. Shows one churlishness is always but a breath away. And I hope you won't mind dear chap getting me a mere pack of ten. That kind of thing would send one in pursuit of rich American divorcees. By god then you'd soon see some bloodstock in my ruddy paddocks. But my dear chap the secret is never be less than compassionate. How do. How are you. So desperately glad to see you.'

Rashers greeting new arrivals. Appearing between our every sip of champagne. Faces one sees at the races. And in other pubs and in other lobbies. Streets like the halls of some vast country house. All just as Miss von B once said it was. Except they've not fought, washed off the blood, shook hands and fought again. And o my God. There just entered, I see through the waving heads. The Marquis in his tartans and the blonde tresses of Baptista Consuelo. Amid the crowd and din. Back slaps and laughter. Sit here. Swept away. Out to sea. On a raft of blossoming dreams with all these people. Their gaiety. And the self assurance of those who have won at the races. Drinks coming hard and fast. One wants so much to know. Where are you. Miss von B. And to ask. Where is Mr Arland. Where is his Clarissa.

'But I think the time has come for you to say something, my good young chap. For a start, what shall I call you. I really must call you something.'

'Macgillicudy.'

'Ah. One could never ask for a name more portending in promise of great future fortune hunting than that. Let us drink to it. Macgillicudy. Cheers.'

'Cheers.'

'To both our fortunes. To white ties. To our swallow tail coats. To that girl in pink. Just over there. When I was a handsome undergraduate at that university down the street. In my rooms in New Square. I had every morning. Two young ladies call. And she, radiantly beautiful dear girl, from a family of rich fishmongers, was one. Both were members of the school of modern languages. The other girl was the daughter of an eminent surgeon. But one does sometimes prefer the successful mercantile class of Dublin society. Surgeons are such bullies when they get you on the operating table knocked out cold. Slashing you often in the most vulnerably wrong places, in a hurry to play golf. Of course I speak from wretched experience as a failed medical student. Doing my bit of stabbing as well. But my dear chap. These girls were vying to make me breakfast. While I disported bollocks naked in the altogether. One's frozen testicles giving one's penis the most marvellous pneumatic bounce as one went to close the shutters to passing prying eyes. Hungering over my rashers. The latter after which of course I am unfortunately named. And women are so marvellous. The way they will utterly tolerate jealousy to snare some poor bugger. June in Trinity week, on the day of the College Races, I rogered both in continuo. As one groaned the other rejoiced. We three, we loved each other. I shall remember that day till I die. Trinity Week Dance at the Gresham Hotel. Both of them. One on each of my arms. So staggeringly beautiful in their gowns. Days my dear chap. Days never to come again. The Lawn Tennis Championships in College Park. God. Too soon does ecstatic beauty and joy pass from one's life. Too soon. And damn too soon without warning does sadness descend. To pinion in death the most utter beauty of all.'

Tears welling in Rashers' eyes. As he turns his head away. Lips quivering. The light of his smile faded. The world dark. Heads turn and talk. With hardly a murmur of love. Or whisper of compassion. Or a thought for those sorrowing or hungering. Just horses. Bashes. Hunt balls. Last night's larks. And champagne.

'Forgive me my dear chap. That was most uncalled for. What I have just said. I do think I was attempting to impress you. One's youthful moments of love. I suppose fills one some times with the most terrible longing. To go back. Back on those graceful college squares. But I don't tell you these things to be a showoff. Rather be it known I am a man of compassion. I say it with all sincerity. Persistent pecuniary impoverishment has driven one to the precipice of the un- principled. And I have jumped downwards. And one upon occasion has even landed among the gurrier element. Among whom I have, in too numerous an extremity, had to reside at the Iveagh House. That most practical but somewhat humb- ling premises over on Bride Street. Ah but let me introduce, my friend here.'

A massive man. Lurching like a tottering tower. A pink cravat at his velvet collared throat. Brows frowning, eyes blinking to see in my direction. And attempting to fix some- where on one's face. As he bows.

'This is Macgillicudy, Leo.'

'I am charmed. Charmed to meet you sir. Have a drink.'

'Of course Macgillicudy, Leo paints ladies' portraits with every bit as much artistry as he does when he fucks them.'

'I object Ronald to your mentioning my two professions as if one depended on the other. However, bartender replace that bottle in Ronald's cooler if you please. With another of the same brand and vintage. And who is this. Behind me. You madam. Please. Don't split your infinitives and leave your gerunds dangling so uncomfortably close.'

A woman in black standing behind this giant man's shoulders. Who pushes forward between the elbows. A black sequined purse clutched in her hand. Her mouth darkened with lip paint.

'I shall not from you you big bear, take any of your semantic battering in this Buttery.'

'Ah madam you are in every respect in the ablative absolute. And I beg your forgiveness.'

Feel the champagne less and less as one consumes more and more. Wonder now in the heady delight, was there ever such a thing as loneliness, and despair. Up out on the street darkness overtaking the late afternoon. These voices bubbling. The laughter. Turn one's ears in any direction. Hear of horses, hernias, holocaust, heroes, harlots, hashish and hell. An abyss widening all round. To jump across. Or be swallowed up. And one is swallowed. As more and more of these euphoric come. To whom I am introduced. As the son of a baronet. Then a baron. Till the present bottle of champagne emptied. And one was a viscount, up to town selling cattle. A moment ago I was an earl, up to town for a new scarlet coat. And now, Rashers Ronald has just conferred upon me the entitlement The Marquis of Delgany and Kilquade up to town for the racing. Said I was the highest ranking peer there. That Major Jones the Mental Marquis was merely titled in the French peerage. And this black engowned lady. Comes swaying close.

'You darling. You absolurely gorgeous darling. What eyes. Absolurely magic. Absolurely medieval. Good lord. You're a leprechaun. Out of what celtic ether have you come. I invite you right this very moment absolutely virginal as you are to later take me in your arms.'

'Well thank you.'

'Thank me. Don't dare thank me like that. Even though I have said I shall go willingly I shall fight bitterly but helplessly. I'm to be taken. Conquered. Swept away.'

'Well I am not quite, I mean I'm rather not, I should say.'

'What indeed should you say. Have you something to say. Have you.'

'No. I haven't.'

'Ah that is what I love. Silence. Still waters my dear boy run deep. With my body enclosed about your own. You darling absolutely gorgeous creature. Crush you to death like a woodland flower. Squeeze from you your nectar. Who bred you. What vibrant man stallion covered your mother. Stunning creature she must have been. Of course in mourning with my hair dyed black, one does look gloomy, wearing only black gems. Is that why you are wide eyed looking at me. Do you know who I am.'

'No.'

'I am one of four scandalous sisters. And better known as the Black Widow. Now only three of us are left. As Ireland's most beautiful creatures we are totally wasted on this utter desert. What have we to choose from but boorish big handed farmers. All with their favourite hounds peeing round the baseboards of their bedrooms and sharing their fleas with their masters in bed. Wouldn't you like to put your hand upon my breast. Press your lips to my throat. As I lay.'

'Well,'

'I mean figuratively my dear boy. Figuratively. Well. Would you.'

'Well.'

'Well bloody what.'

'Well madam I just don't know what to say to your overtures.'

'Overtures. What overtures. I speak my dear boy. Of love. Indeed not Irish love steeped in the greed of money. I mean great love. Love that destroys dynasties. Love that sacrifices thrones.'

'But could that not be lust you speak of madam.'

'Do you have the nerve to stand there in this Buttery and use the word lust to me.'

'Well.'

'There you go again. You're totally repetitive. Must I take out your tongue and teach it to speak. Must I.'

'Why are you doing this to me madam.'

'Doing to you. I'm not doing a damn thing to you.'

'Well you are rather acting like a femme galante.'

'Of course I am. Because you are the most darling gorgeous creature I've seen for days. Don't you find me as attractive as I find you.'

'Yes. But you are extremely forward too.'

'Can a woman be any other way in a land of wife beaters and onanists. I say Ronald I shall have champagne.'

'Of course you shall my darling. And you have I see haven't you, met my most marvellous friend. His Lordship the Marquis of Delgany and Kilquade. Not that either of us give a damn about Debrett. But I saw him darling, perform the most excruciatingly delightful triumph above our heads, on the black and white lino tiles of this hotel's lobby. Which has long been the altar upon which the most sacred of Irish society have been either worshipped or sacrificed. A treat.'

Darcy Dancer hardly able to move. Crunched elbow to elbow. The lady Black Widow turning to other faces. Voices roaring. Eyes smarting in the smoke. Drinking one's dreams. The present future rearing marvellously. And racing away out of one's past. A green tweeded gentleman. Called the White Prince. His face as black as a lump of Welsh coal. Rashers's wine cooler again and again refilled. Bottle after bottle. Making him look ever more benign. Leaning in towards my ear to confide.

'Of course my dear chap, that's the secret, one gets a first bottle and my Ardagh Chalice does the rest.'

'But who are all these people.'

'Ah. Marvellous question that. Marvellous. Your naïveté is stunning dear chap. Never lose it. In a nut shell. They are for the most part the multitude and many from the landless class. And then there are the singular and few of the landed class. The former mingling with and chancing their arms with the latter. He, with his ears sticking out, is a gas meter reader. Whom I dare say is in search of intellectual stimulus. Or more likely, free drink. That bousy looking chap who just poured his drink over his head is a housepainter from Crumlin. That more obnoxious bastard there is a wall plasterer from

Dolphin's Barn. Who propounds his sensitive nature as he curries favour among the bloodstock breeders from Meath and Kildare. But ah. There. That chap. He has just come in from the Stock Exchange. Over in Anglesea Street. Of course it's only a ruddy room with a circle of chairs enclosing barely enough space to decently fart in. But dear me, nice work if you can get it.'

'But why are they all here like this.'

'Ah marvellous question that. Marvellous. But for your recent performance one would by your question think that you were only the most recently arrived of arrivistes. They want, my dear chap. Simply to get each other's goat. However that chap. The stunted one, thin and all hunched up. Euphemistically one refers to him as the Royal Rat. He wants your money first. Made his first roulette wheel out of an old car tyre. Since then the Royal Rat has in various dungeon basements, helped relieve chaps of their fivers. He actually pawned his dying mother's bed. Chucked her on to an old pile of burlap to breathe her last. I thought it damn cruel. Sensible chaps like myself of course take a damn dim view of him having profitlessly to the spirit, encouraged as he does the frittering away of chaps' inheritances in his dingy dank casino. But ah, dissipation. That's what it's all about. Hold death away by intemperance, unchastity and extravagance. Then death is welcomed. Those entering these Buttery precincts do so to squander their fortunes to the wind. Scattering fivers like autumn leaves. It's too sad sometimes. To then see them slink off with their tails between their legs. That's the marvellous thing about not having been left a bean. One does not spend. One only helps to spend.'

A baggy grey suited chap. Cigarette dangling between his lips. Pushing himself forward to squeeze in behind Rashers' back. His hand up to the side of his mouth as he whispers. And Rashers turns and roars.

'You blatant cunt. And I hate using the word. But regrettably it is the only one which applies. Coming to whisper about the plight of the creative artist in my ear. Can one imagine anything more ghastly. In the Buttery. As if I gave one boring damn about your awful nonsense. Had a rhyme published in your local country village newspaper, have you. And now you bring your abysmal ignorance to Dublin. Expecting for your pathetic lyric scribbles to be patted on the back and be thrown free lamb chops from one's dining table. Fuck off.'

The baggy grey suited chap. A sickly smile on his face, blending back into the voices. The teeth. The eyes. The laughs. And sighs. Rashers transporting a cigarette from some one's gold proferred case into the end of his ivory holder. Dragging the air down the length of former elephant tusk. His haughty musical voice sounding from his rather rabbit looking mouth.

'The arts like Catholicism is a disease of the mind, my dear chap. Although I was born a papist I was saved from its worst corroding consequences by a childhood in India among the untouchables. A decent public school situated on a well known English river saved me as well. But of course one stands by the Romanists when Orange men up north there are thundering their drums and threatening to interfere indiscriminately with Catholic testicles. One then shall fight. One doesn't give a damn how one's human rights are infringed. It's one's animal rights one doesn't want mucked about. But damn. One does above all prefer the rich ladies. Even to willingly placing one's lips upon their au blet thighs. Leaving thereon the white indentation of one's fevered mouth. And even some small pleasure is to be found in one's pressured caress of the unresilient flesh of riper ladies' haunches. Better than contretemps any time. Dear me. But the bad name of the Irish spreads all over the world and is only improved when they become a laughing stock.'

'I hope you realize Mister Ronald that I am Irish and some of your remarks are not awfully flattering.'

'You my dear chap. You. Macgillicudy. Marquis of Delgany. Prince of Kilquade. You are a genius. It matters not at all that you are Irish. And if I were not tainted that way myself, I would be bereft of my unerring sense of theatricality which enabled me during my too few undergraduate years to win wagers by running up and down Grafton Street in the thick of the morning shopping throngs. With one's corpus spongiosum hanging loose wagging up and down. Which thankfully it did thereby riveting the attention of all. Which prevented one's face being recognized. Let me fill up your glass, Macgillicudy. And by god I am Irish, you know. It was those damn penal laws gave us our wretched inferiority. Then my good chap, with the flight of the Wild Geese departing for saucier shores. It left what you now see surrounding you here in this Buttery. And the greatest of ironies. Protestants liberated us. Freed us from the British yoke. And then by god left installed straight down Molesworth Street our marvellous gobshite bureaucracy. But it's a blessing. While they have their thrilling time putting their sticky fingers into tight government circles, us sybarites can play splendid with our perversions and appetites. Of course my father accused me of ratting on the war. Disinherited me of his pitiful chattels. Said if I would not fight for king and country I could not have his spoons and saucepans. I of course promptly purloined his Purdey shotguns and delivered them to the appropriate broker. Bash on regardless. That is the cry dear chap. Through the funerals of friends. Trampling the rose gardens of enemies. Bash on regardless. The cry of any self respecting member of the élite.'

The Buttery suddenly emptying. Darcy Dancer following Rashers Ronald up the steps to the street. The Black Widow just behind me. The portrait painter Leo waving a bottle of champagne and roaring out something about diphthongs from the hotel entrance. Baptista tugging the Marquis behind her by the kilt. The stockbroker removing a club from under his coat and flattening unconscious in the gutter the plasterer from Dolphin's Barn. A punch out of nowhere landing on the face of the grey baggy suited artistic chap as he made an attempt to enter a motor car. His cigarette smashed flat between his teeth. The élite piling in over the prostrate bodies. The waiting vehicles packed like sardines. And now roaring off with springs squealing laden with entwined bodies. A pair of lady's feet sticking out in front of the driver's face.

Speeding over the roadway in the black night. Swerving around corners. Shadowy gable rooftops flash by out the window. Someone distinctly tampering with my fly buttons. Here I am. Flying. Through this low life. In some strange secret womb of the damned. In this city. Not a time to be particular. Impossible to tell if a male or female hand is tinkering with my balls. Whose brain knows or cares. The Black Widow pointed a finger at me. Her voice. Loud and clear.

Bring him
He's
Divine

The crystal clear night. Stars out. Speaking. Deep in their black blue beyond. Smell of burning rubber. Wind pouring in the window. Limbs poking in all directions. A voice groaning in rapture. Another screaming in fucking discomfort. Someone said there's Bull Island. Lips kissing my throat. Unable to move to see who it is. And whoever it was, has now let go of my balls. And is pulling my prick. Just as we all crush backwards motoring up a steep hill. Thought I saw the masts of boats. And I do. Down there in the harbour.

Darcy Dancer retwisting his arms and legs back into shape as the bodies separate. Up here in the salty air the line of motor cars unload. A rocky hill covered in heather and gorse. Stand in front of this rhododendron shrouded big house perched up over the sea. Try to adjust one's dress. Finally saw the hand coming out of my flies. Belonging to a chap called Cecil. Who winked at me. Step down through the oily leaved shrubbery. With this arriving crowd. Towards this massive door opening. And this stark naked man whom last I saw on a pavement flattened in a puddle of stout. And now erect once more bowing in the guests.

'Come in my dear darlings. Binky greets you. Come in. Quickly before I'm frozen.'

A long wide hall of black and white tiles. A grand staircase circling upwards at the far end. Through an ante room. One of Lois's pudenda paintings on the wall. And further. This large drawing room. The guests gathered. Corks popping. A gramophone playing. And beyond the shuttered windows hear the ocean waves below go crash, go booming. The Black Widow woman. Comes with her thin wristed arm aloft to take me waltzing out across the floor. Kissing my neck. And three gentlemen on the side lines growl.

'Don't mind them dear boy. They're jealous fliers from the Royal Air Force. You are what I have been waiting for this whole entire evening, you absolurely gorgeous darling. So young, so young, so young. But that is not an invitation for you to say that I am so old so old.'

'I was not about to say that.'

Darcy Dancer swirling on the parquet. Right past Lois in a mattress thick green sweater and skirt. Dancing with Binky. Whose skinny shanks and long spare body made one think of an undressed butler. Lois's head resting with her eyes closed on his shoulder. As one ventures to ask this Black Widow.

'Who is that person Binky. He looks like an undressed butler.'

'But my dear, that's what he is, my butler.'

'Does he always go without his clothes.'

'Only after ten p.m.'

Sound of more arriving guests. Arms stacked with parcels of bottles. And a roar of Leo the painter at the drawing room door.

'Begorra Sodom and Gomorrah.'

And the Black Widow swirling Darcy Dancer in a wild spinning circle. The lights go whizzing past one's eyes. The faces loom. And this largest of the three Royal Air Force gentlemen tapping me on the shoulder.

'My turn to dance my dear fellow.'

Lady Black Widow facing him. Blocking him away. Raising her splendid profile.

'Ah all you lovely men. And you, my dearest Wing Commander or is it Group Captain. Who fought and won the war. I do like you. I do so really absolutely like you. But you see. This gorgeous creature here. I love him.'

Snorts and harumphs erupting from this large broad shouldered chap. The Black Widow swirling me away.

Round one last time and then out over the threshold. Away from the smouldering anger. And the getting of each other's goat. Into the hall. Where a bottle was smashing down on the back of the head of the Royal Rat. Who pitched forward on his face. Roars and shouts raging. And a figure. My god. The gunman. Unleashing a fist. Socking the man with the bottle in his hand. Sending him flying footless back the length of the hall. Over a table. A white pottery lamp crashing to the floor. And the man crumpling into a stand of canes and umbrellas. Rashers in the centre of the mêlée announcing.

'Bottles as weapons you cad are simply not cricket.'

Just as the front door opens. And the Count my former dancing master, surrounded by companions as he stands in a camel hair polo coat arms outstretched surveying the carnage. As one is led half way up this curving marble staircase of this big old house. To hear his voice ringing out.

'O my dears. You have so naughtily disgraced yourselves again.'

The Black Widow tugging my arm. And one so wants to watch. As more fists are now suddenly flying. A gentleman in a rather loudly checked jacket and bright red, white and blue bow tie. My god is flattening people in their tracks. Hardly even see his fists move and hear a thwack and down they go absolutely flaked out.

'O my dear Macgillicudy, let us get away. From the noise and the people. Come.'

'Where are we going.'

'Away from the battlefield. To where we may make love my dear boy. To where we may make love.'

Sound of wind groaning and whistling. Shiver along this dark hall. Led by the hand. Her skin feels cold. Her eyes look dark and then close up they were a yellowish green. Thundering crashes and more screaming below. And in the brief lull comes the music and dancing and jiggling. The Black Widow pushing closed an iron barred gate. It shuts with a heavy clank across the hall. She turns a key in the big lock.

'You see my darling this is the party door. On that side are the noise and the people. On this side. It's you and me. My husband who adores rough social gatherings also likes his privacy. We are as it were in our own little fortress. Protected if not from the sounds at least from the splattering gore. Should one lose this key there is no escape but a drop straight into the sea out the windows.'

Her bedroom hung with tapestry. A parrot in a cage. Large Blackamoor Figures either side of her chimney piece. We stood to kiss under a chandelier she said came from the Court of the Russian Tsars. And a shot gun leaning against the wall. Shoes all over the floor. She takes off her black dress. And silky black underthings. Flings them back over her shoulders. The shadows haunt and rise up through my bones. The sea thundering. The windows trembling. Stands with her naked bony body. Tiny slender waist. And the largest nipples I have ever seen. On her so white bosoms. That I am terrified to touch.

'Why is that shot gun there.'

'It is kept handy so my husband can shoot my lovers.'

'Thanks a lot.'

'Take off your clothes my gorgeous darling. Don't leave me naked like this just standing here.'

Felt for my fiver still intact in my waistcoat pocket. A light out there on the sea. Comes flashing up through the windows and across the walls. She waits there. Swaying. Or my head reels. Keel over into disaster. Get killed here tonight before I ever atone for all my past misdeeds. The first awful things one has done in life. Severed strands in the rope which held up Edna Annie's laundry drying frame so that it would when she raised it, fall and crash the wet wash down on the old crone's head. Felt dreadful for days. Even wept. Between laughing my head off. She used to frighten me as a little tiny boy. Grabbing my wrists and squeezing them cruelly hard when she'd find me on the servants' stairs. Step now naked towards this Black Widow's arms.

'Macgillicudy you're so virginly beautiful. You have the body of a gazelle. Just the right thing for me. To wake me up out of doldrums. One can't hide away from the world. Or close one's eyes to life and live nevermore. Touch me.'

Stacks of magazines on the floor. Four large photographs on her dressing table. An escritoire with its pigeon holes stuffed with papers and its fall front piled high with more magazines. Her mouth opens wide. Pulls my head down upon hers. Miss von B said that even for such a short time that we were together. At least we lived. What more can there be. But to just make it as long as we can. And this Black Widow makes high pitched little grunts and groans. As we stand embraced. My prick pressed hard up into her belly. Her nipples sticking hard into my chest. And Black Widow. Wish you were. My Miss von B. As we were. Back in my life. Home. Together surrounded by my green parklands. Astride our mounts galloping in the fierce madness of the winds. Instead of this body. My desperate lust makes me clutch. With miles of utter meaninglessness between. Only the Marquis's fiver left to stave off the impecunious days. Foolishly taking drinks up to my mouth through an entire afternoon. Amid the endless flattery. Lifting one's spirit. From one round of drinks to the next. And now jump out of my skin. A voice screaming out in the room.

'Fuck you ducks.'

'Don't mind. That's just my parrot Stinky speaking. He simply insists on saying those words at the most inappropriate times.'

Stumbling over her shoes to the bed. Climb in and slide between the chilly sheets. Her love calls. Her purrings. To be on top of her. Pushing between her legs. Pressing. The feel of her fingers. And the circle of her muscles tightening. And thinking. Thinking of a day. Out hunting. Raring to go. With the field waiting. When the pompous Master of Foxhounds turned to tell me that in future I should not jump ahead of him. And I waited. To see him fly at a hedge. His horse tripping and somersaulting over wire. Sending the Master catapulting headlong in his scarlet coat between his mount's ears. White breeches. White gloved. To splatter headlong into the brownest, creamiest lake of cow flop one had ever seen. Mixed to such magic consistency. To leave just a back bit of the mahogany of the Master's boots unsullied. And one feels one has just plunged. Splat. Into life in Dublin. Just as Miss von B said it was. Drinking. Fighting. Washing off blood. Shaking hands. To rear up fighting again. And O god. In her groans. My lust. Dies. Taking something from my body. That fills me with fear in giving. As she screams to give her every drop. Shoot it into me. Gorgeous darling Macgillicudy. And I'm buried. In the sweet smell in under her hair. Her fingers pushing through mine. The chords of the sea. Lying here in the darkness. Listening to her voice.

'My husband may come home. At any moment. Find us like this.'

'Then I must go.'

'O no I'm just joking. I just wanted to feel your body quiver. I'm sure he's still in London. Where he's supposed to be buying guns for a safari but is no doubt gambling and partying. Isn't it all so foolishly sad. He worries I'll squander his fortune before he does. He kept a taxi waiting for him once night and day for six weeks. God you are adorable. And I'll never see you again. More probably you won't want to see me. It's always parting. And it's not sweet sorrow, it's damn misery. One man should be everything a woman needs. Only I need different men. And I need so many. The dearest, the loveliest and the wildest of my sisters. Found just one. And then threw herself out a window. Fell stabbed to death by the railing spikes on the pavement. In love poor girl with an impecunious scholarly gentleman. He lived holed up in squalid digs somewhere down Mount Street. What on earth could she see in him. And why. When every rich man in these isles was throwing his fortune at her feet. And she went walking, o god, can you imagine walking, holding hands with him.'

'Why did she kill herself.'

'I don't know, over the stupidest triviality. And some stupid letter he wrote. He saw her through a window. While he was passing on Stephen's Green. She was having dinner with just an old beau. And indeed flirtatious she was. He must have thought the worst. He wrote her a letter. And left next day on the mail boat. The letter came on Christmas eve. She was found. That marvellous girl was in her prettiest frock. A fence stuck through her lovely body. Because she must have loved him.'

'What was your sister's name.'

Clarissa

29

Darcy Dancer. Bed covers pulled up to the eye. More days gone. And the worst coming. Hotel management demanding settlement of my bill. By latest tomorrow morning. Lay listening to the wireless. Till breakfast is brought. And one thinks back, O god the real goodies of life. Of cook Catherine's late summer picked bramble jam slathered on her fresh made and hot toasted soda bread with the yellow butter melted deep down into the flecks of wheat.

And read of the day's impending races. The fat little maid now remembering to put my newspaper on my tray. After two weeks of telling her. Kept thinking I hear the sea pounding up cliffs outside the window. Those sunless people. Back on that hilltop. As cold in their souls as the ocean waves. Yesterday walked and walked. With every step. Hearing the words spoken by Clarissa's sister. Spikes of a fence. Up through her white alabaster body. Mr Arland. Would be broken in tears. As mine went down my cheeks in the wind fresh on my face. The scent of turf smoke from the grates of the houses I passed walking to the cemetery. And the green of the spring. With a cold rainy winter in one's life. As I looked down on the ungrassed sods over Clarissa's grave.

Darcy Dancer with a last sip of tea. Tear back the covers. Go in my unpaid for dressing gown and slippers to the water closet. Sit. Unable to move my bowels. As I have been every morning after the night of the Black Widow. When I unloosed her arms. Put them back sadly crossed on her breast. Could see the contours of Clarissa in her face. And as she slept I lay awake my head turned to the dawn coming up over the sea. The endless booming waves. And the Black Widow's snoring. And me hoping her husband wasn't coming through the party gate. To fly in blasting with his new safari guns. A ship anchored out beyond an island. On the slate green grey sea. My lips dried. My head frozen and stunned. The key on the dresser. And silver framed photographs of all four sisters. And Clarissa. I dressed staring at her. She looked so unposed unlike the others. Even though her cheek was leaning on her bent hand. String of pearls round her neck. Her face seemed so fresh and open as if she'd been blown in by a sea breeze. And as I tiptoed out. The parrot screamed again. Fuck you ducks. I unlocked the barred door. Went down the stairs. Just as pale sunlight fell on all the bodies, slumped and piled over furniture in the hall. One of which was the irate Master of Foxhounds. Who chased me out of Jammet's. His hand gripping a club with the business end studded with nails. So unconscious was he I even nudged him with my toe. And figures were still wandering. Putting bottles back up to their lips. And one turning to me whose face one remembered from the Buttery. And whose artistic overtures were rejected by Rashers Ronald. And who was out in the street so unceremoniously punched straight on the kisser. And seemed now the only person left able to speak. Through his bruised bloodcaked swollen lips. And delighted to smilingly impart his observations.

'Ah you're wide eyed at the carnage and wreckage. Well let me tell you. An American was loose among us. Knocking dentures flying. Flipping the innocent on their backs. And screaming he was a fighting amphibian. Took a dozen of us to subdue him and we're still waiting for cars to ferry the injured to the hospital. And all that was said to him was, wasn't Hollywood films full of rubbish. And by god he laid into us.'

I stepped to peek into the darkened shuttered drawing room. And still dancing. Binky and Lois. Now both naked. Foxtrotting to the tune of a song saying something like Johnnie doesn't give a damn any more. In my inebriation of the night before I was momentarily loose from the Black Widow and confronted Lois. She slapped my face. Merely for quoting Rashers Ronald. Who had said her paintings were the ravings of an alley cat in heat. I would have thought that such remark was appropriate as she was always going on about her fertile period. God some people are so hard to understand. Also overheard someone talking about Uncle Willie. That he'd gone to London to be a ponce. And I was ready to smash the speaker's face until it said that recent rumours and gossip had it he'd gone to Monte Carlo. Gambled away twenty thousand pounds in one night, and won thirty the next.

Darcy Dancer flushing the toilet bowl. One's reminiscences finally moved one's bowels. And nip smartly down this hotel corridor to the bath. Have perfected twiddling the taps off and on with my toes. Soak away all one's morning worries. Shave away the dark stubble on cheek and jaw. Take in my shoes from the hall. And nicely shined by the Boots. Attire in silk. To dress stylishly gives one such confidence. Polka dotted brown tie. My west of England tweeds. Trilby hatted. Binocs slung over a shoulder. This is my last day of comfort. My hotel bill now large enough to cause actual whispers as one passed out through the lobby. But one was sure it was only because of a solicitous curiosity concerning my where-withal. The staff on the whole have been simply sterling. My picnic lunch neatly packed ready at the porter's desk. Such dear good chaps. Remember them in my will. Times like this of course one must only be even more extravagant. And ordered for late supper after the theatre tonight, duck, wild rice and champagne. With the Marquis's fiver still tucked in my waistcoat pocket. To go today to Punchestown races.

Darcy Dancer walking his brisk way to the station. Cross Duke. Down Grafton. Twenty past noon on Trinity's blue gold clock. The portico of the bank. And plunge smack into Rashers Ronald his rabbit teeth sunnily smiling.

'My dear chap. Hello and how are you. Believe it or not you've stumbled upon me buying seedlings. That's why I'm blushing. With this parcel. That other night. I found myself without warning in charge of a motor car. With someone's drunken head lolling all over the steering column I rammed down someone's garden wall. Flattened two baby palm trees. Demolished a bird bath. But I successfully navigated out on the road again. Only to be brought to a stop by these awful people's tennis net enmeshed in the car's undercarriage. They came screaming out at me in their pyjamas. They want garden reparations made. Awful bore. See you later in the Buttery.'

Darcy Dancer watching Rashers waltz off in his morning suit much needing a pressing and repairs. People look so different outdoors. Just as they do when attired for hunting on a horse. Now pass the smells of coffee of another Bewleys. A dragon emblazoned in tiles at its front door. Turn left up along the Quays. The Ha'penny Bridge. Four Courts across the river. A green dome. Exacting justice. Throwing debtors into prison. All these buildings housing solicitors. And one of whom may be on my trail. Mouldering buildings of merchants. Georgian fronts. Red bricked. Gay painted doors. Bookshops and auction rooms. Antiques and furnishings. A Franciscan church. And soon I'll have so many women in my life that I will because of their numerous number start forgetting them.

Darcy Dancer striding quickly now to catch the train. Past the big brewery. A grey granite barracks across the river. Flying my country's flag. What a marvellous day for racing. White fluffy clouds blown across a sky so blue. The Phoenix Park. Top of the obelisk sticking out of its new green trees. Buy my ticket. First class on this packed train. Pull away out the tracks. On which one had come to Dublin. The big country houses hidden now in all the spring leafage. Click clack over a warming land. To this popularly attended race meeting.

Darcy Dancer with two other racegoers taking a taxi from the station. Nearly crashed us into a ditch or hedge at every turning on the road to the course. And there it was. This track. Spread on the green grasses to the horizon. Pennants blowing. The tiers where people sit and stand. The rich, the poor. The élite and untouchable. The parading horses. The bright fluttering silks. The ladies' big gay hats.

Darcy Dancer standing in the mild breeze. Loud speaker announcing. Tweeds pass all round one. So many familiar faces. Hard to know quickly enough the ones to hide from. Their membership badges flying from lapels, sitting sticks and leather cases. Much as one wants to be with the right people one won't splurge to go into the most expensive enclosure. Instead, in soft fond memory of Miss von B. Put an extra large bet on Blue Danube at fourteen to one.

Darcy Dancer's light hurrying feet. Back to the bookie. Wait in this joyous tiny line. To collect. On the first race, a winner. Watch the peeling off of these thirteen pounds. Now in my pocket. To suddenly have money. To hell with form. Just choose another sentimental name. Moonhatter. Ten to one. Get to the bookie. Hop back to the rails. And my god. Back to the bookie again. For there in the sight of one's binocs. This filly stampeding home. Sixteen lengths out front past the post. And I am forty pounds ahead.

Darcy Dancer's eyes darting from face to face. Everyone at the races. And ghosts. Out of one's past. Priest and parson friends of my mother's. Up in the pavilion. As I stand with a wad of winnings amid the throng in front of these bookies. A fortune made. Put a fiver on Amphibious at twelve to one. Take an egg sandwich out of my picnic. For a bite and breather from the agony. Of watching the big bank where the horses climb to jump down. Uncle Willie said that with so many shenanigans going on that picking winners was something that comes out of your insanity. Creeping to tell you from way out on the edge of the world. But never before today has it ever told me anything twice.

Darcy Dancer dodging back and forth through the crowd. My hand feels so snug and warm in my pocket wrapped around money. Stand at the rail. They canter down. Amphibious is alive and kicking. So mild so sunny. The breeze blowing me luck. Prosperity after all these days. Makes everyone around look so charming. If my nerves simply will take it. But like my vagabond days. And in my moments of defeat. The words are. Press on. And they're off. Stare down at my toes. And look up in the deafening roars. Wake again with the strange soaring elation. Amphibious by a nose. Collapsing me happily in a few seconds of marvellous heart failure.

Darcy Dancer dancing to the parade ring. With packed now in his tweed pockets over one hundred pounds. Walk on air. In one's element. One's demeanour takes on a totally new elegance. Stable lad as I once was. Now watch them leading their horses. Owners disporting in their natty suitings. Wives and daughters in the latest from ladies' gazettes of fashion. My goodness. The Slasher sisters. Each in an umbrella sized straw hat. Trainers in cavalry twill. The jockeys mounting in their bright silks. And along the rail. A face. Staring at me. Matt. From the Awfully Stupid Kelly stables. Who catches my eye. And like a wounded animal moves away. Then looks back suspicious over his shoulder, not sure if it was me.

Darcy Dancer moving out from the rail and along by the backs of the crowd. Closer up to Matt. To see him in a shabby baggy brown suit. Unlike the racy tighter tweeds he wore. Bending over to cough. Hacking and spitting. His lungs heaving. Looking like he might die in a paroxysm. His shirt dirty. Collar ruffled and his cap torn. As I tap him gently on the back he turns to look.

'Hello Matt.'

'By god it is you. Sure you wouldn't know you were the same person at all. I seen you there now at the bookie's collecting a big win and as sure as I was it was you I was just as sure it wasn't. You look now as if you'd had a bit of luck for yourself.'

'I appear at least for the moment to be managing quite well.'

'Well some of us are not. Turned on me they did.'

'Who turned on you Matt?'

'Would it be anybody else but those gombeen curs. Sacked me without even a week's notice. Wasn't but a day after you left. The ungrateful blackguards. You sweat your guts out. Give them your best. Sure the new butler stole them blind. Shifting stuff out of that place now, you wouldn't believe it. Giving parties for his friends while they was away. You're dolled up.'

'Well I have rather bought a few things I needed.'

'Ah now I'm not looking me best. Went on a bit of a skite. Drinking drinking everything I could lay me lips to. You might say I'm down a mite on me luck. Now I'm sorry I went that bit hard on you. Sorry I did that. Regretted it many a time. And you being a great horseman too.'

'That's nothing to worry about Matt. Come along with me. And I'll get you something to eat. Or would you like a bit of my picnic.'

'Ah I'm alright, thanks the same. But I'll wait now till after this next race. Even though I haven't had a bite to eat since yesterday. With only the few coppers I've got left in me pocket. Some of the lads give me a hand that I'd meet in the enclosure. But you couldn't make me the lend of a quid or two could you. I'm gathering together what I can for the last race.'

'Of course I could Matt.'

'Ah thanks. My god though, I thought you might turn on me. But I can see now. You're a gentleman. Real gentry. Grown now fine straight and tall. Not like them gombeen gobshites. But I'll tell you what you do now. Beg borrow or steal. Every last penny you can. And bet to win. That's what I'm here for. No other reason. Sure I reared that Tinkers Revenge meself in the gombeen bogshites stable and I know the trainer well and once he's let go he'll show his heels to the lot of them. I don't usually give a hoot about pedigrees but he's got the blood of the great stallion Dancer in his veins. And an engine on him like the London to Glasgow express. Take no notice of that hundred to one. Some of the rest of us will benefit from that gombeen man's cunning. And be fast before that gobshite puts his own bets on and reduces the odds.'

Matt moving off. The crowds flow back to the enclosures and stands. Darcy Dancer for light relief, putting twenty pounds on the favourite. Embroidery. Even money. Matt to meet me later. And everyone here from everywhere. Even the timber merchant I'd chased out of Andromeda Park. Passed by in the paddock. His face glowering when he saw it was me. And he turned to whisper to the man behind him. Our swarthy ruddy agent. Under his bowler hat and with a pretentiously tightly furled umbrella. Sneaking looks back at me over his shoulder as he and the timber merchant scurried away through the crowd. Rather nice feeling to find one can throw fear into somebody. As well as watch the favourite come in by three lengths.

A dark grey bank of clouds coming up out of the west. The air blows chillier. Gusts whirling programmes and betting slips up into the sky. Hailstones raining down. Racegoers running for cover. Darcy Dancer proceeding along the line of bookies. Standing up chalking in the changing odds on their signs for this last race. One did have a sinking feeling. To peel off these notes. So rarely won. To plunge all but the price of dinner at Jammet's and a bottle or two of champagne. In do or die.

'Ah you'll have to try somebody else with a bet that size at a hundred to one. I'm not here to get skint.'

Dear me. Unpleasant fellow refusing to take my bet. Try this next chap. Certainly. That's what I'm here for. I'll take a hundred pounds at one hundred to one. And the next bookie took twenty pounds at eighty to one. My whole immediate future. Haberdashery and hotel bills. Laid on Awfully Stupid Kelly's father's horse. Only ever been heard of to come in last or next to last. Now in a field of fourteen runners of some of the best steeplechasers in the land. And he'll no doubt fall on his head and send his jockey to kingdom come. And me back to an abattoir. But one's luck is in names today. And that's why mine's Dancer.

The black grey clouds blowing over. Hailstones sprinkled white and melting on the gleaming green turf. A moment's sun splashing on the horses led round the parade ring. One slinks in behind the heads. Awfully Stupid Kelly's mother dressed for some kind of operetta in the centre of the paddock. Primrose satin cape. An emerald satin dress. And would you believe it, a mauve parasol and pink high heeled shoes. Just as garish as her racing colours. And turning this way and that as if people were dying to see every side of her and photographers from *Tatler and Sketch* were clicking cameras recording her for social history. O god they are such know it alls. Stupid Kelly's father sporting a suede waistcoat with gold buttons and having a conspirational talk with a rather impatient jockey. Who now mounts and sits adjusting his stirrups. This chestnut stallion number twelve upon which my future comfortable habits rest, is at least lean and narrow gutted. But slightly sloping in the quarters. And good lord also dishing its front hooves. Whoops. Rears flashing out legs. And kicking Kelly's mother's parasol flying right out of her hands. And that's distinctly a better sign. Of get up and go. But O god. The favourite. Led out. With its rippling muscles. One's heart sinks at the sight of its dancing light strides. Looks like the sheer winner it's supposed to be. As they each go off. To the track. Breaking into a canter. Tails flowing. Pounding down the soft meadow. To size up the first hurdle. This may be Matt's way of dealing me some final blow.

Darcy Dancer walking back to the stands. Another patch of blue sky. Polish off my last egg sandwich. Chew a nice bit of parsley. Look back up there under this race course roof. Where Awfully Stupid Kelly's family and guests now stand behaving as if they own the place. With their binoculars, at the ready. And mine too. And the bill as yet unpaid. Focus a moment. My goodness. They are in the company of seemingly high ranking Army and Garda Siochana officers. And a face I recognized from their disastrous dinner party. Of the woman down whose cleavage the poet dived after the pea. Awfully Stupid Kelly is a brave little bastard to tolerate such parents. And now one distinctly stiffens. Voice on the loud speaker. They're under starter's orders. Flag is up. And they're away. Sledge hammer words hitting the heart.

Darcy Dancer dropping his binoculars. And putting one's hands placed back both over ears and eyes. If one only could bear to look. And now tremble raising one's binocs back to the eyes. The names reeling off over the loud speaker. And what a name for a horse. Tinkers Revenge. Matt said they should have called it gombeen gobshite after themselves. All safe over the first jump. Two down at the second. The favourite setting a fast pace, already out by six lengths in the lead. On the first circuit of the course. Can't bear to put the binocs up. Where the devil is the horse. The stupid bloody beast. With my one hundred and twenty pounds on its back. Damn and sod it. As Mr Arland used to say.

Darcy Dancer turning to look up in the tiers of people.

Scan them with my binocs. To the owners' box. Just to see if if I can determine an equally crestfallen attitude on Stupid Kelly's father's face. And now in the middle of all the heads. The one I hate. My father. With that woman I saw that day up the stairs. The agent and timber merchant standing just behind them. As the announcer's voice thunders on. Coming round the second circuit of the course. The favourite now a long way clear. Leading by eight lengths. Beginning to swing left handed, turning for home. Five fences left to jump. The crowd's roar rising. Raging in one's ears. It's Ulidia Prince. Still making ground coming into the straight. Screaming now. The name Ulidia Prince. And for me. It's back to the abattoir. O christ, one hundred and twenty pounds. My whole dignified salvation, down the drain. On Awfully Stupid's bloody horse. Which at last has just been mentioned by name. O my god. He's still running. Tinkers Revenge. Moved up from last to next to last. Isn't that wonderful. With furlongs to go. Get up. Get up. Over that next ruddy fence you bloody god damn nag. Up. And two more horses down. Squeals of horror. Bury my face. In my hands. O my god my heart. Never again. Just reserve my strength to climb the steps to the owners' box and punch Awfully Stupid Kelly's family and guests one by one in the nose. You damn critter. Peek once more in my binocs. He's over that fence. One is even talking like a cowboy film in one's desperation. O god. Tinkers Revenge has moved up. Into seventh place. Cannot watch any more. Listen to the announcer. Who's in a real lather. It's Ulidia Prince now. Three fences to jump. It's Ulidia Prince, from Intrator. Leaping Lizard, Hindustani, followed by Dictionary, Hilary, Kilcullen and Donadea. The rest are nowhere now. It's Ulidia Prince. O my god. Tinkers Revenge is out of it. Back to something like ninth place. Pause from the announcer. Must have dropped his sheet of names. Ah. He's talking again. And coming now, on the outside. Still in the race. Donadea and Tinkers Revenge making ground. Two fences to jump. Intrator's down. He's down. And it's Ulidia Prince. Hindustani second, Dictionary third. And on the outside now. Making ground. Tinkers Revenge. Donadea coming fifth. And still coming to the last. It's Ulidia Prince. Definitely easing up the pace. Hindustani, Tinkers Revenge, Dictionary. The only ones left in it. And on the outside. Coming fast. It's Tinkers Revenge. Good lord. The announcer is just as hysterical as me tripping over his words. This rank outsider. Neck and neck Ulidia Prince and Tinkers Revenge. O god I've got to look. Stride by stride. The whips raining down on the quarters. Legs stretched. Thump and pound. My god. Tinkers Revenge. Pulling away. And at the post. Tinkers Revenge. By half a length. The world is over. One is now more than just flesh bone and blood.

    I'm
    Rich

30

       What a glorious morning. Turning my haughtibility on the management when they thought I was making a break for it. When it was only Matt helping me carry my parcel of money from the Hibernian to the bank. Safely situated with its great grey pillars across from Trinity College. This marvellous giant room. Two gentlemen in their black banking cloth. I could nearly see his lips forming the words. Have you robbed a bank. And I spoke reassuringly.

'Had a rather good day at the races.'

One with a winged collar. Much delighted hand rubbing. Presenting me with a chequebook. The assistant manager, overseeing the reckoning of the massive stack of notes. One bookie was ashen faced paying me out. Kept peeling off the notes. As if waiting for me to say, that was enough. Had to tell him about five times that it wasn't. And he was nearly sobbing. But the other bookie by the time we got to him was hurrying to pack and go home. Till Matt raised a fist at him and he undid his bulging satchel and began counting.

Take a horsecab to the Shelbourne. Waltz in. With not a soul racing instantly in my direction screaming, there he is. Chequebook out. And the merest shade of suspicion concerning my oversight.

'I do believe there is an account of mine outstanding.'

Darcy Dancer jauntily emerging from the side Shelbourne door. Crossing straight over the street for a haircut and manicure. To lie back. Flush faced in peace. In revenge. Gave a shawled tinker lady following the races five pounds. As Uncle Willie had once bid me do if ever I were in luck. And taxi ride back to Dublin. In a vehicle held together with bits of wire and string. With a flat tyre before we went a hundred yards. Ran out of petrol in the first mile. Then the radiator boiling over. With the driver's constant reassurance.

'Ah sir I'll have you back in Dublin in no time.'

In no time the window of the back door fell out on the road. And coming around a turning we rolled over a farmer's wife's three ducks. Then hit an irate cow who promptly gored out his head lights. Ah but one's discomforts and delays were all merely events in which to take exquisite delight. And laughter. When the taxi finally stopped along the Quay. Paid the exorbitant fare. And just as the driver pulled twenty yards away his decrepit vehicle blew up. Making the world safe again for other road users. Ah but this gentle life. In pursuit of comfortable habits. My fingernails soaking in this manicurist's dish. And after one's safe delivery from the exploding taxi, took tea with Matt at the Four Courts Hotel. Listening and relistening to the retelling of his whole sad tale. Of his past life and especially most recently. When he put my loaned fiver and the rest of his borrowed money on the previous race and lost it all. His hands shaking as he lifted his cup to his lips. Steadied finally by a large brandy. I bid him to allow me book him a room. Where he could stay at my expense. Wrote a note for him to give my gentleman friend at the haberdasher. To outfit him in suitable clothes. And to report to me at the Hibernian. So blissful now to have one's head rubbed by the big wheel brushes they lower whirring from the ceiling. And one's troubles ended. Just turn to determine who the wearer of a kilt is. My god. The Marquis is in the next chair. Busy slinking down low. The barber plying him with sets of hair brushes and tonics. Slipping in the words, Your Lordship between that of Major and Jones. By my swift addition. He's now bought eighty seven pounds and seventeen shillings worth of hair emoluments and dressings plus sundry scalp and hair grooming utensils. And poor man he groans as I now lean towards him with a five pound note.

'Good grief what's this.'

'It's five pounds I borrowed from you Major Jones.'

'O it's you. By jove that's unexpectedly good of you. I

don't mean by that any offence. For a moment there I thought you were serving me with a writ.'

One took a modestly larger front bedroom with an attached sitting room facing down Molesworth Street. More befitting one when one was such a plutocrat. But I spent a somewhat terrified whole night clutching my valuables. Thought there were awfully noisy burglars in the next suite. Was in the middle of adding my couch to the writing desk, footstool and table I had just stacked against the adjoining suite's locked door, when I heard a prolonged high pitched giggle. One's eye had to navigate a double key hole. But one could easily put together in one's mind those things which passed before it. With all the glimpses adding up to an overall sight. The Marquis. And Baptista. Both totally unmindful of the comfort of other guests. And both already rumoured to be next season's joint Masters of Foxhounds. Both of them in the altogether, whooping and hollering. And one imagined Baptista delightedly bringing the whip down on the Marquis's haunches. Then the Marquis taking a gallop. Exercising his mare Baptista. With her saddle worn held on her back with a cinch strap of pure silk. Nothing a courageous hunting gentleman enjoys more in a woman than her ability to walk if she cannot trot on her all fours across the bedchamber floor. Heinous of me. But one did shout shut up through the pair of locked doors.

Matt agreed to be my temporary chauffeur of my motor car. Formerly the property of an Ambassador. With lovely chromium ripples across the radiator. Over which each morning I ran my hand as it pulled up waiting for me in front of the Hibernian. Where now one stood this day. On the steps of this dignified most comfortable hotel. With dowagers passing in pursuit of coffee and buns. And country gentlemen idly twiddling thumbs before lunch. The weather report on the wireless. Sunny periods this morning. In the afternoon, cold and cloudy with rain or drizzle at times. With wind increasing to gale force in Sole Shannon and Fastnet.

Matt improving the dazzle with a cloth leaning over the bonnet of this six cylinder touring vehicle. Envious citizens admiring its gleaming black dignity. The world has taken me in its arms at last. Kissed me in this sunlight. Beaming down Molesworth Street. Gates at the far end lead into where the the government of my country steers this emerald ship of state. Brimming with its oats and barley. Its strong high couraged horses out of the lime green grass. Its creamy butter and deep orange yolked eggs. And here he comes. Smiling fifty feet away. Sauntering along the boulevard. Rashers Ronald. Very washed and brushed up. In top hat, white gloves, striped trousers and tail coat. Ready for another bash. Onwards regardless.

'My dearest chap. How good to see you. Just let me stop here on this lowest step and regard you up there on the highest. My, if only I had your assurance and dash. You know you do appear as one who has been sent out into the world from the nest of family life with pecks on your cheek and all the little cossetings. While my damn unfeeling daddy merely grunted goodbye to me without looking up from his *Times*. Can you give me the loan of a pound.'

Darcy Dancer taking from a large black wallet a five pound note. Which generosity seemed to nervously speed Rashers away. Down turning into Duke Street. Obviously to the Turf Accountant's. And me. I wired Sexton and Crooks to come by train today. To meet them at three at the station. Sexton will oversee the two window boxes on the sill of my sitting room. And sine dubio will know instantly what's wrong with the soil producing such stunted little flowers. And Crooks will do for me. Knows exactly how one takes one's tea. Brush my suits down. Lay out my silks. And I shall by motor go collect my paintings from Lois. Sit further for my own portrait. After my insulting her she was so thrilled to be commissioned. Told me her visiting English couple had sent her a thank you note for tea. And how much they had enjoyed her exposing them to the arts in Ireland. By clonking their heads through canvases.

Darcy Dancer turning his dark head south up the street. A tram bell clanging. A seagull flies floating over the rooftops. A chill gust. A raindrop falls. And last night I had a dream. Stood below in the front lawn meadow field of Andromeda

Park. Looking up at the grey stone house and its chimneys poking from the slate roof. A sun setting westerly in a cold white sky. Heard my sisters' voices playing in the woods. I had come back searching for my mother's jewels. All the years rumoured hidden somewhere near her grave. And found them. In the coffin of a little sister of mine who had died. Before I was born. The box resting on the crypt's topmost musty corbel. Smashed the lock and opened the heavy lid and there amid the tiny white delicate bones were my mother's necklaces of diamonds and pearls. And as I looked up. I was suddenly kneeling. On the other side of the orchard wall. Knees sunk in the soft moist grass. Praying to Sexton's stations of the cross. Each with its own carefully painted little sign. Jesus falls the second time. Jesus is stripped of his garments. And in front of the sixth. Veronica wipes the face of Jesus. And the image left on the towel was Mr Arland's Clarissa. Her body of the softest whitest skin. Pinioned on the railings. Cold rain falling on her lifeless face. Her blood dripping down the black bars of the fence. Gave life to his life. Then death to her own. And that Christmas eve. When I was dying alone out lost cold in the countryside. Clarissa too was dying. While I dreamt she had come to my funeral. That very nice stylish looking couple. So smilingly happy. Waiting to wed. And in one of his low moments, Mr Arland said he would join the lighthouse service. Sit out his years in isolated solitude reading his favourite books while the wild seas pounded up all around him. Miss von B said love was like catching a train, don't be late. And I was. And I hear Mr Arland's voice. Kildare, don't be negatory. Where can I find him. In his sadness. Gone.

Step stylishly down these steps. Into all the cunning and conniving. Amid the chancers and cads. The gay girls and the solemn women. Arrange with Bewley's to post a weekly box of fudge to Awfully Stupid Kelly. Grit blows along the street. Bombards the eyes. More raindrops. A cloud moves a shadow across the city. Comes far from the west. Out of the hush of that lonely sky. Where the winter brown young beech leaves rustle. And fuchsia hang their red flower bells. The donkey brays. Night lowering on the hills. Lose no nerve when unhorsed. Mount again. Go well. Fly fence hedge and wall. Till the huntsman's blowing his long slow notes. Turn home. At end of day. Under the heaven's grey greys. Split pink across by a sinking sun. Go home. Across the dewy meadow grass. Go home. Earthstoppers sleep. Not tonight shall we find him. Curled up below ground safe from the fierce mad winds and fangs. But another day. Disturb his tranquillity. And chase. Call by tongue. Yell by name. To out beyond. In his destiny. For he discourses somewhere.

That Darcy
That Dancer
That Gentleman

More About Penguins and Pelicans

Penguinews, which appears every month, contains details of all the new books issued by Penguins as they are published. It is supplemented by the *Penguin Stock List*, which includes around 5,000 titles.

A specimen copy of *Penguinews* will be sent to you free on request. Please write to Dept EP, Penguin Books Ltd, Harmondsworth, Middlesex, for your copy.

In the U.S.A.: For a complete list of books available from Penguins in the United States write to Dept CS, Penguin Books, 625 Madison Avenue, New York, New York 10022.

In Canada: For a complete list of books available from Penguins in Canada write to Penguin Books Canada Ltd, 2801 John Street, Markham, Ontario L3R 1B4.

J. P. Donleavy

The Ginger Man

'I set out one June near the sea in Co. Wicklow, Ireland, to write a splendid book no one would ever forget. I knew then that the years would come and go and the book would live. It has taken more years than I ever could have imagined and more battles than I ever felt I'd have to fight but the fist I shook and the rage I spent has at last blossomed and before it should fade I'd like to say that I am glad' – J. P. Donleavy

'In the person of *The Ginger Man*, Sebastian Dangerfield, Donleavy created one of the most outrageous scoundrels in contemporary fiction, a whoring, boozing young wastrel who sponges off his friends and beats his wife and girl friends. Donleavy then turns the moral universe on its head by making the reader love Dangerfield for his killer instinct, flamboyant charm, wit, flashing generosity – and above all for his wild, fierce, two-handed grab for every precious second of life' – *Time Magazine*

'No one who encounters him will forget Sebastian Dangerfield' – *New York Herald Tribune*

J. P. Donleavy

The Beastly Beatitudes of Balthazar B

Balthazar B is the world's last shy elegant young man. Born to riches in Paris and raised in lonely splendour, his life spreads to prep school in England. There he is befriended by the world's most beatific sinner, the noble little Beefy. And in holidays spent in Paris Balthazar B falls upon love and sorrow with his beautiful governess Miss Hortense, to lose her and live out lonely London years, waking finally to the green sunshine of Ireland and Trinity College. Here, reunited with Beefy, he is swept away to the high and low life of Dublin until their university careers are brought to an inglorious end. They return to London, there to take their tricky steps into marriage, Beefy in search of riches, Balthazar in search of love.

'Marvellous, as always, Donleavy's language embellishes incident piled on hilarious, marvellously invented incident – encounters with sly Trinity proctors, disportings, disappointments, scenes of domestic life and strife, sexual spectaculars, small joys and further sadnesses. It is Donleavy at his best, eloquent, roguish and also at one with his world and the terrible sadness it contains' – *Newsweek*

J. P. Donleavy

The Onion Eaters

On a grey cold day in a damp gloomy city Clayton Claw
Cleaver Clementine of The Three Glands descended directly
in the male line with this medical rarity intact sets off
westwards to take up residence in the vast haunted edifice of
Charnel Castle. Clementine, a polite unknown unsung
product of the new world and recently recovered by a
miraculous cure from a long decline, alights at an empty
crossroads. Standing lonely on its windswept hillside the
great turrets and battlements rear in the sky. Clementine
destitute but for his monstrous dog Elmer and a collection
of toothbrushes enters this ancient stone fortress. Bedevilled
by rats and rotted floors Clementine stands unbelieving as an
unpaid staff assembles out of the woodwork and guests
appear barefaced on the tiles of the great hall with their
equipment of audiometers, waterpipes, onions and other
venomous reptiles. Bills run up, debts accumulate, confusion
mounts and the Army of Insurrection threatens while the
definition of clarity is ringingly declared as 'that force given
to a fist sent in the direction of a face that when hit has no
trouble seeing stars'.

Madness triumphs over love, beasts over man, chaos over
reason and for the moment life over death.

'The freshness of the writing, the enthusiasm for language,
the sheer joy of the imagination all make a mockery of
traditional modes of novel writing' – *Sunday Press* (Dublin)

As
The circus
Continues
More crazy than cruel
One of us now
Will spin like a top
On the end
Of his tool.

J. P. Donleavy

The Saddest Summer of Samuel S

'It can't be, you're not, are you?'
'Not what?'
'Samuel S.'
'You don't know me.'
'You are. Gee, I mean I've never seen a picture of you, but somehow I wouldn't miss you anywhere. You know a friend of my uncle who's a professor at NYU, he knows you. He said you were one of the points of interest in Europe.'
'Despair is the word.'
'Gee it's true, that's just, ha ha like what he said you might say . . . by the way, I'm Abigail.'

'Donleavy's dialogues become a miracle of writing . . . There is a certain comic innocence' – *Sunday Times*

A Fairy Tale of New York

'Fantastically inventive . . . madly funny. He is an original and almost irresistible writer' – *Sunday Times*

'Cornelius Christian is J. P. Donleavy's new hero, person, protagonist, figure-head, creature. He struts and weaves and shrugs and punches his way through the pages of *A Fairy Tale of New York*. I think he is Mr Donleavy's best piece of man-making since Sebastian Dangerfield in the good old ginger days. The book is fast, funny and addictive' – Robert Nye in the *Guardian*

'Irony, farce, satire and lyric' – *Spectator*

J. P. Donleavy

Meet My Maker the Mad Molecule

When the going
Is too good
To be true
Reverse course
and beat it.
That's Franz F, fearful and put upon, cleaning out the
cockroaches for the arrival of lissome Lydia (his first
woman) but afraid she'll send her husband to blow his
brains out.

'Beep beep'
That's George Smith, the original 'Singular Man' hoping
to get by without actually talking to anyone ever again.

'In this book of short pieces Donleavy has given us the lyric
poems to go with his epics. They are almost all elegies – sad
songs of decayed hope, bitter little jitter-buggings of an
exasperated soul, with barracuda bites of lacerating humour
to bring blood-red into the grey of fate. These stories and
sketches move between Europe and America, New York and
Dublin and London. America is always the spoiled Paradise,
the land of curdled milk and maggoty honey. The place that
used to get you in the end, but that now does it in the
beginning' – *Newsweek*

'The stories are swift, imaginative, beautiful, and funny,
and no contemporary writer is better than J. P. Donleavy
at his best' – the *New Yorker*

J. P. Donleavy

A Singular Man

'Thank you spider.'

(George Smith to the spider that caused him to comfort marvellous Miss Martin.)

'She's a tall girl with gold hair.'

'This is no missing person's bureau.'

'She swings her hips when she walks.'

'What are you, desperate, mister?'

'Yes.'

(George Smith trying to find much more marvellous Miss Sally Tomson.)

'Bump.'

(George Smith's heart after marvellous Miss Sally Tomson said –)

'Yesh.'

His giant mausoleum abuilding, George Smith, the mysterious man of money, lives in a world rampant with mischief, of chiselers and cheats. Having side-stepped slowly away down the little alleys of success he tiptoes through a luxurious, lonely life between a dictatorial Negress housekeeper and two secretaries, one of whom, Sally Tomson, the gay wild and willing beauty, he falls in love with.

'George Smith is such a man as Manhattan's subway millions have dreamed of being' – *Time Magazine*

'A masterpiece of writing about love' – *National Observer*

'. . . an utterly irresistible broth of a book' – *Daily Telegraph*

J. P. Donleavy

The Unexpurgated Code

A Complete Manual of Survival and Manners
Comprising:

Social Climbing
Extinctions and Mortalities
Vilenesses Various
The Pursuit of Comfortable Habits
Perils and Precautions
and
Mischiefs and Memorabilia

No stone is left unturned in this ruthless guide to social etiquette, no left turn unstoned; even the most shameful and embarrassing occasions can be used to your advantage. With this book in your hand, Duchesses cease to appal, long- and well-lost friends to mystify; at a word, with Donleavy's help, you can smash a rival's social pretensions and vindicate your own with ease. Donleavy shows that the race is not always to the swift – especially if it suits you to turn up five hours late – nor the battle to the strong. Whether you're puzzled by the meaning of life or merely lacking the basic human decencies, rest assured that you can reach the top, Socially Registered or not. For Donleavy shows you how!

'Extremely funny' – *Listener*

J. P. Donleavy

The Plays

Four Plays (*The Ginger Man*, *Fairy Tales of New York*,
A Singular Man, *The Saddest Summer of Samuel S*) which
demonstrate the dazzling wit and mercurial prose of a king
among comic writers.

The Ginger Man

Presented at the Fortune Theatre, London, in 1959.
Presented at The Orpheum Theatre, New York, in 1963.

'A bawdy, blasphemous, rich, ragged, monstrous masterpiece'
– *Daily Express*

Fairy Tales of New York

Presented at the Pembroke Theatre, Croydon, England, in
December 1960 and then transferred to the Comedy Theatre,
London, in January 1961. Winner of the *Evening Standard*
'Most Promising Playwright of the Year' Award in 1960.

'A chain of theatrical pearls nourished by a master of comic
dialogue' – Kenneth Tynan

A Singular Man

Presented at the Cambridge Arts Theatre, Cambridge,
England, in October 1964 and at the Comedy Theatre,
London, later that month.

'One of the funniest and one of the saddest plays' – *The Times*

and

The Saddest Summer of Samuel S